THE CRUEL KINGS of CASTLE HILL ACADEMY

RICH
VS.
Boys
POOR
Boys

BOOK I

DEVON HARTFORD

NO BAD BOY IS TOO CRUEL FOR THIS SCHOOL

COPYRIGHT NOTICE

Want to find out about my next book before everyone else and get free novellas not available anywhere else? Then sign up for my mailing list!

Sign up here:

devonhartford.com

DEDICATION

To my fans who wanted me to write again. I can't thank you enough for your support and love over the years.

You know who you are.

Rich Boys vs. Poor Boys

To my loyal readers:

If you've read my other books, you know you always get your HEA (Happily Ever After). In the Cruel Kings of Castle Hill Academy, heroine Mary Angerman will eventually find true love, but it's a rollercoaster getting there. She will meet many young men along the way, some of whom aren't exactly easy to get along with. Because we all know that in the real world, men often aren't, no matter how easy they are on the eyes.

Also like real life, the teenagers in Rich Boys vs. Poor Boys frequently use graphic language, some underage drinking does occur, and there are some sexual situations, all of them consensual. The main characters are age 16 or over.

As for the bullying, it doesn't get any more real than that. Who hasn't been bullied? Whether you're young or old, it happens to all of us throughout our lives in countless different ways, big and small. It's how you deal with it that makes all the difference.

Never give up and never let them get you down.

Mary Angerman never does either.

Buckle up and hold on tight.

It's going to be a bumpy ride.

Devon

Prologue

"You lied to me!" I scream at them.

Them are the four gorgeous Poor Boys watching as a squad of Hill County Sheriff's deputies drag me across the castle's immense courtyard with my arms handcuffed behind my back.

Standing off to the side are the academy faculty.

Entering the courtyard from every direction are other students woken by the commotion. It's dark and the moon is hidden behind sudden storm clouds.

I keep screaming at the Poor Boys, "You said we wouldn't get caught! You said you'd take the fall for me if we did!" I fight viciously against the strong lawmen, but I'm handcuffed and can't break free. "I'm falling now! Why aren't the four of you falling with me?! You're in this too! This was your guys's idea! Not mine!"

I direct my angry glare at one Poor Boy in particular. The tallest and most muscular of the group with the broadest shoulders and slimmest hips, the one who's the most stupid handsome. Painfully so. Dark hair and dark brooding eyes that have a weight to them. Standing still, he is a dark streak of danger.

Rob Fletcher.

Their leader.

When I first saw those guarded eyes three months ago, they carried a hidden sadness I recognized from my own mirror. The moment our eyes met, I got him and he got me. Two halves of a whole soul, broken apart by the ravages of time and reunited after an aching eternity. I knew then we were made for each other.

Or so I thought.

I trusted Rob would always catch me if I fell.

He isn't now. He's just standing there stoic as a stone.

I used to think his stoicism was a shield for his pain. Now I know better. It's a shield for his lack of character and his relentless deception. His eyes don't guard hidden sadness. They guard hidden lies. If you were to cut him open, that's all you would find.

Lie upon lie upon lie.

Millions of them writhing inside him like the worm he is.

I shout, "Say something, Rob! Tell them this was your idea! Tell them you're the mastermind!" Rob doesn't respond. "I put my faith in you! I did exactly what you said! Look what happened!" He won't speak. "Don't you have anything to say?"

Rob's stoicism gives way to the curl of his cocky grin. The one that's just a little bit wicked, the one I let myself fall in love with but never should have. Trust me, it didn't happen all at once. I resisted. For months I fought it. But he was persistent.

Now I know why.

He was making plans to use me all along.

"Damn you, Rob! Say something!"

Then there's that glimmer lighting up his eyes, the usual one that says he knows something no one else does. Something important, something grand, something that if he ever shared it would lift my spirits out of the gutter of my life and into the clouds. No, the only thing that glimmer ever hid was how he would bring this cruel ruse of his to fruition tonight, and at my expense.

I'm absolutely crushed when I realize the real reason for his glimmer. The angelically beautiful and blonde Elizabeth Morgan-Hearst.

She's making him glimmer.

Don't let her beauty fool you. She is the original snake in the grass, the one who offered the apple to Adam. Eliza-bitch is proof that the Devil in the Garden of Eden wasn't a man. She was a woman. I don't even go to church, but I know damn well only a woman could be so scheming.

Elizabeth is that woman.

The one Rob is wrapping his muscled arm around right now. He rests his hand possessively on her flared hip, pulling her to his side. They're the perfect couple. Two snakes intertwined. Okay, so I was wrong about the Garden of Eden. It obviously had a snakey She-Devil hiding behind the snakey He-Devil telling him what to do. And here they are.

Elizabeth nuzzles into Rob and he tips his head down. They kiss, serpentine tongues coiling together. Make that slithering like snails.

Disgust hits me like a hammer.

With that nail, my betrayal is complete.

I should've known better, known that Rob and Elizabeth have *always* been a thing. I denied it from day one, but I was wrong. *So* wrong.

How could I not have seen it?

Because honest *genuine* love is always blind.

I fight back tears as the weight of his ultimate betrayal settles heavily onto my shoulders. "You never cared about me, did you, Rob?! You only cared about what I could do for you! I never should've trusted you!" I flail against the deputies, but they barely notice and keep dragging me along. "I hate you, Rob Fletcher! You're dead to me! Do you hear me?! Dead!"

Elizabeth laughs. The bitch laughs!

Rob's eyes glimmer again.

He is evil. Pure reptilian evil.

Rob finally breaks his superior stare and turns his back on me. His smirking asshat Poor Boy friends follow. They never look back.

At that point, I stop fighting against the deputies.

I never *ever* should've said yes to Rob and his friends, the other three wolves in wool suits, the gorgeous Poor Boys always by Rob's side. They're no better than he is, and no less beautiful.

If only I could've seen past their luxurious exteriors to their rotten cores. If only I could go back in time and make a different decision. Too late for that now.

Now I'm going to prison.

An actual adult women's prison.

My heart is shattered and I'm dying inside but hiding it as the deputies lead me out of the gatehouse to the visitor parking lot. It's buzzing with patrol cars, their red and blue lights bouncing eerily off the castle's tall stone walls.

"WAIT!" a strong baritone voice booms out.

It's Prince Lancaster.

The preeminent Rich Boy on campus.

Blue eyes, blond hair, tan, well-muscled and well-heeled, Prince would be the picture of the perfect California surfer if he wasn't always wearing his custom-tailored school blazer and slacks. Underneath his clothes, he is a hard and masculine Calvin Klein cologne model in the flesh. Imagine him cliff-diving gracefully off impossibly tall rocks into a cobalt ocean because he has, hundreds of times and lived to tell the tale. Proof lies in the videos on the internet. Not his. He never records himself, but others always do. The man is a magnetic sensation wherever he goes. In civil society, Prince is the picture of affluence and entitled attitude at all times, a walking work of art, a Ralph Lauren fashion campaign come to life.

Don't let Prince's civil image fool you.

In the academy's water polo matches, he's the opposite. Prince is vicious in the pool, a swift shark leading the charge. Ask his battered and broken opponents after every game. He also knows how to lead his teammates as their fearless captain, marshaling them to victory time and again. Seeing him standing poolside in a Speedo and dripping wet after winning a game is enough to make Michelangelo blush, and every single girl at Castle Hill squirm in their rolled-up uniform skirts where they sit on the hot metal bleachers. I know because it happened to me the first time I saw him spur his team to victory.

"I SAID STOP!" Prince shouts.

The deputies dragging me along halt suddenly as if Prince is the one in charge. I'm not surprised. Wherever Prince goes, he projects an aura of authority that everyone obeys.

Prince rushes up to me and demands, "Are you okay, princess?"

"I don't know," I whimper. Prince has that effect on me. He steals away my hardened exterior with zero effort. When I'm around him, I'm not the badass bitch I show the rest of the world. I'm his princess.

When he hears my words, Prince's blue eyes storm over. He glares restrained rage at the deputies and his voice cuts like a bloody sword. "Did you hurt her? So help me, if any of you hurt Mary, I will kill—!" He bites off the rest. He was going to say he will kill these deputies.

For me.

Those words of his keep my dying heart alive.

Somehow, he restrains himself, holding back a whirlwind of murder, which is probably for the best under the circumstances.

"Ow!" I shout as one of the deputies holding me inadvertently twists my wrists too hard, causing the handcuffs to bite into my bones.

Prince launches himself at the lawmen, tearing them off of me like paper dolls. A flurry of action follows. Prince punches two men before four more take him to the ground.

"Let him go!" I gasp when Prince hits the slick pavement hard. I try to break free from the two men holding me, but they're too strong and I'm still handcuffed.

One deputy is stabbing Prince with a stun gun while another ratchets handcuffs around his wrists.

Prince fights back hard, ignoring the pain.

The four men weighing him down are barely enough to restrain him, but they do.

Suddenly, two other brash bad boys rush up to help. Prince's best and most loyal friends.

Duke and Chase.

Both are tall, dark, handsome, and as delicious as Prince. With him, they should be the rightful royal princes of Castle Hill Academy, but they aren't. Everyone knows Rob and the Poor Boys are. They're the selfish, soulless, cruel kings who're only out for themselves and their criminal schemes.

Now, Duke and Chase bring the muscles and mayhem as they try to pull the four deputies off Prince. This is what loyalty looks like. No, love. Prince and his friends truly love each other, would do anything for each other, unlike Rob and the selfish Poor Boys. Those four wouldn't know love if it tore their hearts out and stomped all over them like they did mine.

More deputies pour into the courtyard and restrain Duke and Chase, pinning their arms behind them and pulling them away from Prince. Duke and Chase keep fighting, but there's too many men for them to overpower.

Prince lies with his face smashed into the pavement, still fighting and roaring, "I will have your fucking badges for this! I own this town and you know it!"

The deputies hesitate because it's true.

Duke shouts, "Don't worry, Mary!"

"We've got this!" Chase adds.

"We'll take care of you!" Duke says.

The six deputies push Prince toward a patrol car, but he resists.

"The fuck off me!" he roars.

The deputies pause.

Prince locks eyes with mine and says, "Don't worry, princess! I've got your back! I'll always have your back!"

"*We've* got your back!" Duke adds, eyes angry and dark, flashing his irritation at Prince for not including him in his pronouncement.

"The three of us!" Chase shouts.

Duke roars, "We'll tear down the whole fucking jail if we have to!" Classic Duke. Such a drama king, but I know he means it. His family has the finances and political connections to do anything they want, no exaggeration. For them, the law does not apply.

"Stay strong, Mary!" Chase encourages. Always the supportive one, the peacemaker, the glue that holds those three together.

"I'll take care of this, princess!" Prince insists as he's shoved inside a patrol car. "If it's the last thing I do, I'll take care of you!"

In this moment, there is no one I'd rather hold my safety and well-being in their hands than these three kings, the rightful kings of Castle Hill Academy.

Prince, Duke, and Chase.

I have to smile.

Maybe one day I'll finally get that fairytale ending I'm always dreaming about. The only question is which Prince Charming I'll choose to be my forever after savior?

Now I'm grinning.

Do I *have* to chose?

Chapter 1

A few months earlier, my life went off the rails and took me with it. If it hadn't, I never would've ended up at the exclusive, secretive, and somewhat sinister Castle Hill Academy.

They say you can't run away from your problems.

I used to think "they" were wrong.

Nope.

"They" are right.

"I'd kill myself if I looked like you, you ugly bitch," Emily Calhoun sneers behind me.

"We can help, Mary," her cheerleader friend Kaitlyn Sharp says with acid compassion. "Just say the word." She isn't talking about giving me a makeover.

I ignore them and keep walking, heading toward the gate in the fence across the field and just past the bleachers.

Emily, Kaitlyn, and their two reptilian friends Riley and Megan follow like a pack of velociraptors scenting blood.

An hour ago, I waited inside the Roosevelt High school library after sixth period ended to avoid this exact confrontation. Maybe I didn't wait long enough, or *maaaaybe* I shouldn't have been talking to Emily's boyfriend Booth at lunch today.

Guess who saw us?

Emily, the Reptile Queen.

What can I say? Booth is rockstar hot. Spiky hair, spiky tattoos, spikes in his ears and full lips. We have English III, aka American Lit, together. For whatever reason, he decided to sit with me in the cafeteria and ask me what I thought of The Catcher in the Rye, which we're reading. It was the first time Booth ever talked to me in or out of class. I thought he didn't know I existed. Was I supposed to tell him *not* to sit with me and talk about class?

Now the raptors are right on my heels.

I speed up my walk. My battered Doc Martens kick through the green grass on the field in quick flicks.

Emily says, "Booth doesn't like you, you dog face bitch! He just wants help on his English paper."

Kaitlyn adds, "Booth only fucks dogs like Mary doggy style."

"Shut up, Kaitlyn!" Emily hisses.

"What?! It's true!" she mutters.

Someone shoves me from behind.

I stifle my surprise and stumble forward but keep walking. I'd turn around and start clawing eyes out and kicking shins, but I've already been suspended twice for fighting, and I'm desperately trying *not* to get kicked out of yet another school. I swear, at every one I've been to, it's always like this. The ass-tampons like Emily and Kaitlyn and their cruel cronies always seem to find me and devote themselves to making my life miserable.

Like the gullible girl I am, I hoped when I transferred here to Roosevelt three months ago (Go, Eagles! — Not.), I might make some friends for once. So far I have zero. It's what happens when they boot you from one foster home to the next.

Thank goodness I have my book boyfriends. They keep me company wherever I go. You know, the usual hooligans. First it was Harry. Then it was Edward and Jacob, then Gale, then Four, then all the rest. Now it's Holden. Maybe next it'll be Booth, and he's real. Sadly, none of them are here to banish Emily and the reptiles behind me. If I had Hermione's wand, I'd do it myself. Too bad she keeps it for herself in the pages of a billion books, and yet, it doesn't effing exist. That's magic for you.

Hurrying, I make it past the bleachers and go through the gate.

The reptiles follow me off school grounds into the neighborhood. Houses, parked cars, and empty sidewalks. Not a single person to save me if something happens.

What else is new?

Two blocks later, the raptors attack.

I hear them make their move and I start running.

I'm fast, but Emily is faster. She runs track and it shows. She grabs me by the backpack and pulls hard. I'd shrug off my backpack and let her have it so I can run faster, except it holds everything that is precious to me. Living in foster care, you learn to keep anything valuable on you at all times.

Somehow, I manage to tear free of Emily's grip and keep going. I'm running as hard as I can, but she's right behind me every step of the way.

When I turn a corner, she knocks me down.

I go tumbling onto someone's lawn.

Emily lands on top of me and starts swinging.

I protect my face with my arms. Good thing I'm wearing my studded leather jacket. It's not just for show. It's armor. The studs are also great weapons. I swing back, trying to clock Emily in the face with my fists or forearms, whatever I can hit her with.

The other three reptiles arrive.

"Two of you hold her arms!" Emily screams. "Someone sit on her legs!"

They do.

I literally can't move.

Emily reaches over my head and I hear ripping noises. I think she's pulling out my pink mohawk by the roots until she shoves clumps of grass in my face. I clamp my eyes and mouth shut to keep the dirt out.

Six blades of hot hate rip down my cheeks.

I have so much adrenalin pumping through me, I barely notice.

"Stay away from Booth," Emily snarls and jumps off.

Someone kicks me between the legs and it hurts so bad I want to die. I've never been kicked between the legs before. I thought it was only supposed to hurt this bad for guys. Guess not. I'm writhing in agony while Emily and the other raptors sprint away to safety.

When the pain finally subsides, I sit up and spit dirt out of my mouth. That's when I realize my cheeks are burning. I reach up to touch them gingerly.

Blood.

Bright red and wet.

I can't tell without a mirror, but I'm pretty sure Emily clawed my cheeks open with her nails. I won't know how bad it is until later.

I hope I don't need stitches.

That night, I run away from foster care.

Care is too nice a word because my foster parents Dwight and Shayla *don't* care. Per usual, they're both blackout drunk and snoring in their own filth on the floor of their trailer, same as every Friday night since I moved in with them 122 days ago. Of course I counted. When you don't have your freedom, you're always counting the days until you do.

On my way out, I stop in their fake wood-paneled war zone of a living room. Half-assed Dwight and Shayla are sprawled on the floor like victims of a bar fight, which they basically are. They always go at each other whenever they get loaded. Broken liquor bottles and crumpled cans are everywhere. An exploded bag of potato chips coats everything with salty snowflakes. Food flung against a wall sticks and glistens. Furniture is turned over. A window newly broken.

Wait, is that the kitchen sink sticking half out the wall?

Kidding. Only about the sink.

I swear, I've slept in better dumpsters than this place. Not exaggerating. That is literal fact. A clean dumpster is better than a tent. I'll tell you about it some other time.

I'm about to walk out when something catches my eye. Is that a baggie of coke on the glass coffee table? Coke as in blow?

Nah, they can't afford upscale drugs.

Crystal meth, frequently. But not coke.

I step toward it and stare at it.

I know it's poison, but I might be able to sell it.

No, I've got enough problems tonight already, and I'm barely getting started. The last thing I need is to get caught carrying drugs.

I take it anyway, then rifle through Shayla's dirty purse. All I find is change. I take that too. Every coin counts when you're running away.

I crouch over Dwight.

He's snoring like a chainsaw.

I carefully grab the metal chain attached to his belt and give it a tug.

He groans.

I cringe.

He goes back to chainsawing.

I get his tattered leather wallet out and pop the snaps.

Six greasy damp dollars. Probably change from Sticks, Dwight's favorite dive bar. He always preloads there before coming home to drink more here and fight with Shayla.

Whatever.

I crumple the bills and stuff them in my backpack with the change, coke, and my crappy Cricket phone.

I sneak out of the trailer to steal Dwight's dusty old Kawasaki motorcycle. He never rides it.

But I know how.

Kade taught me. He taught me a few other things too. Ever since I can remember, I've flirted with every boy who rode a motorcycle for obvious reasons. But also so they'd teach me how to ride. I was never satisfied only sitting on the back. Okay, *maybe* I enjoy wrapping my legs around the slim hips of a broad shouldered boy who knows what he's doing. Or man. Age is just a number and I never keep score.

Standing outside in the night, I sling my grass-stained backpack over my shoulder. I'm wearing my studded black leather jacket over a random band shirt and ripped jeans. You can't ride in a skirt. The wind won't behave.

Oh, don't forget my pink punk mohawk, plenty of piercings, and enough eyeliner to offend a family of raccoons. Anything to ugly myself up. Most guys think I'm a lesbian, which is the whole point. When you hit puberty living in foster care, you learn real fast to downplay anything feminine. It's safer. I've known more than one creepy foster dad who lived up to the stereotype. Same is true for running away. Going ugly is the only way to go.

I swing my leg over the seat of the Kawasaki. It's a little tall for me, but I manage. I hit the ignition again and hope for the best.

The engine spits and barks to life. I sigh with relief. It sounds a little ragged, but it doesn't quit on me. If it manages to get me where I'm going tonight, anywhere other than here, it'll be the only thing that hasn't in the last seven years.

"What the fuck are you doing?" Dwight grumbles sleepily as he whacks the screen door open.

Okay, I was wrong about his degree of drunkenness.

"You can't ride that! You don't have a license!"

That's where he's wrong.

I may not be old enough for a license, but I've never let anyone else's rules stop me from taking care of myself. Since the system won't, and no one else will, it's on me.

I twist the throttle and slice into the night.

Dwight shouts after me, "Get back here with my bike, you little piece of shit!"

Keep dreaming, you big piece of shit.

I'm out.

Chapter 2

Two hours later, I run out of gas on a lonely road in the woods. It's graveyard dark and dead silent. Slivers of moonlight cut through the trees and carve ghoulish shadows on the ground.

Great.

Time to start walking.

Not a single car or truck passes me in the next twenty minutes. No owl hoots, no growling coyotes, no curious raccoons. Not even crickets.

Just woods.

Until I find the motorcycles.

Four of them parked just off the road. I would've missed them if the moon hadn't glinted off bare metal. I push through bushes and creep past trees to get a better look. Wow.

I'm not a gearhead girl, but I can tell these are sweet bikes.

Racing motorcycles.

Midnight black from wheel to wheel.

Bigger and faster than anything I ever rode on my own. Men's motorcycles. Too big for a girl like me. What are they doing out here?

I walk softly toward them, admiring their lines. Sexy as hell. I run my hand across one of the gas tanks, wondering whose they are. The heat on my legs tells me the engines are warm. Someone road these recently. I'd sure love a riding lesson from whatever bad boys own these.

The chill night air gives me a shiver.

As much as the mystery of these motorcycles and their riders intrigues me, I need to keep moving. I don't want to freeze out here.

I head back to the road and continue walking. Around a curve, I see a car parked on the gravel of the shoulder with its trunk open. A classic muscle car. A Pontiac GTO, I think. I have no idea what year, but it's old. Looks like the driver had a flat or a breakdown or whatever?

"Hello?" I call out then regret it.

I'm a girl all alone on a midnight road.

There's no telling which serial killer's car this is.

Better keep moving.

I glance in the open trunk as I pass.

No way.

Is that?

I unsling my backpack and pull out my Cricket phone. I'm out of minutes but not battery. I flip it open and shine it in the trunk.

No. Effing. Way.

There's like a *million* dollars in cash in the trunk.

Just sitting there in open black duffel bags.

My heart races.

This is enough money to live on forever.

Crap. I can't carry it. Maybe I can steal the car?

I lean in the open driver window and look for keys. Don't see any. Hmm. Aren't these older cars easier to hot wire than a modern racing motorcycle? Crap! Why didn't I watch any YouTube videos about hot-wiring classic muscle cars when I had the chance?

I bite my lower lip and think.

I don't need *all* the money. I'm not greedy.

I dash around to the back and reach into the trunk. Pick up a bundle of cash that's four inches thick, tied together with fat rubber bands. I riffle through a corner and see nothing but twenties. How much money is four inches of twenties? Thousands of dollars? Tens of thousands?

I have no idea, but I'm pretty sure my backpack alone will hold enough money for me to effing retire!

Using my phone for a flashlight, I unzip my backpack and start throwing out the clothes I don't need to make room. Bras, panties, socks. They may be essential, but I can always buy more!

This is in-freaking-sane!

"The fuck you think you're doing?" a gravely voice crackles behind me.

I gasp like a heart attack.

Another voice says, "Put that the fuck back, or I'll put you six feet under, bitch."

I turn slowly and see two big and scary men holding handguns at their sides. In the darkness, their faces are nothing but evil alligator eyes and flashing fangs. It's not what I see that scares me. It's what I feel. Pure, cannibalistic hatred.

Oh, crap cakes.

When in distress, flirt.

"Hey, boys." I flip my broken mohawk out of my eyes and stick my chest out. "What're your names?"

The first man rushes me, grabs me by the throat, and hurls me into the trunk. The other slams the lid, locking me in total darkness on a mattress of money.

"Get in the car," one grunts outside.

I kick the lid with my Docs and scream, "Let me out of here, assholes! You're not kidnapping me!"

Two car doors slam.

The engine rumbles to life.

Backfires twice.

"Let me out!" I scream, kicking with everything I have. "I said, LET! MEEEEE! OUUUT!"

The engine turns off.

Dead silence.

Boots grinding gravel, coming toward the trunk.

I ready my flashlight to shine it in their eyes. It's the only thing I can think. Distraction is all I have at this point because I'm literally cornered.

The trunk pops open.

Three men look down at me. Three *different* men dressed in black and leather. In the light of my phone, they're scary gorgeous. Youngish, but older than I am. They're eighteen? Maybe twenty? Twenty-five? I can't tell.

One guy is gigantic. Big as an NFL linebacker, his shoulders so broad he doesn't even need pads, but he's handsome, has close-cropped blond hair and emerald eyes, the epitome of big beastly beauty without any of the galoot.

The middle guy has short-cropped hair maybe a quarter inch long. On him, the look enhances his rugged charm and leads your eyes right to the wicked gleam in his sparkling sapphires. He's not nearly as big as the giant, but he's wearing a black tank top that shows off his very muscled shoulders, which are strapped with tattoos.

The third, who's the slimmest and trimmest, has dyed scarlet red hair dangling over chocolate eyes, and lush red pierced lips, giving him a mysterious allure I desperately want to kiss. He's the pretty boy of the bunch.

Wowie-wow wow-wow, these boys are beautiful. Total Baldwins.

Red says, "What's with the war paint?"

I reach up toward my cut up cheeks but don't touch them. "Erm, long story." When smitten, flirt. I grin at them, "What happened to the two cannibals?"

Wicked Eyes locks eyes with me and smirks, "You guys can have the cash. I'm taking the girl."

The giant chuckles, "Not so fast. I saw her first."

"I *claimed* her first," Wicked Eyes insists.

Claimed me? Who said I was claimed?! I'm nobody's property! Not that I wouldn't consider it, under the circumstances.

Giant says, "We split her three ways."

I giggle nervously, "Nobody's splitting me."

Wicked Eyes grins, "He meant we'll split you three times. I split first."

"*Split* me?" I snort, mildly offended because I'm pretty sure I know what they mean by split, and it isn't cannibalistic. He means the animalistic kind of splitting. The kind I should find offensive considering they don't even know me, but instead find intensely appealing. What can I say? They're *that* hot.

Red says, "Ignore these two douches. They'd rather fight each other than wrestle you. Me on the other hand…" He flips me a sexy wink and offers his hand. "The pleasure is all… yours."

"Mine?!" I titter. How can I resist? I take Red's hand and he helps me out of the trunk.

Wicked Eyes does a wolf-whistle as he looks me over.

"Would you stop?" I shift from boot to boot on the gravel.

"I'm just getting started, babe," he says.

I almost tell him not to call me babe, then I realize I like it.

Wicked Eyes fingers the lapel of my studded leather jacket.

"Nice hair," Giant says, and tousles my broken mohawk.

Before I can even react, Red pulls me away from the other two, still holding my hand.

Did I mention my hand is on fire? The one Red is holding? Flames rush up my arm and light up my heart. I did say he's the prettiest. If he wasn't holding my hand, I'm pretty sure I'd swoon. My knees are melting from the heat. When I catch the heady scent of rosewood and spice, they nearly buckle.

"Who are you guys?" I ask. As sexy as they are, I'm a trifle terrified by their rutting and wolfish eyes. "And what happened to the two other —"

Two backfires crack the night silence. Wait, the GTO's engine is off. They can't be backfires, unless it's some other car off in the distance. Or gunshots. Hold on. Were the two backfires I heard earlier actually backfires too? Or were they—

I glance over at the GTO.

The two cannibals are slumped in their seats. It's too dark to see if they're bleeding or… Without thinking, I blurt, "Did you guys just—"

"It's best not to ask," Red says, positioning himself between me and the front of the car, and flashing me the most sultry smile I've ever seen while arching what has to be a recently sculpted eyebrow, it's that precisely shaped.

Before I can swoon, two men with handguns rush from the darkness, slowing when they see me and the Baldwins.

"Get behind me," Red mutters in my ear.

He doesn't have to tell me twice. I'm frightened but hiding it when I slide behind him. He's much taller than I am, so I have to peer around his shoulder instead of over it.

"What'd you do to them?" the third cannibal demands, motioning at the GTO.

"Ask them," Red says, tipping his head toward Giant and Wicked Eyes.

For some reason, I expect those two to step up behind Red as a show of force. They don't. They lounge leaning against the GTO, amused smiles on their faces.

"Out of ammo?" Red asks.

"No," the third cannibal snorts.

"Then shoot me already. I'm not armed."

I mutter behind him, "Are you insane?"

"Quiet, pussy riot."

"Don't call me that!" I hiss. "Wait, are you talking about the Russian girl punk band?"

"Shh," Red says. "Not now." In a louder voice aimed at the two standing cannibals, he says, "Go ahead and reload. I'll wait."

I'm starting to realize Red really is insane. Or too smart for his own good. Me, I'm scared out of my mind. I'm pretty sure strong enough bullets can go through at least two people, if not three. My heart is thudding in my chest and telling me I'm crazy for standing here instead of running for it.

"They're out of ammo," Giant says lazily. He and Wicked Eyes don't seem scared at all.

"Somebody do something already," Wicked Eyes says to everyone. "I'm falling asleep over here." To Giant, he mutters with amusement, "I'll give you two to one odds on those two winning."

"Them?" Giant chuckles. "No, man. Four to one. A quarter of our shares."

"Half."

"Deal."

They bump fists.

I glare at them and whisper, "Why aren't you guys helping your friend?!"

Wicked Eyes shrugs, "Who said he's our friend?"

I gape at him in complete disbelief.

Red sighs audibly and is probably rolling his eyes, but I can't tell because I'm cowering behind him. He mutters to me, "Go stand with them, Debbie Harry."

I hesitate.

"Go already."

I trot over to the GTO and hide behind the far side, worried about getting shot. Giant and Wicked Eyes barely look at me and they don't bother hiding.

"Who's first?" Red asks the two standing cannibals.

They don't waste any time with small talk, hurling themselves at Red, who is half their size. Red ducks, kicks a knee with a savage crack, spins low, sweeps the leg of the other guy, and both cannibals are down on the ground, writhing in pain. From the sound of it, I think Red might have broken the first guy's kneecap and the second guy's ankle.

"Pay up, asshole," Giant laughs, waving his hand expectantly.

"They looked like they could handle themselves," Wicked Eyes says to himself, amused.

Red turns to me and flashes his luscious smile. That spicy rosewood scent of his tickles my fancy like he wants to put a bun in my oven.

"You okay?" he asks, brushing a thumb across my chin.

My skin lights with butterfly fire where he touches me and I blush. It takes a moment to collect my thoughts. Just when I have them in hand, I notice his thick lashes and dreamy eyes climbing into mine, and my thoughts slip through my fingers like so many rose petals.

"I asked if you're okay," he grins, his eyes half-lidded.

I giggle, "Um, yeah. Where, um, where'd you learn to fight like that?"

"I was a famous swordsman in a former life," he winks.

"But you don't have a sword," I snicker.

"Check my pants. I'm like sheathed steel just looking at you, Debbie Harry."

I know he's referring to the punk rock icon. I'm totally flattered, but I say, "My name's Mary. What's yours?"

"Call me—"

"What the fuck are you still doing here?" a hoarse voice grates from the darkness, somewhere in the trees across the road.

I clench my teeth in fear, but Red casually turns to face the newest arrival. All I see is his silhouette. The new guy is big. Not as big as Giant, who's almost too big, but larger than Red and Wicked Eyes, and he's dripping alpha male confidence. I can feel it coming off him in agitated waves as he strides into the road.

"We need to get the money and go," Alpha says.

That wakes up Giant and Wicked Eyes, who jump into motion.

Alpha freezes when he sees me, stopping in the middle of the road.

That's when I see the blood. In the moonlight, it's almost black. I tell myself it's motor oil, but that tangy coppery smell hits my nostrils and I have no doubt what it is. I also see slick black smears on Alpha's face, which is mostly shadowed, except for his burning bright eyes.

"Who's this?" he commands, glancing at me.

Red says, "We found her in the trunk."

"Is she with them?"

"No!" I blurt, not wanting to end up like the four cannibals. "I was just—! I ran out of gas! My motorcycle is back a ways! I was looking for help when I found the car. Those other guys tried to kidnap me." My voice trails off as I say it. This is more crazy than I'm used to, and I'm used to quite a bit.

Alpha strides up to me and grabs my chin hard, turning my face this way and that.

I can't see his face because the moon is behind him, but I feel his hard eyes burning into mine with brutal disdain. I can't decide if I like it or despise it, but it's clear to me that this man doesn't give a damn what anyone else thinks, least of all me.

"Careful," I warn, offended.

"Who cut you? Was it them?" He obviously means the cannibals and the scratches on my face. "If it was them, I will fucking—"

"No!" I interrupt, not wanting Alpha to murder anyone in front of me. I can't take any more drama tonight, let alone that level. "It was these bitches at my high school."

"Bitches?" He grunts in frustration, like if I'd said men, he might hunt them down and kill them. Don't ask me how I know, I can just feel it, which is totally weird because I don't know this guy and he doesn't know me, and it's hard not to take the look on his face as anything other than hate for me and the rest of the world.

I sigh, "Emily and her snooty cheerleader entourage. They jumped me today. You should see what I did to them," I lie like I got more than zero good hits in. "It's fine. I'll heal."

Alpha growls, "What the fuck are you doing out here?"

"I told you, I ran out of gas." Are those tattoos on his neck? Hard to say in this light. When he releases me with a savage grunt, I feel and smell wet blood on my jaw from where he was touching me, like I've been marked. I don't know how else to explain it.

"We need to bail," Alpha says to his men.

The other three men busy themselves zipping up duffel bags of cash in the trunk.

Red says, "Let's take her with us."

My chest seizes briefly at the idea. These four mysterious men and their money? Taking me who knows where? To do who knows what? Let's just say, this girl knows how to dream!

"We'll take turns," Wicked Eyes says, sounding entirely entitled.

"Hey!" I warn, as if any of these four guys would ever listen to what little old me had to say, but I say it anyway.

"Shut up," Alpha barks at Wicked while his hard eyes stay on me.

"Nobody's taking any turns and we're not taking her with us."

Am I disappointed? Of course I am! So what if these guys are obviously outlaws?

"This is our problem, not hers," Alpha adds. He barks at me, "Do you have a phone?"

"What?!" I can't figure out why he's asking.

"Do you have a phone?!" he snarls.

"Yes! No! I mean, I don't have any minutes! It's a Cricket."

"Take mine. It's in my pocket," he commands.

"What?!"

"Reach in and get it! I lost my gloves. I don't want to leave any DNA."

I'm mystified.

"Stick your hand in my pocket and take my goddamn phone!"

"Okay," I whine, staring at his pants. "Which pocket?"

"The left one."

I reach for it.

"The other left!" he barks.

"Sorry." I pull on the appropriate pocket. His pants are rather tight. "Should I? Or do you want me to?"

"Quit fucking around and take it!"

Every time he yells at me, something explodes in my chest. Fear? Arousal? I can't tell, but it's intense. No man has ever made me feel this way before. It's intoxicating.

"Take the damn phone!"

"Alright, alright!" I carefully slide my fingers into his pocket, feeling for the phone. My fingers bump something hard and large. It's not just hard, it's—

He grunts.

"Is that your...?" I'm afraid to say it, but I swear I can feel his heartbeat throbbing against my fingers.

"Take the fucking phone," he groans.

I hastily dig deeper and find the sharp corner of what is most definitely not him, I mean, is most definitely a phone. I slide it out.

"It's a burner and it has plenty of minutes. Get rid of it as soon as you get help."

"Why?"

"Just get rid of it!"

He's already off and running, grabbing a black duffel bag of cash from the trunk of the GTO, zipping it, and strapping it over his shoulders. The rest of his pack does the same and chases after.

Red trails in the rear and hollers over his shoulder, "Hey, War Paint!

Don't let those cheerleader bitches get you down!" Obviously, he overheard my conversation with Alpha. "Next time they come at you, bomb their lockers!"

"What?!" I laugh, not sure if he's kidding.

He might not be. He stops long enough to blow me a kiss.

It's the sweetest thing I've ever seen and I pretend to snatch it from the air and press it against my lips.

He smirks, "I'd love to blow you more than that, but that's your job!"

"Shut up!" I laugh.

He salutes me and says, "See you around, War Paint!" He throws something. "Here, catch! You look like you need it!"

"Need what?!"

A small dark blur sails toward me and I snatch it flapping out of the air. There's just enough moonlight to see it's a stack of twenties. About a half inch of them. I'll have to count it later because I'm ready to swoon as I watch him sprint after his friends down the road back the way I came. Not ready to say goodbye, I trot after them, but they're impossibly fast and I couldn't catch them if I tried. Minutes later, four fast shadows blast past me, engines screaming.

The four motorcycles I saw earlier. They don't have any lights on. How can they see when it's this dark? I can barely see my hand in front of my face, but they're racing down the road like it's daylight. What, do they have night vision or something? Are they *actual* werewolves?

No, I snicker to myself. That is totally ridiculous.

Everyone knows there aren't any werewolves for *real* real.

I'm just letting my imagination run away with me.

I wish *they* had let me run away with them.

When the sound of their motorcycle engines fades to nothing, I look at the burner phone in my hand. At least they didn't strand me when they abandoned me. I punch in 911. Before I can hit the Talk button to connect the call, I see blue and reds sparkle, gemming the dark woods behind me. That was quick. I haven't even talked to the 911 operator. Then I hear the helicopter.

Oh, crap.

I'm standing here with two injured men and two more who might be dead. If you include the blood on Alpha's hands (the same blood he left on my jaw), there might be even more dead people in the woods. I smear the blood off my jaw with the inside sleeve of my leather jacket.

Time for me to run!

Straight into the woods where I can hide until the commotion blows over.

Chapter 3

Turns out the sheriff's department helicopter has night vision cameras like every other police helicopter these days. They find me within minutes hiding in some bushes. They also find the coke or meth or whatever it was I'd taken from Dwight and Shayla's trailer still in the pocket of my leather jacket. I totally forgot about it.

The sheriff isn't too happy about that.

I am. It makes the perfect cover story. When they get me to the sheriff's office, they don't mention the car or the cannibals, but they do grill me about what I was doing in the woods in the middle of the night with drugs and $2,320 in twenties.

I almost blurt out, "How much?!" in surprise, but don't. Instead, my heart sprouts angel wings and flutters around inside my chest for a few moments as I think about that handsome devil Red. Tonight he gave me more money at one time than I've ever had altogether in my entire life, and he did it like an afterthought. Such a charmer.

When the deputies press me for an answer, I play dumb and say it's my life savings (it is now), and I was hitchhiking and hid when I heard what I thought was gunshots on the road.

They believe me about that part.

I ask if it *was* gunshots.

That's when they get weird and shifty and turn the topic back to me. They ask where I got the drugs.

I'm like, "Someone gave them to me?"

"Can you give us a name or a description?"

"A short guy at a bar?" Dwight is short, and the trailer may as well be a bar most nights.

They're like, "You don't look old enough for bars. Are you a minor?"

And I'm like, "Coal and gold, dude. Coal and gold." I mime like I have a pickax. "When the veins play out, I'm down by the river panning by hand. Then it's drifting to the next town looking for prospecting work wherever I can find it, you know?"

They don't think that's funny, and they're like, "What happened to your face?"

"Fight with a girl over a boy." I don't say who.

They believe that, but they're like, "Who're your parents?"

"Don't have any," I say truthfully. "I lost them when I was ten."

They ask a hundred other questions about where I live, who takes care of me, and gabba, gabba, hey.

I say nobody and nowhere, which is basically true.

They drop that topic and ask me about Dwight's stolen motorcycle, which they found, obviously. I left it on the side of the road in plain sight. Guess who reported it stolen?

I'm like, "What motorcycle?"

They're like, "Is your name Mary Angerman?"

And I'm like, "Courtney Love?"

They don't like that answer, or the next ten names I give them, so they stop asking.

Since I'm not talking, some sleepy deputy calls CPS. Nobody wants to come out and get me in the middle of the night, so I end up in the drunk tank. Get my own private cell. At least it's quieter than Dwight and Shayla fighting back at their toilet of a trailer.

Oh, the irony.

I lay there alone, a warm blanket of wicked sensations comforting me as I think about my four dark saviors. Red, Giant, Wicked Eyes, and Alpha. Those boys were this girl's fantasy made flesh. I wish I'd seen more of theirs. Too bad I'll never see them again. That night, I yearn for what might've been had they taken me with. Trapped in this cell, fantasy is all I have.

What a way to spend my sixteenth birthday.

Oh, did I not mention that?

I guess my sweet sixteen got lost in the shuffle of the shit storm that is my life.

Silly me.

At least Red gave me a birthday gift. Assuming I get it back and it doesn't go into the evidence locker or wherever.

The next morning, CPS shows up and has me shipped off to juvi. Guess I was wrong about running away from my problems, and "they" were totally right. I just ran into a much bigger one that won't let go.

Chapter 4

"KICK THE BITCH'S ASS!"

That bitch is me. I've been locked up in Juvi for the past three days. My limp pink mohawk hangs over my eyes like unruly bangs. They don't let us have product here in lockup. Did you know hairspray is a deadly weapon? All you need is a match.

"KILL HER!"

"MAKE THE BITCH BLEED!"

The screeching hyenas throwing shade in my face right now are my best frenemies here in juvi. The Constance Q. Montforte Juvenile Detention Center, to be exact. Don't ask me what the Q stands for, but with a dusty old name like that, I'm thinking add a U, a couple Es, and one other letter. I'll let you guess which one.

"Fucking slut! Stole my shampoo out the shower!" the big white hyena snarls as she charges.

"You weren't using it," I snark then dodge.

It's true. Queen LaQueefa's straw blonde hair is matted and clumped in oily locks. She thunders past, her large arms missing me by a mile.

I've always been fast on my feet because I was born running. Still moving, I try to break out of the surrounding circle of girls in orange jumpsuits. They shove me back into the ring. So much for my escape plan. Guess I'm fighting my way out like always.

"Get back here, slut!" the Queen screams. "I'm gonna tear your tits off!" She whirls and hurls her claws at me like she means it.

I duck under and punch, a pink flash as I attack.

Crack!

I hit LaQueefa right in the eye.

Her head snaps back briefly, but it doesn't bother her.

I'm already throwing another punch.

Which she catches in her ham hand.

Shit.

I may be quick, and I may be strong for my size, but I'm not cavewoman strong.

She has me by the wrist and ninjas me to the dirt ground of the yard, knocking the wind out of me. Then she drops on my chest, squashing my breasts as she sits down with all her weight.

I thought I didn't have any wind left to wheeze, but I do.

Now I really can't move and my vision stars.

Next thing I know, she has one hand on my throat, and the other is holding a toothbrush like a knife, pointing the sharpened handle an inch from my eye. Her hateful lips peel back over cemetery teeth and she cackles, "Bitch, you gonna get it now."

The toothbrush is so close to my eye, it's blurry.

Did I mention I've always dreamed of being a badass lady pirate with a sexy eyepatch?

LaQueefa snarls, "I'm gonna blind both your eyes out, you punk-ass little bitch."

I didn't say two eyepatches!

"Blind them right out!" She smiles a hateful grin.

I'm ready to piss my panties, but I'm not giving up either eye for this witch. Time to bitch-slap her smile into submission. Hard as I can, I slap cupped hands over her ears.

LaQueefa screams in pain and rolls off me. Her fingers explode open and she drops the toothbrush so she can cover her ears. She rolls writhing on the ground and I grab the toothbrush.

I spring to my feet and spin a circle, expecting her friends to jump me from behind.

"Break it up, break it up!" the guards shout as they rush over.

What do they find?

LaQueefa on the ground with blood dribbling out her ears and me standing over her with a deadly plastic prison shank.

<(—)>

"Felony assault with a deadly weapon and attempted murder," the tired public defender says as she reads over the charges from the paperwork laying on the table between us. She's older and wears a cheap navy skirt suit. Her name is Nadine Something.

I can't remember what because I'm a little frazzled. I say, "I didn't try to murder her! I was trying to get her off me!"

Nadine levels a look at me over her reading glasses and purses her lips. Her eyes say she's heard it all before. Her mouth says, "Her ears were bleeding. She has two punctured eardrums. You were holding a sharpened toothbrush. Six witnesses say you stabbed her in the ears."

"I did not! They're lying! That toothbrush isn't even mine! It's hers!"

Nadine arches an eyelid because she's been arching the eyebrow over it ever since she came in here, and the eyelid is all she has left to work with. She says, "It doesn't look good."

"You have to believe me!" I plead.

"I'm not the one you have to convince, Mary. It's the jury I'm worried about."

I shriek, "Jury? What jury?!" I know from extensive experience that juvenile cases are decided by a judge, not a jury. They only use juries when—

"They want to try you as an adult."

"No!" I gasp.

"I'm very sorry, Mary."

"Not half as sorry as I am! This isn't right! That big bitch attacked me! She had the shank! I was just trying to save my own ass because you people won't!" Now I am crying. I can't help it.

Nadine reaches across the table and gives my wrist a motherly squeeze.

"Don't touch me!" I bark and yank my arm away. Having spent nearly half my underage life getting kicked around in foster care, and I hate being touched unless—

((((pitch black))))

((((pain))))

—I'm warned at least a week in advance.

"We'll get through this," Nadine encourages softly.

"We?!" I sneer and shoot to my feet, "Oh! Are you going to jail with me, Nadine?! Are you going to be my cellie?! Are we going to spoon together every night so none of the other women try to rape me?! That's right, Nadine! Female rape is a thing! You don't need a dick to do it! They use other things! Sharp things! Oh wait, let me guess. You've never been to jail, have you?! Have you?!" I'm inches away from her face because I'm so damn mad and scared at the same time.

Nadine gives me a pained look. "I'll do everything for you I can, Mary. I won't let you down."

"Bullshit, Nadine! That is total bullshit and you know it! The system has let me down my whole life! That's not changing now and we both know it!"

The door to the interrogation room opens and a big deputy sticks his head inside. He says, "Everything okay in here, Nadine?" They know each other.

She says over her shoulder, "I'm fine, Jeb. It's a lot for her to process right now. You understand."

I barely notice because I'm freaking the fuck out about spending years in a women's prison. Years. Everyone knows American prisons *ruin* people. I'm already ruined enough. I don't need *more* ruining. For once in my life, I need less.

You know that saying, "When you hit rock bottom, the only place to go is up?"

It's bullshit.

When you hit rock bottom, you still haven't hit prison.

I eye the open door. If I wanted, I could slip under Jeb's arm and make a run for it down the hallway. I tense my legs under the table, ready to spring from my seat.

A commotion in the hallway attracts Jeb's attention. His eyes glance to the side.

Time to make my move.

Before I can launch into action, some stuffy old dude in a fancy suit is beside Jeb and blocking my exit. Stuffy's skin is so pale and translucent, it's almost vampiric. Not that that's a thing, but you never know.

Stuffy the Vampire makes eye contact with Nadine and says, "A moment, if you please."

Nadine frowns, "Who're you?"

"I'll explain outside," Stuffy says.

"Are you from the DA's office? Jeb? Do you know him?"

Jeb shakes his head.

Nadine glances at me.

I roll my eyes because I've never seen Stuffy before in my life.

A very serious looking middle-aged man in a rumpled suit steps up behind Stuffy like he's catching up to the man.

Nadine says to Mr. Rumpled, "Colin? What's going on?" Nadine turns to me and says, "Colin works at the courthouse. For the district attorney."

"Is that a good thing?" I ask.

"I don't know." Nadine shakes her head uncertainly.

"Shall we?" Stuffy asks the room.

Colin gives Nadine a nod.

She says, "Is this in regards to Mary?"

"It is," Stuffy says.

"Okay then," Nadine nods, stands, and brushes down her skirt. On her way out she says to me, "I'll be right back. Hang tight."

"Take your time," I smirk. The longer the better.

Jeb closes the door.

I immediately start looking for a way out. I'll climb through the ceiling if I have to. No, it's solid. So is the floor. Anybody have a jackhammer? Like, a team of hot muscled sweaty construction models from Abercrombie & Fitch or wherever to dig me out of here? No? Not today? A girl can dream.

In lieu of that fantasy, I wrack my brains for an escape plan.

<(—)>

When they come back in, I'm clutching a paperclip from Nadine's papers in my fist. It's the best I could come up with on short notice. I can use it to pick a lock later if I have to. Not that I know how, but necessity is the mother of invention and desperation is her cheerleader.

Nadine is beaming a smile when she sits down. I know that look. Seen it a thousand times. It means I'm not her problem anymore.

"Good news," she gushes.

I try to perk my resting bitch face up into a smile, but I just can't. I know better. "What?"

"Nothing like this has ever happened before…"

"Tell me about it," I grumble.

Nadine glances at Stuffy, then smiles to me, "Mr. Ralston has arranged to have your charges dropped."

Stuffy is obviously Mr. Ralston.

I snort a laugh at him, "Whose dick did you suck to make that happen?" I know how the system works.

Nobody laughs.

"Sorry," I mutter under my breath. "I should've said blood." I don't believe in vampires, but Mr. Ralston is seriously pale. "Whose blood did you suck?"

They still don't think it's funny.

Flustered, I hiss, "I'm kinda stressed out, okay? Sorry!"

Nadine regroups and weaves her fingers together, clasping her hands on the table. She says cheerily, "As I was saying, Mr. Ralston would like to make you an offer."

I almost blurt out that I'm not sucking his dick for any price. He's grandpa old. Ew, just, ew. I sigh, "And?"

"And," Nadine nods and smiles enthusiastically, "you should really hear him out."

He steps up behind her all smiles and says, "Allow me to introduce myself, Miss Angerman. My name is Mr. Ralston and I am the assistant to the headmaster at Castle Hill Academy. I have come here today to offer you the opportunity of a lifetime."

"Which is?" I prompt, folding my arms across my chest.

Mr. Ralston puffs up proudly. "In exchange for the dismissal of all charges, we at Castle Hill would like to take you into our custody."

"I don't like the sound of that," I say cautiously, trying not to think what sort of custody Mr. Ralston has in mind. I don't like the word headmaster either, and when I hear the word castle I think dungeon, which is obviously worse than prison, because dungeons have actual torture chambers with toothless torturers who are ready and waiting to do their worst. I'm already seeing sizzling hot pokers aiming for my fingernails.

Mr. Ralston smiles, "I can see by your reluctance that you misunderstand my meaning, Miss Angerman. We would like to offer you admission into our program."

"What program?"

"The Castle Hill Academy work-study program."

I frown, "What's Castle Hill again?"

"Why, it's one of the most prestigious preparatory academies in the world, if not thee."

"*Thee* what? Most prestigious?"

Winking at Nadine, Mr. Ralston chortles, "She has a keen mind, this one. Exactly the sort of pupil we prefer."

I say, "Are you for real?"

"Very much so, Miss Angerman. As is our offer."

"Why me?"

"Examination of your school records indicates that you have untapped potential."

The only potential I'd like to tap is the potential to get the F out of here.

"With your permission, Miss Angerman, I would like to take you to the academy post haste. We are already three weeks into the first term of the school year, which according to your records is your second year in high school. Am I correct?"

"You are."

"Good. I wouldn't want you falling any further behind than you already are. Based on your impressive test scores, I have no doubt you can handle the course load and catch up with your classmates, but I would like to ensure you have the time you need to familiarize yourself with our little quirks before too long."

"So, erm, am I stuck at the school—"

"The *academy*," he's quick to add.

"Yeah, that. Will I be stuck working there for like, ever?"

"Certainly not. Upon completion of your junior and senior high school years, you will receive a high school diploma."

"Then I'm out?"

"No," he smiles. "You will remain in our custody another two years while you accrue two years worth of college credit, at which time you will be granted an associate's degree in your chosen field."

"Wait, *I* get to choose?"

"You do indeed. At the completion of your four years, you will be free to go, armed with the finest preparatory education the world has to offer. If you play your cards right, the contacts you make at Castle Hill will provide you with entré into the most prestigious universities in the world."

I smirk, "I'll never be able to afford one of those."

"If you maintain a 3.9 GPA or above for all four years while at Castle Hill, you will be eligible for our scholarship program, which will cover the cost of two years worth of tuition, room, board, and books at the university of your choosing."

I snort, "Any university? Like Stanford or Harvard or wherever?" I know those schools are crazy expensive, but I like to set my sights high, even if I never get where I'm going.

Mr. Ralston nods enthusiastically, "Yes, Miss Angerman. *Any* university."

I blurt a laugh.

This is literally too good to be true. In other words, I don't believe a word he's saying. He must've bribed the sheriff or something. It's the only explanation.

I arch an eyebrow because everyone else in the room seems to have forgotten how, and I say, "Okay, if you're for real, what's the catch?"

Chapter 5

Mr. Ralston leads me out to the parking lot of the Constance Q. Montforte Juvenile Detention Center. Such a weird name.

I can smell freedom already, and it smells like sunshine and blue skies. Today is going to be another hot end-of-summer day. A warm wind is already billowing through the trees. They gave my clothes back, but it's already too hot for my leather jacket, which I have slung over one shoulder. My backpack is slung over the other.

I'd make a run for it if deputy Jeb wasn't beside me. I'm not handcuffed, but with him here, it's best I behave. Later, when it's just Mr. Ralston and me at a gas station or wherever, I'll bolt then. He's too old to stop me. Unless he's a vampire, which he isn't, obviously and thank goodness. Too bad I didn't have garlic for lunch.

Mr. Ralston opens the back door of a brand new big black Mercedes.

I climb in and he shuts the door.

"Oh shit!" I gasp and clutch my backpack to my chest like a shield.

There's a huge scary dude sitting beside me in the leather backseat. From the side, he looks mean. Prison mean. Tattoos crawl up his neck from under his jumpsuit like monster vines trying to eat him alive. The hard look on his face says he doesn't care what they or anyone tries to do to him because he'll eat them first.

He doesn't scare me, but he does make a snake spiral up my insides. When it wraps around my heart and squeezes, I try not to squirm.

I say, "You're too old for juvi."

He obviously is. At least twenty, maybe even twenty-five. Total man. He left boy behind forever ago. I may be boy crazy most days, but some days when I'm not paying attention, I go man crazy. And this one? Oh god, this man is *so* hot. Painfully.

I glance over my shoulder out the back window and see Mr. Ralston talking on his phone while Jeb walks back into the building.

"I said," I say to Mr. Prison, "you're not from juvi, are you?"

He doesn't answer, just stares straight ahead like he's a statue. Then his scent hits me.

Leather and motor oil.

This man smells like a freaking motorcycle. He certainly is the human version of one, a walking rocket waiting to explode. All you have to do is twist his throttle and the magic happens. Or so I've been told. Ahem.

I look over his clothes. Auto mechanic's navy blue coveralls that stretch over his muscled chest. You can't miss it. Worn black leather work boots. Hard hands. He's got five o'clock shadow and it's not even noon. Swoon. The stitched patch on his boulder of a shoulder looks like a badge. Some sort of elaborate family crest.

The gothic letters say Castle Hill Academy.

That's when it clicks.

I say, "Did Mr. Ralston make you an offer too?" Mr. Prison is way too old for juvi, but maybe he's from the men's jail? I know it's not far from here. "Um, hello? Did you like, get out of doing prison time because of Mr. Ralston?"

Mr. Prison's jaw muscles tick and he heaves an irritated sigh like he can't stand my existence. Not even looking at me, he rumbles, "Stop talking." His voice hits like a whip.

That snake of his wrapped around my heart rears its fangs and bites down before quickly slithering away. I snort a gasping laugh, "Sor-*ry!*"

He goes back to being a stone statue. Not some delicate marble thing in the Louvre, more like a hard gargoyle keeping watch over Notre Dame, ready to swoop down and devour any intruders, except his skin is tanned a golden brown and exudes masculine vitality.

Gulp.

I'm not scared of him. I'm not.

Okay, maybe a little. But he's ignoring me so I look him over some more and see an elliptical patch on the far side of his chest. A name tag, but I can't read the embroidered letters from here. I lean forward to see.

"Rob? Is that your name?"

His head turns stone slow to face me and he growls, "Shut. Your—" His eyes meet mine and he suddenly swallows. "Mouth." His dark mahogany eyes fire and his face goes to war.

I'm speechless and I swallow too.

Why is he looking at me like that?

I can't tell if it's hate or rage, but it isn't happy and nice and let's be besties, that's for sure.

That heart snake comes back in a flash. This time, instead of coiling around my heart and biting, it coils around my chest and squeezes hard. I literally can't breathe. I'm stunned but my heart is racing.

He's freaking gorgeous, his finely sculpted face a work of hardened art, the lines refined, the planes perfection. I'll say it. He's too good looking to be true, but here he sits, his eyes devouring mine with relentless abandon.

Squirming and nervous, I say, "Are you doing the work-study thing like me?" Notice how I slipped in a subtle suggestion there at the end? Like me? Because I sure hope he does. Like me, that is. Fair is fair.

Eyes pinned forward, teeth clenched like fangs, he hisses low, "If you don't shut your mouth, so help me I will—"

Oh no. No, no, no, no.

I already know where this is going. Nobody talks to me like this twice and gets away with it. I don't care how big and dangerous he is. Total ass-helmet. Just as I'm about to cut *him* off and tell him to F the F so far off he Fs his way out of this car and off the planet, I recognize those eyes. And the neck tattoos. And the motor oil.

I blurt, "You're that guy from Friday night!"

He freezes stone cold.

"Oh my god!" I gasp. "It is you! I remember your eyes! You're Alpha!" I dreamt about those eyes all night, but I don't mention that. I'll *never* tell him that.

"Shut up," he hisses.

"You were at the car with the money! With your three friends!"

Alpha, aka Prison Rob, or whoever he actually is, lashes out so cobra fast, I never see it coming. With his big hand, he locks my entire forearm in a crushing grip.

White hot hammers smash my bones. It hurts so bad, I can't even squeal. Pain has taken over and I'm completely at his mercy.

He flicks his eyes out the back window at Mr. Ralston still on the phone, then gets right in my face. His eyes are blood fire. His face knots with rage. In a hiss so faint a snake might miss it, he says, "I don't know what you're talking about, Mouth. We have never met. You don't know me and you never will. Do you understand?"

I'm in so much pain I can't answer. My leather jacket offers no protection. The stud backs on the sleeve make it worse, digging into my skin like spikes. Doesn't seem to bother his hand any, and he's getting the pointy ends of the studs, but it's killing me.

"Do. You. Understand." It's an order, not a question and he growls, actually *growls* like a grizzly bear.

The only thing I can manage is the weakest squeak.

He relaxes his death grip on my wrist slightly and says, "Yes or no, Mouth? Do you understand?"

"Y-y-yes," I whisper-whimper.

He releases my wrist and sits up statue straight, eyes forward like nothing happened.

I cradle my arm to my chest. I don't need to peel off my leather jacket to know I probably have bloody marks in my skin from the stud backs. Even if I don't, I'm sure my entire forearm will be bruised come morning. What an ass!

I'm about to let vent my anger at him for being so harsh when I think better of it. Another peep might be the death of me. But I want to reassure him I would never tell on him, never rat him out to the sheriff or anyone else. I want to tell him I've got his back. Assuming that *was* him Friday night with Red, Giant, and Wicked Eyes.

Was it?

I know Rob isn't Red or Giant or Wicked Eyes. I got good looks at those three with the light from my phone Friday night. I never really saw Alpha except in shadow. I mean, I *thought* I saw neck tattoos, but it was really dark, it could've been a trick of the moonlight, and everyone has neck tattoos these days anyway. With Rob sitting down beside me, I can't even compare his size with my memory of Alpha's size Friday.

What about his reaction now?

That was damning.

Does it mean he's Alpha?

Not necessarily, but he's acting very guilty of something.

Mr. Ralston opens the driver door in front and folds himself creakily into the leather seat.

"My sincerest apologies for the delay," he gasps from the effort.

Even I know old vampires don't gasp from effort, they're super strong. Ergo, he isn't a vampire.

Unless he's faking.

"Are you two settled in?" His eyes meet mine in the rearview mirror.

"Uh, yeah, I guess," I mumble.

Mr. Ralston's eyes narrow, "Something wrong with your arm, Miss Angerman?"

"Uh, no," I lie. "It's fine." I lower it to my lap and try not to wince. "Perfectly settled and ready to go."

"Excellent." Mr. Ralston starts the car.

With ass-helmet Prison Rob sitting next to me, it's scientifically impossible for me to be settled. The only thing now is figuring out why. Is it because after the way he grabbed me just now I insta-hate him, or after what he and his friends did Friday night, it might be insta-luh—

Ha.

As if.

"Are we there yet?" I whine dramatically an hour later, half joking, half not.

Mr. Ralston says, "In due time, Miss Angerman. In due time." He says "due" like "dyoo." It's funny. So are his leather driving gloves and driving cap. It's not like we're in a convertible. But this is the closest I've ever come to riding in a limousine.

I'm sitting in the back of his big black Mercedes and he's been driving the whole time. Rob is next to me. I swear, he hasn't moved a muscle since we left juvi. He may as well be a stone slab.

My arm is feeling better, the pain no more than a dull throb, which might just be me because sitting next to Rob makes me throb all over. What can I say? I like danger.

It's hard to stay angry at Rob because he doesn't seem to care about whether or not I exist. I know, that sounds pathetic in more ways than I can count, but his wall of disinterest is a reminder he never would've touched me if I hadn't pestered him with questions.

I mean, yeah, he *totally* over-reacted, unless you consider that I may have witnessed him and his friends steal a million dollars and maybe kill some people Friday night. No big whoop.

During the drive, Mr. Ralston asks me a few friendly questions to break the boredom. I answer reluctantly. It's awkward with Rob listening. If he wasn't here, I'd be more likely to talk because Mr. Ralston seems nice enough, and you can never have too many friends, especially when you have zero. Those four werewolves Friday night don't count because I'll never see them again.

Unless Rob *is* Alpha?

Too bad he's such a chore.

I wish his three funner friends were here instead of him.

Sigh.

I look out the window at the passing trees. I have no idea where we're going, other than to Castle Hill, wherever that is. Somewhere way, way, *way* out in the country, obviously.

This whole time, I've been clutching my forgotten backpack in my hands like a shield. Blame Rob. He'd make a welcome mat defensive. When I realize I'm holding it, I rip the zipper open and dig through clothes until I find the money Red gave me. Still there. All $2,320 of it. It's a freaking fortune and it's all mine!

Next, I check for the other precious cargo I've been carrying around with me since forever:

A dog-eared library copy of The Voyage Out by Virginia Woolf. I've read it a dozen times.

Grayson's knife. When I stole it two homes ago before running away, I left him one of my earrings so he'd know it was me. A little silver dagger. A knife for a knife. It's symbolism. Sometimes I imagine him keeping my dangling dagger earring like I kept his knife. But you know boys. They lose everything that isn't attached. That's why I never gave Grayson my heart. I wanted to, but I knew he'd lose it.

My journal, which has the one remaining picture of my birth parents stuck inside. It's a nothing photo. Just them as high school sweethearts. It's so normal, which is why I love it so much. You can tell they're best friends. They're kissing and smiling while holding soft serve ice cream. My mom's cone is tipping over and the ice cream looks like it's about to spill off, but she's too focused on kissing my dad to care. Same for him. They're smiling so big, the kiss is more teeth than lips. It's awkward but it's honest.

That's why it's perfect.

Someone took the picture for them. I don't know who. One of my grandparents? I'll never know. They're gone too. Both sets.

In the background of the photo, you can see a fairy tale castle. It's the one from Disneyland or Disney World. I can't tell which because I've never been to either. At the rate I'm ruining my life, I probably never will.

I also have my birth mom's engagement ring and my dad's wedding band in a frayed velvet box. Those rings are the only things left of either of them besides this one picture.

I miss them so much it guts me.

Every night when my head hits the pillow, I think about them. Close my eyes and send my thoughts out to them, hoping they catch one or two. They've never answered back because that *is* a fairy tale. I know it's stupid, but that never stopped me from trying. Sometimes a stupid dream is all you have.

I find my copy of The Voyage Out near the top of my backpack. I have to dig for the ring box. When I open it a crack to peer inside, I hunch over it, acting like Rob might try and steal it or my money. When I see the rings, I breathe a slight sigh of relief and stuff them away.

Does Rob look?

Of course not.

When I dig out my journal and find the picture of my parents inside, my relief is complete. I press the picture over my heart for a moment, then look at it.

Mom! Dad! You're never going to believe the news!

I don't quite believe it either.

As far as I can tell, Mr. Ralston is legit. But you never know. Could be he *is* a vampire, and Rob is his mindless human muscle. No, that's stupid. Life isn't that show NOS4A2.

Either way, I fish through my backpack looking for Grayson's knife.

It's gone.

That's not good.

I immediately feel a trickle of fear, and quickly whip my head around to make sure Rob isn't about to suffocate me with a rag or plastic bag or whatever.

He isn't. He's still nothing but a handsome gargoyle looking straight ahead. Do vampires use gargoyle henchmen? Is that a thing? I don't know. But I do know you should always have a knife. No matter where you go, or who you're with, carry a knife. Grayson taught me that, and I couldn't agree more. More importantly, that knife is the only piece of Grayson I have left. I really want it back.

I say, "Mr. Ralston, did they give you back my knife?"

"They did." Mr. Ralston tosses a quick smile over his shoulder before putting his eyes back on the road.

"Can I have it back?"

"In dyoo time."

"How long is that?"

"Patience, Miss Angerman. Patience."

For a second, I think I see Rob's cheek curl into a ghost of a smile, but that must just be me. Everybody knows stone gargoyles *can't* smile.

<(—)>

They weren't kidding about the hill.

Going slow, it takes us like two hours to drive up a long and winding mountain road before we reach the summit.

They weren't kidding about the castle either.

I see the flying Spanish spires long before we get there. When we finally do, the place reminds me of the pictures I've seen of the legendary Hearst Castle in San Simeon, but more grand and much larger. Almost like a Spanish Hogwarts, but this place is real, an actual stone castle in the middle of nowhere. Then I see the terraces and columns and green gardens climbing up the hillside. They add a uniquely Greek or Roman flair that most definitely isn't Hogwarts. I almost don't want to use the word castle. It sounds too medieval, too grungy and dirty.

This place is… palatial.

Elegant and immense, delicate and strong at the same time, the sparkling picture-postcard of every girl's fairytale castle made real. How have I never heard of Castle Hill Academy before? Anyway, if Disney or Universal Studios or whoever knew about this place, they'd sell tickets.

I say, "Do you guys have rides?"

"Come again?" Mr. Ralston replies from behind the wheel.

"You know, roller coasters and stuff."

"Oh, no, certainly not," he chuckles. "But I do believe you will find your academic studies more than thrilling."

That's a laugh. Studying isn't thrilling. Unless…

My eyes light up and I suddenly say, "Wait. You guys don't teach students how to be wizards, do you?"

"No, Miss Angerman," he laughs. "Nothing of the sort. But our graduates frequently go on to shape the world as we know it."

"Huh?"

"In dyoo—"

"Dyoo time, Miss Angerman," I finish for him in my best upper-crust impression of him. "In *dyoo* time."

"Indyoobitably," he grins.

You know what?

I like Mr. Ralston. If the teachers at the academy are anything like him, I'm going to love this place.

As for Rob, it's like I don't exist.

Whatever.

I don't care because freaking Spanish Castle Magic is right in front of me! Yeah, Dwight is heavy into classic acid rock and he plays Jimi Hendrix every time he bites the bong, which is every day he isn't drinking. But I don't care anymore! I'll never see Dwight again! Or Shayla! Or Emily and Kaitlyn and their reptile friends!

This is my new home!

Bye, bye, Roosevelt High!

Say hello to Castle Hill Academy!

I couldn't be happier.

The sad part is, had someone told me what I was about to get myself into here at the academy, I would've opted for prison.

Chapter 6

"Thank you for the company, Mr. Fletcher," says Mr. Ralston. He's talking to Rob, who I'm assuming is Mr. Fletcher. We're parked in the Mercedes somewhere in a massive modern underground parking structure underneath the castle. We all climb out. "Mr. Fletcher, would you be so kind as to guide Miss Angerman to see the headmistress? I shall catch up in a moment. My bladder isn't what it used to be, I'm afraid." Mr. Ralston finishes with an embarrassed smile.

"Sure," Rob nods and Mr. Ralston goes the other way.

When my sunlit eyes adjust to the darkness underground, I can't believe what I'm seeing. The parking structure is so clean and white, doctors could operate, and it's bursting with the most expensive cars I've ever seen. Ferraris, Lambos, Bugattis, Bentleys, Aston Martins, Rolls Royces. By comparison, the Porsches, Jaguars, Mercedes, Range Rovers, and BMWs here look embarrassingly cheap.

"Whose are these?" I blurt in total awe. When Rob doesn't answer, I turn and see him walking away. "Hey! I asked you a question!"

He ignores me and keeps going.

I shout, "Were you in detention the day they taught manners class?" That doesn't stop him. I need to up my game. "Or just out behind the bleachers getting high?" Still nothing. "Skipping school and stealing cars?" He's still walking. I almost laugh because this guy is ridiculous. "Doing doughnuts in the football field with the groundskeeper's pickup truck?"

He stops. Turns. Glares, "Are you done?"

"What?" I snicker. "I'd totally do that. We can do it together. Do you know where he keeps his truck?" Yes, I'm flirting. Because, look at him! After we do those doughnuts, who knows what he might do? Or who. I know, it's stupid. He's too temperamental to bother with, but I can't help myself.

"You're wasting my time." *Because you're a waste of time.* He doesn't say it but his face does. "I have more important things to do than babysit you. Get your ass moving."

"Screw you! You can't talk to me like that!"

He explodes. Marches toward me like the Terminator or some other psychotic cyborg that cannot be stopped. It's either the sexiest thing I've ever seen, him coming at me like this, or the scariest. No, after the way he grabbed me in the car it's... Okay, I admit it's both.

My heart races and I rip my backpack open, digging for my knife, which I don't have because Mr. Ralston took it! Shi—!

A hard hand clamps down on my right wrist, the one that's not sore, before I can finish my thought. I fight hard, trying to break free, but his hand is a handcuff. I should've run!

"What are you doing?!" he demands.

"Let go of me! You're hurting me!" He isn't, but I whimper like he is. Never show your strength until you have to. Another thing Grayson taught me. "Would you let go already?!" I'm pulling as hard as I can, using my whole body, but he doesn't budge.

Rob tears my backpack out of my hands and digs through it, letting go of my wrist.

"That's mine! You can't do that!" Now I'm worried about my journal, my parents' photo, and their rings. "Be careful already!"

"Your knife," he grunts. "Where's your knife?"

"Mr. Ralston still has it!"

Rob's shoulders relax, but his eyes are dark fireworks. He shoves my backpack at me even though I'm still holding it, towering over me like a monument.

Now I really do want to run, but I'm paralyzed by those eyes.

His face changes, full lips peeling back over clenched teeth. I want to say fangs, but that's not quite right. His teeth are too perfect for fangs, but no less dangerous. He clamps his hand back on my wrist.

"Ow!" I whine for effect.

"Listen to me," he hisses. Glances furtively over each shoulder. What's that about? "I know what you did."

"Oh yeah?" I cock my hip defiantly. "I know what *you* did."

His snout does that hot werewolf thing and he glares at me. Two can play at his game.

I sneer, "I was there, remember? I *saw* what you did."

His snarl relaxes into the cockiest smirk I've ever seen and he says in a surprisingly friendly tone, "Really? What? What'd I do, Mouth? Tell me. Tell me everything you *know* that I did. Don't guess. Tell me the facts. What facts do you *know*, Mouth?"

"I… Well… You… Uh…" I release my breath, which I didn't realize I was holding in fear. I also realize he keeps calling me Mouth, and I can't decide if I love that he gave me a nickname or hate it, because who wants to be called Mouth? It's bad enough for a guy, but when you're a girl? It conjures nothing but sluttishness.

"You don't know shit, do you, Mouth?" His smirk gets cockier, if that's even possible. "You know what I know? I know the sheriff charged you with attempted murder."

I roll my eyes, "That's not what happened."

"That's what I heard."

"How would you know? You weren't there. What facts do *you* have, *Rob?*" Another thought barges in as I piece things together. "Wait, did Mr. Ralston tell you why I was in jail?"

Rob's eyes ice over, "This isn't a game, little girl. You're lucky as fuck you're in the work-study program and not lockup, same as me. If anyone finds out why you're here, they will kick you out faster than you can blink."

I snort, "That's ridiculous. They *know* why I'm here. Mr. Ralston signed the papers himself. I guess he told you, didn't he? I mean, about why I was charged?"

"Stop talking, Mouth. Listen like your life depends on it. Mr. Ralston isn't the problem. *They* are."

"Who's they? Has anyone ever told you you sound like a movie? You like conspiracy theories, don't you?"

Rob's nostrils flare like he's going to roar in my face so loud it blows my hair back, like the king T-Rex in Jurassic Park loud. He doesn't. "I'm not talking about the faculty."

"They know too," I say like I would know, which I don't, but they must. It wasn't like Mr. Ralston snuck me out of juvi. All those contracts and paperwork he and the notary had to sign with the people at the Sheriff's office? My case file is probably a matter of public record at this point. Everybody knows.

"The Alumni don't. The students don't. The parents don't."

"What parents?"

"Can you shut your mouth for more than two seconds? Is that possible?"

I'm already opening my mouth to reply when I clamp it shut and silently sneer at him, arching an annoyed eyebrow.

The evil crinkles around his nose decide to relax a tad. His meaty grip on my wrist doesn't, and now it is actually starting to hurt. His hands are really hard.

I *almost* say something, but think better of it.

He whispers, "Do not tell anyone why you're here."

"Who anyone?"

His eyes fire.

I roll mine and mime zipping my lips. When he doesn't say anything, I again arch an annoyed eyebrow, waiting.

"How are you not dead, Mouth?" he asks with unguarded sincerity.

"Mm?" I'd say more but my lips are zipped.

Suddenly, he's a different person. "PTSD."

"Mm?"

He nods. "Ralston said you were in foster care before juvi."

I shrug.

"How bad was it?" he asks.

((((pitch black))))

((((pain))))

I shrug again. What I can't figure out is, where did Prison Ass-King Rob go? Now he's like... Mr. Robbers Neighborhood Rob. Robbers because he could *never* pass as straight-laced Mr. Rogers, not even if you lasered off his neck tattoos. Rob exudes attitude and danger. Public Television wouldn't know what to do with him.

"Don't want to talk about it?" he asks with real concern.

I never want to talk about it. And no, I don't have—

((((pain pain pain))))

((((it it it))))

— PTSD. That's ridiculous. I sigh through zipped lips and let my head loll a slow roll to show how bored I am. When I'm done, I glare at him and snark sharply, "When did you get so nice?"

Out of nowhere, his Mr. Robbers nice guy look is clobbered away by a wall of fury, and his hot mahogany eyes fire once again. He looks ready to attack.

I cringe.

He says, "Did someone ever..." He can't finish his sentence, like spitting the words out would be like spitting out barbed wire.

I know, because I know *exactly* what he was going to say just now when he asked if someone had ever—

((((hurts hurts hurts))))

—had ever, you know, but didn't finish his sentence.

This Rob is giving me emotional whiplash. I can't decide if he hates *me,* or if he... I don't know what. But this thing now isn't hate.

"Did they?" he asks softly.

I know exactly which they he means this time.

((((please no))))

"No," I mutter meekly before I make the mistake of stupidly telling him the truth. If I do that, I might start crying and never stop.

His hand wrenches down on my wrist.

"Stop it!" I squeak. "What is wrong with you?!"

"Sorry," he says and releases me instantly. "It's just that when I... it makes me want to... if anyone ever... to you... I would..." His angry eyes prowl through mine, latching onto the truth even though I don't want him to.

He knows.

Damn it, he—

((((pain pain pain))))
((((it hurts!))))
—knows.

I don't even know Rob, but he seems to know me, like he's *always* known me, which is total romance novel nonsense. There's no way he can know me. We just met. But I feel it anyway, a warm rainstorm of hope washing away the hate and hurt in my heart, cleansing my soul to the core, seeping past my defenses in a hot torrent of—

That's when I panic.

Two horses pull me apart, one trying to steal me away to safety, to run away where I never have to think about the past. The other horse wants to take me and Rob to some fairy tale future where there is no pain, only love. Knowing that place definitely doesn't exist, I jump on the first horse, ready to flee.

The moment I turn my back on Rob, he grabs me from behind, spins me around, and pulls me into him. For a second, I think he's attacking me, but he isn't. He's holding me in the tightest, warmest, *lovingest* hug I've felt since losing my parents. He's really and truly hugging me with everything he has. The only way to describe it is as a *safe* embrace.

That's why I know it's a lie.

Since losing my parents, no embrace is ever safe.

I struggle against Rob's powerful arms and try not to whimper.

He won't let go.

I don't know if I want him to, and for a second I clutch the chest of his coveralls and—

Let me go!

I don't want to be held by anybody!

His arms are lying!

When I try to tear myself away, the sound of high heels clack across the concrete, startling both of us.

"Who're you raping this time, Rob?" a conniving female voice laughs.

Rob instantly lets me go, and practically hurls me out of his arms while spinning me around.

I'm thinking: Rape? *This* time?

Please don't let that be why Rob is here at the Academy.

Please don't let rape be his crime.

Please.

Chapter 7

Three female fashion models strut down the parking aisles between the luxury cars. The only thing they're missing is the catwalk lighting, but they nail everything else. The walk, the couture clothes, the heels, the hair. They've got the hot, the haute, and the haughty attitude.

Except it's not *actually* couture. They're wearing prep school uniforms, but they're so fashionable it's hard to tell. Pleated plaid burgundy skirts riding high enough over black silk stockings to show garters. Double-breasted navy blazers with flared cuffs, the blazers dangling open over half-buttoned blouses, starched and white. Loose burgundy neckties hanging like an invitation over what has to be breast implants for all three. Their boobs float like they don't need bras, the black lace of which you can see popping out, obviously. Lastly, patent black leather stripper heels. Stilettos. As deadly as the rest of their costume, because that's basically what they're wearing. The Halloween version of slutty prep school girls, but everything is so obviously expensive and high-end, I know it's the real deal.

As one, they stop and cock hips like they've practiced this move a thousand times. Before I can ask who their choreographer is, the blonde in the middle snorts, "Another one of your sluts?"

The brunette sneers, "Or does this one make you pay?"

The redhead giggles, "Rob never pays. He rapes."

Are they joking? I sure hope they're joking.

The loud popping of knuckles causes me to glance at Rob beside me. His fists are straining white at his sides. How to describe his face? I've never been a matador, but I can easily imagine the look in the black eyes of a bull before it charges and gores you with its horns because that is the *exact* look on Rob's face right now, except his eyes are twice as dark as those bull's.

The blonde teases, "Aren't you gonna say something, Rob?" There's a familiarity in the way she says it. Something almost too familiar.

I can't pin it down, but it's there. Are they a thing? No, that's ridiculous. She'd never be into someone like him, or him her. She's saving herself for an eighty year old billionaire. Rob doesn't look like he's saving himself for anyone or anything.

The brunette snarks, "This scratched up alley cat has his tongue." Her hateful gaze says I'm the alley cat with the face scratches and the tongue is… Rob's, and its location is—

"Right where she wants it," the redhead adds, looking me over like

I'm slutty scum.

The blonde is taking in my outfit with a sneer. "Isn't this one a little too dykey for your tastes, Rob? I know you like them young, but... this dykey?"

I glance down at my band shirt, ripped jeans, and studded leather jacket. What's wrong with being a lesbian? Or looking like one? Nothing.

I glare at the girls.

Beside me, Rob is cracking his knuckles and looks ready to bull-charge and start goring these whores with his horns.

No need.

I'll handle it.

I set down my backpack and march up to the blonde because she's obviously the leader, and slap her across the face as hard as I—

Except Rob stops me before I connect, hooking his arm around mine from behind. My fingernails are short, but come within an inch of clawing the blonde's nose off. The wind from my hand makes her blink her eyelash extensions and smoky eyes.

"Did she just...?" the brunette asks.

"I think she did," the redhead gasps.

I'm already kicking out at the blonde with my Docs, but Rob is pulling me back too quick for my boots to kick her professionally whitened teeth in.

"Leash your dyke dog, Rob," Blondie says, her perfect lips curling in disgust. Otherwise, she appears unfrazzled.

Brunette says, "Do it quick. I think she has rabies."

"And syphilis," Redhead adds.

"She's not mine," Rob growls and I'm crushed.

Not that I want to *be* his, but who doesn't want to be wanted?

"Someone oughta neuter her," Redhead says.

"It's spay!" I snarl. "Spaying is for girls! Neutering is for boys!"

"Like I said, dyke," Redhead smirks.

I admit, my mohawk isn't exactly feminine. But it is pink. "What're you doing!" I snarl at Rob. "I can take all three of these bitches! Let me go and I'll show them!"

"SHUT UP!" he roars, pulling me far enough away that the Silicones are safely out of reach.

"No!" I shout. "Why are you protecting them?!" I am so mad at him right now. "They deserve it!" I'm not usually this un-ladylike, but Rob and I were having a moment that was a little bit mystical, and they barged in and ruined it in the meanest way possible. I didn't make it this far in life giving in to entitled plastic Barbies like these three.

Rob hisses in my ear, "Do you want to get kicked out of here?"

"I want to kick their teeth in!" Since I'm too far away to do that, I spit. I don't have much spitting practice, because I'm not *entirely* un-ladylike, so my spit falls short, landing on the pavement a foot away from Blitchy the blonde bitch.

Blitchy's eyes slit and she scowls, "Do that again, and I will have you removed. Permanently."

"You and what army!" I yell. "I'm not afraid of you and your platinum blowout! Those are extensions, aren't they! As fake as your boobs! I can tell!"

"Muzzle her," Blitchy threatens Rob. "Or I will have her sent back to whatever garbage dump you took her from."

Rob's eyes lower like he's afraid to meet her gaze. "She doesn't mean it," he says, meaning me, that I am the she who doesn't mean it.

But I do! I really do! I'm practically gnashing my teeth when I say to him, "Don't apologize for me! She's asking for it!"

"Shut up!" he hisses in my ear. "Do you wanna go back and stand trial? Is that what you want?"

"Oooooh, I get it," Blitchy sneers. "She's in the work-study program, isn't she? Yet another one of your disposable Connie Convicts."

"Screw you!" I growl at her, noticing Blitchy has a delicate silver nose ring circling one nostril, and a silver tongue stud, both of which I would absolutely love to rip out. In a very ladylike way, of course. After, I'd hand them to her nicely and even curtsy for the honor.

"Let's go, girls," Blitchy says to the other two and they pile into a nearby Bentley. The car's engine purrs to life and it backs out of the space, pulls alongside us, and stops. The power window lowers silently. In a calm but commanding tone, Blitchy says, "I'm not kidding, Rob. Muzzle this bitch or she's done here."

I say, "You're the bitch, you Barbie-faced bitch! I dare you to step out of your limousine and fight me! No? Too scared? That's what I thought, you prissy little bitch!"

Blitchy stares at me, her face relaxed like she's on the verge of falling asleep, like she hardly notices my existence. It's probably from too much Botox. She yawns, "Are you done?"

I roll my eyes.

She frowns, "Don't you roll your eyes at me, gutter slut. I own this place and I own you, and don't you forget it."

"You don't own me!"

"Don't I? Lesson one, gutter slut. No back-talk to your betters."

"Screw you," I growl.

Blitchy twists in her seat, grabs what at first appears to be a Starbucks cup, but the logo actually reads Castle Hill Cafe, and peels off the lid.

Before I can react, she splashes the cold coffee at me, hitting my face and drenching my band shirt and studded leather jacket.

"Bitch!" I shriek, and launch myself at her, but Rob holds me tight from behind. "Stop protecting her!" I rage at him and kick for her car, trying to scuff the paint with my Docs. If only they were steel-toed. Either way, I can't quite reach the car, but I flail anyway.

"STOP FIGHTING!" Rob roars.

"I told you! It has rabies!" Brunette squeals gleefully.

"It does!" Redhead laughs.

At that point I realize I have a hint of whipped cream from Blitchy's cup stuck to my face. I can see the white fluff from the corners of my eyes.

Inside the Bentley, Blitchy and the Silicones laugh their asses off.

Again, I try to tear away from Rob and attack them, but he won't let go. Eventually, I give up.

"Pick that up," Blitchy says, glancing at the coffee cup on the pavement.

"Screw you!" I snarl.

"I wasn't talking to you, gutter slut. Speak only when spoken to. Rob, pick up the cup."

"Don't do it!" I plead. "She threw it!"

Rob growls behind me, clamps one hand around my bicep like a vise, and leans down to grab the cup.

"No!" I moan, coffee dripping off me. "Why'd you do that?"

Rob doesn't respond. He doesn't even look mad. He looks… vacant.

Honestly, I'm embarrassed. I mutter, "How can you let them treat you like that?"

A wicked smile spreads across Blitchy's plump lips and she says, "Because he knows his place. You'll learn yours soon enough, gutter slut."

I'm humiliated.

<(—)>

The Silicones laugh and I watch the car drive slowly out of the parking garage, glaring daggers at the Bentley's tires in hopes that they'll pop, which they don't. Mr. Ralston already said they don't teach wizardry here, but this girl never stops dreaming.

Rob is fuming beside me, his body a coiled spring.

I say, "You want to hit something, don't you?"

"What?!" he barks at me.

"Punch one of these cars. It'll make you feel better."

He looks at me like I'm stupid.

I smirk, "Don't believe me? Here. Watch." I dig into my backpack until I find the key to Dwight's Kawasaki, which the deputies let me keep for some reason. I hold it up so it catches the light. "Is one of these other cars those other girl's? The brunette's or the redhead's maybe?"

Rob glares.

I stroll over to a nearby Range Rover. "How about this one?" I'm about to drag the key along the front fender when Rob leaps forward and stops me, grabbing my wrist again. This time, it's gentle but firm and sends a spiral of desire sizzling through my body and I don't want him to ever let go.

"Put that away!" he whispers. "They have cameras everywhere!"

I wait for him to make me, to wrestle the key away or something equally foreplayish.

Instead, he lets go of my wrist, but he's mad. "How many times do I have to tell you, Mouth? Stop fucking around! If you do one wrong thing, you'll get kicked back to jail. You're already on Elizabeth's shit list. If you piss her off again, you're gone. She wasn't kidding. You're lucky you caught her on a good day." Now he's lecturing me and I can't stand it.

I snort, "That was her on a good day?"

"Are you hearing me, Mouth? This is serious."

"Fine! Whatever!" I stuff the key in my backpack, secretly gleeful he's again calling me Mouth. "I don't care what she thinks."

"You better start caring."

"Screw her. Eliza-*bitch* can suck my lady dick."

Rob's brows are knit into an angry frown, but one of the seams pops and he tries not to smile. "What did you just call her?"

I giggle, "You heard me."

"Eliza-bitch?" He's grinning like he's never heard anyone say it.

"Has no one seriously thought of that until now?"

"They think it, but nobody has the balls to say it that I've heard. If word got back to... *Elizabeth*—" he says it like he wants to say Eliza-bitch, but he's afraid to, "—she would go ballistic. Heads would roll."

"Literally? Like off with their heads? Because she seems like the type. You guys don't have guillotines around here, do you?"

He smirks, "What would you call going back to jail?"

I don't have an answer for that. "Wait, would *you* go back to jail if you pissed her off?"

He arches an eyebrow that says yes.

"Is it because you're in the work-study program?"

"And I'd like to keep it that way."

I almost cut in and ask him if he ever raped anybody like the Silicones said, but I seriously don't want to know. No, I don't need to know. Mr. Robbers here would never rape anybody. He's too nice under his hardened exterior. I can tell. When he saw into my soul, I saw into his.

He finishes, "So don't go pissing off Elizabeth or her friends."

"The other two? The brunette and the redhead?"

He nods, "Victoria and Jacqueline. They're not worth it. Doing your time here and walking away with a diploma is."

"Don't you have yours? Your diploma, I mean?"

He totally looks old enough for a degree, let alone a diploma, but he shakes his head, "Not yet. Still working on it." There's no way he's not eighteen.

"How old are you?"

"Old enough. Forget about me. Focus on not pissing off Elizabeth."

After what he did since we got in the parking garage, I could never forget a man like him, no matter how old or young he is, diploma or no diploma. In a weird way, I realize that a minute ago, he wasn't protecting Eliza-bitch from me, and he wasn't protecting me from her wrath either. Not literally. He was protecting me from *myself*. It wasn't like she was going to fight me. I could tell. Other than throwing drinks at you, rich girls like her never lift a finger. They pay people to lift their fingers for them. If Rob hadn't pulled me off Eliza-bitch, I would've slapped her nose job off, and then some. You can bet your best bra Eliza-bitch would press charges if I'd clawed her eyes out. Except Rob stepped in when it counted and literally saved me from jail. This man is much more complicated than I thought at first blush, and that's not counting whether or not he is or isn't Alpha. You know who isn't complicated? Eliza-bitch. She's a walking cliché. "Is she like, the Queen Bee-word around here or whatever?"

Rob smirks, "Close enough. Whatever you call her, don't say it to her face or anyone else."

"Anyone?"

"Not anyone. Do what she says or she will have you kicked back to jail. I mean it."

"Seriously? She can do that?"

He says cryptically, "At Castle Hill Academy, Elizabeth Morgan-Hearst can do anything she wants."

I don't know it at the time, but I will soon find out how right he is. Blitchy bitches be like that.

Rob says, "Keep your head down, Mouth. Life here isn't so bad if you follow orders. And do me a favor."

"What?"

"Learn to pick your battles," he winks. "I've got a thick skin. Elizabeth doesn't. I mean it when I said you caught her on a good day. I've never seen her this nice."

"Are you serious?" I laugh.

"Deadly."

"What, did she get laid last night? Or this morning or whenever?" I'm suddenly wondering if Rob is the one who laid her. No! No effing way! He'd never do a bitch like her!

"Probably," he smiles wide and tousles my limp mohawk like I'm a little kid.

I hate that he's treating me like a kid, but I love, no, I mean *like*, that he, I don't know… likes me enough to finally smile at me like maybe he likes *me*, even if it's just as a friend. And what a smile it is. It pulls at my soul, slipping past my defenses and cuddling up with my heart and spooning it before I realize he's doing it.

"Let's go," Rob grins and starts walking.

"Yeah," I titter and follow willingly.

Another thing I don't know at the time is that Rob's kindness is a blatant lie, his smile a traitorous thing no one should ever trust, especially not a gullible girl like me. If only I'd known better, but he tricked me. Hit me where I'm most vulnerable. Right in the feels.

I told you hugs are lies.

Chapter 8

Rob takes me up an elevator from the garage. Just me and him. Inside during the ride, I desperately want him to push me up against the wall and kiss me.

He doesn't.

I'm not exactly sure why. He's all over the place emotionally, he may or may not be a murderer or worse, but he's a walking wall of masculine perfection, we're alone, and he's irresistible. Isn't that good enough?

When the doors open, he walks me out to a gorgeous courtyard. Blue skies, tall palm trees, more marble columns, intricate red brick inlayed walkways with colorful patterned tiles, a round fountain with a statue of a patinated Poseidon or Neptune surrounded by nymphs, all of them lounging or frozen in mid-frolic on a raised dais held up by giant seahorses ridden by mermen. On every level, countless hanging flowers splash over balcony railings like rainbow waterfalls. In the distance, the vast cyan expanse of the ocean. I can almost smell the surf.

This place is paradise.

At the moment, I don't see any people around. Class must be in session. My mental lightbulb flips on sun-bright, and I say, "What did you say Elizabeth's last name is?"

"Morgan-Hearst."

"As in *the* Hearsts? Like, Hearst castle Hearst? Did they build this place? It totally reminds me of San Simeon."

"No, the Morgan-Hearsts are a different branch. No relation. From what I've heard, her family came over *before* the Mayflower got here. We're talking the oldest money in America, going way back. Back in the day, they had tobacco slave plantations all over the south. They had to get rid of the slaves after the Civil War, but they never got rid of the tobacco fields or the plantation mindset. These days, that means vaping products."

"Makes sense someone so vapid is into vaping."

"Yeah," he snickers.

"Wait, her family owned *slave* slaves?"

He smirks, "Where do you think she got her attitude?"

I grin, "From her weave being too tight? Botox on the brain? Her boob implants leaked silicone into her heart and hardened it?"

He chuckles, "Good breeding, according to her."

"What, is she a horse? Because she looks like one." That's totally not true. Plastic surgery or not, Eliza-bitch is wicked good looking, which makes her all the more hate-worthy.

"No, but her family has owned half the horses to ever win the Kentucky Derby."

"What?! That can't be true."

He nods. "Rumor has it, the Morgans and the Hearsts have royal blue blood coursing through their veins."

"What, like British Royals?"

"Who knows. European for sure, but with both sides of her family coming over so long ago, they could be British, French, Dutch, German, Russian. It's anybody's guess."

"Her family really owns Castle Hill Academy?"

"They built it shortly before the Civil War, so yeah."

"Wow. How rich is she?"

"Put it this way. When God needs a loan, he asks her family."

"Uh uh," I laugh.

"For real. Pick any exploding American industry, and they were in it from day one. Tobacco, cotton, steel, rail, banking, weaponry, electronics, computers, pharmaceuticals, the internet, artificial intelligence, and whatever other secret shit they're investing in."

"How do you know all this stuff?" I'm thoroughly impressed with Rob's insight. He's not just some pretty boy prison thug.

"Been here a while. You pick things up when you're the janitor. People talk."

"Is that your thing for the work-study program? Janitoring?"

"Yes, and janitoring isn't a word," he smirks.

My eyes light up and I snicker, "Listen to the word nerd nerding out over here."

"I don't plan on being a janitor forever." He smiles and his dark eyes light up with kindness and good humor. "You shouldn't either."

"Wait, is that what I have to do for my work studying? Janitoring?"

He grins, "Who knows. They'll assign you to something. It's random."

Suddenly, a mellifluous male voice calls out with friendly familiarity, "Well, well, well. If it isn't Rob Fletcher and his latest Connie Convict." Whoever it is sounds almost like Justin Timberlake singing, his voice is that handsome, but there's a cool cruelty to it you can't miss.

I lean around Rob to look.

The hottest bleach-blond surfer-tan boy you can possibly imagine comes sauntering up wearing a prep school suit. He's tall, broad shouldered, trim of hip, his blue eyes are lightning sapphire, his hair spun gold, his skin melted caramel, his cheekbones chiseled, his teeth and smile the most lickable looking candy confection I've ever seen. His tailored suit isn't half bad either. The jacket's gold buttons are diamond studded, the tie a silken shimmer, the gold piping and Castle Hill crest so vibrant, I almost think they're running rivulets of molten gold. The jacket material is a jeweled ultramarine blue, the slacks a royal purple so deep, it's almost black, but in the sunlight, the purple hue shines through.

Royalty.

That one word encapsulates everything this boy is.

He says, "Elizabeth told me about you, Connie." You meaning me.

He's still far enough away, and I'm hidden behind Rob, so I whisper, "Are this guy and Elizabeth a thing?"

Rob mutters, "Whenever he's not banging someone else."

"How often is that?" I ask.

"You mean how often *isn't* that."

"Is he one of those?"

"He's one of those," Rob answers.

In other words, manwhore.

I step out from behind Rob, who is standing tall, but his head hangs like he's bowing, his eyes studying the intricate brick pavers beneath his work boots.

Me on the other hand, I stare right at His Highness. Honestly, I can't take my eyes off him. Are my hands shaking? Yup, they're shaking. So is the rest of me. This young man is a walking icon of masculine perfection, the refined kind, everything every girl ever dreamed of.

"Eyes down," His Highness commands, a bitter slap.

"What?!" I snort.

"Eyes down!"

Rob hisses, "Don't look at him."

I laugh, "Are you serious?"

"Deadly," His Highness seethes, glaring at me with pure hate. "Put your eyes on the pavement, Connie, or I will put them there for you."

"My name's not Connie," I sneer. "It's Mary. What's yours? Prince Prick?"

He smiles, "Close. It's Prince."

"No it's not."

"Prince J. Lancaster the third. It would be customary for me to add at your service, but you, my luscious strumpet, will be at *my* service, always at my beck and call. Now do as I say. Eyes down. Now, strumpet."

"No," I snicker, staring right at him.

"No?" He cups my chin with a soft hand, his thumb lovingly caressing my jawline.

"No," I mutter. I'd tell him to let go of me, but I'm stopped by a bloom of pure pleasure sizzling down my neck. It swirls in my breasts, melting my resolve. I swear, I start to float. I'd look down to see if my feet have left the ground, but I can't look away from his beautiful blues. That doesn't stop me from adding, "Has anyone ever told you you sound like the middle school version of a bad Shakespeare play?"

A slow smile eases across his full lips. He leans in, inches from my ear. This young man reeks of affluence and privilege, but he smells divine, sandalwood and a hint of cinnamon that hits me with a shiver. As much as I hate to admit it, this guy is a god.

He whispers, "Oh, strumpet. Do you realize how happy you just made me? What a pleasure it will be to break you." His voice is a soft song, a lullaby that hides the lie. I've known boys like Prince. And men. They've never been this polite or picture perfect, but underneath they're all the same. He sniffs my neck, so close I can feel his heat. "*Mocha* strumpet, Myyyyy *favorite*," he sings, savoring the words. "What a pleasure it will be to butter your crumpet and eat you, my little strumpet." You don't need a dictionary to know what kind of eat he means, or which crumpet he intends to devour.

Without thinking, I reach up and slap him.

Smack!

This time, Rob doesn't stop me, but he is wincing like he was the one I hit, and he's obviously hiding his shock.

Oops.

I was kinda counting on him to grab me before I did something truly stupid. Too late now.

Suddenly, Prince's caramel skin burns red and his sapphires ice over. "You shouldn't have done that, strumpet. I was going to break you in gently, but that's not what you want, is it?"

Am I an idiot if I admit my heart is hammering at the thought of him breaking me in? That my blood is simmering with what I can only assume is lust, and part of me wants to tell him no, that is *exactly* what I want? Gentle, not gentle, I don't care which, as long as it's him? Not that I would, but I sure am thinking it. Does that make me a disgrace to women everywhere? No, it's not like he touched me. I was the one who hit him. He's just using words, and they're not even technically insulting. He's just being an arrogant ass, acting like he owns me, which he doesn't. No one does.

He says, "Kiss my shoe."

"What?" I giggle.

"Kiss it."

"No! Are you crazy? I'm not kissing your shoe!" I look to Rob for support.

He's stone still, same as when we were in Mr. Ralston's Mercedes. No, that's not quite right. Rob's exhibiting an imperceptible shiver. Every muscle is flexing like he's an earthquake waiting to happen, on the verge of cracking open like a giant fault line about to go 9.0.

The last thing I want to see is Rob fighting Prince. No matter who won, it would end badly for Rob. Me too, because I wouldn't just stand here and watch. Then it would be back to jail for the both of us.

Desperately wanting to avoid that disaster, I look around the courtyard for some authority figure, some adult who'll step in and stop this nonsense, but there aren't any. It's just me and these two brooding bad boys.

Prince says, "As much as I'd like to see you down on your knees, strumpet, I have a better idea. Rob, kiss my shoe."

Without hesitation, Rob grunts, "I'll kiss your shoe if you promise to leave Mary alone."

Prince laughs, "I don't bargain with you. Kiss my shoe."

"Don't do it, Rob," I say. Nobody deserves to kiss anybody's shoe. "This is so stupid. Don't!"

Rob bends down on one knee.

Prince extends a shiny leather loafer in a courtly pose. The shoe is a rich ombré mix of purple blending into ebony. It's so polished, it's practically mirrored, and catches the reflection of the deep blue sky, adding another jeweled hue to the overall palette. I've never seen anything like it. It must be priceless.

Rob leans forward, his weight on his fingers, his lips an inch away.

"Don't leave a smudge," Prince smirks. "This one shoe costs more money than you earn all year."

Something tells me Prince isn't exaggerating.

To my utter amazement, Rob actually leans forward and kisses Prince's shoe. Then he's back on his feet, head bowed down obediently.

Prince turns to me, "Your turn, strumpet. On your knees."

"No!" I blurt. "You can't—"

"O, but I can, strumpet. On your knees, or it's back to the big house for you."

I gasp, "Rob, he can't!"

Rob is completely obsessed with his work boots.

I glare at Prince, "This is wrong!"

"And yet so right, strumpet. Classism in action, with me on top and you exactly where I want you. On the bottom." He wears his expression of superiority and cruel amusement with pride. If he wasn't so good looking, it would be disgusting. But he is. "Kiss it, strumpet."

I know better than to fall for looks. "You can't make me!"

"The rules say I can. On. Your. Knees, strumpet."

Meanwhile, Rob is literally standing there like a stone.

"No, just no!" My eyes flick between him and Prince.

"Now, strumpet. I don't have all day." Prince is loving every bit of this, savoring my desperation like priceless wine.

Just when I'm about to go down, because I don't know what else to do—

"Miss Angerman!" Mr. Ralston calls out from across the courtyard. "I've been looking all over for you!" He rushes over. "Ms. Skelter is waiting! Rob! What *are* you doing? I told you to bring Mary to her office straight away!"

Prince is standing between me and Mr. Ralston. If I had thought Prison Rob was bad before I realized he was also Mr. Robbers Rob underneath, this Prince prick is a million times worse. I give him a last glance and flip him off.

"It would be my pleasure..." Prince mutters quietly then silently mouthes the words, "...*to fuck you.*"

"That's not what I meant!"

He chuckles, "In that case, I am very much going to enjoy making you regret that gesture, strumpet. I will repay it in kind, but I won't be using my finger."

The sick thing is, I can't decide if I like the sound of that or not. No, of course I don't like the sound of that! Not at all! Then why am I so flustered and shaking? I've had guys say things ten times worse than this. Okay, I admit it. They never looked as good as Prince, nor spoke with so much poetry, but they said worse.

Rob puts his big hand on my lower back to guide me toward Mr. Ralston and away from Prince. Rob's hand is almost touching my ass. A hot liquid sensation pours out of his hand and rushes around to my front, bouncing up and down my body. It's tender and protective and thrilling enough to make me a little bit giddy.

"Not so fast, Fletcher," Prince insists, stepping directly in front of me and Rob. "I can take it from here. You have work to do. Unlike the ruling class, you *always* have work to do." There's an implication in there that Prince never has work to do. You can't miss it.

The bull is back in Rob's eyes and I'm caught in a standoff. My chest seizes as I wait for him to charge Prince. I'm torn between wanting to cheer Rob on and protect Prince from certain death at Rob's manly hands.

"You're dismissed, Fletcher," Prince says with authority.

Rob doesn't budge. He's furious, jaw muscles ticking, knuckles popping again, his granite fists clenched at his sides.

Prince says, "Be a good little janitor and go find a mop or a broom and do what's expected of you while I escort Mary here to— Where is she going again, Mr. Ralston?"

"To see the headmistress," Mr. Ralston says, now standing beside us.

"Of course. She needs a bit of discipline, doesn't she?" Prince's terrifying eyes roam over me and pull at my clothes.

It's an awful invasion that part of me... welcomes.

"I'll take her," Rob seethes in a voice that is almost deadly silent.

I nearly gasp, imagining angry Prison Rob taking me... wherever and however he wants. And then I realize Mr. Robbers means take me *away* from Prince, not *take* me.

"You still here?" Prince quips, staring down his nose at Rob through carefree and drowsy half-lidded eyes. Suddenly, Prince scowls. "What's that foul smell? Is that you, Fletcher? Or the toilets you should be cleaning?"

Rob is shaking so hard he's about to snap. His face is bright red and his neck tattoos are writhing tentacles as his big muscles clench. He hisses, "If you—"

"If I what, Fletcher?" Prince challenges. "If I have you thrown out of Castle Hill Academy? Have you sent back to prison? How many years did they give you for what you did?"

The war on Rob's face turns into a massacre. Not Prince's. His. There's nothing Rob can do and it's obvious he's dying inside where he stands.

Meanwhile, I'm a mess of mixed emotions. I'm also stunned that Mr. Ralston isn't doing anything. Is he as afraid of Prince as Rob is? Sure seems like it.

"Run along and plunge a few filthy toilets, Fletcher," Prince says. He reaches out and tenderly grabs my wrist, pulling me away from Rob and toward him. For reasons I can't explain, I go willingly. "Get your hands dirty and do your *dooooty*." Prince chuckles at his own wit.

Mr. Ralston finally speaks, no, cowers, "I suggest you do as he says, Mr. Fletcher. Mr. Lancaster and I can manage Miss Angerman without your assistance, I think."

Rob's eyes dart to Mr. Ralston and he growls, "Make sure she gets where she needs to go."

"But of course," Mr. Ralston smiles.

"You may go, Fletcher." Prince taunts.

Rob gives me a last desperate look before spinning on the heel of his work boot and charging off. If there were any fearless matadors waiting with red capes, they're long gone when I look. No doubt too scared to face off with Rob. Shortly after he turns a corner, there's a slam followed by a boom, and I picture Rob punching his fist through a steel door or knocking down an entire wall with one punch, but that's just my imagination.

Prince sniffs the air and smiles, "Much better. Mr. Ralston, you might want to go check on Rob. Make sure he's not destroying anything irreplaceable. We wouldn't want Elizabeth mentioning it to her parents, would we?"

"Certainly not." Mr. Ralston nods dutifully, "I'll go make sure nothing is amiss. You will escort Miss Angerman to see Ms. Skelter, won't you?"

"With pleasure, Mr. Ralston." Prince's sensual smile is undeniable.

Chapter 9

I am so stupid.

Now I'm all alone with Prince and we're walking down an isolated walkway with a roof on top, a wall of bushes on one side, and columns on the other. Past the columns is a long hillside that drops quickly down into a river valley. The only sound is the warm summer breeze blowing in and the chirping of birds as they flutter and flap from one bush to the next.

If I knew Prince better, and knew he wasn't a complete prick, this moment might be romantic. Instead, it's totally scary. Then again, I wouldn't be here if Prince wasn't so scary hot. If it wasn't for that, I would've run already or insisted Mr. Ralston take me with him. Anything sensible except this.

But no. Prince's presence scrambles my lady brains. Okay, that isn't quite true. The way he asserted his power back there, I'm afraid of him. For my sake and Rob's. After you spend the night in an adult jail, and narrowly avoid getting charged with a felony, you quickly realize the people in power can do just about anything they want to you, and it's best to do what they tell you.

I have a pretty good idea what Prince wants from me, and it isn't sending me to jail. When you're faced with a choice between that or living with the likes of Queen LaQueefa, the choice isn't too difficult. It's shameful, but it isn't difficult.

I mean, look at Prince now. See the breeze blowing through his blond locks, making them dance across his face in mesmerizing swirls. Not even anime hair is this picture perfect. I'm dying to run my fingers through his.

Even so, I just can't do this.

Prince ordered me to kiss his shoe. He *made* Rob kiss it.

That is a hundred different flavors of effed the eff up.

My impulse now is to scream for Rob, but I don't need Rob. I can run. If Mr. Ralston hadn't taken Grayson's knife, I wouldn't even bother to run. I'd wait for Prince to try anything unwelcome, and if he did, I'd cut his dick off.

"What do you think of the view?" Prince asks nonchalantly, stopping to look at the birds and bushes.

"Erm, what?"

"The view. The birds are always more active this time of day when the winds start to blow. The hillside creates an updraft. They love to play in it."

I snort a confused laugh, "Are you serious?"

"Why wouldn't I be?" He offers a million dollar smirk.

"It's just, I'm, are you, why'd you take me here?"

"To see the birds."

I can't make sense of this young man. My head and heart are spinning like runaway yo-yos. I blurt, "That's bull crap! That's not why you took me here."

His eyes, which I had mistaken for a deceptively cool blue until this exact moment, suddenly harden and darken into what is most definitely a cold cobalt. His smirk flattens into a tight white line and he glares at me.

Looking at it actually hurts.

He chuckles, "You're right. I took you here to have my way with you."

I'm shocked. I can't believe he actually says it!

I tense, ready to run.

Before I do, he slides his hands into the pockets of his tailored slacks and that smirk is back. "Well?" He just stands there waiting.

"Well what?" My anger explodes. "What is wrong with you?! Why would you say something like that?!"

"Why not?"

"Do you hear yourself? I'm not your toy! I'm a person! Why do you treat people like this?! Me, Rob, Mr. Ralston! You're an asshole, Prince! A complete jerk!"

His lips loosen into a full smile and he snorts a laugh, "Did you think I was serious, strumpet? Do you think I would risk my future on you? For what, a quick tryst here in the portico? You are sorely mistaken, and you're not half as bright as I hoped. Let's go. Ms. Skelter is waiting." He turns his back on me and walks away. His ass is perfection in those tailored slacks. He stops after a few paces and glances over his shoulder, his blond locks hiding a genuine smile. "I suggest you come quickly." This time there isn't a hint of innuendo. "Ms. Skelter doesn't like to be kept waiting."

"Who's Ms. Skelter again?"

"The headmistress." He resumes his walk, which seems... strained? It's the only word I can think of.

Did I... did I *hurt* his feelings?

Is that what just happened?

Did he actually bring me out here to show me a bunch of stupid birds? If he did, that's... actually romantic. But he couldn't have. He was going to... No, he didn't even try anything.

"Move it, strumpet," Prince hollers without looking back. "I may not have you sent to jail, but if you keep her waiting, Ms. Skelter certainly will. She's a bit of a bitch." This time he stops and turns. His nose crinkles in a genuinely charming smile that I can't resist.

Screw that. I *can* resist it.

Why? Because this Prince is psycho.

Psycho hot, but still psycho.

What did I get myself into coming here?

Have you ever watched one of those really old black and white movies, the romantic gauzy ones with the elaborate sets, the impossibly long night gowns, the dashing men wearing tuxedos to breakfast, and thought you would do anything to step inside that world and live there for a minute?

I just did.

Prince takes me into one of the Spanish mission-style buildings where everything is overly ornamented in gold, stone, and dark hardwood. The impossibly high vaulted ceiling is like the Sistine Chapel, except instead of being covered in oil paintings or frescoes or whatever it has, it's coffered and carved wood, hundreds of bas-relief royals, one king after another, each one in repose on an elegant throne. And that's just the ceiling. Instead of a chapel, it's a dining hall, and there are in fact waiters in tuxedos setting places at an impossibly long dining table.

"Who eats here?" I ask.

"Your betters," Prince says flatly.

Before I can ask what that means specifically, Prince takes me deeper into the building and we cut through a huge kitchen. I'm expecting fast food uniforms or something, but everyone is wearing fancy kitchen whites that are impeccably clean, and the chefs wear those tall hats like it's a gourmet kitchen.

The men ignore us but the women's admiring eyes are all over Prince.

He winks at every one and they blush or giggle like you would expect.

Then we're out and crossing a courtyard, and into another building through brass and glass doors. The decor here is different. More modern, but equally embellished, this time in straight lines, like I've stepped into an Ayn Rand novel set in the early 20th century.

There, Prince tells me to take a seat in a square chair of hardwood and leather.

Across from me, several women sit behind fantastic wooden desks typing. On actual typewriters.

I kid you not.

Ticka-ding! Ticka-ticka-ding!

Prince chats with the women young and old alike, some of them grandma old, obviously flirting shamelessly with all. He may be a classist ass, but at least he isn't ageist. Eventually, he walks back to me.

"I told them you're here," he says.

"Thanks." I lean toward him and mutter, "Why don't they have computers?"

"Ms. Skelter is old-fashioned. It's not just the typewriters. We have to write our term papers by hand. They don't just grade you on your content, they grade you on your handwriting. If they don't like it, they make you take a penmanship class."

"No way. Do you have to write in cursive?"

"If you don't, they make you write with a calligraphy pen and make you grid out the letters so they're spaced perfectly." He curls a grin.

"Really?"

"No," he chuckles. "Just cursive. In fountain pen." In an official sounding voice, he says, "Black ink only. No ball point, gel, pencil, or otherwise. I'm quoting the student handbook on that."

"What about printing? My printing is really neat."

"Nope." He shakes his head, "Cursive only. Like I said, Ms. Skelter is old-fashioned. She blames computers for the decline of civil society."

I like the woman already. I also realize I like this version of Prince just fine. If he had acted like this from first impressions, we could be friends. His loss.

"Good luck, strumpet," he says abruptly. "You'll need it."

Before I can ask why, he's gone.

I sit back in the square leather chair and wait.

"There you are, Miss Angerman," Mr. Ralston says as he walks in. "Shall I assume Prince was a perfect gentleman?"

I blurt a laugh because I have no idea how to answer. "I guess."

"Excellent. I have a few things to attend in my office. When Ms. Skelter is ready, I will join you in her office."

"Okay, great."

While I wait, my mind drifts back to Prince. To Rob kissing his shoe. When Rob knelt down, I could see his big back muscles straining his coveralls. They swelled against the rugged material like they might split it apart. Underneath his clothes, Rob is a beast, but he hides it. I'm pretty sure, if it was him and Prince in a fight, Prince would lose, hands down. Erm, unless Prince knows ninja moves like Red when he fought those two cannibals at the GTO. Because even in a tight tailored suit, Prince obviously has a killer swimmer's body. I have no doubt he's cut and chiseled underneath those clothes, but I still think Rob would easily beat Prince in a fair fight. Especially if Rob is really Alpha. I remember his glistening hands black with blood.

If Rob *is* him, why didn't he stand up to Prince?

And why am I embarrassed for Rob, whether or not he's Alpha? He didn't even say anything about *not* kissing Prince's shoe. He just let him humiliate him like it was business as usual. I mean, I know why on a mental level, but it made Rob look pathetic. Like Rob is a big wimp who can't stand up for himself. I know that's ridiculous, because look at Rob. He would seriously give the Terminator a run for his money. But... I don't know. Some part of me, which I know I should be ashamed of, is telling me Prince is the better man.

Before you call me crazy, seriously, who won that duel?

Prince did.

He made Rob kiss his shoe.

So what if Rob did it willingly?

It's... ew.

I'd never do it.

I know it's wrong to think that about Rob, but seriously.

Ew.

His shoe?

I know, I know. I'm terrible. But I can't deny my feelings, even when I know better. If you're a girl, you can relate. Sorry, guys. Not sorry.

"Ms. Skelter will see you now," says one of the women behind the typewriters.

Chapter 10

Mr. Ralston darts out of his office and leads me past the typing pool to a very large office. It's half art deco library and half art deco museum. Bookcases, abstract paintings, elegant streamlined statues. The hardwood floor is laid out in an intricate geometric pattern that obviously cost a fortune.

A frail old woman sits behind a dark wood desk with a design that combines curves and lines. She has gray Greta Garbo hair that could be a wig or her real hair, I don't know which.

She is writing with a fountain pen in a leather-bound ledger. Probably the "permanent record" where everyone's demerits go when they misbehave. I couldn't care less. The only "permanent record" I'm worried about is the one the state keeps for felony convictions, whether or not you do time.

"Is that her?" I whisper to Mr. Ralston.

He doesn't answer.

The old lady continues writing as if we aren't there.

I whisper, "Is she hard of hearing? Does she need one of those old-timey ear horns?"

Mr. Ralston cringes and shakes his head imperceptibly for my benefit. A warning.

The semi-skeletal woman caps the fountain pen with a click, sets it down on the green desk blotter, and closes the ledger respectfully. She stands up from her desk and says with authority, "I am your headmistress, young lady, and you will address me as *Mizz* Skelter." Her voice is so strong, I expect it to shake her bones apart.

Mr. Ralston cowers slightly at the power of her voice.

Not backing down, I smirk at her, "Is that with one Z or two?"

Her eyes fire. She walks around the desk wearing not the Victorian-era dress I would expect on someone like her, but something a 1920s flapper would wear. Silk, sequins, and tassels. It actually shows a little bit of leg below the knee. She probably bought the dress *in* 1920. News flash! Your dress doesn't make you look twenty! It makes you look ancient!

That doesn't stop her from wearing it with confidence. And her shoes? Her heels are so high she's practically on her toes like a ballerina. Like, she actually was a ballerina at some point. It would explain the stylized ballet statues mixed in with the rest of the art deco statues.

Me, I hate heels. I can't imagine walking in her shoes, and I'm not even a living skeleton. I don't know how she does it.

She stops inches in front of me and asks, "Pardon me, Mizz Angerman?"

"*Mizz*," I quip. "Do you spell it with one Z or two?"

She clasps her hands together and her face tightens into an evil smile. "You can audition for the theater on your own time, Mizz Angerman, not mine. Perhaps they'll give you the part of Puck in next year's production of A Midsummer Night's Dream."

"I can't act," I say seriously.

"I beg to differ. You have already demonstrated a native talent for playing the fool."

This bitch is good, I'll give her that.

Headmistress Skelter continues, "Has Mr. Ralston explained your work-study arrangement with the academy?"

"Not really," I admit.

She nods, tosses an eye dagger his way, which causes him to flinch, then says to me, "If he *had*, he would have informed you that your continued enrollment here is contingent upon three things. One, you must maintain a three point five GPA or higher."

"No problem. My GPA is a three-nine," I say casually because my GPA has never slipped below a 3.8 since sixth grade after I lost my parents. That counts all of middle school and freshman year in high school too, and that was with me bouncing from one public school to the next since I started foster care.

"Don't interrupt. Two, you will work twenty hours weekly. Three hours daily, Mondays thru Fridays. An hour before classes each morning and two hours after classes each evening. Five hours each Saturday, from seven each morning until noon. Sundays are yours to use as you see fit. I suggest you devote yours to your studies."

"I can do that." I'm not afraid of hard work. It's all I know.

She disregards my second interruption with restrained annoyance and says, "Three, you will strictly adhere to the student code of conduct at all times. Do I make myself clear, Mizz Angerman?"

I smirk at her.

She smirks back, "*Now* you find your manners?"

I shrug and stay silent.

"I require a verbal answer, Mizz Angerman. Do I make myself clear?"

"Crystal," I say, still smirking.

"Finally, it should go without saying, Mizz Angerman, but I will say it anyway for your benefit. The commission of any crimes from this day forward, be they merely in violation of the student code of conduct, or more seriously, in violation of the laws of this state resulting in criminal prosecution, be they *either* a misdemeanor *or* a felony, shall result in your immediate and permanent expulsion from both the work-study program, and Castle Hill Academy."

"Duh. Obviously," I grumble.

"If it was so *obvious*, Mizz Angermen, then *why* was it necessary for me to send Mr. Ralston to fetch you from juvenile hall today?"

I hide my embarrassment with an annoyed sneer.

She returns the sneer with ample superiority. Her eyes give me a quick once-over that is dripping with disdain. She says, "We will have to do something about your hair. It simply won't do."

"It looks better with product in it." My floppy pink mohawk is hanging over one eye like bangs. I blow it a puff of breath for emphasis.

"And those piercings of yours. You look like a pin cushion. Pull them out." She offers her open palm expectantly.

"What?" I balk. I have a bunch of ear piercings, but that's it. Nobody even notices ear piercings anymore, which is why I've been debating about getting a lip piercing or something more edgy than effing earrings. It's not like I have tapers or spirals or gauges or whatever. It's just freaking earrings.

"Your jewelry, Mizz Angerman, is in violation of our dress code, as is your hair, which are sections three-b and three-c of the student code of conduct."

"No they're not," I scoff. "I saw Eliza-bitch Morgan-Hearst wearing a nose piercing, *and* a tongue ring! And have you seen *her* hair? It looks atrocious!"

"Watch your tongue, Mizz Angerman! I will not have anyone using such foul language in my presence!"

"Atrocious?" I snort. "That's foul?! Oh, you mean because I said Eliza-*bitch*." I sneer, "Well, she—"

Skelter cuts in, "Is none of you concern, Mizz Angerman. Now hand it over!"

"No!"

Ms. Skelter lowers her arm and her eyes bore into me with a hateful smile. She keeps her glare locked on me as she says, "Mr. Ralston, if you would be so kind as to return Mizz Angerman back to juvenile detention? I believe the district attorney's office is ready and willing to press charges for attempted murder."

Mr. Ralston dances nervously, "Are you sure, Ms. Skelter? Can't we just—"

"NO! We can't JUST anything, Mr. Ralston! Mizz Angerman will follow the rules or we will turn her over to the authorities!"

I blurt, "You can't do that!"

Ms. Skelter sneers at me, "I can do anything I please, Mizz Angerman! I am the headmistress of Castle Hill Academy! While you are under my care, you will do what I tell you! If you do not, it's off to jail with you!"

"Prison," I grumble.

"Whot?!" She actually says "whot."

"Prison," I insist. "You don't go to jail for attempted murder. You go to prison, whot." I mutter the word whot.

She glares at me for a long time. She heard. Once she comes to a boil, she blusters, "I don't care where you go, Mizz Angerman! As long as it is out of my sight this instant!"

I glance at Mr. Ralston.

The uncertainty knotting his face suggests he knows his place.

I say in a low voice, "Is she serious?"

"Always," he mutters.

Ms. Skelter offers a victorious smile. Once again, she lifts her palm, waiting for me to hand over my jewelry.

I glare at her hand. "Fine!" I start ripping earrings out of my ears. Drop them on the floor one by one until I'm done. "There's your stupid *jewelry*," I saw as haughtily as she did.

"Excellent," Ms. Skelter smiles. "Your next task will be to pick those up."

"What?! I'm not picking them up! You pick them up!"

"Mr. Ralston! Remove her from my office immediately!"

Mr. Ralston takes a step toward me then stops. He doesn't want to do it. "Ms. Skelter, she's new. She's learning the rules. She's—"

"MR. RALSTON! SHALL I HAVE YOU REMOVED TOO?!"

"No, ma'am." He bows his head. Then walks over to me and says pathetically, "My sincerest apologies, Miss Angerman. It wasn't right to bring you all this way. I'll get your things."

I'm shaking with hatred and fear. Hatred for *Mizz* Skeleton, yes, Skeleton, because that's what she is, an evil skeleton, and my fear of going to prison. I'm about to scream in her face and tell her to fuck the fuck off and shove her witch's broomstick up her cunt when I remember Queen LaQueefa and juvi. They're the least of my problems. If the state tries me as an adult and a jury finds me guilty, I won't be going back to juvi. I'll be going to a maximum security women's prison.

Is my pride worth that?

No way.

Life has taught me that it will always break you. No matter how hard you fight it, something or somebody else always wins. If I have to choose between losing in prison and losing here, I'd be an idiot not to let myself lose here.

"Fine!" I nearly scream and drop to my knees. "I'll pick up your stupid *jeeeewelry*," I mock, my face burning with rage, my entire body an inferno of impotence.

"It's not mine," Ms. Skelter says archly, watching me like a hateful hawk.

When I have my collection of rings in hand, I unzip my backpack and prepare to stash them inside.

"You will give them to me, young lady." Ms. Skelter waves a hand.

I consider slamming my rings into her wretched skeletal palm in hopes that I'll poke holes in her thin skin. I'm about to do it when I hear Rob warning me in my head, *Keep your head down, Mouth. Life here isn't so bad if you follow orders.*

He would know better than I.

With an annoyed sigh, I pour my rings into Ms. Skelter's hand.

Guess who won that round?

All of a sudden, I understand exactly why Rob kissed Prince's shoe. That wasn't half as traumatic as what *Mizz* Skelter just put me through, and I didn't even have to kiss her shoe. I also realize Rob is much tougher than I gave him credit for. What was it Grayson always said about fighting? *You can hit all you want, but if you can't take a punch, you aren't a fighter.*

If kissing a shoe counts as taking a punch, Rob stepped right into it without batting an eyelash. I was the one avoiding it like a sissy.

That means Rob is wiser than I am. He better be. He's at least five years older than me, maybe even ten. Now I see what he meant by pick your battles. I'm drained, and what do I have to show for it?

Nothing.

Except my very own nickname. Mouth. Technically I already have two, but I'm not counting Prince calling me strumpet, because I can't decide if I maybe kinda sorta like Prince in a weird way, or if I absolutely despise him.

Rob I like, no question, and that makes me smile.

But I won't be smiling for long.

Prince didn't go far enough when he called Ms. Skelter a little bit of a bitch. Gigantic is the word I'll be going with shortly.

Yes, she gets worse.

Chapter 11

"Now we'll take care of your hair," Ms. Skelter says.

Perfect. I hate wearing it limp in public, especially on the first day at a new school. There's nothing like having foot-high pink spikes on your head to warn the bitches off. If I'd had them when I'd met Eliza-bitch earlier, she might not've said anything.

Ms. Skelter leads me to the academy's very own tiny salon. We cross a courtyard, pass yet another fountain, go up curving brick steps to an elevated patio with two French doors. Inside is the super cutest two-chair salon I've ever seen. Like a storybook. I don't know how to describe it. Colorful, comfy, and chic at the same time. Even has a view of the distant ocean. At the moment, there's no one in the salon.

"Who's this for?" I ask.

"Anyone at the academy," Ms. Skelter says.

"How much do you guys charge?"

"For staff such as yourself, salon services are gratis."

My eyes light up, "Shut up!"

Ms. Skelter's eyes pop with rage, "Mizz Angerman! You will not take that tone with me!"

I backpedal, "I meant in a good way! Like, shut up because that's awesome!"

"I know what you meant, Mizz Angerman." She's calmer now. "But I will not have you slaughter the English language with such utter disregard. Say what you mean and mean what you say."

Pick your battles, I hear Rob say.

I sigh, "Okay, I get it."

"Now try again."

Apparently, English class is in session. "Erm, no way?"

Ms. Skelter frowns a warning.

I cringe, "No, that doesn't make sense. Yes way? Erm, no. That's great." I smile. "Gratis is great."

"Much better," Ms. Skelter says, folding her hands together.

A young woman walks out of the back.

Ms. Skelter greets her, "There you are, Luna."

"Hey," Luna says shyly. She's hispanic and wears a basic black stylist's uniform that has the Castle Hill Academy crest high on the breast. Her lustrous black hair is back in a basic chignon and her makeup is minimal. It's impossible to get a sense of who she is from that, but she's beautiful. A natural beauty, unlike the Silicones. I wonder if we could be friends? At the rate my day is going, I could use every friend I can find.

Ms. Skelter says, "Luna, I'd like to have you tend to Mizz Angerman's hair, if you please."

"Sure," Luna nods.

I sit in the chair.

Luna wraps the cutting cape around my neck and says, "What would you like?

I look at myself in the mirror, turning from side to side as I say, "I was thinking we put up my mohawk? Fan it or spike it? You might need egg whites to do the spikes right, or we can just fan it with hairspray, I guess. Whatever works. What do you think?"

Luna offers an impish grin, "I say we fan it."

Ms. Skelter laughs, "No, I'm afraid we'll have to shave it. Luna, get your razor."

"What?!" I blurt. "No! You can't shave my mohawk! It's my hair!"

"It is in direct violation of the student code, Mizz Angerman." She walks over to Luna's station table and picks up an electric razor. When she flips it on, it buzzes like a hornet's nest aimed at my heart.

"No! Just no! I already gave you all my *jeeeewelry!* I'm keeping my hair!"

Ms. Skelter's lips purse into an alligator handbag, "Would you prefer I have Mr. Ralston return you to the penitentiary?"

I'm not going through this again, but I glare at her for a moment before growling, "Fine! I'll do it myself!" I stand up and yank the razor out of her hand and hastily shave my head. Even though it's an electric, I manage to nick my scalp in several places, I'm so angry. My pink mohawk falls off in limp locks that flutter to the floor. I don't even bother with the quarter-inch of stubble growing out already, just leave the bleeding bald streak running down the middle of my head. I turn to Ms. Skelter and bark, "There! You happy now?!"

"The sides."

"What?!"

"Do the sides." Her eyes say, or else jail.

"Fine!" I finish the sides, leaving scattered patches, and slap the razor into Ms. Skelter's waiting hand.

She smiles like a skeleton. "Much better."

Is she serious? I look like my head lost a fight with a lawn mower.

Total bitch.

Luna's face says, "Sorry" in the nicest way possible.

I roll my eyes to say it isn't her fault. I'm ready to storm out of there.

"Come along," Ms. Skelter says as she heads out the door.

I dig into my backpack and peel a twenty from my stack of cash and hand it to Luna for a tip.

"What's this for?" Luna asks. "I didn't do anything."

"For the trouble," I smirk. "Take it."

"We can't accept tips."

I see that Ms. Skelter has disappeared around the corner and can't see me and Luna. "Nobody'll know," I whisper.

Luna shakes her head and mutters, "Cameras."

I frown. Rob said the same thing about the parking garage. It's ridiculous. What's wrong with a tip? "Are you sure?"

Luna shakes her head, "I can't. I don't want to get in trouble. Sorry. It's the rules."

"Screw the rules," I sigh but put the money away. It's yet another sign this place isn't as innocent as it seems, that it's far more sinister beneath the surface, but I won't put the pieces together until much later on. "Next time you need coffee or whatever, it's on me."

Luna smiles at that, "Thanks."

"It's a date," I grin.

"Mizz Angerman!" Ms. Skelter barks behind me so loud I jump. "I don't have all day! Neither do you!"

I groan for Luna's benefit before heading out the French doors.

<(—)>

"I'm not wearing that," I laugh.

"We can't have you walking around stinking of coffee, young lady," Ms. Skelter says, turning up her nose.

The coffee Eliza-bitch threw at me dried already, but you can't miss the smell. I'm a walking Starbucks, which actually isn't so bad.

Ms. Skelter and I are several buildings away from the salon, now standing inside the Castle Hill Boutique. It's like a tiny dress shop with two headless mannequins wearing academy uniforms. One male, one female. I have to say, the female uniform looks like the less slutty and less expensive version of what I saw Eliza-bitch and her friends wearing. The one on the mannequin is nicer than anything I've ever owned, but not as nice as the ones the Silicones have. And that's why I won't wear it. I don't want to be a lesser version of them. No, I don't want to be *any* version of them.

Ms. Skelter says, "While I do appreciate your spirit, Mizz Angerman, I do not appreciate your lack of *school* spirit. This uniform has been worn by great young women for generations, women who went on to have historical significance. If you desire to join their ranks, you must wear their uniform."

I say, "The only thing I want to do is avoid prison time."

"Then wear the uniform, Mizz Angerman. It's as simple as that."

I sigh and feel the pleated plaid burgundy skirt. "It is sort of punk rock. Can I thrash it and attach a bunch of safety pins?"

"You may not."

"What if I tear it by accident?"

"It will be replaced immediately and the fee deducted from your stipend."

"What's that?"

"As a work-study student, you will receive a bi-weekly stipend to cover expenses such as these. Your first uniform and accessories are paid for courtesy of the academy. Replacements are not. Don't waste your stipend on a frivolous fashion statement."

"Fine."

Barbara, the middle-aged woman who works in the boutique, picks out clothes from the shelves and racks, measuring me by eye. She hands me a gray plaid skirt and a darker charcoal gray jacket, not the burgundy plaid skirt and navy jacket I see on the mannequin. I remember the Silicones were wearing burgundy plaid and navy too.

I say, "How come I get gray?"

Ms. Skelter says, "Burgundy and navy are reserved for tuition students. Gray is for work-study students."

"Can't I wear orange?" I smirk. I'm thinking of prison jumpsuits: orange, gray, take your pick. I'm surprised Skelter doesn't make me wear black and white stripes.

Ms. Skelter glares, "I find your sense of humor entirely lacking, Mizz Angerman."

I wasn't trying to make her laugh. It's bad enough I can't dress punk rock. Now I have to announce to the other kids I almost went to jail and I'm working off my debt to the academy by wearing gray? Welcome to serfdom, I guess.

Ten minutes later, I walk out of the dressing room wearing the academy uniform, which fits perfectly, thanks to Barbara. Except for the gray scarf, which I hold at my side. I'm not wearing a scarf. It's too hot.

Ms. Skelter says, "Do you need assistance with your pussybow?"

"My what?" I snicker.

She motions at the scarf in my hand. "Your pussybow. I'll help you with it." Before I can protest, Ms. Skelter takes my scarf, wraps it around my neck (she's taller than I am even without her stilettos), and ties it expertly around my neck in a flouncy bow.

It's stifling. I tug at it. "Can't I wear it untied? Elizabeth and her friends weren't wearing theirs tied." They also had their button-down blouses half open showing their bras and boob jobs.

"Mizz Angerman," Skelter warns, her eyes sharp. "If it was good enough for the late, great Coco Chanel to wear her pussybow properly tied, it's good enough for you."

"Fine," I sigh. "I'll wear your stupid *pussy*bow!"

"I think it's rather smart," Ms. Skelter grins, straightening it and fluffing it. She smiles, "Much better. Now you look the lady." She turns me to face a full length mirror.

Except for my bald head, she's right. I've never looked this feminine, unless you count the princess dresses I wore as a little girl, but that was forever ago. Even the cheesy knee-high white stockings aren't terrible. They didn't give me lingerie and garters like the Silicones have, but these stockings work with the new low-heeled black shoes Barbara gave me. Now that I see the gray skirt and jacket on me, I actually like it.

I hate to admit it, but I don't look half bad.

"What about my old clothes?" I glance back at the dressing room where I left my leather jacket, concert shirt, ripped jeans, and boots.

"They will be taken to your quarters," Ms. Skelter says.

"Quarters? What are those?"

"Your room in the Convent."

"The what?!" I laugh. "Who said anything about me becoming a nun?" I'm horrified by the idea.

"No one. The name is merely a historical holdover from the earliest days of the academy. During the Civil War, the Convent was exactly that. A refuge for young women in trouble, women such as yourself who chose to devote themselves to a higher purpose. Then it was the lord's work, now that purpose is learning and service."

"Oh. Right. I can do that."

"I should hope so," Ms. Skelter chortles. It's a warning, a veiled reminder of where I'd be if she hadn't shown me mercy not once, not twice, but three times.

I roll my eyes and sigh.

Before leaving, Barbara also gives me an official Castle Hill Academy leather book bag. It has buckles and straps and looks vintage but isn't. I also get a Castle Hill notebook. The unlined paper is practically parchment, bound in a booklet, and removable from the soft leather cover that has its own leather belt to keep it closed. I guess so you can put in a fresh one when you fill the first. Last, I get a Castle Hill fountain pen kit with extra nibs and ink cartridges.

It's quite the haul for a foster kid like me.

I guess this place has some perks.

We'll soon see if they're worth it.

Chapter 12

Now that Ms. Skelter has beaten the rebel out of me (or so she thinks), I think she's comfortable not hovering over my shoulder because she hands me over to one of her underlings back at the administration offices to set up my schedule.

Yes, everyone there pretends not to stare at my bald head. I refuse to ask Ms. Skelter if it's a violation of the student code for me to wear a wig. I'd rather walk around bald. In a place like this, with its ridiculously cisgender uniforms, it doesn't get any more punk rock than that.

The woman sitting behind her typewriter tells me her name is Joan and says she's preparing my schedule. She slips a fresh sheet of paper into her typewriter and twists the clicking dial thing before typing.

Tikka-tikka-ding!

I wait while she does her thing, sitting in the leather chair in front of her desk. I pull out my Cricket from my backpack to check it out of habit. The battery is dead. I put it back. Wait. And wait. *And* wait. Is this what people did back in the day? Wait all the time for every little thing? The weird thing is… it's kind of relaxing not checking my phone obsessively. Who knew?

Eventually, Joan looks up and says, "And what would you like for your elective, Mary?"

"I don't know. What do you have?"

"How about computer science?"

"Ew."

"Personal finance?"

"I don't have any money."

Joan snickers at that. "There's always public speaking."

"After the day I've had, I need to do less of that," I joke.

"How about drama?"

"You mean theater? Like plays and musicals or whatever?"

Joan nods, "This year's big production will be Romeo & Juliet."

"That'll work." Knowing I have to work twenty hours a week, maybe they'll give me one of the minor parts. No, the chorus. Then I won't even have to talk. I can just move my lips while everyone else does the talking for me. No, I'll be backstage crew. I hate being in front of an audience. I can do lighting or stage-handing or whatever.

Joan clacks a few keys, then spins the typewriter dial, ejecting the paper, and hands me a freshly typed schedule of my classes for this term.

Period 1 - Physical Education

Period 2 - AP Physics
Period 3 - AP US History
Period 4 - AP English
Period 5 - Trigonometry
Period 6 - AP Spanish
Period 7 - Drama

"Are you shitting me?" I groan.

Joan frowns.

"Sorry. I mean, um, what's the Skelter-approved word for, um, S-ing?"

"Kidding, I would venture," Joan offers.

"Right, Kidding. Are you kidding? I have to do all this *and* work twenty hours a week?"

Joan smiles, "Ms. Skelter said this course load is similar to what you were enrolled in at your previous school."

"Yeah, but not AP classes. Can't I take non-AP classes?" I know the best colleges and universities expect you to take AP classes, but at no point in my high school life did I ever think I could afford one of those. I don't care what Mr. Ralston said, I just want to get my diploma and associates or whatever, get out of here, get a job, and never look back. I only keep my grades up to keep my mind off everything else. The point of school was never to work my ass off. That's what jobs are for. They pay you for your hard work, unlike school.

Joan smiles apologetically, "We don't have any non-AP classes here at Castle Hill."

"Oh? Okay," I sigh. "This is a lot, Joan. Erm, Mrs. Joan? Miss Joan? Sorry, I don't know what to call you."

"Joan is fine," she smiles.

I whisper, "I don't know if I can do all this and keep my GPA up. Ms. Skelter says I need to keep a 3.5 or you'll kick me out. If I didn't have to work, I could totally do it. But I don't know." I'm really and truly worried. Ms. Skelter hasn't cut me any slack so far, and she sounded serious about me keeping up my GPA. I really *really* don't want to go back to jail because I flunk one math quiz or can't remember my Spanish vocab.

Joan leans across her wood desk and whispers, "Ms. Skelter wouldn't give you anything she thought you couldn't handle."

"Okaaaaay. If you say so." I look over the schedule again. At least I won't have to work hard for drama if they put me on curtain duty like I hope.

"You can do it, Mary. You're smart, I can tell." Again she whispers, "Only the smartest ones get under Ms. Skelter's skin like that."

"Thanks." I want to say Skelter doesn't have any skin, only bones, but I don't.

Joan offers a friendly wink, "Don't worry. If you need help, we have plenty of student tutors ready and willing to help out."

"Are they cute boys?"

Joan blushes, "I'm sure some of them are."

I almost ask if Prince is a tutor, then decide I don't want him to be, for obviously asshat reasons.

Joan says, "Now let's get you to class. The day's almost over."

"What period is it now?"

"Seventh is about to start. I'll have one of the work-study drama students show you the way." Joan picks up an old phone receiver from the old black phone on her desk. It has a dial. She spins her finger around the circle of numbers so many times I get dizzy, and it takes her like twenty minutes to place *one* call. How did people manage back in the day? It's ridiculous. When she's done, she hands me my very own copy of the student handbook (Yay! Not yay!), and asks me to sit down and wait in one of the square chairs near the door.

So I do.

I know period six is over when I hear a church bell ring, and coming through the open windows in the administration office, the sounds of students flooding the courtyards between buildings. I can practically feel the excitement. I've always liked school. No matter how bad any school was, it was always better than foster care with people like Dwight and Shayla. Let me tell you, they weren't the worst. The worst was—

((((*it hurts!*))))

((((*please not again!*))))

—I forget what the worst was, but this place?

As bad as it's been today, it's actually pretty good.

"Hi," someone says shyly.

I look up into the eyes of Eliza-bitch herself. She's my escort to drama class? Somebody made a mistake. I'm not going anywhere with her. No, no, no! Not after how she treated me and Rob.

In a demure voice, she says, "You must be Mary. My name is Azielbeth, but you can call me Azzie."

"Um..." I say, totally confused. I glance over at Joan. She smiles and gives me a nod like everything is on the up and up. When I look back at Elizabeth, I finally notice she's wearing a gray work-study academy uniform like mine. Instead of her boobs hanging out like before, she's buttoned up to her neck. I blurt, "When did you change?"

"I'm sorry?" she giggles.

"Your clothes. You were wearing a burgundy plaid skirt earlier and a navy jacket."

She frowns, "I was?"

"Yeah. When I saw you in the parking garage. With your... *friends*," I say with disdain. "Victoria and Jacqueline."

Her brows go up and she giggles like a bashful anime heroine, holding her fingers over her mouth, "You're thinking of my twin sister Elizabeth."

She's *totally* lying. I mean, she *has* to be. This person *is* Eliza-bitch. I got a great look at her earlier and this is her. I'm not buying it. I admit, her nose ring is gone, and so is her tongue stud, but those are as easy to remove as her smoky makeup. I narrow my eyes, "What did you say your name was again? I mean, your full name?"

"Azielbeth Morgan-Hearst."

"How do you spell your first name?"

"A-z-i-e-l-b-e-t-h. It's weird, I know." Is she kidding? Azielbeth is *so* obviously an anagram for Elizabeth, and not a very good one. "It was the name of my great-great-great-*great* grandmother or something like that." She giggles and smiles sweetly, the picture of innocence.

"Of course it was," I say dripping with suspicion.

"I know what you're thinking. My sister and I are alike on the outside, but not the inside. I promise."

Okay, this is beyond bizarre. Either she's crazy or I'm crazy for believing anything she says. Isn't Aziel some ancient historical name for some devil or something? One of the ones from Dante's Inferno or whatever? I'd check my phone if I had any minutes or battery, but I don't. Not that I need to. This is Elizabeth or my name isn't Mary Angerman.

"We should get to class before the bell." She does another anime giggle that is only slightly insane when you see someone doing it for real. "So we're not late."

"Whatever you say..." *Elizabeth.* My words are fake sweet but my thoughts are not.

She doesn't notice.

I follow her outside.

On the way to drama class, Azzie and I cross campus and pass hundreds of kids along the way. The girls in the colorful couture of the paying student uniforms generally ignore us. Like Eliza-bitch and her friends in the garage, their expensive outfits often make them look more like strippers than students. Their shoes in particular stand out. Gucci,

Miu Miu, Alexander McQueen, Jimmy Choo, Christian Louboutin. I don't know any brands by sight, but Azzie does and points them out like a jealous downtown shoe whore on her first trip window shopping uptown. Her shoes are the same academy-issued low-heeled numbers I wear. She says she's dying to get her own pair of Manolo Blahniks some day.

I couldn't care less. I'd rather have my old Docs back. For all I care, she and the rich girls can sit on their Manolo Blah-Blahs heel side up.

The only time the rich girls don't ignore us is when we don't get out of their way.

"Move it, skeeve," says some beauty queen with utter disgust. The rich girls with her laugh like catty crows.

"No, you move, you..." I stand my ground, trying to think of a witty retort. I don't need to read the student handbook to know fighting is off limits, but hurling insults isn't. I should've had a retort at the ready.

Azzie yanks me out of the way before I can say anything.

The Skeeve Queen and her minions blow past.

"It's not worth it," Azzie warns me. "If you don't do what they tell you, you'll get in trouble."

"For not getting out of their way?"

Azzie nods ominously. "This isn't regular school."

"Don't remind me," I grumble and we keep walking.

The rich boys don't ignore us. They can't stop staring at us. Obviously, Azzie-Elizabeth is stunning. Quite a few boys grab at her, tugging at her hair, her arms, even the hem of her skirt. She giggles demurely and does nothing. When the rich boys don't listen, I shout at them to keep their hands off and swat them away. It doesn't matter if Azzie is Elizabeth or not. Girls need to stick together when it comes to rapey boys like these. And I thought it was just that guy Prince. No, it's all of them. They're shameless with their grabbing. The rich ones, anyway. By contrast, the work-study boys in the drab gray uniform blazers and slacks *are* respectful, which is a huge relief.

"Thanks," Azzie says, embarrassed, like she can't stand up for herself or doesn't know how or I don't know what.

"Haven't they heard of hashtag MeToo around here?" I whisper.

"It doesn't apply to us."

"Why not?"

"Because they know we can't do anything."

"Because we're work-study?"

She nods. "Get used to it. They're untouchable."

Me they taunt, calling me Baby Bald, Virgin Vadge, Gray Gash (because my gray uniform?), Red Wendy Woundy. It's disgusting, really.

At least they aren't grabbing me.

Until they are.

When I feel my skirt pull up in back, I spin around swinging.

A group of little rich boys laugh and jump back and I punch nothing but air. They're young, probably fourteen year-old freshman, if that.

"What is wrong with you?!" I shout at them. Honestly, I can't believe this sort of behavior is tolerated. The worst part? None of the rich girls get treated this way. From what I've seen so far, the rich boys are super respectful when it comes to them. "Go away!"

One of the rich boys sneers, "Not until we check your panties!"

"Check them for what?!" I bark.

"If you're wearing any!" the lead boy snivels.

I can't believe what I'm hearing. Did I get time-warped back to the Dark Ages or Ancient Mesopotamia or whenever?

"We want to see!" they plead.

A commotion draws their attention.

Rounding a Spanish-tiled and stuccoed building walks Prince Lancaster surrounded by an entourage of adoring and giggling beautiful rich girls. From the way they shamelessly vie for his attention, you'd think Prince is an Emmy-winning pop star fresh off his latest world tour. In actual fact, he's telling some story about surfing. I can't quite hear all the words because he's not close enough, but it involves a very large wave off the north shore of Oahu, and him chasing the barrel while being chased by a great white shark swimming in the wave with him.

He is such a liar.

His gaggle of admirers "Oohs!" and "Aahs!" and they tell him how brave he is.

Azzie whispers, "He is *so* dreamy."

"He is a walking cliche," I complain and roll my eyes because I refuse to admit out loud I somewhat agree with her. As it is, I'm barely willing to secretly admit it to myself. But my feelings don't lie. Seeing Prince like this makes me all fluttery inside, and jealous because he's showering these bimbettes with attention but not me. Like everyone else, I'm a victim to my traitorous hormones.

"I wouldn't bother with these ants," Prince says as he approaches me and Azzie and our boy tormentors, the Panty Checkers, who paused their perverted pursuit of our panties the moment they heard Prince and his giggling bimbettes coming around the corner.

I mutter to Azzie, "Did he just call us ants? Like, bug ants?"

"That's what we are," she whispers.

"Ants?"

"Sort of. It's short for either peasants or servants, I'm not sure which.

Both, I guess."

"Oh."

Prince slides his amused eyes across Azzie and I, then says to the Panty Checkers, "Stay away from these two. You might catch something you can't cure. This world has enough ill-bred dirty bastards already. It doesn't need more." He jabs me with a hateful scowl.

My jaw drops. Is he serious?

One of Prince's rich bimbettes says, "Why does Castle Hill need criminal ants anyway? Can't we hire maids that *aren't* slutty drug whores?"

"We could," Prince smirks, "but if we did, we would have to treat them with some measure of respect. I'd much rather be at liberty to abuse them however I see fit."

I expect his bimbette to giggle dumbly and say, "Tee-hee, what?! Big words are hard!" She doesn't because she probably takes AP classes like everyone else here at the academy.

Instead she says, "Oh, right. I'd much rather treat them like trash."

"Or step on them like insects if they get in our way," warns another rich bimbette, glaring expensive jewel-encrusted designer eye-daggers at me, or is that just her eyelash extensions and colored contacts?

Prince smirks at me in disgust and says, "Let this human filth clean up your filth for you, ladies. Filth is what they know best. When they outlive their usefulness, dispose of them as you see fit."

"Totalleee," they laugh as they leave and Prince starts on another surfing story.

For obvious reasons, the Panty Checkers heed Prince's words of wisdom and disperse. They obviously look up to him. You could almost call what he just did chivalrous, intervening on my and Azzie's behalf, except for the part where he blatantly insulted and demeaned me and her as less than human, dirty ants to be smashed underfoot without concern.

I was foolish to think earlier in the office that Prince has a hidden softer side underneath his shiny candy shell. I'm over it, it as in him, because I don't think he qualifies as human after this. He's just a shitty it.

Whatever.

Azzie and I continue toward class, passing more kids. Overall, there seems to be a similar ratio of rich kids to work-study kids. That's good because the work-study kids aren't jerks. Quite a few smile and greet Azzie as we pass. She introduces me to a several of the girls (but no boys for whatever reason). I don't remember the girls' names because I'm laser-focused on whether or not any of them call her Elizabeth.

None do.

If I remember right, Prince said earlier that Elizabeth told him about my arrival, probably through text, and he didn't acknowledge Azzie or even wink at her a moment ago. The growing body of evidence is suggesting Azzie and Eliza-bitch really are two different people.

Or this is some elaborate gaslight aimed at me and everyone here is in on it? No, that sounds crazy on the face of it. Who does that? It's not like I'm some rich heiress and they're trying to swindle me out of my $2,320 fortune. That's crazy. I'm just being paranoid.

"Shouldn't the class bell have rung by now?" I ask.

Azzie says, "We have afternoon break for twenty minutes between sixth and seventh periods. We also get one between periods two and three."

"What about lunch?"

"It's forty-five minutes between four and five."

"Oh. Good to know. Hey, what's that white tower over there? I keep noticing it wherever we go." It's so tall, you can see it anywhere you stand on campus.

"That's the Ivory Tower."

"What's that?"

"Castle Hill has four secret societies that run the school. Each has their own building. The Golden Circle, The Hidden Eye, The Locked Door, and The Ivory Tower."

"That sounds like Harry Potter," I snort. "When do we try on the Sorting Hat?"

"Never. We're not allowed to join any of the secret societies."

"Why not?"

"Because we're work-study. Only Fundies can join."

"Fundies? What's that again?"

"Trust fund kids who pay tuition. *A* Fundy. Or multiple *Fundies.*"

"Aren't you one of those?" I smirk.

"No," she says, feigning embarrassment. "I'm work-study like you."

I still don't quite believe Azzie when she says she's not Elizabeth, but for the sake of simplicity, I'll pretend she isn't, that she is Elizabeth's twin sister. Unless she's an evil clone cyborg sent to sabotage me or whatever. No, that's ridic. "You were saying only Fundies can join the secret clubs?"

"Secret *societies.* Yeah. Just them."

"But not us?"

"Uh uh," she shakes her head.

"That's wrong."

She shrugs.

"We should make our own secret work-study society," I muse.

"That's against the rules," she warns, eyes flicking from side to side like we're being watched.

"What, no organizing?"

"I'm sorry?" she giggles.

"You know, no organized labor unions. No working class uprisings or strikes against management for better pay or whatever?" I snicker.

"Oh," she giggles. "I guess not, no."

"That sucks. I'm not surprised after the way Ms. Skelter treated me. I am surprised I didn't get whipped," I laugh.

"Don't say that!" Azzie whispers.

"Why? Do people actually get whipped around here?" I swallow the rock suddenly floating in my throat, because now I'm wondering. "Does this place have corporal punishment?"

She hesitates. "I'm not... sure."

That's a weird answer. When she doesn't say more, I shrug, "I'll try not to get whipped. So, if we can't join these secret societies, does that mean any rich kid can?"

"No. They have to get tapped."

"Tapped?"

"Chosen. They do it the first week of school in the quadrangle inside the Palace every year."

"The Palace?"

"Where the Fundies live. The quad is in the center. Tapping is when everyone gathers in the morning on a certain day each fall and they mill about, waiting to get tapped. If someone comes up to you and taps your shoulder, you go with them to join their group." She says it with reverence and awe, as if she wishes she could join one of the clubs herself.

"And you care because...?"

"They pretty much run the school."

"Isn't that the job of the administrators?"

"Sure, they do the day-in day-out stuff of teaching the kids and keeping the lights on, stuff like that, but the secret societies make a lot of major decisions, like when to build new buildings, what to name them, what teachers work here, what electives are taught, changes to student conduct codes to keep them up with the times."

"The *students* decide that?"

She shakes her head, "Not just any student. The Fundies in the secret societies. They also vote on who can go here and who can't, that kind of thing."

"Isn't that something parents usually do?"

"Alumni parents, yes."

"Who're they?"

"The parents who went here when they were young *and* joined one of the four secret societies as kids. Once a member, always a member. They make academy decisions too. Them and their kids. The secret societies pretty much control everything."

"And they vote who goes here?"

"Uh huh."

"Wait, did we get voted in? Us work-study kids?"

"No. They don't care about us. They vote on which tuition kids can go here." She bites her lower lip and her eyes water ever so slightly. Either she's a really good actor, or she's hiding something, I mean, other than that she's actually Elizabeth.

"Who votes us in?"

"Ms. Skelter chooses the work-study kids based on suggestions from juvenile courts across the country."

"You went to juvi?"

Azzie lowers her head in shame. In a tiny whisper that a mouse would struggle to hear, she says, "Can we not talk about it? Please?"

"Sure." After the way she let the rich boys grab at her, I feel bad for her. She doesn't need me making her life more difficult.

Chapter 13

"Here we are," Azzie says. "The Lancaster Auditorium."

I say, "Wait, Lancaster? As in *Prince* Lancaster?"

She nods, "The same. His family donated the funds a few years ago. They built it before I got here."

"It sure is nice." I admire the architecture, which is totally in keeping with the overall San Simeon theme, with modern hints but lots of rich historical flavor. "Should we go inside?"

"Not until the Fundies do." Azzie glances at the steps. There are two flights of stairs leading up to a terrace and the entrance doors beyond. Kids congregate on either flight in two distinct groups: one gathers on the various steps and the terrace on top, the other remains on the ground at the bottom. Guess which kids are on the steps and terrace? Not the ones in the gray work-study uniforms. Those kids are on the ground. The prettiest kids wearing burgundy and navy are spread out on the steps from bottom to top, with less and less the higher they go. "The higher up on the steps you are, the richer and more powerful and more popular you and your family are."

I've been a loner since I lost my parents. I have no interest in climbing the pyramid of popularity. But I'll be damned if I let some ridiculous social hierarchy stop me from climbing a stupid staircase.

I start toward it.

Azzie grabs my arm, "Don't. You have to wait for the Fundies to go first. You're not allowed on the steps until they leave."

"Says who? Ms. Skelter?" I sneer. "Is it in the student code?"

"Yes."

"No it's not," I laugh.

"It is," she says with total sincerity.

What do I know? I haven't read the student handbook, which is weighing down my book bag like an old and unnecessary telephone book. I smirk at Azzie, "Aren't you one of the Fundies?"

"I was…" Her blue eyes go gray with pain. "It's complicated."

"I'm sure it is," I say with more sarcasm than I intend. I don't mean to be rude, and her feelings seem to be genuine, but I can't escape the feeling she's a total liar.

"We should just wait until the bell."

"Screw that." I walk past several work-study kids. When I step foot on the stairs, they gasp. The boy Fundies on the stairs goggle and the girl Fundies glare, snort, and snark as I march my way past them to the top.

"Nice hair," one titters.

"Thank youuuuu," I gush sarcastically and keep going. I have to hop a few tripping feet, which is harder in low heels than my Doc boots, but I make it to the last step and the landing without falling. Call it a symbolic journey.

Grating giggles catch my attention.

Vicious Victoria and Jack-*ess* Jacqueline, the female jackass. The brunette and the redhead from the parking garage. Eliza-bitch's friends. Or Azzie's. Anyway, the two of them are leaning against the railing between the two flights of stairs and hanging off some guy. I can't see his face because Victoria appears to be kissing him and her hair extensions are in the way, but I can see the guy is wearing the standard men's dark gray work-study uniform. It has a white Castle Hill crest over the breast pocket, and black piping along the edges. I almost want to say his uniform looks like an anime prep school uniform, but it's too nice for that.

Curious, I step past a few hateful gazes to get a better look at the boy. He breaks the kiss with Victoria and looks right at me. When I see his scarlet red hair draped over his dark chocolate eyes, I literally can't believe mine. I blurt, "Red?"

"War Paint," he grins. "What're you doing here?"

I reach up absently to the scratches on my face but make sure not to touch them. Him calling me that is proof Rob *is* Alpha. I don't care what Rob says. I wonder if Wicked Eyes and Giant are here too? That would be fantastic. Even if they're not, Red being here means I have at least one friend, two if you count Rob.

I can't help but notice Victoria's glittery lipstick is smeared all over Red's face. Er, wait. Based on the color, and the smudges on Jacqueline's mouth, it might be hers too. "Were you just—?" I stop myself from asking Red if he was kissing both of them.

The sultry smirk on Red's full mouth and smoking hot chocolate eyes both say yes.

I feel a stab of jealousy. What is he doing kissing *them*? If he should be kissing anyone, it should be me.

"The trash is back," Jacqueline sneers, glowering at me.

"Shouldn't you be cleaning something, ant?" Victoria asks, eyeing my gray uniform.

I smirk, "I have drama class."

"You have no class," Jacqueline laughs.

"*Li*-trally," Vicious giggles.

"No," I snort, "I *literally* do have class. This one right here. Drama class."

"What happened to your hair?" Red asks.

"Ms. Skelter," I say sourly and feel the hot flush of embarrassment.

Vicious titters, "Did she put your head in a blender?"

"No," I scowl. "I cut it myself. I can do your hair if you want."

"Hmph. I wouldn't let you touch my hair with someone else's hands, gutter slut," Vicious sneers and spits out a wad of bright pink gum at me. "Pick that up, ant."

"Screw you," I drawl. "There's a trash can *right* there," I point.

"You were closer," Vicious giggles, arching a superior eyebrow.

Red sighs, "Was that really necessary, Vick?"

"What?" she sneers. "I was done with it. Pick it up, gutter slut."

"Do your job, trash," Jackess Jacqueline adds.

I glance at Red, expecting him to come to my rescue because that's his thing.

He shrugs and smirks a cocky grin at me, "It's not going to pick itself up, War Paint."

My body lights up with surprise and a hint of rage. Did he actually say that? I thought he was on my side.

"That's a good boy," Vicious purrs sensually and goes back to kissing Red.

He happily obliges.

Jackess says, "If you don't pick it up, trash, I'm calling Ms. Skelter."

"Go ahead," I bark. "She's the one who spit out the gum. I'm sure Ms. Skelter will be happy to hear about that." I fold my arms across my gray uniform jacket, which is either too hot for summer, or I'm burning with righteous anger because of these two Silicone nitwits *and* the way Red chose now to totally throw me under the bus.

"Oh, you think?" Jackess challenges. "You think Ms. Skelter'll listen to you, ant?"

"Gutter slut," Vicious mutters, still kissing Red, who seems to have forgotten my existence as his tongue twines with hers.

I can't decide which is making me angrier: them kissing or how the Silicones are treating me.

"Yeah, gutter slut," Jackess says. "Do you think Ms. Skelter likes it when the help disobeys? How about I call her and we find out together?"

I'm about to say go for it and laugh in her face. Instead I have flashbacks of arguing with Ms. Skelter. She was *this* close to sending me back to jail, and she meant it.

"Pick it up, gutter slut," Jackess chides. "Go ahead. You can do it. Bend over and take it. I know you're good at *that*." She and Vicious both laugh.

Red keeps on kissing, grabbing Victoria's unbuttoned blouse like he's ready to rip it open in front of everyone and kiss the rest of her. I bet she'd like that.

I know I wouldn't. No, scratch that. He can have her. Red is no better than them. A rope of disgust ties my guts in knots. I tell myself the way he treated me the other night was a fluke. A one time thing. I get it. He doesn't need me, obviously, and I definitely don't need him. Even as I think it, I know I only half mean it. Who wouldn't want a man like Red? I hate myself for thinking it, but it's true. He's gorgeous, he literally saved my life, and he can be generous to a fault, tossing me $2,320 like it was nothing to him. He didn't have to, but he did. Was he being kind? Or just teasing? Why do I even care? He's kissing Vicious like he *likes* her.

"My turn," Jacqueline whines, pulling on Red's arm.

He finally breaks the kiss with Vicious. Then he attacks Jacqueline with abandon.

Victoria watches, giggling and blushing bright red, biting her lower lip like she's hungry for more. It doesn't take long for her impatience to get the best of her and she tugs on Red's arm.

He turns to her with sleepy sex eyes and chuckles low in his throat, leaning in.

"WHAT THE FUCK YOU THINK YOU'RE DOING TO MY GIRL, SKILL?!" A baritone voice barks from behind me.

I'm so startled I practically jump out of my sensible low-heeled shoes in surprise.

Chapter 14

As I'm spinning around, I hear the rustling of clothes as two broad-shouldered tall boys in academy uniforms rush past me, both of them burgundy blurs. Victoria and Jacqueline scatter, leaving Red on his own with his back to the railing. Behind him, it's like a two story drop to the paved bricks below. The two bigger boys hover over him like they're dying to throw Red over. If I was them, I'd be worried. I saw what Red did to those two cannibals the other night.

One of the Burgundy Boys cocks his arm back and clocks Red across the jaw with a meaty thwack.

Red's head snaps back violently.

"Stop it!" Victoria screams. "You'll hurt him!"

"That's the fucking point," the Burgundy Puncher growls and punches Red in the gut.

Red collapses around Puncher's fist with a loud oof. I wince in shock. Why isn't he fighting back?! He knows how!

"Leave him alone, Duke!" Victoria pleads, pulling on his burgundy jacket. "You'll get kicked out!"

"For hitting this peon?!" laughs the Burgundy Puncher, who I guess is named Duke? "I can hit him all I want!"

Is that true?

He punches at Red again.

Red dodges and rolls sideways over the wide Greek-style railing. Jacqueline and Victoria both gasp. Everyone leans over to look. My heart is in my throat as I watch Red drop a few feet. He slaps his hands on the edge of the terrace level like he's doing a pull-up, slides his shoes down the face of the wall until he's hanging halfway down to the ground, then drops, his leather shoes slapping the bricks. When he lands, he looks up, smirks and salutes, then trots off, disappearing around the corner of a distant building.

"If I ever see that prick again," Duke growls, leaning against the railing, "I'm going to kill his ass." He whirls on Victoria and glares, "Was he kissing you?"

"No!" she lies. I'm assuming she and Duke are a thing. Unless he's her over-protective brother? No, they look nothing alike.

"*She* wasn't," Jacqueline insists. "*I* was."

Duke glares at them both, not sure who to believe.

I notice other kids smirking behind the backs of Vicious, Jackess, Duke, and the other Burgundy Boy. The kids know the truth. So do I. I consider throwing Vicious Victoria under her boyfriend's bus. It's the least she deserves for spitting her gum at me.

No, I can't do that. Their drama is not my problem. I turn to go. Someone grabs my arm and turns me around.

The one named Duke.

I finally get a good look at him. He's so tall, I have to crane my neck to see his face. The first thing I notice are his eyes. Dark and burning black. Not in a bad way. They have an endless depth you could lose yourself in, and I swear, they're not hiding rage. They're hiding pain. His features are sculpted but rough. I can't explain it. His face is a precise balance of hard strength and vulnerable compassion, like it hurts him that he cares so much. His spiked hair is dark too, definitely black and a dangerous counterpoint to the emotion in his eyes.

Quiet, almost embarrassed, he says to me, "Was Vicky kissing Skill?"

"Who?"

"The peon with the red hair. The jumper. Was he kissing Vicky?"

I guess Red is Skill? "Oh, uh..." I glance at Vicious Vicky. She's glaring warning daggers at me from behind Duke. I did say I don't want to get sucked into their drama. But Duke is... he's freaking beautiful. Who cares what Vicious thinks? I blurt, "Yes. She was all over him before you got here."

Victoria's eyes bulge like they're going to explode.

Duke's eyes go dim like he's dying inside.

I want to tell him she's not worth it, I am. But I can't say that! I would never say that!

"Is that true?" Duke whispers, his eyes begging me to change my answer.

"She's lying!" Victoria shrieks and charges toward me, her claws out.

Considering my face is already gouged up, I don't need more gouges. I duck and dart to the side. Smash right into the other guy. Duke's burgundy brother. This guy isn't quite as tall as Duke, maybe an inch shorter, but he's at least six feet tall and solid. A wall of muscle and abs I can feel through his burgundy jacket.

I look up into his smoky topaz eyes. Oh, wow. He's fashion model material. His brown hair is a luxuriant umber and it's screaming at me to run my hands through it. I would if he wasn't grabbing my wrists. He exudes the exotic and mesmerizing scent of musk and myrrh and it's making me giddy. In a seductive voice, he mutters, "Where do you think you're going, little miss mugshot?"

I titter, "I was just—"

"Throw the lying bitch over, Chase!" Victoria rages. "I was *not* kissing Skill! Throw her!" She means the railing. "Toss her onto her head!"

What is wrong with her?! She's acting like I'm lower than any animal, *less* than an ant, a mere microbe, and she's the queen of all creation.

Mr. Mugshot grins at me with his smoky eyes. "Should I?"

"Throw me over?" I giggle, quickly forgetting my fears as I'm hypnotized by this boy's beauty. No, he's hardly a boy. He's older than me by at least a year, if not two.

"Throw her, Chase!" Victoria demands. "It's the least she deserves for lying about me! I would never cheat on Duke!"

"She's just a gutter slut, Chase," Jacqueline adds. "Nobody'll care."

Clearly, Mr. Mugshot with the smoky topaz eyes holding me is named Chase.

"I'll care," Chase says, eyes locked on mine. "I haven't had my fun with her yet."

"What?!" I snort.

"You heard me," his low voice a steamy secret suggesting dark places and wet hot throbbing.

"You did not just…" I can't even finish my sentence because I almost like the sound of whatever it is he's suggesting, which is absurd because he's toying with my life like I'm the devil's plaything, meaning him. Ohmygod! What is he doing to me?!

"Not yet," he winks. "Later. When you clean my suite."

I crinkle my nose and snort a dismissive laugh, "I'm not cleaning your anything. You can chase your own tail for all I care."

"Knock it the fuck off, Chase," Duke barks and rips me out of Chase's arms, spinning me around like a rag doll. "What happened, peon?"

"Don't call me that," I sneer.

Duke's dark eyes bore into mine, "Tell the truth, peon, or I'll tell Ms. Skelter you attacked Victoria and Jacqueline."

"She did," Jackess says, examining her nails. "See? She broke one of my nails."

"I didn't break your nails!" I say.

"Yeah you did. You broke this one." She flips me off with a perfectly French-manicured fingernail.

"It's not even broken!" I groan.

"I hope you like jail, gutter slut," Victoria hisses viciously.

My heart starts to pound. I have no doubt these four Fundies won't hesitate to have me kicked out. I'm already on thin ice with Ms. Skelter as it is. Azzie *did* say the student handbook says we can't upstage, or should I say upstep, or should I say *upset* the fragile little Fundies. Whatever the rules, the last thing I want is to crack through Ms. Skelter's thin ice and fall into the frigid depths of prison where I'll drown in a cold ocean of human ruin.

"What happened, peon?" Duke demands.

I know what he wants to hear and I spill my guts like a spineless coward. In general, I try not to lie, but my life in foster care has taught me that lies are often necessary for survival. Now they come rolling out. "I was kissing Red."

"No she wasn't," Jacqueline snorts. "He'd never kiss this bitch."

Duke and Chase glare at her.

I say hastily, "I mean Skill. Whatever his name is. The guy with the scarlet red hair. We were kissing. These two weren't." I toss the lie to Victoria like a life preserver.

"See?" she sneers at me. "Once a gutter slut, always a gutter slut. She'll kiss anything with a dick."

Amused, I snort, "I wouldn't put it quite like that."

"I would," Victoria insists. "That's why you're here, isn't it? You slept with one of your teachers, didn't you? Back at that trashy public school you went to before here."

"No I didn't." Thought about it. Mr. Vaughn at the last school I was at before Roosevelt was a Marine for eight years before he got into teaching. As hunky hot as he was, I never actually did anything with him outside of my journal. He was way too old. Like thirty or something. Still, he's a total DILF.

"She didn't," Jacqueline says, which surprises everyone. "She *said* she did. He went to jail because of her. Statutory rape."

Victoria looks happy that Jackess upgraded her lie for her. Nothing ever happened to Mr. Vaughn that I know of.

"That's a lie!" I laugh. "You guys have no idea what you're talking about."

"It's public record," Jacqueline sneers.

"How would you know?! You don't even know my name!" I protest.

"It's in the student directory. I Googled it, bitch. She also stole a motorcycle from her foster parents and deals drugs."

I don't know what to say. The part about the motorcycle is all true, and the drugs is vaguely true. However you slice it, Jacqueline had to've at least Googled me to know that, if not dug a little deeper. She's a lot smarter than I gave her credit for, which is not good. Dumb enemies I can deal with. Smart ones are dangerous. Considering Joan told me they only have AP classes here at Castle Hill, I shouldn't be surprised.

Duke has his arm around Victoria. She leans into him and glares at me, silently mouthing something at me that I can't quite figure out, but it clearly contains several F-bombs. She should be thanking me. If it wasn't for me, her boyfriend would know she's literally a two-timing slut. Slut because it clearly wasn't in the contract she signed with Duke. The part about the contract is a joke. Obviously, the part about her staying faithful to Duke isn't. To him, anyway. To her it obviously is.

Chase is standing alone. For some reason, I expect Jacqueline to be nuzzling up against him. She's not. But she's looking at him like she wishes she was. I can't blame her. He might be the finest Fundy I've seen so far.

"What're you looking at, Chemo?" Jacqueline smirks when she catches me looking.

Chase chuckles to himself. Total ass.

"Chemo?" I scoff. "They made me shave my hair! I don't have cancer!"

"Nobody better fuck her," Jacqueline warns, flicking a glance at Chase. "Chemo got cervical cancer from HPV. From fucking that teacher."

"None of that's true!" I bark because I realize everyone is staring at me like, well, like I'm *diseased.* "I don't have HPV! Or cancer! Ms. Skelter made me shave my mohawk!"

Mutters of doubt from the crowd.

"She's lying!" Why am I defending my hairstyle? Because it's easy to tell yourself you don't care what other people think when you're always running away. When you're forced to stay and look them in the eye, you realize what they think not only matters, it shapes your life in ways you can't control. "I've never had HPV!"

The Fundies start to turn their backs on me.

Victoria says, "Go back where you belong and take your HPV with you, gutter slut."

"Go, Chemo," Jacqueline says.

"Screw you!" I'm so mad it takes everything I have to hold back the tears. I've had kids at other schools do some pretty mean things, but nothing like this. A few scratches on my face from Emily Calhoun I can deal with. Having my reputation destroyed in a matter of seconds in front of half the academy? I'm about to make my case when Chase and Duke both approach me.

They take me by the arms, one on each side. For a second, I think they're saving me, protecting me from the insane web of lies tightening around my throat like a silken noose. I want nothing more than to collapse into the safety of their loving arms.

"Get off the terrace," Duke says quietly. "Stand with the rest of the peons." He gives me a gentle shove.

I give Chase a pleading look.

He smirks, "Get going, ant. Down to the bottom with the other insects."

My eyes say, "Are you serious?" but my mouth says nothing.

"Go," he grumbles.

Heartbroken, I stumble down the steps.

"Chemo!" the other Fundies laugh, the girls and boys. "Gutter Slut! HPV! Cancer cunt!"

"I don't have HPV!" Now I'm begging for them to believe me. Nothing like having a couple hundred kids hating you with everything they have to break you down to nothing within minutes.

"Sure you don't, cancer cunt," some random Fundy girl sneers and kicks me in the shin.

"Ow!" The pain is intense and I stumble down the steps, dropping my book bag as I fall and tumble to the bottom, nearly smacking my face into the bricks as I land on my hands.

More laughter.

It hits harder then I would've thought possible, tearing away at my heart and peeling back my skin even though it shouldn't. I'm tougher than this. Somehow, it just does. Their words are acid and lashing whips, their laughter salt in my wounds. How is any of this happening?! I look around briefly with watery eyes, sensing their cackles attacking me like a physical thing, biting me with monstrous teeth, like they're all orcs and goblins underneath their finery. No surprise there. Who knew that laughter was the cruelest weapon of all?

I grab my book bag and ready myself to run.

Someone kneels beside me. Gentle hands steady me and help me to my feet.

I look into the eyes of Azzie.

"I told you not to go up there," she whispers apologetically.

"Let go of me!" I'm convinced she really is Eliza-bitch, and she's not apologizing. She's gloating. Somehow she planned all this in advance. Brought me here to set me up for a literal fall. "You're one of them!" I shove her away and run.

Who says you can't run away from your problems?

"Them?"

You know what?

"They" can suck it.

As long as you still have working legs, running is always an option.

Chapter 15

Tears blur my vision as I turn randomly, running across the campus. At some point, the church bell rings, signaling the start of class. Guess I'm ditching out on drama. The class, not mine. Like I care. I just want out of here.

The fancy buildings give way to tennis courts, a huge pool with mammoth bleachers, a red rubber track and green field with stadium seating, more sporting fields, an equestrian center, what is probably an indoor sporting arena for basketball and stuff like that, and past all that, some big modern industrial looking buildings with a bunch of trucks and vans parked outside. The spotless trucks and vans have Castle Hill Academy logos on the doors and the words Plant Services stenciled underneath.

A couple guys wearing navy coveralls and work boots are walking in the big open doors. They say something to a huge guy in coveralls walking out and share a laugh without stopping.

The big guy sees me running and calls out, "Where are you going?!"

I ignore him and jog past the big building.

"Hey! Come back! You can't leave!" The big guy is shouting and jogging after me.

He's wrong. I *am* leaving and never coming back. I'll live in the woods like a lone wolf if I have to, but I'm never going back to Castle Hill. It doesn't take long for me to reach the end of the paved road I'm running on. I'm stopped by a gate and a wire fence. Signs on the fence and gate say WARNING! HIGH VOLTAGE.

Is this an electric fence?

I don't care. I'm about to grab the gate and climb over when rough hands stop me.

"Don't! You'll fry yourself!" the big guy says behind me.

"Let go of me!" I try to jump onto the gate, but he stops me, grabbing the back of my academy jacket.

"There's enough current in that gate to fry a grizzly. You'll kill yourself." There's real compassion in his voice.

"I don't care!" I scream and reach for the gate, clawing the empty air.

He picks me up under my arms with my feet dangling in the air like I'm weightless and walks me back up the road.

"Put me down!" I growl, trying to pry his fingers off. They're like steel. "I'll bite you!" I crane my neck down, trying to reach them, but they're too low. I bite the air anyway.

He chuckles, "I'm just trying to help. You would've fried yourself." He sets me down and turns me around.

I look up into the eyes of Giant. He's Alpha and Red's friend from the other night. Or should I say Rob and Skill? I'm immediately aware of Giant's friendly lemon and lavender scent. It's calming.

Giant looks me over and frowns, "Hey. You're that kid from—" he stops himself short. "I didn't recognize you without the mohawk. Rob said..." He reaches into the pocket of his coveralls. "He told me to give you this if I saw you." It's a Castle Hill Academy navy-and-burgundy knit beanie.

I stare at it in confusion, "Rob told you?"

"Yup."

"But he didn't see me get my hair cut."

Giant grins, "He knows Ms. Skelter and the school rules. No pink mohawks or anything edgey. He said it was inevitable they'd make you hack yours off," he chuckles. "Here, take it." He proffers the beanie.

I do, holding it forgotten at my side.

"Me," Giant chuckles, "I don't think you need it." He gives me a wink. "You're Mary, right?"

"Yeah," I sigh.

"Name's Jonah. Jonah Biggs."

I look up into his genuine emerald eyes. They project a friendly energy. Right now, it's like oxygen and I can't get enough. His hair is dusty blond and cut somewhat short but long enough to part and sweep slightly to the side like he puts a little product in it. It's a good look.

Concern tightens his brows. "Something happen? You look like you were crying."

"No," I sniff and wipe my nose, looking away.

"Course not. Girl like you never cries." His eyes are laughing, but in a good way.

"Shut up," I giggle and swat his chest, which is like slabs of concrete sidewalk attached to a man. Jonah is the largest person I've ever stood in front of. It would be freaking scary if he wasn't so... nice. I realize he's the epitome of a Gentle Giant, which is exactly what I need right now. He didn't seem so nice the other night when he and Wicked Eyes were making bets about Red winning that fight against the cannibals or not. "Hey, is your other friend here too? The one with the buzz cut?"

"You mean Tucker? Yeah, he's here. Probably in the kitchen prepping dinner for the Fundies."

"Wait, so all four of you work here?"

"Yup."

"Where do you work?"

"Plant services." He hooks a thumb over his shoulder at the big modern building with all the pipes.

"Do you go to school too?"

He nods.

"You guys are in high school?" I gasp. They don't look nearly young enough.

He shakes his head, "College."

"All four of you?"

He nods, "At the rate we're going, we'll each have enough credits for a four year degree by the time we finish our sentences."

"Sentences?"

"We're here same as you. Work-study. We weren't exactly well behaved little boys out in the big bad world before we landed here."

"I'll say," I snicker, thinking about what I saw them doing the other night. "Wait, how are you guys allowed to leave—"

"Careful, kid," he cuts in, emerald eyes flickering intensely.

"Oh, sorry, I was…" I was going to ask him how they're allowed out to freaking steal a million dollars from those rabid cannibals, but he probably doesn't want me talking about that. Duh. Rob said they have cameras everywhere. They might have microphones too. "So, um, yeah. I was going to say, you and your friends are, um, *allowed* to work here in the work-study program like me?"

His intensity melts into a big grin, "Took the words outta my mouth, kid." He takes the beanie from my hand and tugs it onto my head.

I smirk, "I thought you said I don't need it."

"You don't," he winks. "But the rich kids here are dicks. I wouldn't want them hassling you any more than they have already." His eyes darken to a dim forest green. "That's why you were crying, right? Some Fundy pricks giving you a hard time about your hair? Fucking dicks."

"Something like that." I don't want to go into it.

He lifts my chin with a huge thumb. "These scrapes make you look badass, Mary. No wonder Skill called you War Paint."

After the way Skill, aka Red, treated me outside the drama building, I don't give a crap what he thinks or says or does. He's dead to me. But Jonah can call me War Paint and I won't mind. I giggle a bit more bashfully than I'd like and break eye contact before I do something dumb. Jonah has a sneaky charm I can't deny and probably can't resist if he pushes it.

"You have class now, right?"

I nod. "Drama."

"With Mr. Klein?"

"Erm, I guess."

"If it's drama, it's Klein."

"If you say so. Don't you have class too?"

"Later. College classes are on a random schedule. They're not every day either."

"That's rad."

He smirks, "Until you have a class till ten o'clock at night one night, then another first thing in the morning the next day. Then it blows. We better get you back before Mr. Klein marks you absent. Wouldn't want that on day one."

I want to say I don't give a damn because I don't plan on being here for day two, but he's probably right. I can try to live in the woods all I want, but it would only be a matter of time until I get caught and hauled back to juvi, jail, and then prison.

Stupid infrared helicopters already caught me once.

As huge as this place is, they probably have their own flying around scanning the hillsides every night for runaway work-study kids. Based on what Azzie said, they probably also have a bunch of barking German Shepherds and mean guards helping hunt down the runaway work-study kids. Can you say human tranquilizer darts? No, it wouldn't be mean guards. It would be the rich Fundies chasing us on horseback with their expensive customized tranquilizer rifles and laughing at our misery, one of them would be blowing a hunting bugle over the barking beagles (they'd have those too), and the Fundies would get extra credit for every work-study kid they capture.

No, they don't need any of that. They just need a deadly electric fence. Like the one in front of me.

I heave a sigh.

"Come on, Mary," Jonah says. "Let's get you going." He puts a big hand behind my back and moves me toward the main buildings.

I go willingly.

It's not so bad here, right?

Not when Jonah literally has my back with his gigantic hand and I guess Rob is watching over me from who knows where and gifting me a much needed beanie.

There's worse places.

Chapter 16

"You're late, Miss—" Mr. Klein stands on the empty stage of the auditorium. Well, almost empty. There's a podium center stage, and a big projection screen hangs behind him. On it is a photo of a circular stone Greek theater. Mr. Klein checks some papers on his podium and finishes, "—Angerman."

Every kid in class turns their heads to stare at me from where they sit in the sloped rows of theater seats. The Fundies in navy jackets glare hate, the work-study kids beam sympathy. They sit only in the back two rows. The Fundies are scattered all over the auditorium, sitting wherever they please, except for an open row between them and the work-study kids. Call it no-man's land. Even so, quite a few Fundies are crammed into the corners as far back from the stage as possible. It's ironic because the work-study kids get the treasured slacker back rows all to themselves, which appear to be off limits to the privileged Fundies. Or is it the Fundies don't want to sit in the *back* back because it'll make them look third class? Who knows.

I consider flipping off all the glaring and gawking Fundies, except what would be the point? I grab the first seat I find. Right next to Azzie, who saved me a seat by the aisle. She lifts her book bag and motions with a smile.

Great.

I drop down next to her.

"I saved you a seat," she whispers.

"I can see that, thanks," I smirk.

Mr. Klein uses his stage voice to call out, "It *is* Miss Angerman, isn't it?"

"Yes," I sigh because everyone is still staring at me.

He marks something in his notebook on his podium. "Don't be late again, Miss Angerman. You're allowed one tardy per term. Any more than that, and you will forfeit your right to be here."

Is he serious? I've never heard of anyone getting kicked out of class because of two tardies. Er, wait. Does he mean kicked out of the academy? I hate to think, but knowing Ms. Skelter, I wouldn't be surprised. I need to ask. "Mr. Klein, do you mean—"

"Your hand, Miss Angerman."

"What?"

"If you have a question, raise your hand."

"But I'm already talk— I mean we're already talking to each—"

"Your hand, Miss Angerman," he insists.

The class laughs.

I heave a sigh and raise my hand.

It takes two years for him to point at me and say, "Yes, Miss Angerman?"

"Did you mean two tardies gets me kicked out of class or..." I'm afraid to say it.

"Two tardies in one term will lead to the forfeiture of your tenure here at Castle Hill Academy."

"Are you serious?" I groan.

"If you doubt me, Miss Angerman, please consult your student handbook. You did get one, I assume?"

"Yes."

"Good. Now, as I was saying, a festival was held each year in Athens in honor of the god Dio—"

"Mr. Klein?" I ask.

"Your hand, Miss Angerman," he says with increasing irritation.

Is everyone here a rules Nazi? I raise my hand again.

He points at me, "Yes, Miss Angerman?"

"Did you mean two tardies per class?"

"No, Miss Angerman. I mean two tardies in toto."

"In what? Oh, sorry." I raise my hand.

"In toto, Miss Angerman. It's Latin. Perhaps you should have taken that as your elective instead of this." He starts to speak then stops. "Are you finished? Or would you prefer to do all the talking henceforth? Perhaps I should turn the lectern over to you."

More hateful laughter from the class.

I sink into my seat and do my best to disappear.

Mr. Klein goes back to lecturing about the history of Greek Theater.

While taking notes in my school-approved notebook with my school approved fountain pen, which Azzie helps me assemble despite me not wanting her help, I can't help but notice her penmanship is precise, like calligrapher precise. Her class notes are a work of art. I'd be jealous if I didn't think she was Eliza-bitch.

I also notice the auditorium. That word doesn't do it justice. This place is like a grand opera house, except completely modern. Sleek and state of the art with artful acoustic panels suspended from the high ceiling, a balcony overhead and elevated theater boxes on the sides. Talk about extra. Most schools I went to didn't even have dedicated theaters. They did plays in the lunch room.

At some point during the lecture, which I'm actually enjoying, a wave of titters flitters across the students in their seats. They're reacting to—

"Do you hear that?" Azzie whispers.

"Hear what?" I whisper back. "I'm trying to take notes." Fountain pens take some getting used to. The ink just runs and runs.

"Listen!" she hisses.

Then I hear it.

Moans. Male and female.

"It's coming from one of the boxes," Azzie offers.

A nearby work-study boy says, "It's coming, alright."

The kids next to him all giggle.

Mr. Klein is so busy booming away in his stage voice and describing the slides in his PowerPoint presentation, he doesn't notice until the moans are so loud and obnoxious they're impossible to miss. He hollers, "Whoever is up there, stop what you're doing and show yourselves!"

The moaning turns to screaming. The sexual kind.

"Yes, Chase! Yes!" a young woman squeals.

The kids in the auditorium laugh.

"Mr. Wendingham!" Mr. Klein roars. "If that's you, I'll—!" More moans. "Stop what you're doing and return to your seat immediately!"

"Don't stop!" the young woman squeals.

"Mr. Wendingham!"

I'm assuming Chase's last name is Wendingham?

"It's not Chase!" squeals a reedy male voice from the box that sounds nothing like the Chase I met earlier. "It's! It's! It's *Tinsley!*"

More laughter and all eyes are on a nerdy looking Fundy kid with big glasses who's blushing like mad.

"You hear that, Tinsley?" A jocky looking Fundy chuckles. "You're finally getting laid."

Geeky looking Tinsley appears to be in love with the idea, but everyone laughs at him and his hopeful blushing turns to embarrassment then humiliation as Fundy kids throw wads of paper at him.

"I know that's you, Wendingham!" Mr. Klein shouts and spins on the heel of his loafer and marches off stage. A backstage door slams open or closed, I can't tell which, then all goes silent.

One of the Fundies laughs, "You better go, Chase! Klein is coming for your ass!"

Sure enough, Chase stands up in the elevated box and belts his slacks. His tie hangs loose and his shirt is unbuttoned. He grabs his jacket off the floor with one hand, and a beautiful blonde Fundy girl with the other. He pulls her to her feet by the wrist. For a second, I think it's Eliza-bitch, but Azzie is sitting right next to me. The blonde in the box hastily pushes her skirt down and wraps her arms around her unbuttoned blouse and jacket. Chase rips open the door at the back of the box and hauls the girl out.

"Wait! My panties!" she gasps in panic, lunges, grabs them off the floor, and the two of them dash out the door.

Everyone in the auditorium laughs.

You can hear pounding shoes from the hallway behind the auditorium walls.

Seconds later, Mr. Klein bursts into the box. "Where'd they go?!"

More laughter from the audience, because this has turned into a classic farce, you know, an episode of I Love Lucy or The Carol Burnett Show, both of which I used to watch with my mom and grandma on DVD when I was little because Mams grew up on those shows.

"They dropped over the railing!" one of the Fundies shouts from below.

Mr. Klein grabs the railing like he's going to launch himself over and give Chase a chase. Everyone gasps, but he's only looking, eyes searching for the guilty moaners.

Another Fundy shouts and points at the back of the auditorium, "They went thataway!"

More laughter and the farce is complete.

Mr. Klein tries to look, but the main balcony is blocking his view of the main doors on the ground floor. "Someone stop them!" No one moves. Mr. Klein grumbles in frustration and runs out the door at the back of the box. More thudding footsteps as he presumably chases after Chase.

I turn to Azzie and ask, "Who was that blonde with him?"

"With Chase?" She giggles demurely and covers her mouth. "I'm not sure."

"Was it your sister? Eliza—" I almost say Eliza-bitch. "Elizabeth?"

"I couldn't see." She is such a liar.

Everyone saw.

Not that it matters. Who cares what Chase was doing up in that balcony? I'm not even hot from thinking about it. Not one bit. Balcony box sex during class? Really? With a guy who may as well be a fashion model? Like anybody cares about that. Probably the only person who does is that kid Tinsley, who looks like he wishes *he* was Chase up there with that blonde. Me? I couldn't care less who that blonde was. Or what Chase was doing to her—

At that point, I finger my pussybow, trying desperately to loosen it because it's suddenly stifling in here.

Chapter 17

After class, Azzie leads me to the Convent. I try to decline, but she says we have to work tonight.

"Are you serious?" I groan as we walk across campus in a rush with the other work-study kids while the Fundies lounge around outside in the perfect summer weather, laughing it up and relaxing, many of them swiping away at their smart phones and smiling. Did I mention I haven't seen a single work-study kid with a smart phone? Are you surprised?

"Completely," Azzie says, pulling me along. "Joan told me to make sure you got your work assignment as soon as class was over, and make sure you get set up with a room."

"She did? Like a dorm room or whatever?"

"Mm-hm."

"Oh, good. I'd like to put my book bag and backpack somewhere safe."

"Can I carry one for you?" she says kindly.

"Oh, I'm fine. You've already got yours." And I don't trust her with my stuff.

The Convent building looks like exactly what you'd expect. A 19th century Spanish convent with a red brick roof that matches the other buildings here. Azzie leads me inside to a small office. A stocky woman sits behind the desk wearing black. No wimple or anything overly nunnish, but she sure looks like one. She's punching buttons on an antique adding machine. She has to keep cranking a lever on the side to make the machine rattle. Each time she does, another quarter inch of paper spits out, forming a long roll curling onto the desk.

"Ms. Braunschott?" Azzie asks politely.

"One moment!" Ms. Braunschott barks without looking up. She punches buttons and throws the lever several more times, jots down something in a ledger using a ragged pencil that looks like it was sharpened with a pocket knife, and finally looks up. "To what do I owe the interruption?" Her smile is white with irritation, but her cheeks bake red with rage.

"I brought the new girl," Azzie offers. "Mary Angerman."

"I can see that," Ms. Braunschott scowls. She steeples her fingers on her distressed wooden desk and looks me over like she's apprising a side of beef. She glares at Azzie. "You may go, Ms. Morgan-Hearst."

"Yes ma'am," Azzie whispers, does a quick curtsy, and leaves.

"Close the door," Ms. Braunschott commands.

"Um—"

"Now, Miss Angerman."

Not another one. Ms. Skelter was bad enough. I sigh and turn. My backpack is currently slung over one shoulder and I'm holding my book bag in my other hand, so I set it down on the floor and close the door with that hand. Then I face Ms. Braunschott.

"Your bag, Miss Angerman."

"What about it?"

"Did I give you permission to set it down?"

Is she serious?

"Answer me, Miss Angerman." Ms. Braunschott has gunmetal gray hair pulled back in a severe bun so tight it's strangulating and serves as a makeshift facelift. She also has a burly longshoreman quality that Ms. Skelter lacks. Like, Ms. Braunschott could beat up adult men without breaking a sweat. It's scary, really. "I don't have all day, Miss Angerman."

Flustered, I shake my head, "What were you asking?"

"Your bag. Did I give you permission to—"

"Oh, right." I turn to grab it.

"DON'T INTERRUPT, MISS ANGERMAN!" Ms. Braunschott barks louder than a bazooka.

She's so loud, I'm literally scared straight and stand bolt upright at attention because it seems like the right thing to do when the devil is your drill sergeant.

Her voice cuts low, "Did I give you per—"

"I'm sorry, I was just," I quickly grab my book bag off the floor before this gets any worse. When I realize I just interrupted her *again*, I cringe at attention, expecting the worst.

Ms. Braunschott looks ready to bite a chunk of solid wood off her desktop, which is at least an inch thick, chew it up, and spit wooden bullets at me.

It takes everything I have to stand facing her. The only thing stopping me from running out of here is my deep desire to not get shot in the back by a wooden bullet.

Eventually, Ms. Braunschott grumbles, "Are we going to have a problem, Miss Angerman?"

"No!"

Ms. Braunschott re-steeples her fingers. "Good."

She turns in the squeaky metal chair behind her desk and opens a wooden filing cabinet. Busies herself doing who knows what while I stand there. Lays papers on her desk. Writes stuff down.

What is she doing?

Do I just stand here until forever?

She looks at the tick-tock clock on the wall. It's some old vaguely German looking cuckoo clock, I think. That makes three, if you ask me. The clock, Ms. Braunschott, who is obviously a nut job, and me for being crazy enough to actually stand here instead of bolting to the nearest CPS office to file a complaint. This scared straight tough love stuff plays great on TV, but I can't believe it's allowed in this day and age.

Ms. Braunschott picks up the handset of an old black phone and dials, which takes forever. Finished, she waits for someone to pick up on the other end, which I swear takes twenty or thirty rings before someone answers (I guess they don't have voicemail?), then she says, "Have someone send Miss Barker to my office immediately." Then she hangs up. Wow. Talk about rude. Who's the one with no manners now?

A few minutes later, there's a knock at the door.

"Get that," Ms. Braunschott says without looking up from her pencil and papers.

I want to ask sarcastically if I have her permission, but I don't want her to kick my ass with her dockworker galoshes, or whatever she's wearing under her old wooden desk. For all I know, she has army tank tracks for legs, because she's clearly at least half machine, if not more. I turn and open the door.

A girl about my age with auburn hair steps inside.

Ms. Braunschott levels looks at the two of us, "Miss Angerman, this is your new roommate, Miss Barker. Here is your key. Don't lose it." She holds it out. "Miss Barker will explain the do's and don'ts, won't you, Miss Barker?"

"Yes, Ms. Braunschott," Miss Barker curtsies.

"Like you, Miss Barker, Miss Angerman will be on cleaning detail until further notice. I'll have a uniform sent to your room immediately. You may go."

What a bitch. I turn to go.

"Your key, Miss Angerman," Ms. Braunschott grumbles behind me.

I roll my eyes for the benefit of Miss Barker, then turn around and take the key from Ms. Braunschott. "Do I curtsy, or...?" Oops. It just slipped out. I didn't mean to sound so sarcastic, but I did. Probably because I was trying to impress Miss Barker with my rebellious disregard for what any adult in a position of authority thinks.

Ms. Braunschott's eyelids flutter like she's holding in an explosion. "Miss Angerman, you are not the first smart mouth to pass through that door, and you will not be the last. If you desire to remain here at Castle Hill, you will learn your place, or that will be the end of you." The way she says it makes me think she would stomp my head with great glee rather than bother with sending me back to jail. "Use your intelligence for your studies, not to amuse yourself and your peers."

Curtsying for her makes me want to puke, but I do it anyway.

"See how easy that was?" Ms. Braunschott grins like an ogre.

I force a smile.

"You may go."

Gee, thanks.

<(—)>

"I'm Mimi," Miss Barker says, leading me down a dingy hallway into the bowels of the Convent. There aren't any windows in the stuccoed walls, just a few old lightbulbs that barely cut the gloom. Mimi is wearing a gray work-study uniform like mine. "You'll get used to Brawny."

"Who?"

"Ms. Braunschott?"

"Oh," I giggle.

"Everyone calls her Brawny behind her back. Everyone says she was a German lumberjack before she came here."

"Totally," I laugh.

"As long as you follow orders, she'll leave you alone."

"Good to know. I'm Mary, by the way."

"Nice to meet you." Mimi has a warm smile that is a huge relief. "What year are you?"

"Junior."

"Me too, dude!" she smiles and offers her fist, which I bump.

I rarely make female friends because I hate catty drama. Since I'll be living with Mimi, I hope she isn't too catty.

"Here it is," Mimi says and opens a creaky wooden door that looks ancient. It's recessed about a foot into the white stucco, and we passed a bunch of other doors and alcoves just like this one along the way here.

"Let me guess, this door is from before the Civil War."

"That's what they say," she grins.

"So, is this like the dorms for the work-study girls only?" We passed a few other girls in gray uniforms coming and going on our way here.

"Yeah. The Fundies live in the East Hall and West Hall off the Palace."

"They live where?" I laugh.

"I'll show you in a minute. We have to change first." Mimi leads me into the room.

It's depressing.

Two wooden cots, one on each side of the narrow room. I can see the ropes holding up the thin mattresses and scratchy wool blankets. The pillows are an inch thick. One bed is made. Probably Mimi's. The other has the bedding folded in a tight pile on the center of the ropes like someone aligned it with a ruler. At the foot of each bed near the door are two plain desks and two flimsy wooden wardrobes set catty-corner to each other, so the desks are opposite the wardrobes. I notice one desk has books and writing supplies, the other is empty. At the end of the room is a single square window the size of a piece of paper. Tiny for a window. It has two iron bars in a cross shape but no glass. It literally looks like an old-timey jail cell. If it wasn't for the irregular white-stucco walls, which look original to the Convent, I'd say it was.

It's also a bit too claustrophobic for my tastes. I try to avoid—

((((pitch black))))

((((pain))))

((((it hurts!))))

((((please not again!))))

—small spaces when I have the choice. No reason, really. I just don't like them. Since I don't have a choice, I'll have to suck it up. I say seriously, "They don't lock us in our rooms at night, do they?"

"No," Mimi laughs. "Make yourself at home."

"If I must," I grumble and set my bags down on the rope mattress of my bed. At least it's not actual jail. There's a way out of the room if I need one. "What about the Convent? Do they lock that?"

"Yeah. The outer doors are locked at curfew every night. Are you working up an escape plan already?"

"Already drawing up sketches."

"Really?"

"Nah," I laugh.

"Don't worry. I'll show you my underground tunnel after lights out."

"Wait, you have a tunnel?" I gasp.

"Mm-hm. It's got mine carts and everything," she laughs.

Now I know she's joking, which I like. "Where's the bathroom? Don't we get our own toilet and sink or whatever?"

"No. There's a group bathroom down the hall."

"Do we share it with the boys?" I hike an eyebrow and offer a hopeful grin because I'm picturing Rob and his friends soaping themselves up in the shower.

"I wish," Mimi giggles. "No, they live over in the Monastery."

"Wait, for real? Like an *actual* monastery?"

"Totally. You wouldn't know it from all the work-study hotties they have here."

"Right?" My eyes light up, "It's crazy. Like, where'd they get them all? And some of the Fundies are just a little bit gorge."

Mimi crinkles her nose, "They're not my faves."

I titter, "I know, they're horrid, but gosh, they're hot."

"I know, right? I could spill tea over who's shipping who all night, but—" A sound in the doorway distracts both of us.

The room door is still open, and a random work-study girl holds up a reusable vinyl garment bag. "I have Mary's uniform."

"Oh, thanks." I take it from her.

She's gone before I can say anything else.

Mimi closes the door to the room, opens her narrow wardrobe, kicks her low-heeled school shoes off, and starts stripping out of her work-study uniform and hanging it inside. She's already down to bra and panties.

I'm used to sharing rooms with other girls in foster care, so I don't think anything of it, and get busy undressing. I quickly realize why the wardrobe are catty-corner to each other. There's barely space in the narrow room for both of us to change at the same time, but we manage because our wardrobes aren't facing each other.

When I unzip my garment bag, I laugh, "They can't be serious." I'm holding a skimpy black-and-white French maid's outfit by the hanger. When I turn around, Mimi is already wearing hers and tying the apron strings behind her waist. "Are we maids?"

"It's better than jail," she grins.

"Is it?" I snicker.

"For me it is." She's pulling on black stockings and attaching them to garters under her skirt.

"Do the boys wear Chippendale's outfits or whatever?"

"You mean like white collars, tuxedo pants, and nothing but rock hard abs?" She offers a wicked grin.

"Yeah."

"I wish. They wear coveralls."

"That is so sexist!" I gasp.

"Welcome to real life. Now get dressed." Mimi is already stepping into her high heels.

"We're supposed to work in heels?"

"It's not as bad as it sounds. Your calves get a great workout." Mimi has great legs, those long slender coltish legs I'll never have, but she does have a point about the workout. She pins her lace headpiece into her auburn hair. "Hurry up! If we're late, Ms. Braunschott docks our pay."

"We get paid?"

"Didn't they tell you about your stipend?"

"They did. I thought they were kidding. Wait, do we actually get paid?"

"Not if we're late we don't. Now shut up and get dressed. I'll help."

To my surprise, everything fits. Mimi zips me into my dress and I step into my shoes. "The shoes fit too! Where'd they get my shoe size?"

"Jail," Mimi says, tying my apron behind me.

"Really?"

Mimi simply nods.

I say, "The dress is a bit breezy, don't you think?" I'm not used to wearing skirts of any length, let alone a micro mini like this.

"Work it, girl! Put the head piece on."

"Over my beanie?" I'm still wearing the knit cap Jonah gave me.

Mimi bites her lip, "Probably not. I guess skip it?"

"The hair piece?"

"No," she laughs. "The beanie."

I pull it off.

Mimi cringes, "What happened to your hair?"

"Ms. Skelter," I grumble.

"I hate that bitch," Mimi scowls. "Put the hoop on."

I set my headpiece into position.

"Perfect," Mimi smiles.

"Liar," I laugh. "Don't we have mirrors?"

"There's one in your closet."

I check. It's hanging in the back and it's *smaller* than a piece of paper. "I meant a real mirror."

"That's all we get."

I sigh and check myself. "Does the headpiece go with my war paint?"

"Your what?" she giggles.

"War paint." I point at my scabby scratches.

"Is that what that is?"

"No. Some bitch scratched me at my last school."

"Did you cut a bitch?" Mimi titters. "Oh, wait. Is that why you're here?"

"Nothing that badass. I ran away from foster care and stole a motorcycle from my foster dad," I say honestly. Mimi strikes me as someone I'm going to like, so why lie?

"You can ride a motorcycle?" she gasps.

"Uh huh."

"That's badass. Can you teach me how? I've always wanted to learn."

"I guess." I remember seeing Rob and his buddies ride like racers. "Wouldn't you rather ask a sexy boy? That's how I learned. I'm sure there's some here at the academy that know how better than I."

"Who?"

"Uhhh…" I titter. I almost mention Rob and Jonah by name, but I don't want to get them in trouble by accident, and I kind of want to keep them to myself. I consider mentioning Red, I mean, Skill, but he's an ass and I wouldn't wish him on Mimi or anyone else except Ms. Braunschott and Ms. Skelter. They can have a three-way and give him what he deserves. I laugh at the image.

"What?" Mimi grins.

"Nothing."

"You're thinking of a boy, aren't you?"

"No," I giggle. "Sort of. Don't we have to go?"

"Oh, right."

I glance at the mirror and groan, "I look ridiculous with a bald head and this stupid hairpiece."

"You look great," Mimi encourages.

"Liar," I snicker.

"It'll grow out," she admits.

"See!" I laugh. "I look like a giant baby!"

"No you don't. You're gorgeous!"

I roll my eyes.

"Let's go, sistah. We have work to do."

Her calling me sister pretty much makes up for my lousy day. Finally, a friend, *and* she's my new roommate. I call that a win.

Chapter 18

"We have to do what?" I cringe as we step out of a fancy brass and glass elevator.

"Clean the Fundies' rooms and bathrooms," Mimi says. She pushes a cleaning cart down a long hallway that reminds me of a luxury hotel. "We have to do the entire floor before they're done with dinner."

"Please, no."

Mimi grins, "It's just one floor. I had to do all of it myself before you got here."

"Oh. Wait, is this the boys dorms or the girls?"

"We're in the West Wing, so it's boys. Which means we get to snoop."

"In boys' bathrooms?" I grimace.

"Trust me, the girls are worse."

"Nuh uh," I shake my head vigorously and my hair piece almost falls off. I grab it and fix it. "I've lived with tons of boys in foster care. Boys are disgusting."

"Yeah, but you didn't live with Fundy girls."

"How's that different?"

"They make messes on purpose."

"Ew."

She purses her lips, "Exactly. That's why we have these." She pulls out heavy duty red vinyl gloves.

"Why are they red?" I ask innocently.

"I'll give you one guess."

"Oh. Oh! Wait, what, do the girls, like—?"

"You don't wanna know."

"I guess not. Wait, if we're cleaning the boys' bathrooms, shouldn't our gloves be, I don't know—" I snicker, "—brown or something?"

"They will be later," she laughs.

"You did not!" I gasp.

Mimi laughs like a songbird and opens the first door with a key.

"Is that the one you got from Ms. Braunschott on our way here?" I ask. There was a line of work-study girls in maid uniforms waiting to get their key, and I watched Mimi sign a sheet of paper like all the other girls before Ms. B handed over the key.

"Yup. It opens every room on this floor, but only this floor. I have to check it back in to her as soon as we finish our shift."

"When's that?"

"The sooner the better. Dinner goes for two hours. There's fifteen rooms on this floor."

I'm stunned. "How many?"

"Fifteen, but don't worry. It's more than enough time with me helping. I'll show you what to do in the first one. It's easy." Mimi pushes into the room.

My jaw drops. The room is more luxurious than the hallway. You know those pictures you see of upscale hotel rooms online? The ones in faraway countries like Paris or London that you'll never afford? The ones where movie stars and world leaders stay when they visit? Those look like this. "This is a *dorm* room? It's like a penthouse suite."

"You should see the ones for the college kids. They make these look like hovels."

I snicker, "What does this make *our* room look like?"

"A jail cell," she smirks.

"No, ours doesn't *look* like one because ours *is* one."

"True," she grins. "Enough jibber jabber. We need to clean, sistah." Mimi makes quick work of cleaning the first bathroom, which has a huge shower with five hundred different shower heads, recessed lighting, and a sound system with waterproof buttons and a full color screen for selecting songs.

I can see the waterproof speakers in the ceiling. "This takes singing in the shower to a whole other level, doesn't it? What happened to the antique decor I saw in Ms. Skelter's office? And Ms. Braunschott? And all the stuff about penmanship and old telephones? Shouldn't they *not* have MP3 players in their showers, or whatever this is?"

"Record players."

"This is hooked up to a record player?"

"No," Mimi snickers. "I was thinking like jukeboxes or whatever."

"That's what this is hooked up to?"

She laughs, "It should be. The Fundy kids demand modern amenities in their dorm rooms. They store their music on the network or whatever. It's supposed to be all digital."

"Oh. Obviously. But we get a jail cell with no bathroom and share a prison shower with I'm guessing no piped-in music?"

"Sort of. The music comes in through the bathroom air vents. There's an old piano in the Convent. A couple of work-study girls who take choir gather around the Convent piano every night and sing songs so we can hear it while we shower."

"Really?"

"No," she laughs. "Brawny wouldn't approve. Having fun is against the rules for us ants."

"Seriously?"

Mimi doesn't answer. Instead, she explains how to clean. Lesson one: don't clean what isn't dirty. Within minutes, she's done a once over of everything including swabbing the toilet and wiping down the shower, put a few things like toothbrush, toothpaste, shaving cream, and razors back in the medicine cabinet, and rearranged the toiletries around the vessel sink, which looks hewn from a solid chunk of dark red marble and has a brushed gold spigot shaped like a curve of flat metal that is rather elegant. Last, she picks up the wad of white towels piled on the floor *beside* the hamper.

"Why don't they use the hamper?" I sigh. "It's empty and it's *right* there."

"Because they know we pick everything up," she smirks.

"That is so effing lazy."

"That's Fundies for you. Let's go. We've got fourteen more rooms to do."

"When does the snooping start?"

She rolls her eyes. "Let's go."

Was she joking about that? Probably, because after handing me my own bucket of cleaning supplies and tools, she's back on me like a hawk, checking constantly to make sure I'm getting everything done in each room and reminding me Ms. Braunschott will have our asses if we don't do a good job. It isn't exactly rocket science, but Mimi's had practice and is faster than I am. When I have two rooms to go, she sticks her head in the door and hollers, "I'll get the last one for you, Mare Bear! We're almost out of time! The boys'll be back any minute!"

"What?" I holler. "Oh, okay! Thanks!" I busy myself with the toilet bowl because it has a noticeable ring. I've already poured in the blue cleaner and am vigorously scrubbing away with the brush in silence because Mimi explained you need a code to activate the sound system if you want music, and it's different for every room and she doesn't have it. The least they could do is let us have music to work by.

"That's a good look for you, mugshot," says a manly voice.

I scream in surprise and stand up suddenly because this stupid maid costume is so freaking short, I know my panties are hanging out in the wind. I'm so startled, I throw the toilet brush spinning wetly through the air, spraying blue toilet water splattering across the mirror. The brush hits the ceiling, spraying more water on my bald head, then clatters to the floor.

Chase laughs from where he leans casually against the doorframe like he might fall over if it wasn't there. He's just as good looking as I remember, and his thumb is hooked in the belt of his slacks, dragging down the waist band just enough to show the tiniest triangle of tan skin between the tails of his button-down shirt, which is tucked into his pants, but not for long at the rate he's pulling on his belt.

"What're you doing?" I blurt before tearing my eyes away from his crotch.

"Enjoying myself." His fingers are splayed over the front of his slacks. They're not moving or doing anything inappropriate, but they're in a very inappropriate position. "Didn't I say earlier I'd have some fun with you when you cleaned my suite?" He's got me there.

"You've had your fun, so get the F out so I can finish."

"I'd rather watch."

"Screw you, Chase."

"That's my job."

My cheeks burn in response. "Will you go away? I have a job to do. Shouldn't you be like, I don't know, studying in the library or something?"

"I'd rather study you."

I'll admit, being studied by the likes of him, here, now, has a certain... inappropriate appeal. "Get out, Chase. We have to get the key back before Ms. Braunschott bites our boobs off."

"She'd like that," he chuckles. "But I'd rather do it myself." Chase closes the bathroom door and stalks toward me.

Am I scared? You better believe it. This French maid outfit is like wearing next to nothing and my heart is racing. But I'm also, I don't know, Chase is so... those topaz eyes of his are smoldering... and a lock of umber brown hair is dangling over those smoky eyes, bouncing hypnotically and I can't look away, like that hair is demanding I push it back into place before I regain the ability to think straight.

He gets within a foot of me and I feel his heat right before his musky scent mesmerizes me. "You like fun, don't you, mugshot?"

I laugh stupidly, "I have HPV, remember? And cancer of the who-ha." It's the only thing I can think of because his intentions are completely transparent.

"I had the vaccine and cancer isn't contagious." He cages me with my back to the sink, hands planted on either side of me on the countertop. His lips are inches from mine. No, make that one inch. He's getting closer and closer. Half an inch. His minty breath washes over me in sultry seduction.

I can feel the cool marble of the sink against my butt because again, sexist costume. I should be shoving him away and ordering him to stop and lecturing him that no means no, but I haven't said no, have I? I don't think I could say it if I wanted to. At this point, a one syllable word is more than a mouthful. I don't think I could manage a single vowel if I tried. My knees are melting to jelly, and that's not the only part of me that is.

The bathroom door bangs open.

"Mary, we have to—" Mimi stops herself and gasps, "Chase! Get off her!"

His lips can't get any closer without his nose bumping into mine. His warm breath caresses me as he says, "How about I get you both off, then you both return the favor?"

"Chase!" Mimi barks. "Stop it or I'll tell Ms. Skelter!"

"Get her too and she can join in," he chuckles. "You know she still has a tight ballerina body under those old lady clothes she wears."

"Have you seen it?" Mimi blurts.

Chase offers a sly wink.

"Ew, Chase! Ew!" Mimi shivers. "Ms. Skelter is grandmother old! That's disgusting!"

"Don't tell her that," Chase chuckles. "She's not too old to enjoy a little fun."

"Get out of here, Chase!" Mimi orders, irritated.

"It's my room," Chase drawls, not taking his eyes off me.

I can't take mine off his either. I'm shivering in anticipation.

Mimi says, "I meant the bathroom! Wait for us to finish."

"Oooh," he purrs suggestively. "Can I watch you two finish each other off?"

"Out, Chase!" Mimi practically shoves him out the door and slams it. She whispers, "Can you believe him?"

It takes me a moment to collect myself and stutter, "Yes. I saw him in the balcony box in drama class today with some blonde Fundy."

"What were they doing?"

"What they weren't supposed to be," I giggle.

She rolls her eyes. "Did you see who he was with?"

I almost ask why she cares so much. Does Mimi have a thing for Chase? I mean, who doesn't, but he did seem overly familiar with her and let her order him around. Then again, he was being overly familiar with me and probably every girl here at Castle Hill. I shake my head, "Just some blonde. I thought it might be Eliza-bitch Morgan-Hearse, but..." I think of Azzie, who I'm convinced is actually Elizabeth, but I don't say that because if they're the same person, and Azzie was sitting next to me, that means Chase was up in the box, that's not a pun, with another person whose box he was up in, that was *not* her. "I think it was someone else."

"Did you just call her Eliza-*bitch*?" Mimi laughs.

I nod, "And Morgan-Hearse with an e, you know, like one of those funeral cars, because something tells me she'll be the death of me if she ever gets half a chance."

"I can't stand her," Mimi scowls.

"Who, Eliza-bitch?"

She nods.

"Can anyone?" I quip.

She laughs. "Only her stupid boyfriend."

"Who's that?"

"Prince Lancaster the *turd*," Mimi giggles.

I laugh at that even though that little detail about him dating that female fiend is slightly annoying for no rational reason whatsoever.

"Have you met him yet? Prince Turd?"

I nod, "Definitely a turd."

"Tell him I told you that."

"Next time I see him," I wink.

"No don't!" she laughs.

"What's so funny?" Chase calls through the door.

"Go away, Chase! We're working! Mary, we need to finish and get the key back. It's almost seven."

It takes minutes to finish up, but that's more than enough time for the moaning to start outside the bathroom.

"Is that Chase?" I hiss.

"Who else," she replies.

"What is he doing?"

"What or who?"

"Wait, really? I was guessing he was— you know, doing *things* to himself."

Mimi rolls her eyes, "Chase *never* does anything he can get a girl to do for him."

When Mimi drags me out the bathroom door, she grumbles, "Avert your eyes."

I try not to look but I do.

Chase is lounging alone on his enormous king-sized bed. He wears boxers and nothing else. One muscled arm is draped over his head. His other hand holds his... tablet. He's reading something on it and has books and papers scattered around him.

"What're you doing?!" Mimi gasps.

"Studying," he grins. "I could use some trig tutoring, if you guys have a minute. It's... really... hard..." he purrs suggestively and his sultry voice is like the Pied Piper pulling my eyes straight to his—

I can't decide if he's referring to his abs, which are deliciously carved in hard angles, or his—

"Put some clothes on, Chase," Mimi snarls. "Let's go, Mary." She yanks me out of the room, pausing long enough to throw Chase's dirty towels in his face.

"What was that for?" he chuckles, catching them with ease.

"For you to clean up after yourself."

I have a vague idea what she's talking about and an increasingly less vague suspicion she's either into him or they're hooking up. Or both. Mimi is certainly beautiful enough with those long legs of hers, her slender body, and her runway-ready face.

What I can't figure out is whether Chase was serious about me. I mean, I don't *want* him to be, he's just a manwhore, but I'd be flattered if he was. Don't tell any feminists.

On our way out of Chase's room, Mimi and I pass a bunch of gawking Fundy boys. They hoot and holler but Mimi plows past them with our cleaning cart, knocking boys aside like upscale bowling pins as we make our way to the elevator.

<(—)>

"Ugh! Can you believe him?" Mimi asks.

"Who, Chase?" I whisper.

"Who else?" she says bitterly.

"What's the tea on him?"

"Oh, let me tell you. If rumors are true, he's slept with everyone at Castle Hill."

"Even the teachers?" I snicker.

"Them too."

"Seriously?"

"I don't know," she laughs.

"What about you?" I blurt it out before I can stop myself.

Mimi blushes guiltily.

"Is that a yes?" I titter.

"That's an I wish."

"Who doesn't," I chortle.

The two of us are lying in our beds with the lights off. As soon as we got back from cleaning the West Wing and gave our key to Ms. Braunschott, Mimi showed me the bathroom and shower situation and hooked me up with towels and toiletries. Bar soap and government issue shampoo-plus-conditioner in one refillable bottle with no label. Mimi explained there's a huge jug in the Convent Exchange if I need free refills, or I can buy my own from the salon using my stipend when I start earning money. I don't care because I have no hair and free is better than prison. We both took quick showers.

After, while Mimi studied in silence for three hours, I wrote in my journal, jotting down copious notes about today's craziness. Who knows, maybe someday, I'll write a novel about my experiences here, only I'll make everyone vampires and werewolves. Like, obviously, Rob and his friends are savage werewolves who live in a forest stronghold, while Prince and his are stylish vampires who live in a gothic castle, and they've had a blood feud going for centuries when little old me stumbles into their clutches.

I also made a list of the beautiful boys I met today, starting with the Poor Boys:

Alpha = Rob

Red = Skill

Giant = Jonah

Wicked Eyes = Tucker???

I'm not sure about Tucker because I haven't met him yet, but I just know he's him.

Then there's the Rich Boys:

Prince

Duke

Chase

For the heck of it, I listed the Silicones because every vampire story needs some bitchy witches as the villainesses, and they're perfect for it. I can totally see them magically cursing the main characters and making things generally miserable for the peasants or whoever.

Elizabeth Morgan-Hearst

Victoria the Vicious Bitch

Jacqueline the Jackess of Heartlessness

When I finally put my journal away a half hour ago, Mimi was still studying, so I went to bed then. By the time she turned her desk lamp off and climbed under her covers, I was dozing under my scratchy wool blanket and dreaming I was back in Chase's bathroom, just me and him.

A minute ago, Mimi's bedtime questions about Chase and the ensuing gossip tugged me reluctantly awake.

Now, I say, "Is Chase always like that? Hitting on every girl he meets?"

"Yes! What is wrong with him?!" Mimi groans. "He's like a walking hard on!"

"Aren't all boys?" I try not to picture Chase walking around with his boxers off, but he was pretty much doing that in my dream, so it's hard not to.

"I know! But Chase is always in your face with it."

"With *it?*" I snicker.

"I mean," she laughs, "you know what I mean!"

I giggle guiltily, trying not to picture that either.

Mimi starts laughing with me, and it's this easy joyful laugh I envy. I can't remember laughing like that since I was little. It's so loud she covers her face with her pillow to muffle the sounds. Her laugh slowly fades to a sigh and she puts her pillow behind her head. "I'm so glad you're here, Mare Bear. It was getting super lonely all by myself. It's about time I have a bestie."

"Yeah," I mutter, careful not to let myself like Mimi too much too soon. Every time I make a friend, I'm always saying goodbye soon after. I tell myself if I *don't* make friends, I don't have to say goodbye. It's been that way since I lost my parents. If all goes well, I'll be here four years, unless I do something stupid and get kicked out. Or Mimi gets kicked out for whatever reason. You never know. I hope we both stay. It'd be nice to put down roots for once.

Mimi is breathing evenly across from me.

It's soothing and I slip into slumberland.

That night, I dream.

About boys, about friends, about my parents. We're gathered in a summer park somewhere, all of us having the perfect picnic. The beautiful boys are ever so easy on the eyes. Everyone is laughing because Lucille Ball and Carol Burnett are there getting up to their usual unladylike and wacky shenanigans and we're all having fun and wearing white suits or dresses and summer hats, floppy straw for the women, rigid straw skimmers for the men. The day and the fresh lemonade never seems to end, and if I didn't know better, I'd say it was heaven.

It's the best most restful sleep I've had in forever.

Chapter 19

The tea about me, Mimi, and Chase alone in his room last night quickly boils over the next morning and the resulting rumors "Chase" us (ha, ha) all week like wild hyenas biting at our ankles. Getting my school books and locker assignment (our textbooks are huge and so is campus and there isn't time between classes to go back and forth to the Convent to switch out books so we get lockers), and getting to classes on time every day while avoiding the rampant rumors is almost more than I can manage. The only time it lets up is when Mimi and I are cleaning in our French maid outfits. Who thought that would be a relief? Turns out it is.

The Chase rumors aren't the only ones making the rounds.

Guess who broke up Monday night, aka my first day here?

Duke and Victoria.

Guess who gets the blame?

Me.

The gutter slut. The kissing cancer cunt. Mary Mugshot.

Guess who's gunning for me? That's the big surprise. According to the rumors, Duke *and* Victoria both have it out for me. We'll see who hunts me down first to exact their revenge. From what I've heard, they're going to slit my throat in my sleep and dump my body in a ditch somewhere in the hills around campus so the coyotes can eat me.

We'll see about that.

I'm happy to report no one kills me by the time Friday rolls around. I'm not happy to report first period PE blows! Because guess what? Not only do Mimi and I do the maid thing every night while the Fundies eat in the luxurious Palace Dining Hall in the converted chapel building (while us work-study maids eat after cleaning in the dingy Convent Commissary, aka The Cave because of its awful ambiance), we maids also have to get up at 5:00am every morning to vacuum classrooms and offices!

Going to gym class after that is completely unnecessary, but according to our PE teacher Mrs. Boobuster (her name's actually Mrs. Gillespie, but I swear she's doing everything in her power to bust our boobs in the name of perfecting our volleyball skills), you can never get too much exercise. Or boob bouncing because I'm not wearing a sports bra the first day of PE and it is a painful experience, let me tell you. After a while, I try to move as little as possible. Luckily, Mimi has a spare which she shares and I hand wash it every night in the communal Convent bathroom and hang dry it on the cross bar in our little jail cell window like Mimi does hers.

Do *we* get access to the campus's full-service laundry facilities like the Fundies get for their clothes? No, we hand wash. If I ever get transferred to the laundry department, I told Mimi I'll maybe accidentally not on purpose ruin a few Fundy clothes.

Anyway, it only takes a few days before I'm waking up exhausted every morning. And they don't serve coffee! Not to the work-study kids, anyway. It's forbidden. I'm always seeing the Fundies sauntering around with those Castle Hill Cafe cups in hand. It turns out they have a shop here on campus *and* in downtown Castle Hill, which I have yet to see, because guess who isn't allowed off campus? The work-study kids.

I told you this place is jail.

Not complaining, but come on! When you're surrounded by entitled rich kids who get everything they want, get to do anything they want, and get away with social murder, it's just a teensy weensy bit annoying as fucking hell.

Don't let my glibness fool you.

It's just for my journal (which you're reading now).

During the day, the Fundies really do make my life a living hell and the Poor Boys (I've heard some of the Fundies calling Rob and his friends that) aren't helping. Rob and friends may've saved my life the night I ran away, but they haven't done shit since, not that I'm expecting them to, but it would be nice. I'm not holding my breath. Life has taught me that people are never there for you for long. I'm used to it.

Azzie is always trying to be supportive during drama class, but I'm not buying whatever she's selling, and I avoid her whenever possible.

The one person who is making a huge difference is Mimi. I've started calling her Meems, and she's always calling me Mare Bear. Some of the other work-study girls have started calling us M&M because the two of us are always together giggling when we're working or in our dorm room studying or wherever. Ms. Braunschott has come pounding on our wooden door almost every night telling us it's lights out and to shut our mouths. We're gaining quite the reputation.

Thursday night we're gossiping about boys until 1:00am even though we have class in the morning. A loud pounding on our wooden door scares the F out of both of us.

"OPEN THIS DOOR NOW!" Ms. Braunschott commands.

"We'll be quiet!" Mimi pleads.

"I'VE HAD ALL I CAN STAND!"

"We're asleep!" I laugh.

"OPEN UP YOU TWO, OR I WILL BREAK THIS DOOR DOWN MYSELF AND MAKE YOU PAY FOR IT!"

"Okay!" Mimi grouses and hops out of bed. "I'm opening it!" She opens the door and Ms. Braunschott fills the doorway, she's so big.

"Get your things, Miss Angerman!" she booms. "Now!"

"What things?" I ask, suddenly frightened.

"Your everything! Your books, your clothes, your uniforms!"

This can only mean one thing.

"What?!" Mimi gasps. "You can't take her! She didn't do anything! It was me! I was the one keeping *her* up! It was all my fault."

I'm grateful Meems is taking the blame, but I'm shaking under my sheets and scratchy wool blanket. I'd do anything to keep sleeping here, but it's past that.

"You can't send her back to jail!" Mimi is crying now. "She doesn't deserve it! I'm the bad apple! Throw me away! Not her!" She's sobbing so hard I start weeping.

"Calm down, Miss Barker," Ms. Braunschott admonishes. "There's no need for hysterics."

"Yes there is! You're taking her away!" Mimi is down on her knees, pulling on Ms. Braunschott's wrist as if it'll make a difference. It won't, but I love her for trying.

Exasperated, Ms. Braunschott says, "Miss Angerman is not being expelled. I'm moving her to another room as far from yours as possible. You have shown you cannot keep your mouths shut after curfew. This is what you get for ignoring the rules. Miss Angerman, get your things. I don't have all night."

Mimi apologizes to me continuously while helping me pack my things. By helping, I mean delaying. Everything I do she undoes until Ms. Braunschott calls her on it. Eventually, I'm packed up and Brawny walks me through the Convent to the far end of the building.

She knocks gently on a wooden door similar to mine.

"Come in," a demure voice says.

When the door swings open, I see Azzie sitting on the edge of her bed in a long nightgown.

Not her. Please no.

Brawny says, "Miss Morgan-Hearst, I trust you can show Miss Angerman how a proper lady behaves."

"Yes, Ms. Braunschott," Azzie nods deferentially. "Mary, I made your bed for you as soon as Ms. B told me we'd be roommates."

"Thanks." I force a smile.

Brawny helps me carry my things inside and set them on my new bed and desk.

"Good night, you two," Brawny says and closes the door behind her as she leaves.

Azzie beams a bright smile and clasps her hands together in front of her chest. "I guess we're roomies now?"

"I guess," I say sourly.

"You're my first!" she gushes.

I hate to think why, but I already have a few ideas. Like, no one wants to live with a lying gaslighter.

The next morning, things go from Azzie to ass-tampon. Are you surprised? At Castle Hill Academy, fun is verboten. Just ask Ms. Braunschott.

"It's your fucking fault, peon," Duke growls in my ear, ambushing me that morning as I make my way alone from the science building where I was vacuuming classrooms and heading over to the Convent so I can change out of my maid outfit before PE. Duke is wearing a traditional navy and burgundy striped rugby uniform short-sleeve shirt with the Castle Hill Academy crest on the breast pocket, and white shorts. His muscled arms and muscled thighs are visible and straining with thick veins.

"I have no idea what you're talking about," I lie, knowing exactly what he's talking about. "And don't call me that."

"I can call you anything I want, peon," Duke grunts, cornering me on an isolated terrace walkway shaded from the rising sun by palm trees and shrubs, and hitting me hard with his familiar fragrant mix of cedar and ambergris as he forces me to back into the stuccoed wall. This man smells like money. He looks it too, a young mogul who wields his wealth and power like a hammer that hits my heart as hard as his striking good looks.

I don't want to be attracted to him, but I am.

Duke is everything *every* woman wants.

"Get away from me, Duke," I sneer, "or whatever your name is." I push my palm against his granite chest but he doesn't move.

"Jacob Pierpont Montforte. You can call me master." He means it.

"Keep dreaming," I snort. Then I remember something. "Wait. Montforte? I know that name." I'm trying to distract him with the truth because I'm more than a little bit scared. I'm genuinely worried Duke is on the verge of murdering me with his bare hands.

Bristling with deadly danger, he growls, "Of course you remember, peon. They found you at the Constance Q. Montforte Juvenile Detention Center. My grandmother paid for that place. I make one phone call and they'll take you back."

"No they won't," I smirk. "I was going to adult jail, dumbass."

"What did you call me?" His black eyes crackle with fury and he stabs me with a truly hateful look.

"You heard me, dumbass," I mutter half-heartedly. My entire body tingles with adrenalin. I can't decide if I want to run or let Duke do anything he—

"If you call me that one more time, I will end you." His voice is so low, so predatory, there is no doubt he means end me in the most horrid way possible. This man is cruelty incarnate.

I swallow hard and nod minutely, but somehow manage not to blather how sorry I am, even though I probably should, I'm that frightened by what he might do if I say the wrong thing. He's a bomb ready to go off.

"Now you're going to fix this shit with Victoria that you caused, or I am going to make your life more miserable than you can possibly imagine. Are you hearing me, peon? Or do I need to carve it into your skin?" He reaches up with a thumb and grazes the scabs on my right cheek that are finally starting to fleck and fade after two weeks. "Looks like someone else already carved you."

Somehow, what should come across as a taunt is startlingly tender. I don't know if it's his change in tone or the careful hardness of his thumb, but he went from crazed to concerned in the blink of his dark eyes, which are no longer crackling. They're seeking something, I don't know what. Not hunting, seeking. It's a subtle difference. I can't explain it. One is terrible, the other is tender. His eyes shine with the latter. My head is telling me that's ridiculous, his only desire is to kill me, but my heart is hinting otherwise.

"Who did this?" he asks, brushing my other scabbed cheek.

"Stop," I whisper not because it hurts. Because it does the opposite.

He lowers his hand but doesn't pull away, leaning one muscled arm against the stuccoed wall over my head. His heat presses against me with a noticeable weight, trapping me inches away from his big rugby body. He asks, "Did someone do this in juvi?"

"No, it was— what do you care?" I glare at him.

His eyes die and he spits, "I *don't* care." He straightens stiffly and backs up a step, clenching his fists and flexing his arms. They ripple with corded muscle and the veins surge with rage. "You fucked things up with Victoria."

"I did?! She was the one who—" I cut myself off. I swore I wouldn't get involved.

"Who what?"

"Ask her," I grumble and fold my arms across my breasts, not protectively, but in irritation. "Don't drag me into your drama."

"You need to fix this!"

"No! You fix it! She's your girlfriend!" ·

"She's my fiancée."

"Sucks to be you," I smirk.

His eyes flash black and his jaw ticks.

"Wait, you're engaged?"

He nods.

"How old are you?"

"Seventeen."

"Don't you have to be eighteen?"

"Not with parental consent."

"You want to marry *her*?"

He glares at me.

"Sorry," I say. "That came out wrong. I mean, why are you guys engaged so young?"

He barks, "Stop asking questions, peon. Fix this shit you fucked up. Everything was fine until you came along!"

"It was?" I huff. I'm about to tell him what I saw Victoria doing with Red, erm, Skill outside drama class the other day.

"Yeah it fucking was," Duke says.

I don't want to argue because the truth hurts and he doesn't want to hear it. So I change the subject and grab the first topic that comes to mind. "Is your name even Duke? I thought you said it was Jacob."

"It's a nickname," he grimaces. "My dad gave it to me."

"Well, Duke, I don't know what to tell you. This thing between you and Victoria is between you and Victoria. I can't fix your break up. You have to do that." Is it weird part of me doesn't want to help him patch things up with her?

"How?"

"I don't know! I'm not a therapist or whatever. You've got money. Go pay a good one to tell you what to do."

Duke's face sours and he glares at me, "Money doesn't fix everything, peon."

"I wouldn't know, Rich Boy."

"Fuck you, peon."

"Fuck you too, Fundy." I can tell Duke has gone from on the verge of murder to confusion and irritation. With my life no longer hanging in the balance, I'm not letting him talk to me like that without paying for it.

Grunting, he spins around and walks away saying, "If I can't fix this, you're outta here, peon."

"Then you better go fix it!" Now I'm mad.

He growls dismissively and turns the corner at the end of the terrace, leaving me to enjoy the view, which I'm in no mood to enjoy.

Do I like knowing my presence here at Castle Hill balances on the knife edge of his shaky relationship? No way! The strange thing is, I *really* don't want to see him getting back together with Victoria. Not because of me, because that Fundy slut is totally two-timing him! Nobody deserves that, not even Duke.

Maybe what I need to do is tell Skill to knock it the F off.

First I have to find him.

Chapter 20

Mimi tells me where to find Skill but not when.

I keep thinking of him as Red, but literally everyone else calls him Skill (is that even his real name?) for obvious reasons, so maybe I should switch over. Either way, since I never see him on campus, my plan is to track him down where he works in Castle Hill's IT department. According to Mimi, he's some kind of computer genius.

Originally, Mimi says Skill was working laundry when she got here a year ago. Then the Academy got hit with a ransomware thing. Yes, this place uses computers for all kinds of stuff behind the scenes, like computer programming, for one. Ms. Skelter's preference for paper and fountain pens only pertains to students and teaching faculty. Pretty much everything else in the academy's infrastructure (and the Fundy dorms) is modernized. You wouldn't know it from the architecture outside, but inside it's obvious.

Anyway, when the school got hit with ransomware, the hackers wanted a million dollars or something exorbitant like that. Mimi says Skill heard about it and convinced the faculty to let him take a crack at it. They stood over his shoulder as he rooted out the malware code or whatever, and told the ransomeware hackers to F the F off. Problem solved.

He's been working in IT ever since.

It takes a week before I actually find him. In the meantime, the Fundy girls add "homewrecker" to their list of insulting nicknames for me. Some of them spit at me after saying it, like some kind of cryptic ritual. If I wasn't so quick on my feet, I might've gotten hit by their spit more than I did. Sadly, you can't dodge when they spit at the back of your head. The first time it happened I didn't know what it was and wiped it away with my fingers and looked at, thinking it might be bird poop or I don't know what. It was definitely slimy and disgusting. I figured it out when they spit again.

I keep telling myself it's better than them picking up rocks to stone me the old fashioned way. Or tie me to the nearest post or flagpole and burn me at the stake.

At least it's just spit. But seriously, can I tell you how annoying and demoralizing it is having people *actually* spit at you like it's okay? I start getting jumpy whenever I see a Fundy. Now I try to avoid them. Doesn't always work. One time, a bunch of freshman Fundy girls chased me into a corner and the group of them spit on me. Evil little vicious witches is what they are. They're the ones who need burning at the stake. I swear, they're possessed.

I keep telling myself this place is better than prison, but I'm starting to think I'm blowing smoke up my own ass. Whenever that thought crosses my mind, I think about Queen LaQueefa. She was literally going to blind me with that toothbrush shank. I wince at the memory of her heavy hate weighing down on me when she sat on my chest and threatened to stab my eyes out.

You *know* I'd be crazy to go back to prison.

Being spit on every single day isn't so bad, is it? Being the most hated social pariah in the entire school isn't the worst way to live, is it?

Is it?

I'm not crying. I'm not. Sniff.

That night after cleaning the West Wing, I skip dinner and go crying back to Mimi's room, planning to spend the night sleeping there, no matter what Ms. Braunschott says. Meems and I whisper until lights out, thinking we've fooled Brawny until she comes knocking.

Guess who was worried I was missing?

Azzie.

Total tattle tale.

She acts all innocent when I go back to her room.

I know better.

Such a gaslighter.

At least Meems made me feel better, however briefly.

One lunch hour, which is obviously only forty-five minutes, *obviously*, duh, I skip food at the Convent Commissary and head over to the IT building. It's locked by one of those keycard thingies. I press the buzzer button and wait until some nerdy middle-aged IT guy who isn't Skill answers the door.

"Yes?" he asks, pushing up his eyeglasses while holding the door open a crack. He's wearing a Castle Hill polo shirt, random slacks, and running shoes, and he's shaped like a potato, but he has a wrinkled peanut face.

"So, um, yeah. Last night in the West Wing? A bunch of the shower sound systems weren't working?" I'm totally lying.

Peanut Face frowns, "We didn't get any complaints about that."

"It's off and on. Someone said I should tell Skill? He'll know what to do? Is he here?" I stand on my tiptoes, trying to look through the crack over Peanut Face's shoulder.

"Yes, he's here," he huffs.

"Can I see him?"

Annoyed, he says, "I can pass the message along for you."

"It's, um, complicated."

Peanut Face frowns, "How is a malfunctioning sound system complicated? If it is non-functional, we'll check the data logs and run diagnostics until we determine the problem. Then we'll implement a firmware solution. If it is a hardware issue, we'll replace any damaged parts with new ones. Simple as that. Nothing complicated about it at all."

"Can I just talk to Skill?" I wish I was wearing my French maid outfit, but I'm wearing my gray work-study uniform, which isn't nearly as flirty. "Please? It's really important."

Peanut Face rolls his eyes like they weigh a ton each and sighs like he's out of breath from rolling them, "Fine. But don't touch anything."

"I won't," I grin.

He opens the doors and leads me inside. There's a second door where he swipes his badge. The sensor bleeps and he pushes inside. The loud sound of fans is nearly overwhelming in the big room. Row upon row of computer stacks are lined up like library bookshelves, except it's all black boxes and flashing lights into the distance.

"This way," Peanut Face says and leads me along a wall of windowed offices. People sit inside at computers doing computer stuff. Several doors down, we stop and P.F. says, "Skill? You have a visitor."

Skill is sitting in an office chair typing away at a keyboard. When he sees me, he spins around and his scarlet hair whips out of his eyes. He smirks, "War Paint," he drawls affectionately. "What're you doing here?"

Believe it or not, I'm actually happy to see him. I glance at Peanut Face, waiting for him to leave. Instead, he walks into the office and sits at a desk opposite Skill. I notice a placard in the window with two names on it.

Arthur Hovarth.

William Rose.

I point at Skill and whisper, "You must be Arthur?"

"I'm Arthur," Peanut Face says without looking away from his computer, his voice annoyed. "Your lady friend says the shower sound system is non-functional and only you can fix it." He's obviously talking to Skill.

"She's probably right," Skill says with smarmy confidence.

Arthur heaves a weighty grumble, pushes up his glasses, and clicks away at his keyboard with his potato fingers.

I try not to laugh.

Skill says, "What's the problem, War Paint? No playback? System lockout?" He's actually talking about the radios.

"It's, erm, complicated."

Arthur grumbles, "Whatever the problem is, miss, I will have to oversee whatever actions Mr. Rose is required to perform for security purposes. You may as well explain yourself while I'm present. Otherwise, Mr. Rose will merely have to convey your information in a lossy process that will waste his time and mine."

Skill mimes holding a gun to his head and shooting himself.

I laugh.

"Why is that so funny?" Arthur demands without looking away from his monitor.

"It's—" I sigh because I'm getting nowhere here. Frustrated, I blurt, "Okay! There's nothing wrong with the stupid shower sound, Arthur! I need dating advice!" I'm lying, but I'm hoping talking about boys will frighten off Arthur.

He turns to face me and smiles from behind his thick eyeglasses, "Why didn't you say so, miss? I would be more than happy to provide you with whatever information you desire. Is it about a boy?"

"No, it's—"

"A girl?"

"No! It's! Can I just talk to Skill in private?"

"I don't see the need, miss. What is your name?"

"Mary."

"Miss Mary, I am a married man." He holds up his hand and shows his wedding band. "I have a wife and four teenage daughters. You will find I am very experienced in the art of love."

I cringe because I *so* don't want to know.

Skill's face is as red as his hair because he's trying so hard not to laugh.

"It's about Skill!" I snap. "Me and him! He and I! We need to talk! About us!"

Arthur's peanut face wrinkles into a smile. "Why didn't you say so, Miss Mary?" He winks at Skill, "Another one of your young ladies, eh, Skill? I know about what you do."

Okay, that is *super* pervy.

"We'll talk outside," Skill grunts guiltily and shoots out of his chair. He guides me past the windowed offices and the stacks of blinking computers to the other end of the loud room.

I glance over my shoulder and see Arthur leaning out of his office. "Why is he staring at us?" I mutter.

"Arthur has to keep an eye on me," Skill says in a normal voice. "Don't worry. He can't hear you over the server fans."

"Is that what these are?" I motion at the stacks of black computer boxes.

He nods. "What is it, War Paint?"

My scabs are almost gone, but it makes me grin he's still calling me that. With my back to Arthur, and the fans blotting out most of the sound, I'm consumed by all things Red or Rose or Skill or whatever you want to call this model of a man. When his rosewood spice hits my nose, all I can think about is ovens and buns and how this bad boy bakes. Flashes of him fighting the GTO cannibals come flittering back. Followed quickly by him sucking face on Vicious and Jackess at the same time. That dirty little secret clears my head.

"Duke and Victoria," I say.

"What about them?"

"They broke up. Because of you."

He smirks, "No, they broke up because of Victoria. Can I help it if she's into me?"

I glare, "Do you realize how arrogant you sound?"

"Just the right amount." His cocky chocolate eyes and lush lips flicker with amusement.

"No wonder you have two girlfriends."

"I have more than that," he chuckles.

"Listen to you!" I goggle, "You've got more manwhore in you than twenty manwhores put together!"

"I'll take that as a compliment."

"Don't," I snort.

"Why are we talking about this?"

"Because Duke ambushed me and ordered me to fix things. I told him I'd start with having you neutered."

"You did?" he chuckles.

"I should have," I laugh. "It would solve everyone's problems."

"Except yours," he practically purrs.

"What?!"

"If you neuter me, you'll die a lonely old woman, childless and forever unfulfilled."

"Wait, what does neutering you have to do with—"

"Me filling you?" His sexy smirk is patently absurd and painfully obvious, but it looks devilishly delicious.

I roll my eyes simply to break my gaze away from his mouth, otherwise I might send the wrong signal.

"We should do something about that, War Paint."

"About Victoria?"

"No, filling you."

"Would you stop?!" I mistakenly swat his chest. Mistakenly because touching him is the last thing I want to do. I fist my fingers and hold both arms stiffly at my sides. Do! Not! Touch! This! Boy! But that isn't quite the right word. This boy is more man than I've ever had.

"You started it, War Paint." He arches an eyebrow. "You never told me what happened to your face."

"You never asked. You were too busy kissing Victoria and Jacqueline's asses."

He grins, "I wasn't kissing their asses. I may've been grabbing them, but I wasn't kissing them."

"Ew. Anyway, you were letting them walk all over me and treat me like dirt."

Skill runs a muscled hand through his scarlet red hair. Like Arthur, he wears a Castle Hill polo shirt and slacks. Unlike Arthur, Skill's arms are toned with sculpted muscle, and his polo shirt is tucked in tightly over his rippled abs, which peek through the material just enough so you know they're there.

"Sorry about that, War Paint. Rob told me about Prince and the shoe kiss. That's the way it rolls around here. Doesn't matter if it's guys or girls, the Fundies treat us work-studies like slaves."

"You didn't have to back them up. You literally told me in front of them that Victoria's gum wouldn't pick itself up. That was really mean."

He sighs, "If I stood up for you, no, even if I hadn't said anything and kept quiet, Jackie and Vicky would've blown their ass-tampons over me not backing *them* up."

"What?!" I snicker at the image of exploding ass-tampons, which is fitting.

"If those two think for a second I like you even a little, they'll go out of their way to fuck with you every chance they get. If that happens, picking up their spit out gum'll be the least of your worries."

"Oh."

"You know how it is around here, and you've been here, what, a couple weeks?"

I nod. I know he's right. Vicious and Jackess, are terminally vengeful.

"This place has a hard hierarchy and we're at the bottom of it."

"What am I going to do about Duke and Victoria? He said if they don't get back together, he'll send me back to jail or juvi or whatever."

"He can do it too."

"That's what he said," I sigh.

Skill nods and combs his fingers through his scarlet hair, thinking. "I'll talk to some people and see if I can't figure something out. If they get back together, you owe me."

"Owe you what?"

His chocolate eyes smile, "Whatever I want, War Paint."

We both know what that is.

I laugh, "That costs extra."

"I already paid you extra." That he did.

I still have his $2,320 buried in my backpack at the back of my dorm wardrobe. I giggle, "I mean, *extra* extra."

"Name a number."

"It's not about money." It really isn't, but I am curious how much he actually has. More than me, that's for sure.

"Then what is it about?" He leans into me until his polo-shirted chest tickles my gray blazer and blouse beneath.

"Um," I bite my lower lip. "Can we work this out later? I have to get to trig class and lunch is almost over." I back up slowly, eyes locked on his.

"Name a number, War Paint," Skill calls over the humming computer fans. "I'll make it worth every penny."

"For who? You?"

"No, War Paint. You. I've always been a giver. You know that."

I do. Giddy, I spin around because I'm blushing and head for the door. Oh, Red Rose William Skill, you're going to thrust your way through my defenses if you try even a little bit harder.

Chapter 21

You know what the first sign is that someone is gaslighting you?

It's that creepy feeling that things are off, but you can't exactly pinpoint how. You just feel it, that greasy sensation of intrusion into your life that won't go away no matter how much you ignore it or tell yourself you're imagining things. You know better. You know someone is fucking with you. You don't know who, or why, but you *know* they're doing it.

Or you're going effing crazy.

That's the whole point.

They want to make you, the victim, worry that you're losing you mind. If they secretly drive you crazy, and you have no idea who's doing it, you can't fight back, can you?

If they succeed, and turn you into a miserable puddle of impotence, a pathetic blob of human jelly that doesn't even have the willpower to beg for mercy, they've got you. If they gaslight you just right, they own you, body, mind, and soul.

You're theirs.

If they can manage that, you will do anything and everything they tell you, and you'll think you're doing their bidding of your own free will. They will replace your desires with theirs and you won't even know it.

That's gaslighting.

I find myself in a mad panic the day I figure out Azzie is gaslighting me. After coming back to my room after classes one afternoon, I realize something is amiss, but it takes a few minutes to figure out what.

When I enter Azzie and my shabby little room, the air feels thicker somehow. It's not a smell. It's a sensation. A tickling of the skin, an ancient mammalian awareness that danger lurks near. A cloying sludginess to the air I can't pin down.

Is it Azzie's perfume?

I don't remember her wearing any.

Does her alter-ego Elizabeth wear it? I don't know. Maybe? Did she sneak in here when I wasn't around to change in or out of her Elizabeth attire? Is that how she does it? Portrays herself as two different people? I know she said they're twins, but that is a freaking lie! I'm living with Eliza-*bitch* Morgan-Hearse, the platinum blonde angel of death!

I have to give her credit. "Azzie" plays the part of the demure nobody to a T. Even though we're roommates, we rarely talk, keeping our conversations to a polite bare minimum. The only sensible explanation for her quick change routine is she does it somewhere else for two reasons. One, I've checked her wardrobe. It doesn't have any of the fancy Elizabeth clothes hanging in it. Two, she couldn't change here in our room because other work-study girls would see her coming and going from the Convent. I suspect she might do it when she cleans the East Wing (she told me), which is presumably where "Elizabeth" has a second fancier schmancier dorm room.

Anyway, I don't smell anything specifically amiss in my room right now. I just feel that feeling.

I set my book bag on my bed.

Stand in silence and listen.

Outside my room, I can hear the laughing, talking, walking work-study kids coming back from class. Inside my room, it's a loud silence I strain to identify.

What am I missing?

What is out of place?

My wardrobe.

Where I keep my old backpack with my journal and my parents' rings. I open the wardrobe slowly, expecting someone to jump out screaming, or slashing with a butcher knife.

Nope, none of that.

At first glance, everything is where it should be.

Still worrying, I pull out my backpack and sit on the bed with it. Unzip it and pull things out, setting them on the bed. Old clothes, my copy of The Voyage Out by Virginia Woolf, and more until I find the frayed velvet box with my parents' rings.

I open it expecting the worst.

My heart sputters as I pry the box open.

Both rings are there like they should be.

Phew.

Next, I pull out my journal. On first inspection, it appears fine. Flipping through it, I see my poetry, song lyrics for the band I'll never have, drawings that will never hang in any gallery, tattoo ideas that I will absolutely wear with pride when I finally get them, a dark and rambling multi-page fantasy tale about a deliciously dangerous man I will never meet or marry, and most importantly of all, my innermost thoughts and dreams. It's my very own illuminated manuscript, meant to shine a light on my gloomy life.

Normally, leafing through it is grounding, now I barely notice the contents. For several anxious seconds, I can't find the picture of my parents kissing over ice cream and I start to panic. I flip through the journal's pages three times before I find the photo where it always is.

Silly me.

Was I imagining things?

Probably.

Oh, wait! My money! The cash Skill gave me! Almost forgot! Since moving in with Azzie, I haven't once looked at it. I don't want her stealing it. I claw through my clothes to find where it's hidden inside the legs of an old pair of jeans, half the money in each leg. I count it meticulously. It's all there. Or is it? I'm about to count it again when I realize this is how they make you crazy. Of course it's all there. I don't need to recount it.

Rolling my eyes at myself, I pack my things into my backpack. The last item is my copy of The Voyage Out.

I frown.

What happened to the dog ears?

I've had this book like forever, and the corners are all bent, the cover scuffed, the pages faded. Except they're not.

Hmm.

That's weird.

I turn it over in my hands. Everything's the same, except it isn't as old as I remember.

What?!

I laugh to myself. That's ridiculous. The only way a book can get younger is if someone replaces it.

Azzie.

Effing gaslighter.

I check inside the front cover for the library stamp. On the very last page it should say Lincoln Middle School Library, which is where I checked it out and never checked it back in.

The stamp isn't there.

Did someone tear the page out?

No, because Azzie took my book.

Replaced it with an almost identical copy.

Why?

To gaslight me, obviously.

Shit. Do I count my money again?

No! I'm not falling for her head games!

Screw her! She probably didn't even find the money, stupid bitch.

She can try and gaslight me all she wants, switch out my stuff till the cows come home, but I won't let her switch out my journal, my parents' rings, or my ice cream photo of them, and there's no way I'm letting her take my money.

Backpack in hand, I march down to Mimi's room and knock on the door.

"Mare Bear!" she smiles when she opens the door.

"Hey, Meems." I walk inside.

"You ready to study?"

"Erm, yeah. In a sec. I forgot my school books in Azzie's room. Before I get them, can I keep my backpack in your room from now on? Azzie is messing with my stuff."

"Oh, totally. You can keep it in your old wardrobe where it'll be safe."

"Thanks," I smile and set it inside myself and say a silent screw you to Azzie as I do. Now all I have to do is keep one eye open when I'm sleeping in Azzie's room. Who knows what she might do to me at night. Eh. I'll deal. I've lived with—

((((*pitch black*))))

((((*pain*))))

((((*it hurts!*))))

((((*please not again!*))))

—far worse.

Azzie is nothing I can't handle.

Too bad Mr. Ralston took Grayson's knife away.

I really need to get that back.

<(—)>

"You want to watch a water polo game after we eat?" Mimi asks on Saturday after we finish working. We're getting lunch in the Convent Commissary.

The work-study kids call it The Cave because that's what it is. Dark, no windows, a few bare lightbulbs. Even during the day it's dim. It's the dreariest place I've ever eaten. Hopefully I'll get used to it. The tables are splintery old wooden picnic tables placed end to end in long rows.

Can we take our food outside and eat in the sunshine? Nope. Against the rules. Too many complaints from the Fundies about having to watch us savages gnashing away at the shoe leather and soggy cardboard we call food.

"Water polo?" I snort while spooning something slightly gray and very sloppy (I think it's gruel, like *actual* gruel) from the cafeteria trough and onto my tray. "Why would I want to watch that? Isn't that a horse thing?" I ask because I know about the equestrian center and how some of the Fundy sports involve horse riding and jumping and vaulting or whatever they do, not that I know a thing about horses other than you have to be a rich Fundy to own one and if you're a poor work-study kid, you have to clean the stables for them. Luckily for me and Mimi, that's something the boys do. Rumor has it the girls also did it long before Mimi and I got here, but that changed when the Fundy girls realized some of the work-study girls were sneaking horse rides on *their* horses, and *liking* it. Gasp! Anyway, now just the work-study boys handle the horses.

"No," Mimi giggles then whispers, "water polo is boys in bathing suits fighting over a ball."

"Whose balls?" I quip. "Their own? Or each others's?"

Mimi laughs, "No, the water polo ball."

"Sounds boring."

"Their bathing suits are tiny."

I stop. "How tiny?"

Mimi holds up her thumb and finger so close together they're almost touching.

I bite my lower lip, "Which boys?"

"Prince and Chase are on the team."

"Hurry up and eat," I laugh, slopping green mush onto my tray, which at one time may have been peas.

We make it to the pool stadium before the game starts. It's like an Olympic stadium, it's so big and futuristic. Mimi and I get in for free because we're students. The crowd is light, so we're allowed to sit close to poolside. Mimi explains when the stadium is packed, work-study kids have to sit in the back. What else is new?

When the teams walk onto the pool deck, I gasp.

"Look at those Speedos," Mimi marvels.

"Are they even wearing any?" I titter, crinkling my eyes like I'm looking hard. "I can't see any."

Mimi laughs.

We both stare at the lithe and muscled bodies of the boys on the Castle Hill team. They're an explosion of tight abs and tighter asses. Prince and Chase immediately stand out as the tallest and tannest and having the best bodies on the team.

At one point, Chase catches us staring, he turns around and stretches his arms over his head, tightening his abs and thrusting his package right in our faces.

"How many abs does he have?" Mimi whispers giddily.

"Every single one," I answer absently, transfixed by his physique.

When he finishes tormenting us, I mean stretching, he flashes us a cocky grin and turns around to focus on the coach, who is jabbering away about gameplay.

Mimi and I tear our eyes away just long enough to gawk at each other and gasp.

"Who needs football?" Mimi snickers.

"Right?" I titter. "What's not to love about water polo? Who knew it was my favorite sport ever?"

"Totally," Mimi laughs.

For the next hour, we watch Prince and Chase both attack the ball, moving through the water like they were born to it, scoring goal after goal on the visiting team. Prince is constantly hollering orders at his teammates, keeping them on target the entire time. Everything about him screams leader. Chase is his right-hand man, often assisting Prince in some impossibly fast passing and scoring.

"They are so good," I say to Mimi at some point.

She says, "I heard their coach coaches the Men's Olympic team every four years."

"It shows," I say, watching the yellow ball sail across the blue water of the huge pool as someone passes it long.

When the buzzer signals the end of the game, the players climb dripping wet out of the water. I swear they go in slow-mo. That might be the rush of my adrenalin that is surging through my body with the help of my pounding heart.

Prince doesn't notice us as he passes on the wet pool deck, but we notice him. Every dripping inch.

Chase notices and chuckles to himself before blowing us a kiss.

Mimi and I both catch it.

"That's mine!" Mimi blurts.

He chuckles, "It's for both of you."

Mimi and I look at each other and break into gasping giggles.

Did I mention Castle Hill Academy just became a dream come true? The dreamy boy kind of dream? I am a smitten kitten. This place is a pretty boy paradise. Maybe it's not as bad as I thought.

I raise a mental toast to that feeling lasting forever.

Chapter 22

"What's this?" I ask.

Ms. Braunschott is holding a slip of paper over the desk in her tiny office. "A voucher for your first stipend check."

"My what?"

"For your work-study work. You receive a voucher every two weeks."

"Oh, right." I examine the paper. It's printed with official Castle Hill Academy information, then there's handwriting in fountain pen noting a bunch of things including my name, the pay period, and the amount, and it's signed in fastidious slashing script which I can barely read.

Brigid Braunschott.

The amount?

Two hundred effing dollars!

"This is mine?" I ask.

"Don't lose it," she says. "You can redeem it as necessary for cash, or you can keep the amount in your student bank account for the duration of your stay. I suggest you find a safe place for your vouchers and keep them there."

"Yeah, totally." I'll have to put it in Mimi's room, or— "Wait, can I, I don't know, leave this in your office? It's always locked. That might be safest."

"You may." Ms. Braunschott stands from her desk, whips out a huge key ring, opens a sturdy wooden cabinet with hundreds of tiny drawers. With a separate key, she opens one. "Place your voucher in the drawer."

I do. "Thanks. May I go now?"

"You may."

I curtsy on my way out.

Walking down the narrow corridor toward my room, I do some quick math in my head. Two hundred for forty hours of work is bit less than minimum wage even after taxes, but I can't complain. If I save it, I'll walk out of here four years from now with like twenty grand! Plus the money Skill gave me it's like twenty-two grand. If I'm stuck here summers and I work full time June, July and August, it'll be even more. Almost twenty-five grand! That's a fortune, if you ask me.

This place really is shaping up to be a dream come true.

An hour later, it's the opposite.

<(—)>

"Jacqueline says Elizabeth told her Kate said Chloe saw you kissing Duke the other day on the terrace!" hisses Vicious Victoria, grabbing my arm from behind and digging in her claws.

"Ow! Would you let go?" I yank my arm away. I'm totally startled because I just changed into my gym clothes and wasn't expecting any Fundy girls to surprise attack me here in the slums of the work-study girls locker room. I thought I'd be safe until I walked out. They must've snuck in and found me.

Victoria is glaring at me and my back is to my gym locker. Jackess Jacqueline stands beside Vicious with another Fundy girl I recognize but haven't had the pleasure of meeting.

"Chloe saw you with Duke, Chemo!" Vicious snarls. "Kate said!"

I don't know why she's still calling me Chemo. I'm not baby bald anymore. My hair is over a quarter inch long. Not long enough to do anything with, but at least I *have* hair. Another inch and it might even look chic. Either way, I don't look chemo at all.

"Chloe saw you!" Victoria reiterates.

"Who's Chloe?" I say. "I don't know any Chloes." I glance at the third girl. "Are you her?"

"I'm Kate, cancer cunt. You should know that by now!"

"Sorry for asking," I grouse.

Victoria barks, "Chloe saw you kissing Duke!"

"I never kissed Duke!"

"That's not what Chloe said," Vicious scowls. She is ma-a-a-ad.

"She's lying," I say.

"She saw you with him, Chemo!"

"Because he cornered me!"

"To kiss you!"

"No, all we did was talk! He's your boyfriend, ask him."

"Ex-boyfriend," she seethes.

I groan, "I don't care what he is. Stop interrogating me and go hassle him. This is your drama, not mine." I try to leave but Victoria and her henchwomen step in front of me and bang me back against the lockers.

"It's your fault we broke up!"

"No, it's *your* fault." Now I'm mad but staying calm. "You were kissing Skill. None of this is my problem." I shouldn't have to deal with this, but Duke did threaten to kick me out of here if I didn't fix things. You know what? I can get revenge on him *and* Vicious by getting them back together. Talk about just desserts.

"That's where you're wrong. This is *entirely* your problem."

Since I'm literally backed into a corner, I should say something.

Where to start? I smirk, "Have you tried apologizing to Duke?"

"For what?" Victoria scowls.

"For cheating on him! Duh!"

"I wasn't cheating!"

"Hello! I saw you! A hundred other people saw you! Jacqueline saw you too! Tell her! You were both kissing Skill!"

Jacqueline blushes and titters, "The only kissing I remember is kissing Skill's luscious lips."

Why does that make me jealous? So annoying.

"Shut up," Victoria glares at Jacqueline.

She snips, "You shut up."

Obviously, they're jealous of each other over Skill. I groan. Why do I feel like I'm talking to toddlers? Because I am. "Victoria, listen to me. Apologize to Duke. Tell him you'll never do it again. You can do that, right?"

"I didn't do anything wrong!" she insists.

"She didn't," Jacqueline says. "It was only kissing. It's not like they fucked."

"Are you hearing yourselves?" I shake my head in disbelief. I'm not talking to toddlers, I'm talking to insane people. "It doesn't matter what you think, Victoria. It matters what Duke thinks. He thinks you cheated on him! No wonder he broke up with you!"

Victoria gasps, "No he didn't! I broke up with him!"

"What?!" I laugh. "I thought—"

"You thought wrong, stupid chemo cunt!"

I almost lose it, but manage to keep myself semi-calm. "Then why do you care if I was talking to the boyfriend *you* dumped?"

"Because he's *my* ex-boyfriend!"

I have nothing to say to that.

"You fucked everything up, cancer cunt! I am going to make you pay so hard for this, you have no idea. NO IDEA!" She whirls and the other two follow her out of the work-study locker room.

How did I get myself in this mess?

A better question is, can I just go back to jail so I don't have to deal with these Fundy freaks?

"They're so mean," a demure voice says. Azzie. She peeks out from around a row of lockers.

"What're you doing here?" I blurt. "You don't have PE first period." After three weeks, I would've seen her by now.

"I got permission from Ms. Skelter to rearrange my schedule."

"Why?"

Azzie bites her lower lip, "I, I don't know. I just—" She shrugs shyly and blushes. Her anime mannerisms are frighteningly precise.

Is she stalking me? And why do I keep seeing Victoria and Jacqueline together, but no Elizabeth Morgan-Hearst? Those three were thick as thieves the day I met them in the parking garage. Now all of a sudden Elizabeth is *never* with them? But Azzie is always trailing me? It's bad enough we're roommates, but she has to have every class I have? It's too much. She's gaslighting me. I just know it. I blurt, "You're Elizabeth, aren't you?"

"No," she whispers, almost embarrassed.

"You are."

"Why would you say that?"

"Because it's true."

Her face starts to quiver, her eyes water and two tears dribble down her cheeks. "No it's not," she sniffs, covering her nose and mouth with one hand. "We're sisters."

"I don't believe you. I've never once seen you and your *sister* at the same time. You're a liar, Azzie. Elizzie. Or whatever your name is."

"We're identical twins," she says meekly.

"That's pure crap, Azzie. I knew some identical twin sisters in grade school. I could tell them apart. But you? You're the mirror image of Elizabeth because you *are* Elizabeth. Admit it."

Her face crinkles in pain and she sobs, "Why are you so mean?! I've never been anything but nice to you! When Ms. Braunschott asked if I'd share my room with you, I said yes because all the other girls said no! None of them wanted the Fundies getting revenge on them for being nice to you!"

I cringe. Is that true? Since I barely talk to Azzie in our room, and the only other work-study girl I really talk to is Meems, and we never talk about anything other than boys or bitch about Ms. Brawny, I don't really know.

Azzie says, "Everybody thinks you're trouble because the Fundy girls hate you! Nobody wants to room with you! But I do! I thought you were nice! You're not! You're no better than Victoria and Jacqueline!" Her face collapses in misery and she turns on the heel of her running shoe and runs into the bowels of the locker room.

I feel like an ass. "Azzie! Wait!" I start after her then stop because it's all an act.

I'm not falling for it.

No way.

<(—)>

Volleyballs bounce off the gymnasium's immense floor and echo off the tall walls. Slaps and whacks and squeaking shoes echo too. I'm hunched over and waiting for the other team to serve. I watch the girl toss the ball in the air on the far side of the court and whack!

Something hits me in the back of the head.

A volleyball goes bouncing.

"What the hell?" I spin around to see Victoria standing in the next court in the service position.

"Sor-reeee!" she smirks a not-sorry smile.

One of the other players runs after the stray ball and tosses it back to her.

"Don't do that again," I warn.

She does. Three more times. Not right away, and not always while serving. After the fourth time, I grab the ball myself and hold onto it, turning my back to her.

"Can we have our ball back?" Victoria calls out indignantly.

I ignore her.

One of her teammates gets Mrs. Gillespie (the aforementioned Mrs. Boobuster) involved and I turn the ball over without explanation. The fifth time Victoria hits me, I throw the ball at her, aiming for her face. I miss. She and Jacqueline laugh.

I march over to both of them, my fingers curled into claws. I can't decide if I'd rather tear out their hair or their eyes first.

They both stand there casually not moving but looking damn good. Even in their gym clothes, they're like pinup princesses, which makes this all the more frustrating.

They won't be pinup-approved when I'm done with them.

"Go ahead," Vicious taunts. "Do something, Chemo. I'm sure Ms. Skelter would be glad to kick you back to jail for fighting."

"It'll be worth it," I scowl, ready to pounce.

A shrill whistle stops me short.

"Ladies!" Mrs. Gillespie calls out from across the gym. "What is going on over there? Why aren't you playing?!"

"Tell her, Chemo," Jacqueline says loudly enough for me to hear but too quiet for Mrs. Gillespie. "We don't mind. Tell her anything you want and we'll see who she believes."

Now, Kate and the three other girls from Vicious and Jackess's team are standing behind them both, a united front.

Kate says, "Stop serving balls at us, Chemo. Keep it in your court."

"Yeah," the other girls echo. "Stop trying to hit us."

Mrs. Gillespie glares.

I look at my work-study team of girls to corroborate my side of things.

They all shrug.

Gee thanks. Seriously, what's the point?

I turn my back on Vicious and Jackess and go back to ignoring them.

The next time they try to hit me, they miss because I'm watching them more than my game. I almost stumble over my teammates a hundred times because of it, which is starting to annoy them. You can't win for trying. The seventh time I never see coming. Right when I'm turning to look over my shoulder, the ball smacks me in the nose. I'm so surprised, I fall on my ass.

Victoria and Jackess laugh.

When I stand up, I see blood dripping on the varnished wood floor. My nose is bleeding. That's it.

I charge snarling.

I slam into Victoria with both hands.

She goes flying into Jacqueline and they both tumble onto the gym floor.

I rush toward them.

Mrs. Gillespie's whistle blows, stopping the fight. This time she's only one court over and yelling, "Miss Angerman! What do you think you're doing?!"

"They hit me with the ball on purpose!" I swipe blood from my nose and hold up bloody fingers. "See?! I'm bleeding! Because they hit me! This is the seventh time!"

Mrs. Gillespie strolls over, frowning with concern, inspecting my nose.

I wait for her to tell me to go the nurse's office or wherever.

"She's faking," Victoria says.

"I saw her hit herself," Jacqueline says.

"I didn't hit myself!" I protest. "You did!"

"You never know with these work-study girls," Kate says.

"They're crazy," another Fundy says.

"She was picking her nose," yet another says.

"She's always picking her nose," says a third.

"That's why it's bleeding," a fourth says.

Now there's a dozen Fundy girls and more coming to back up Victoria and Jacqueline while the work-study girls on my team keep their distance.

I really am being gaslighted by the Fundies, not just Azzie, all of them, only not in a clever way. In the most obvious way possible. It's pathetic.

"They're lying!" I grumble.

"No, you are."

"I wasn't picking my nose or hitting my own face!"

"I saw you."

"That's crazy!"

"You're crazy."

I don't know who's talking because all the Fundy girls are saying things blaming me. Frustrated beyond belief, I look back to the work-study girls on my team. "Aren't even *one* of you going to say something?"

They're too scared. Frightened of retribution from the Fundies, no doubt.

I'm on my own. I turn to Mrs. Gillespie, "They hit me."

"Who hit you?" she asks.

"I didn't see. I turned around just in time to see the ball slam into my face."

Victoria sneers, "You hit yourself. I saw."

"Then you came over and attacked us," Jacqueline adds.

"Because you're crazy," Kate says.

Mrs. Gillespie says, "Miss Angerman, I did see you push Victoria into Jacqueline."

"Yeah," I say, "because they hit me with the stupid ball seven effing times!"

"Calm down, Miss Angerman."

"She can't," a random Fundy says. "She's off her meds."

"I'm not on any meds!" I shout.

"You should be," the Fundy titters.

"Would you shut up!" I growl at her.

"There's no need for yelling," Mrs. Gillespie warns. "Get yourself under control, young lady."

I groan, "Can't you see they're lying?!"

"Miss Angerman, the only thing I see is a hysterical child who can't control her temper."

"Meds would help," the Fundy mutters.

Ignoring her, I roll my eyes and sniff petulantly because of the blood dripping out my nose, not because I've lost my temper or need any effing meds.

Mrs. Gillespie inspects my face, "I don't know what you did to your nose, Miss Angerman, but it—"

"I didn't do anything!" I hiss under my breath.

"Stop interrupting me, Mary! You're disrupting the entire class with your need for attention. If you want to be the star of the show, sign up for the school play!"

"But I—!"

Mrs. Gillespie blasts me in the face with her whistle.

It's so freeping loud I cringe.

"Outside!" She grabs me by the arm and rushes me toward the doors.

Behind us, the Fundies laugh.

Mrs. Gillespie doesn't seem to notice because the faculty *never* notices when the Fundies get away with murder. Or framing me for it.

"I'm going," I whine, trying to fall into step with Mrs. Gillespie so I don't trip and fall.

She doesn't slow down until we're outside at the red rubber track. She gives me a push and lets go. "Start running, young lady!"

"This is—!"

"Go!"

I heave a sigh and start walking.

"I said run, Miss Angerman! That is not running!"

I start a slow jog. Stupid bitch.

"Mr. Perkins!" Mrs. Gillespie calls out to the boys' PE teacher. Mr. Perkins stands at the edge of the field supervising the boys playing flag football. "Keep an eye on Miss Angerman and make sure she finishes eight laps before coming inside."

"Eight laps?!" I blurt. "That's two miles!"

"How about three?!" Mrs. Gillespie challenges. "Twelve laps, Mr. Perkins! Don't let her in until she finishes twelve laps!"

Mr. Perkins nods absently before blowing his own whistle to stop the play on the field.

When I come around after jogging my first lap, Mrs. Gillespie is gone, so I walk. Mr. Perkins doesn't care.

All I can think is, how the hell did that happen? I've literally never had anything like that happen before at any school I've ever been to, and there have been many. For all the bullying I've dealt with, I've never had a group of people gang up on me and outright lie that blatantly to a teacher. It's insane! That doesn't mean it didn't happen.

I'm flabbergasted, actually.

On the plus side, after two laps my nose isn't bleeding. I guess it wasn't that bad.

Later, I don't know how many laps I've walked when the boys on the field jog back to the locker rooms, but I follow. A shrill whistle stops me in my tracks.

"Where do you think you're going?" Mr. Perkins asks. "That was only eight laps."

"But I have to shower or I'll be late for second period," I protest.

"You should've thought of that when you were walking instead of jogging." He checks his wristwatch, "If you run, you won't be late. You can do a six minute mile, can't you?"

I gawk at him. One more tardy and I'll get kicked out of Castle Hill permanently.

"Don't just stand there, young lady! Move!" He's like an effing drill sergeant all of a sudden. "I said MOVE!"

I shake my head in disbelief and start running. Not jogging. I go as fast as I can. Did I mention I hate running? Walking is fine. But running? I'd rather clean truck-stop toilets with my tongue than run. Okay, maybe that's an exaggeration, but you know what I mean. Anyway, I'm sweating my ass off and breathing my last breath when I make it around the final lap and cross the finish line dying for air.

Mr. Perkins is standing there smiling and holding an old-school silver stopwatch in his hand. He clicks it off with a smile. "Five minutes, fifty-seven seconds. Not bad, Miss— What was your name again?"

"Mary! Gasp! Anger! Gasp! Man! Gasp!" I'm bent over, hands on kneecaps and heaving air while trying not to heave my guts up. I've never run that fast in my entire life for that long. They do say motivation is key, and honestly, I'm more afraid of getting kicked out of Castle Hill Academy than I ever was of Emily Calhoun back at Roosevelt High.

"Maybe you should try out for track come spring, young lady."

"No! Gasp! Thanks! Gasp! Can I! Gasp! Shower! Gasp! Now? Gasp!"

"Go right ahead," Mr. Perkins smiles. "Don't take too long a shower. You wouldn't want to be late for period two."

I want to flip him off so bad it hurts, but the knife in my side hurts worse.

I throw up my breakfast when I get to the communal showers.

The water from the shower spout washes it down the drain.

Thankfully, no one is here to see because I'm so late and the work-study girls have left the locker room to get to second period. Lucky for me I don't have any hair to wash. I soap myself up and rinse off as quickly as possible, turning the knob off with a squeak. Water drips for minute, then it's eerily quiet with everyone gone from the locker room, which means I don't have to worry about having my very own "Plug it up!" Carrie moment, and because I know what a tampon is.

The downer about not having a "Plug it up" moment is I don't get to go telekinetic badass on the Fundy bitches. If I had powers like Carrie's, I wouldn't kill the Fundies. I'm not that vengeful. But I would lock Vicious and Jackess and their friends in the gym with like a thousand volleyballs and hurl them at the girls with my telekinesis until I got bored. Imagine all the bruises and bruised egos. *That* they deserve.

I've heard the Fundy girls' exclusive locker room is complete with private showers instead of a big communal one like ours, which is really old, by the way. Like 1950s plumbing or something. They say for the Fundies it's like a modern day spa, everything sparkling and super chic. Of course they get the brand new building and we get the old one. I'd check for myself just to see, but you need an electronic key card to get in and the Fundy girls are protective about that door.

I walk out of the shower in a towel and flip flops which Mrs. Gillespie forces us to wear to cut down on athlete's foot. As you can guess, the Fundy girls say it's because we all have it.

When I get to my locker, it's open and empty.

My gray work-study uniform is gone.

Is this the wrong locker?

It has to be. I'd never leave my locker open like this. I must've walked into the wrong row.

I check the others.

Crap.

That *was* my locker.

Those bitches stole my clothes.

My chest caves in with an overwhelming sense of invasion that presses in around me from every direction and my body gets hot.

It's the adrenalin, I can tell.

It's bad enough they bashed my nose with a volleyball, bad enough I'm late for class and I threw up in the shower after running those laps. But this is worse. They're gaslighting me again! I can't decide if they're trying to get me thrown out of school on purpose, or if they're just tormenting me with no concern for the consequences. No, I can decide. They *don't* care. They only care about screwing with me however they want because they can. They *know* they can get away with anything so they do.

You know what?

Screw them.

I've dealt with way—

((((pitch black))))

((((pain))))

((((it hurts!))))

((((please not again!))))

—worse than this.

This is nothing.

I walk to class in a towel.

It's warm enough.

The only thing I can't figure out is how they got into my locker. No one knows the combo. I memorized it from the paper they gave me, and that paper is in my room in the Convent, I mean Mimi's room, where I left it tucked safely inside my copy of The Voyage Out by Virginia—

Azzie!

I mean Eliza-bitch!

It *had* to be her!

That gaslighting goodie two-shoes!

Two can play at that game.

Chapter 23

Walking discretely around campus in a towel and flip-flops is easier said than done. Each step brings me one step closer to a panic attack. I keep expecting someone to tear my towel off and leave me naked with everyone laughing. Except, there's no one around. It's already past tardy. The church bell in the tower rang two minutes ago. That doesn't stop me from clutching my towel closed with both hands while I hurry to AP Physics. I don't even have my book bag. It's in my regular locker. Unless Azzie broke into that too.

Scattered laughter from around the corner of the next building sends me scrambling for cover, only there isn't any cover here on the stone canal walkway. Yes, there's a canal running through this part of campus with walkways on both sides between buildings, and little arched bridges here and there. It's made to look like Venice, Italy. Even the stones look historical and old. It's actually romantic when you're not late for class and wearing only a towel.

I dash up the narrow arched bridge heading toward the other side of the canal. That's a mistake because two Fundy boys turn the corner between buildings on the other side and walk onto the opposite end of the bridge heading straight for me. I don't recognize them, but I know they're Fundy from their uniforms.

"Look! It's Chemo!" Everyone recognizes me, with or without my uniform.

I'd turn around but I need to go forward to get to class. My plan is to push past these two on the narrow bridge.

"Not so fast, Chemo." The tall kid says and grabs me by the waist.

"What's under the towel?" the shorter kid asks and paws for it.

"Let go!" I twist and rip it out of his hand and spin away from the tall kid. Again, they stand between me and the way I need to go. I fight back the impending panic attack.

"This should be good," a deep voice says behind me.

I glance over my shoulder at Prince.

He's leaning one hip against the Greek-style bridge railing, arms folded across his chest, looking sexy as hell in his royal uniform. As always, he's surfer hot, his blue eyes amused. "Whoever gets the towel first can sit at my dinner table tonight in the palace."

Evil grins peel across the mouths of the two little gibbering grabbers.

"No!" I shout. "No one is taking my towel! Stop them, Prince!"

"What's to stop? They aren't doing anything." Prince stands there like moving is not on his agenda for the year.

The two grabbers are giggling like goblins.

Now that I look at them, they're young. No more than freshman. Fourteen at the most, both of them skinny and geeky. Emily Calhoun and Kaitlyn Sharp back at Roosevelt are bigger than these two. These two I can handle.

I glare at them, "Out of my way, jerks, or I'm pushing you into the canal."

"Oh yeah?"

"Yeah," I growl and run at them.

Wrestling two boys, no matter how small, is nearly impossible while holding onto your towel.

"I got it, I got it!" the short one squeals.

"No, I got it!" the tall one squeaks.

They're pulling on my twisted towel like a tug of war.

Me?

I'm naked down to my flip-flops. "Give that back!"

Now it's a three way tug of war.

"Stop," Prince says half-heartedly because he's obviously enjoying the show. "Stop already," he sighs, still leaning against the wall.

They don't. We're fighting for the towel in a frenzy.

"Stop!" he hollers in exasperation, wading into the fray and tossing the two goblins on their asses and taking the towel. He's about to hand it to me when—

"What the fuck are you doing, Prince?!" someone screams. Everyone turns to look at Elizabeth Morgan-Hearst. "Are you... Are you three *raping* her?" I'm too embarrassed to respond, and too busy covering myself with both hands. Backing into the bridge railing doesn't hide anything. Prince wraps the towel around me. Elizabeth snorts, "Because if you are, don't let me stop you."

I'm stunned. "You think this is funny?"

"Yes," she titters.

Prince glares at her.

I snarl at Prince, "Oh, you're the good guy now?"

His face burns red underneath his tan, "I didn't think they'd actually —"

"Actually take my towel, you ass-tampon?! You *told* them to!"

He runs his fingers through his golden hair and mutters, "I'm sorry, I didn't mean to—"

"Don't apologize to her!" Elizabeth snaps. "She's a gutter slut! *We* do not *ever* apologize to back-talking trash like *her*."

Prince starts to say something then stops himself with a pained sigh.

I glare at Elizabeth, "Mind your own business, *Azzie*."

"Don't call me that." She frowns at me down her surgically sculpted nose, which is as beautiful as I remember and exactly the same as Azzie's. Exactly.

I clutch the towel around myself and get right in her face. "Why not, *Azzie?* You said it was your name."

"Are you insane?" she laughs.

"No, but you are." I realize I didn't see Azzie in PE class after she ran away in the locker room. That means she had more than enough time to change clothes, do her hair, put in her nose ring and tongue stud, and put on the makeup she's wearing now. Unlike "Elizabeth," "Azzie" wears no makeup and pulls her hair back in a ponytail. I'm sure she's got the transformation in either direction down to a science. "You've been gaslighting me since I got here, haven't you, *Elizazzie?*"

Elizabeth frowns at Prince, "What is she talking about?"

He shrugs.

"Don't deny it," I say irately, glaring at Elizabeth.

"Deny what, gutter slut? That you need Lasik?"

"My vision's fine! You're Azzie!" I scoff. "Everybody can tell! It's so obvious!"

She snorts, "I have no idea what you're talking about."

None of the other three seem to know either. See? They're gaslighting me again! "You know what? Screw all of you! I'm late for class!" I barge past them.

<(—)>

When I get off the bridge and turn a bunch of corners and go down to another terrace level, I check over my shoulder to make sure none of them followed me.

"Mary, wait!" Prince is jogging to catch up.

"Oh, no! You get away from me!" My legs are jelly from all those laps I ran, otherwise I'd run faster.

He quickly catches me and grabs my towel, stopping me.

"Let go of me, Prince!" I struggle, but he's too strong and I don't want to lose my towel again. "Let! Go!"

"Would you relax?"

"No! You're a piece of shit!"

"I'm sorry," he sighs.

That stops me cold. "What?"

"I said I'm sorry." He lets go of my towel.

I turn around, "Sorry you tried to get them to sexually assault me?"

"I wouldn't have let them."

"Take my towel?"

"Sexually assault you."

I'm surprised by that but I'm still raging. "Oh, but you *would* let them take my towel."

"I didn't think they'd do it."

"You're a liar, Prince Turd."

He scowls at that.

"I don't even know you, but I know everyone around here kisses your ass. Especially geeky little goblin boys like those. I see the way people always *defer* to you like you're the king. Step out of your way when you're walking. It's disgusting. I'm surprised you don't have them throw roses wherever you go."

He smirks, "I would, but you would have to clean them up."

I scowl, "Is that supposed to be funny? That is not even close to funny. It just shows how far up your ass your head is, Prince Turd."

His blue eyes chill to an icy azure.

"You don't like that name, do you? You're as bad as Duke. No one ever calls you names so you don't know how to deal with it when they do. You're both a bunch of babies, you know that? Grow a pair already." I've got nothing to lose at this point, because seriously, I changed my mind and this place is no better than jail. And I used to think Roosevelt High was bad. That was nothing. I decide to let Prince have it. "You think just because you have money, you're better than me?"

"It's not *just* the money," he grins. Is it a cocky grin? Yes. Is it arrogant? Of course. Is it blatantly flirtatious and incredibly sexy? Everything he does is incredibly sexy!

"Go away, turd," I giggle and mean to start walking away, but I don't. My legs stopped working. Everything below my waist wants to head *toward* him, not away. No, everything below my neck. All of me is thrumming with excitement. It's been a few weeks since stalkery Prince stole me away from Rob and Mr. Ralston and led me to see the birds my first day here. Aside from seeing nearly all of him at that water polo game, I constantly see him on campus in his sexy academy uniform suit, but it's never for long because I'm rushing from one place to the next, and he's always surrounded by a huge entourage of Fundy girls in their unbuttoned blouses. Wherever he goes, it's a festival of boobs. There's no reason he'd notice me. I've pretty much forgotten him (except at night when I dream about him in a Speedo against my will), and forgotten what an ass he is, but my body remembered everything else. "Can I go now, your lowness?"

"Lowness," he chuckles. "You're lucky I like you."

"No you don't," I snort. "I mean, you like me the same way little boys like to fry ants with magnifying glasses or pluck the wings off houseflies, *little boy*. That's what you are. A turdy little boy. The lowest of the low."

"You're quick, strumpet. And you amuse me. Come to my party this weekend."

"Party? I'm not going to any party you throw unless I'm forced at gunpoint."

"That can be arranged."

"Are you serious?" I sneer.

"About you coming *at* my party."

"Did you just say at?" I blurt.

"I did," he grins.

"No! You have a girlfriend!"

"Who?"

"All of them!" I laugh.

He snickers guiltily.

"Why're you laughing?! It's true!" I'm laughing too.

"It's not true. Come to my party," he says, verging on politeness.

"Is that a command, your lowness?"

His mouth tightens, "No, it's a request."

"Why should I? So I can be your girl jester? Do I have to wear a jester costume? Tell riddles and make jokes all night? Or just dance around like a dope and juggle a lot?"

"If that's what you want."

"Screw you, turd."

"We can do that." He leans closer and his sandalwood and cinnamon smell hits me right between the... wherever, and launches an army of angry butterflies in my chest and the rest of me lower down. He tugs on the side of my towel.

I slap his hand away, "Hands off!"

"If you insist." He turns and walks away, hollering over his shoulder, "Saturday night, strumpet! Don't be late!"

"I'm not going to your stupid party! I don't even know where it is!" Why did I say that? I don't want to know and I certainly won't go.

"I'll send word!" he calls.

"Don't send anything!" I giggle.

"Saturday, strumpet! Don't be late!"

There is no way I'm going to his party.

"You *have* to go to his party, Mare Bear!" Mimi squeals. We're in her dorm room hanging out studying. Just because we can't room together doesn't mean we can't study together. "I don't know a single work-study kid, boy or girl, who has *ever* gone to one of Prince's parties! You have to go!"

"No way!" I laugh. "Prince is a lunatic! He probably doesn't even have a party. He's just trying to get me somewhere alone to do… I don't know what he wants to do."

"You know," she says archly.

"Do not!" I pout.

"Do too. And that's a bad thing?" Mimi giggles.

I roll my eyes and drawl out my words, "Evvvveryone knows how hot Prince is, and evvvveryone wants him to want them. Except me. I don't want anything to do with him."

"Your denial is paper thin, Mare. You should totally go."

"Even if I wanted to, which I don't, I don't have anything to wear, and I'm not buying anything. I had to pay for a new uniform after they stole mine, and that took all my stipend and then some. I had to write and sign an IOU to Brawny, deductible from my next paycheck."

"You can borrow anything you want from me."

"I can't fit into your clothes."

"Yes you can. We'll find something that works. Oh, wait. It is October. It must be his Halloween party. Could that be it?"

She's right. I was already several weeks into the term at Roosevelt when I left, making it October when I got here.

"Mare Bear, if it's his Halloween party, it's a once in a lifetime kind of thing. I hear they're epic. Totally off the hook. You have to go. No excuses."

"Do you have any spare costumes?"

"I have a French maid outfit," she quips. "You do too. And yours fits you like a glove."

"More like a giant's welding glove."

She rolls her eyes, "You're going."

"No, Meems! I'm not going wearing my work uniform! If it's Fundies, even if I have a mask, they'll know it's me from my hair. I'm the only girl on campus with a buzz cut. I'll never hear the end of it."

"So what?! You're going! I'd go if it was me he's inviting."

"What if Chase invites you?" I tease. "We could go together."

"He didn't," she pouts. "Otherwise I would. Stop deflecting. You're going."

"I don't even know where the party is."

"I'm sure you'll find out. B-dubs, what happened with Mrs. Vang? Did she mark you tardy for Physics?"

"No, when I walked in wearing a towel and explained everything, she let me off the hook."

"That's a relief. I know two work-study kids who got kicked out for being tardy. You better be more careful."

I smirk, "You mean more careful that no one breaks into my gym locker and steals my clothes?"

"Yeah, that," she grins.

I throw my old pillow at her face and she bats it away laughing. Brawny never gave Meems a new roommate because there's no one to fill the space at the moment. She obviously wanted to separate us because we were having too much fun. It was bad for morale. Our late night laughing and giggling was making the other work-study girls want to laugh and giggle too, which as we all know is verboten.

When I finish studying and go back to my dorm room, I find an invitation waiting on my bed. I don't find Azzie. I haven't seen her all day since the locker room this morning. The invitation is on fancy layered paper with multiple colors and textures, one of them patterned like lace, another fibery and old-timey. The writing is in gold ink. Hand-written calligraphy, of course. It's nicer than a wedding invitation.

Visions of Cinderella's ball flash through my mind. Prince already looks the part of the... prince. LOLs. My heart was thudding as I read it.

You are cordially invited to attend the legendary Lancaster All Hallows' Ball this Saturday evening at ten o'clock. The secret location will be revealed the night of the event. This invitation is your ticket. Do not lose it, strumpet.

Signed Prince J. Lancaster the Turd.

He actually wrote turd.

I snicker to myself.

Did he hand-write this himself? He must have. Only he would call me strumpet. I can't picture his secretary or party planner or whoever writing strumpet.

I laugh and clutch the invitation to my breast.

What am I thinking?

I smell a trap.

Like, a literal trap.

Speaking of traps, I glance at Azzie's bed. The blankets are pulled tight. No one has so much as sat on it since this morning. Where is she? It's almost light's out. She should be here.

The next morning, I wake up at 5:00am and see her bed is untouched. She never came home.

I knew it.

She really is Elizabeth. She probably spent the night in the East Wing of the Palace where the Fundy girls sleep. I'm sure she has her own penthouse suite or whatever. Now that she knows I'm on to her, she'll probably never come back here.

Good.

That means I'll have the room all to myself.

I'd rather share with Mimi, but this is better than having a gaslighting social assassin sleeping in the next bed.

Chapter 24

"You have to go as Little Bo Peep!" Mimi laughs from her dorm room bed a few days later. I already told her about the invitation.

"I'm not dressing as her!" I giggle, sitting across from Meems on the other bed. "Besides, where would I get the sheep?"

"You don't need sheep!" she laughs. "You just need a flouncy dress, the milkmaid hat, and her staff."

"No! It needs to be something more... adult."

"Go as Slutty Bo Peep!"

"No!" I laugh.

"Why not? All the other girls are gonna dress slutty and you know it. Or have you *never* been to a high school Halloween party?"

"I've been to plenty. I know nothing is too slutty for Slut-O-Ween. But I need something better than Slut Bo Peep," I titter.

"It's *Slutty* Bo Peep."

"Whatever!" I laugh. "I don't even know what that is!"

"Bo Peep in a G-string."

"Is that even a thing?"

"It will be when you go as her." Mimi is loving this and has been torturing me with bad ideas for an hour.

"No, Meems! No Slutty Bo Peep, no Slutty Little Mermaid, no Slutty Eloise at the Plaza, and no Slutty Dora the Explorer! And stop trying to ruin my childhood already!"

She laughs, "How about we both go as Slutty M&M's. I'll be red, you be yellow."

"Peanut or plain?"

"Which is more slutty?" she winks.

"No-a!" I giggle. "You're supposed to ask which is *less* slutty, Meems! Less! Not more! Have you *never* been laid?"

"Not lately," she laughs. "Have you?"

I blush, "We were talking about costumes! Not my sex life!"

"Okay, okay. We'll go as peanut M&Ms, minimal slut."

"Now *that* I would do. If I can wear a giant no-slut M&M candy shell."

"Fine, but you have to at least wear high heels and fishnet stockings."

"I guess I can do that. I already do for work."

"See?" she laughs. "We can totally pull it off. You and me as sexy M&Ms. Not slutty. Just sexy."

"Love it. But you don't have an invitation," I pout.

She shrugs. "Maybe Chase'll invite me. We still have a few more days."

"Doesn't Prince have to invite you? It's his party."

"They're friends. Put in a good word for me."

"I will." Then, for no reason whatsoever, I'm overcome by emotion and I tear up. I try to sniff it back, but I can't. The tears pour out of me, dribbling down my face. I wipe them away guiltily. I hate crying in front of other people.

"What's wrong, Mare Bear?" Mimi asks frowning with genuine concern.

"N-n-n-nothing," I sputter, but the tears won't stop. I cry-laugh, "Look at me. I'm pathetic."

"No you're not. What is it, Mare?" She hops from her bed to sit by my side and puts a comforting arm around my shoulder. "What? Tell me?"

"It's just—" I know I'm red faced and ready to break down into blubbery body-wracking sobs. It takes everything I have to hold it back. I haven't had a girlie-girlfriend since losing my mom. She was the best girlfriend ever. When I was with her, it was nothing but dresses and tresses twenty-four seven. It's been very hard not having that sort of feminine connection in my life all these years.

Worse, I never get along with girls my age. Everything always turns catty, they inevitably plot against me, and I end up friendless.

But I get along with Mimi.

She could never replace my mom, but Mimi is easily the next best thing. In this place, having her as my friend is the only thing keeping me going some days. She's a shield from the casual cruelty that permeates the academy. I never let the mean treatment from the Fundies and the faculty get to me, but it builds up, and sometimes you have to let it out like now.

I collapse into Mimi's arms and whimper, "I don't know what I'd do without you, Meems."

"Awww," she coos and hugs me lovingly. "Don't worry, Mare Bear. You've got me. Besties forever, right?"

"Right." That's when I lose it and I *do* sob.

No girl my age has ever called me her bestie.

Not one.

This moment is the shining diamond in the dark and dreary coal mine of my friendless life. I'll never forget it.

Or Mimi's friendship.

It means the world to me.

<(—)>

"How do I look?" I ask Mimi a week later. We're in my and "Azzie's" room, no Azzie. With no full-length mirrors anywhere in the Convent, I need a second pair of eyes.

"Slutty as hell," she grins.

"Really?" I whine.

"Kidding. You look hot as hell, Mare Bear. Totally badass."

"I don't feel badass," I sigh. Or hot as hell. I never do. But I'm not admitting that. I prefer to bask in Mimi's compliment for at least a few minutes before the truth takes over.

"Well, you look it."

We're standing in my dorm room and I'm dressed as Charlize Theron's character from one of my fave badass babe movies, Mad Max: Fury Road. For me, it's hardly a costume. Sleeveless white T-shirt with the neck torn into cleavage. A bunch of leather belts around my waist like a corset, borrowed from some work-study boys Mimi knows. My dark jeans and Doc Marten boots. A lone black shoulder pad stolen from the football team. Don't ask how Mimi got that. She assures me she didn't steal it. Supposedly someone gave it to her, which no doubt involved stealing. The pad is attached to the belt corset with old rope we found in the Convent's storage room. For the mechanical robot hand, we took a leather work glove and spray-painted it silver. I got that stuff from Giant Jonah. He said they had it lying around over at the Plant Services building. For the chainmail skirt thing dangling from the front of my belt, we spray painted a ratty old rag silver. I didn't have anything to make the circle-of-flames belt buckle, but Jonah gave me an old gear he found. Close enough. Jonah really is a sweetheart. It was Mimi's idea to age everything with wisps of black spray paint (also from Jonah) and rubbing it in the dirt outside.

"I can't believe how good it turned out," I say, looking down at everything.

"Where there's a will there's a way," she grins. "I love that you don't even need a mask."

"Yeah." From the eyes up, my face and forehead are black and sooty like Furiosa's. That was easy. Black eyeshadow, mascara, and eyeliner liberally applied.

"That is like the smokiest smoky eye look I've ever seen."

"Right?" I laugh. Now that my scabs from Emily Calhoun are completely gone, and thank my lucky stars there's no scars, we did consider adding some fake ones but I decided not to bother. The eye makeup is more than enough.

"Are you ready?"

"Um..." I'm actually crazy nervous about going to Prince's party alone tonight. We couldn't get an invite for Mimi no matter how hard we tried. This means I'll be going into the viper pit of Rich Boys and Rich Girls on my own. "Sort of?" I offer nervously.

"Don't worry, Mare Bear. Looking like this, you'll slay everyone at the party."

"If I had Grayson's knife, I would."

"Vicious," she giggles. "Don't worry. You're going to have the time of your life. It'll be fine. Just have fun."

"I don't even know where it is yet! We're supposed to find out tonight. The Fundies who're going are probably getting texts on their phones or whatever, but I never gave my burner phone number to anybody."

"Prince knows where your room is from sending the invitation. He'll make sure you know."

"Unless he's pranking me and never shows up."

"He gave you the invitation. He'll be here."

"I hope so."

"I guess we wait?"

"I guess."

We both sit down on the beds.

"Any sign of Azzie lately?" Mimi asks.

"No, but I've seen a lot of her twin 'sister' Elizabeth."

"I know I saw Azzie going out of the Convent the other day."

"Yeah, but did you see her and Eliza-bitch at the same time?"

"No. Maybe they hate each other. You know, they avoid each other or whatever."

"Or maybeeeee... they're the same person! I'm telling you, Meems! It's all an elaborate gaslight."

"Why would they gaslight you?"

"Who says they're just gaslighting me? What if they're doing it to everyone?"

"Why?"

"I don't know. For all we know—"

A loud knock at the door startles us both.

"Brawny," Mimi hisses. "We're being too loud. If we're not careful, she's going to cut our tongues out."

I grimace at that image. "Sorry, Ms. Braunschott! We'll be more quiet."

The knock becomes a pounding.

I jump up with an annoyed sigh and go open the door. "I said we'd be—! Oh, shit!" I gasp and take a step back.

Filling my doorway is a giant lion man holding a cane. He has a massive mane of blond hair and is wearing a royal blue colonial suit with elaborate gold embroidery. His face is leonine and beastly, but in a dreamy way that betrays a certain irresistible appeal. Only the eyes I recognize. Piercing blue.

"Prince?" I ask.

"I'd roar," he quips, "but I wouldn't want to frighten you ladies."

"Nice costume," Mimi gawks. "Is it like, from a movie or whatever?"

"It's from the Manhattan Opera Company in New York. This is one of the rejected designs for the upcoming production of Mozart's unfinished Beauty & the Beast opera."

"Is that even a thing?" I scoff.

"It will be next year," Prince grins.

"Once Mozart finishes it?" Mimi asks.

"Something like that," he says.

I ask, "If it's not out yet, what're they doing giving you one of their costumes?"

"I told you, this is a rejected design. When I found out they weren't using it, I snapped it up."

"How do you know these things?" I laugh.

"I'm well connected," he says with enough arrogance to inflate a blimp.

"The makeup is incredible," Mimi says, admiring his beastly face and mane of hair. She's right about the makeup. If anything, it accentuates his hard charm. There's just enough to shape his nose like a lion's, and give him whisker dots, but the rest of his face, jawline and beard stubble are all his. "Who did it?"

"A makeup effects artist from Hollywood."

"Hollywood?" I snort. "That's nowhere close to here."

"I had them flown in for the weekend," Prince smiles.

"To do your makeup," I say with rhetorical disgust.

"To do my makeup," he agrees with syrupy pride.

I roll my eyes and say to Mimi, "Rich people."

She smirks at him, "You are such a Fundy, Prince."

"I prefer the term filthy rich. My money is my own to do with as I please, ladies."

I snark, "Junior Shakespeare is back in the house."

"For sure," Mimi giggles.

In a perfect Australian accent, Prince says, "Crikey, you two up yourself Sheilas defo need to get your heads outta your lappies and spend less time on Facey and go back to the bush where you can both get stuffed, I reckon."

Mimi and I stare at each other a moment before bursting into laughter.

Prince grins.

"Wait," I say, "you're not Australian, are you?"

"No. I spend a lot of time surfing there when it's winter here. Been going since I was little. I'll be there over winter break. Or maybe Fiji or South Africa, depending on the weather."

"Really?"

He nods.

"Wow. I've never been out of the state."

"I can arrange to change that," he says mysteriously. "Before that happens, we have a party to attend."

"To attend," I mock.

"Yup."

"Okay, I have to ask. What's with the weird Shakespeare thing?"

"Old habits."

"Huh?"

"Freshman etiquette. You spend an entire year learning how to *tawlk prawperly*," he finishes with a crusty British accent. "It's mandatory for paying *styoodents*."

I snicker, "You sound like Mr. Ralston."

"He teaches it."

"That explains it." I won't tell him how impressed I am by his accents. They're really good. He could be an actor.

"As I was saying, we have a party *tyoo* attend." He offers his hand and glances at Mimi. "I'll have her back before the sun comes up."

"Don't look at me," she laughs. "Take her to Fiji or wherever!"

I'm so happy it's a Saturday and I don't have to work Sunday. I'd go to Fiji in a heartbeat.

"Another time," Prince smiles. "Who're you supposed to be, Mary?"

"Your worst nightmare," I smirk.

"I can see that," he grins.

"I'm Imperator Furiosa."

"From Mad Max?"

"Uh huh. Do you like it?" I look down at my costume. "Me and Mimi made it. It's not Hollywood or extra like yours, I know, but I thought we did a good job for it being budget."

"It's terrific. Better than anything I could do without paying someone else to do it for me."

"Humble-bragger," Mimi mumbles.

"I'm never humble about my bragging," he winks at her and offers me his white-gloved hand. "Shall we?"

I take it and immediately feel the heat. Merely touching this young man is enough to make me tingle. Butterflies launch themselves up my arm and swirl around my heart, sending warm rain cascading down to my toes.

Prince leads me out along the empty and narrow Convent corridor toward the exit. It's late, so all of the work-study girls are in their rooms for the night.

Someone jumps out of the shadows and bellows.

"Where do you think you're going, Missy?!" It's Ms. Braunschott. She stands there like a military blockade, one fist on her big hips. Her other hand holds a flickering candle in a brass holder. She wears a tent of a white nightgown, but the sleeves are rolled up to her elbows. Did I mention she literally has Popeye forearms? She scowls when she recognizes me. "Where could you possibly be going at this hour in any sort of official academy work-study capacity?"

"Um, out?" I cringe hopefully. "To clean?"

"To clean, she says," Ms. B snorts to herself. "Where out?"

I look to Prince for that answer.

He says, "To my party."

"Over my dead body," Ms. B says. "It's an hour before light's out. Mary is on thin ice already. She should be in her room, not out with the likes of you." She looks us both over, her face screwed tight in a twist of disdain. "Back to your room, Mary, and I just might overlook what is surely a very bad decision on your part."

Prince says smugly, "I will be taking her with me, Ms. Braunschott, and you will like it."

I hold back a laugh.

Ms. B's eyes bug. "You do *not* talk to me like that, young man!"

"Oh, but I do, Ms. Braunschott," Prince says tenderly. "I can tell my beastly makeup is confusing you, and the candlelight is not enough for your tired old eyes. I am Prince J. Lancaster the third, and you will do as I say."

Ms. B's face burns bright red and she almost glows brighter than the candle light. "Do I need to wake Ms. Skelter? Would you like that, master Lancaster? Do you think Ms. Skelter would approve of your backtalk and flagrant disregard of academy rules? One word from me and Mary here is out on her ear. How would you like that, *master* Lancaster?"

Now I'm worried. Ms. Skelter has the power to kick me back to prison.

Prince says, "I don't *care* what Ms. Skelter thinks, Ms. Braunschott. I am going to take Mary away from here, and you, my dear lady, will say nothing about it. If you do, you will find yourself shipped out on a fishing trawler to Antarctica. I hope you like the cold."

Ms. B's eyes are on the verge of popping out of her skull.

"Good night, Ms. Braunschott," Prince says politely and leads me out of the Convent.

That was F-bombing awesome!

Chapter 25

"So, um, where's the party?" I ask as Prince leads me across the dark campus. At this hour, it's dead empty.

"That is a surprise."

"Oh, crap! I left my invitation back in my room!"

"Not to worry. I'll be your ticket to anywhere you want to go."

"Anywhere?"

"Even Fiji," he grins. "We can go right now, if you want."

"What about your party? And your costume?"

He shrugs, "If you want to go to Fiji, we'll go to Fiji." He sounds serious. "It's just a party. I throw one every year. Do you know how to surf?"

"I wish I did," I sigh. "I've never lived close to the beach."

"Don't worry. I'll teach you."

I can practically see the ocean waves in his blue eyes, and he's surfing them with me. Talk about hot.

"What'll it be, strumpet? Halloween or surf lessons in Fiji?"

"Erm," I laugh. "You're kidding, right?"

He smiles widely, "I never kid about surfing. Surfing is sacred."

I'm giddy just thinking about it. "Don't you need a passport to leave the country? I don't have one."

"I'll make the necessary arrangements."

"Won't that take weeks or whatever?"

"Not in my world, strumpet. I'll have the US Embassy in Fiji make the necessary accommodations to get you into the country. They'll issue you a temporary passport. If we have to, we'll get an official letter of entry from someone in parliament." He looks at his wrist watch. "If we leave now and take my plane, we can get there by sunrise."

"No way," I laugh. "How can you, I mean, it's like, there's no way, it just can't, can you *actually* do that?"

"I can do anything I want, strumpet."

This time, him calling me that doesn't bother me at all. His smirk doesn't hurt. It's truly priceless, a treasured work of art deserving of being immortalized on canvas and hanging next to Mona Lisa's infamous smile in the Louvre.

I am flabbergasted. The most exciting date any boy ever offered me before this moment was Grayson saying he could get us two tickets to either Coachella or Lollapalooza one summer, my choice. We would've gone, but neither of us were old enough to drive and you can bet our foster parents weren't going to drive us there and let the two of us run wild at a music festival. What Prince is offering now is way beyond that. It's something out of a fairytale. "Are you shitting me, Prince?"

"Not one bit of shit," he grins.

"Should we go pack our bags or go in costume?"

Prince chuckles, "It might be a tad bit more difficult getting you into Fiji looking like a Mad Max villain."

"Furiosa was the heroine not the villain."

"I don't care what she was. Which is it, strumpet?"

"Um," I laugh. "I'd hate to throw away all this hard work on my costume. Can we go to Fiji next time?"

"We can. Now let's get you to my party. Shall we?" He offers his arm.

"We shall." I bite my lower lip and hold him by the elbow as we walk along. It takes everything I have not to giggle and lean into him. Prince is dangerously attractive when he's not being an ass.

We end up in the parking garage where all the million dollar cars are parked. He leads me to a black car that may as well be the Batmobile, it's so exotic. It's parked in a corner where there are only three spaces. It's in the middle, and the adjacent spaces are empty, blocked off with orange traffic cones.

"Is this yours?"

He nods. "Bugatti *La Voiture Noire*." He says it with a perfect French accent.

"A what?"

"Bugatti's one-off hypercar, inspired by the legendary Type 57 Atalante."

"I can see that," I lie, having no idea about exotic sports cars, "but what's it called?"

"*La Voiture Noire*." His French accent is impeccably buttery and a little bit hypnotic, with a devilish edge that's definitely delish.

"Translation?"

"The black car."

"That's it?"

"That's it," he grins.

"The way you say it sounds like, I don't know, it should mean 'the dark angel,' or 'the shadow demon.' Not 'the black car'," I snicker.

He grins, "I didn't name it. I just bought it."

"With what? Your allowance?" I smirk.

"No, the profits from the company I sold last year."

"How much was that?"

"The profits or the car?"

"Either."

"The price of the car was a mere nineteen million."

"A *mere*," I mock.

He nods, "The profits from selling my company were substantially more."

"How can someone as young as you have sold a company already?"

"You know how some families start their kids skiing or riding horses or playing piano at age three?"

"No," I snort. "We couldn't afford those things."

He nods. "In my family's case, we start businesses from a very young age."

"What, like a lemonade stand or whatever?"

"For me it was a lemonade *business*. My first summer I was managing twenty stands. A hundred stands by the time I was nine."

"Is that even true?"

He shrugs.

I roll my eyes. "You said this car was a one off? There's only one?"

"Mine," he grins that cocky grin and checks his wristwatch, which matches the medallion on the car.

"Are we late or something?"

"No, I was just getting your door for you."

"With your watch?"

"Yup." He taps the watch screen and the passenger opens slowly backward instead of forward. He grins and walks me around and helps me slide in. The interior is a black leather cocoon that swallows me into the seat. "Don't touch anything."

"Shut up," I frown.

He winks and presses buttons on his watch, closing my door and opening his. He dashes around and drops in. When his door closes it's dead silent inside.

"It's so quiet in here," I whisper.

"That's so nobody can here you scream." He flashes a wicked grin.

"I knew it! You *are* a serial killer!" I laugh nervously because part of me thinks he is.

"I didn't mean that kind of screaming." His blue eyes burn into mine.

A wave of heat hits me, washing over me and penetrating me to my core. Ladies, even with his lion makeup, which really is minimal, Prince is so hot I'd let him do anything he wants right now. The surf trip to Fiji and this car don't hurt his chances either. What am I saying? Get a grip! I'm supposed to be Imperator Furiosa, not Pushover Bendovera!

I break eye contact and snort, "Are we going? Or are you just going to sit there staring at me with that pervy look all night?"

"I'm game if you are," he chuckles.

"Go already," I snicker and wave my fingers at the windshield, refusing to look at him lest I end up hypnotized.

He starts the engine and it rumbles through the car. Not like it's shaking it. Nothing so crude. More like it vibrates straight through to where you're sitting on your—

"Go!" I whine. "I'm getting bored!"

"Is that what you call it?" He inches the car out of the space and we rumble out to the automatic gate. After it raises, the car slides onto the pavement of the road leading out. He winks at me, "Don't get the seat wet."

"What?"

He drops the hammer and I explode.

I mean, the car, it explodes, the engine roars and we shoot forward so fast I'm forced into my seat by the savage hands of acceleration.

I've only been on this road one time with Mr. Ralston, and that was during the day. Now it's night, it's dark, and we whip viciously around one corner after the other. I can't decide if I'm scared out of my panties or… the other thing.

Prince sure knows how to drive. We may as well be flying. I just hope we don't end up dying. There's a few turns where I'm absolutely positively convinced I've died and gone to heaven, but that's just Prince's driving.

Minutes later, we're rolling to a stop in a well-lit parking area for delivery trucks with a bunch of rollup metal garage doors. We're somewhere on the back side of campus, not far from Plant Services. A couple of huge men are standing there waiting in the shadows.

"Who're those guys?" I ask.

"Security."

"For the party?"

"For my car."

"Wait, we're here?"

He nods.

"We haven't even left campus," I laugh. "We could have *walked* here."

"You kidding? A lady can't arrive at a masquerade on foot. She has to take a chariot or carriage at the very least."

"This chariot?" I grin.

"The one and only. Wait in your seat," he commands.

The doors open and Prince trots around to help me out.

I glance back at my seat.

"Did you get it wet?" he quips.

"No-a," I giggle. "I, um, my costume. I forgot. It's kind of dirty. Sorry. I'll clean it up." I turn to start dusting off the leather.

He grabs me and stops me, spinning me around before I start. Then he snarls. The lion makeup enhances the effect. Seriously, he *snarls*. Fangs and everything, like he wants to physically eat me.

"What?" I say timidly wavering on whether or not I'll let him take a bite because I can't quite tell where his head is at. "It's just dirt. I said I'd clean it."

The hot hatred in his eyes turns to humor. "When you're with me, Mary, you never clean *anything*."

"Huh?" I almost think he's offended to be going out with a maid like me and doesn't want anybody knowing. I'm about to tell him to F off when his eyes burst into a soothing blue grin.

"You heard me," he chuckles. "I didn't bring you here to work. It's a party, strumpet. I brought you here to enjoy yourself."

"Now *that* I can do," I grin.

He offers his elbow and leads me toward the building.

"Mary?" says the larger of the two shadowed men. "Is that you?"

"Jonah?" I smile.

"Yeah," he says, stepping into the light.

The other guy steps forward too. It's Wicked Eyes. Er, Tucker, if I remember correctly. It's been weeks since I saw him that night with Dwight's motorcycle and the cannibals' GTO. I wouldn't know he was here at Castle Hill except for Jonah mentioning it. But I haven't forgotten Tucker's gorgeous good looks and his wicked sapphire eyes.

"Nice hair," he winks at me. His is clipped shorter than mine, same as the night we met.

"Yours too," I offer.

"You look badass," Tucker grins and steps boldly forward, fingering the chainmail piece between my legs dangling from my waist belt.

A jolt bolts up my body and puffs of pleasure caress up through my breasts. I titter in surprise, "Stop it!" even though I don't mean it.

Something about Tucker is, I don't know, *raw*. It's very appealing. He doesn't have Rob's restrained rage, or Skill's lady's man charm, or Jonah's monumental and yet soft confidence, or even Prince's dazzling it-factor. Tucker is just hard and raw and I really like it. It's probably enhanced in the moment by his scent of sage and cypress, which I don't remember from the night we met, but it definitely reminds me now of a walking human forest fire ravaging the woods as a horde of shirtless fireman attack the blaze and fight it back, their oiled abs flexing and—

You get the idea.

I'm giggling dumbly as I search Tucker's fiery eyes.

"Stop what?" he chuckles, closing the gap until he's an inch away, practically consuming me with his savage heat.

Before I can respond, Prince barges between Tucker and I and barks harshly, "Hands the fuck off, ant!" He's right in Tucker's face. "I'm paying you to watch my fucking car, not to take a fucking joyride!"

When did I become the joyride?

Tucker swells his chest forward into Prince's and laughs, "I don't give a fuck what you're paying me. This girl is nobody's joyride, princess." He isn't calling me princess. He's calling Prince princess. An obvious insult.

"What did you call me?!" Prince rages.

"You heard me, turd," Tucker chuckles, totally unafraid.

Me? I'm giddy these two are fighting over me, so giddy I blurt a laugh, "I call him that!"

Without breaking eye contact with Prince, Tucker says to me, "You call him turd?"

"Yes!" I laugh because I'm a little bit scared Prince will have Tucker thrown out of the academy for standing up to him, or Tucker might kill Prince with his bare hands. I don't want either happening. To distract, I add, "Does everyone call him that?"

Tucker smirks. "The Fundies don't. They're all pussies for the prissy Prince. Bending over whenever he tells them. Me and the boys, we never bend over for anybody. Isn't that right, turd?" Tucker looks ready to bite Prince's nose off, and he's close enough to do it.

Is Tucker including Rob in the list of people who don't bend over for anybody? Because I clearly remember Rob bending over for Prince the day I got here.

Without backing down a single millimeter from Tucker, Prince seethes at him, "Call me that again and I will see to it that you and your inseparable friends are kicked out of Castle Hill so fast and far you never see each other again. How does that sound, ant? Would you and your precious pals like that? I'll put one of you in Alaska and one in North Dakota so you'll freeze your dicks off. The other two I'll put in New Mexico and Georgia so you'll die from the heat. How does that sound, ant?"

"Like you got an A in geography," Tucker chuckles.

Prince cracks Tucker across the jaw with a blinding fast punch.

Tucker stumbles back laughing and shaking it off like it was nothing. "Are we doing this, princess? I've got nothing to lose and you know it. You? You've got everything to lose, don't you?"

Prince stands there, fists knotted in rocks at his sides. "You've got your freedom to lose, you fucking ant brain."

"Freedom's an illusion, turd." Tucker starts to circle. "You're only in prison if you think you are. Unless you're dead. Then, you're fucking dead. You wanna end up dead, princess?" Tucker's fluid moves are effortlessly dangerous. If he can fight anything like Skill, and it sure looks like it, Prince should be worried.

Prince is turning to face Tucker as he moves, his hands now up like maybe he knows how to fight. In his beastly costume, he definitely looks ready to pounce.

Jonah watches carefully like he might step in to stop the fight, but he hasn't done anything yet.

I have no doubt, if Prince and Tucker fight, and setting aside either young man's survival, Prince will ruin his costume at the very least. I don't want a stupid fight ruining my night.

"You guys," I whine, "It's Halloween! Can we not do this right now? Please?"

Tucker says, "Your call, princess." He's obviously talking to Prince. "You calmed down yet? You already got a free shot. You gonna try for another? See how that works out for you?"

Prince looks ready to roar, his jaw muscles ticking on the fine fangs of his rage, his leonine snout crinkling in restrained fury.

"Prince?" I say gently. "Can we just...?"

Prince slowly closes his eyes and shakes his head. "Fine. Forget it. Let's go inside." He turns and offers his elbow, now smiling. "You know how it is when you get a bug up your ass." He flicks his eyes at Tucker.

Tucker snorts a laugh, "Had to get in the last jab, didn't you? One free shot wasn't enough?"

I roll my eyes and wait for Prince to fire back.

He doesn't. Just smiles at me. "Shall we?"

"Sure," I smile.

Do I glance back at Tucker?

Only long enough to catch him winking at me. I also see Jonah rolling *his* eyes and offering me a sympathetic shrug.

Prince calls out in a friendly voice, "If you two ants want to get paid, keep your eyes on my car, per our agreement."

Tucker smirks and is about to open his mouth when Jonah gives him a solid shove. Tucker goes flying.

Jonah calls out, "Have fun, you two!" He means it.

You gotta love Jonah.

And Tucker, for obvious reasons I'm too guilty to admit I like.

What a night, right?

I have no idea at the time that the drama is just getting started.

Chapter 26

"Where are we going?" I ask.

Prince and I are walking through the bowels of Castle Hill Academy in a long tunnel. Pipes and conduits run overhead into the distance for a really long way.

"To my underground dungeon lair," he growls.

"Obviously," I giggle nervously. "So you can serial kill me. No, torture me in your torture chamber, *then* serial kill me."

"Who told you I had a torture chamber?"

"Wait, do you?"

He simply smiles his leonine smile and leads me deeper into the darkness. The farther we walk, the older the tunnel gets. We're talking *really* old. Concrete turns to bricks and mortar to hewn stone.

"What is this place?" I ask.

"Among other things, Castle Hill was once home to a gunnery battery that stood guard over the coast in the second half of the nineteenth century. These tunnels connected the various cannon emplacements to the magazines where they stored the powder kegs and cannon balls."

"Nerd," I snicker and bump his hip.

"Everyone at this academy is a nerd, strumpet. Have you not noticed? We only accept the best and brightest, not the dimmest and dumbest."

"Is *everything* you say elitist rhetoric? Or is this just your usual claptrap?"

"I see you've been practicing your SAT words," he grins.

We turn a hidden corner and find ourselves at a metal door with bolts around the frame. I can hear loud dance music thumping behind it. Prince knocks and it opens with a creaky Halloween squeal. Someone dressed as Alice's White Rabbit motions us inside. Standing beside him is someone dressed as Jack Skellington.

Prince says, "Welcome to my All Hallows' Ball, strumpet. May it fulfill your wildest dreams."

We walk inside and I'm stunned.

If Alice in Wonderland and The Nightmare Before Christmas were set in a real live dungeon, that would describe Prince's party to a T. Every party I ever went to had only three things: kids, kegs, and plastic SOLO cups. That's it.

This?

This is another world.

I blurt, "Did you like, hire the Disney Imagineers to decorate this place?"

"Some of them," Prince grins.

"Let me guess. You flew them in," I laugh.

He winks, "Right again, strumpet."

It's not just the decor. It's the people. Or should I say aliens from another planet or the crazy beasts you see in your daydreams and nightmares. From classic to fantastic, every costume looks as professional and expensive as Prince's. One guy's even wearing a shimmering suit of medieval armor worthy of a museum.

As good as my costume is for being budget, it doesn't hold a candle to what the Fundies are wearing. Even I'm impressed. Except for the fact that more than a few of the girls are topless. Not in a slutty way. Their costumes are obviously designed to be topless. Let it all hang out, ladies. Are they for real? I mean, half the breasts are obviously fake, but are they for real letting them all hang out just because it's Slut-O-Ween? They are.

Rich people.

I mutter, "Am I the only work-study kid here?"

"As far as I know," Prince answers.

"That's not going to be a problem, is it?"

"Not as long as you're with me."

I hope he's right.

Eerie but danceable electronic music fills the air as we walk through the maze of the massive space. The girls are tossing jealousy bombs at me left and right for obvious reasons. I'm with Prince. They aren't. Sucks to be them. Tee. Hee. I'm happy to report, their jealous bombs disappear into the actual fog floating on the floor and swirling up to everyone's knees. I'm also happy none of them are calling me Chemo or cancer cunt or gutter slut for once. Probably because I'm in costume and they haven't figured out who I am. It won't take them long to recognize me from my hair. Until they do, I'm basking in this moment of reprieve however brief.

Someone dressed as Captain Jack Sparrow from Pirates of the Caribbean is staring at me like he knows me. He looks almost exactly like Johnny Depp from the movie, except hotter. He says, "Is that you, mugshot?"

"Chase?" I ask.

"At your service, m'lady." Chase doffs his pirate hat and bows low, causing the floor fog to billow out around him. I must admit, it's rather magical. So are his abs, which are showing because he isn't wearing a pirate shirt under his pirate coat.

"Wow, Chase! You look great!"

"I always do," he grins, winking a heavily eye-shadowed topaz eye. "Would you like to parley now or parley later?" When he says it, he emphasizes the "ley" in parley with enough innuendo to get an old lady pregnant.

I snort a laugh.

Prince barks, "Back off, Chase. She's my date."

Chase offers a rakish grin. "I don't need to date her. I just want to par-*ley* her."

Before I can say anything, Prince drags me farther into the party. I immediately see someone dressed up as a very imposing and movie-accurate Darth Vader.

"Who's that?" I wonder.

"Darth Vader," Prince quips.

"Duh! I meant, who *is* it?"

"Duke."

"Who's that with him dressed as Katniss Everdeen?" I'm referring to the girl with the perfect body hanging off Duke's arm wearing the Mockingjay movie costume, complete with bow and quiver of arrows. She also has a black masquerade mask hiding her face.

"That's Victoria."

"Are they back together?" I ask innocently.

"Funny you should ask," Prince smirks.

"Did you hear too?" I grouse.

"Everyone heard about what you did, homewrecker," he chuckles and winks.

I roll my eyes. "I didn't do anything! They did it to themselves! It's not my problem they're insane." The spitting from the Fundy girls has subsided in the past few weeks, but I still bear the emotional scars. "You believe me, don't you? I had nothing to do with their breakup."

"Duke and Victoria are very volatile."

"Is that a yes?"

"Yes, strumpet. I don't blame you for their relationship problems."

"Thank you!" I say victoriously. "At least someone around here has some sense."

Prince leads me over to the bar. It's set up like a mad scientist's laboratory. The bottles and beakers are bubbling with a rainbow of colorful under-lit liquids steaming out from their tops. Probably dry ice or whatever.

"Pick your poison," Prince says, motioning to the bar.

I smile, "Do they have any cyanide?"

"No."

"Arsenic?"

He simply smirks.

"You said poison," I grin.

"How about I order for both of us?"

"Don't put any ruffies in it."

"Why would I need to do that? I'm already enough of an aphrodisiac on my own." He offers a flirty wink.

I roll my eyes and try not to laugh.

Even though there are a dozen other people waiting in line for drinks, everyone parts deferentially as Prince steps up to order. Even the bar tender, who looks like Dr. Emmet Brown from Back to the Future, stops what he's doing to make drinks for Prince.

"Here you go," Prince says, handing me a drink glowing green.

"Is this radioactive?" I titter. "How's it light up?"

"There's a green glow stick inside."

"That is so cool!"

"Thank you."

"Who'd you pay to come up with that idea?" I ask sarcastically.

"Myself."

"Nuh uh."

He nods and holds up his drink. "To what do we toast?"

"Um, new beginnings?"

"I'll drink to that." He clinks my glass with his and pounds half of it.

I hesitate.

"Don't leave me hanging, strumpet."

"It's not alcoholic, is it? Drinking is against the student handbook rules. I don't want Ms. Brawny booting me out of the Convent if I come home buzzed, or Ms. Skelter haunting me from beyond the grave or whatever. She is a skeleton, you know. This is *her* night."

"I promise, Ms. Skelter will not jump out of your closet with a breathalyzer and Brawny won't either. Anyway, it's non-alcoholic. I don't want you thinking I need to get you drunk to get in your pants, strumpet."

"You did not!" I gasp a laugh.

"Did too." He flashes a winning grin. "Drink up."

I sniff the liquid. Doesn't smell like alcohol. I taste it. "Yummy! It's like candy apples or something."

"Virgin Appletini."

"I love it!"

"Shall we find a seat so you can sip and stare into my eyes?"

"Sure," I snort.

Like any good nightclub, there's a high ceiling and multiple levels and roped-off areas with seats and tables aplenty where you can watch the crowd and the dance floor from above. The only difference is the stone walls. It really is like a dungeon. We make our way up stone steps past dozens of sitting areas. Hanging from the ceiling are spotlit sash dancers defying gravity, spinning and twirling in their sexy tights.

"I wish I could do that," I grouse jealously.

Prince leans into my ear and mutters, "I'll talk to administration about adding rope dancing to the PE curriculum next term. We'll hire whoever teaches this troupe."

"What?! You can do that?"

Prince leans around so his eyes meet mine. "Do you have to ask, strumpet?"

"You're too much, Prince." It's a good too much.

"My reputation precedes me." He's obviously referring to his skills as a lover. On top of that, his closeness and his heat and impossible promises are hitting me harder than any alcohol.

I sniff my glowing Appletini and take another sip. It really is virgin. You wouldn't know it from the way my head is soaring through the clouds. Imagine the things I could do in life with someone like Prince as my boyfriend?

You know what's sad?

I can't imagine it because all I ever think about is barely scraping by on my own. Prince is offering me the opportunity to do literally anything I can dream of.

Or he's lying to get laid.

Who am I kidding?

Of *course* that's what he's doing! It's what every guy does. Except this place and his car *are* real. Maybe he *isn't* lying? I don't know.

"Here we are," Prince says as he leads me up to the highest seating area in the entire cave. We're eye level with the rope dancers. "My private box."

Elizabeth Morgan-Hearst is lounging in said box. When she sees Prince come up the steps, she titters, "Is that any way to refer to your girlfriend?"

I cringe for a couple reasons. First, she's topless. It would be disgusting if she wasn't so stunningly beautiful. She's dressed entirely in white, some sort of sexy wedding angel. The gossamer gown is bodycon chiffon and slippery satin with white lace wings and a matching veil. If she hadn't turned the slut-o-meter up to eleven with the topless look, I'd say she was the picture of feminine perfection. Okay, her breasts are literally perfect, possibly even real now that I see them, and if mine looked like hers, I'd show them off every chance I got. But still.

I'm also cringing because I distinctly heard her call herself Prince's girlfriend. I knew it.

Knew! It!

He is too good to be true.

And that's why she's up here with her top off.

Prince sighs, "What are you doing here, Elizabeth?"

"Waiting for you, sweetheart."

"I've asked you to stop calling me that. We broke up a year ago, Elizabeth. It's time you move on. If you would be so kind, Mary and I would like the use of my private booth." He motions down the stairs, hinting that Elizabeth should leave.

Elizabeth glares at me. "Who's this garbage? She looks like a walking dump."

"The only walking I'm worried about," he says, "is you walking yourself out of here immediately. Goodbye, Elizabeth." Despite his politeness, his voice comes out cold and cruel, his words a silent slap.

I want to add, "And take your tits with you," but I manage to keep my mouth shut.

Elizabeth shoots to her feet and pouts, "Fine! Have fun with the auto-mechanic! I hope she knows how to turn your crank as well as I do!" She storms past me in a huff, stopping short to glare at me. "Gutter slut. I should've known. What're *you* doing here?"

Prince says, "Go, Elizabeth."

She ignores him and knifes me with her eyes. "Who let you in, cancer cunt?"

I'm not playing into her hand. I smirk sarcastically, "Good to see you too, Azzie."

"Why do you keep calling me that, gutter slut?" She's no less beautiful as her face wrinkles in irritation.

"Because you're Azzie. Duh."

"No I'm not!"

"You are such a liar," I snort.

She sneers, "Has syphilis eaten your *entire* brain already, gutter slut?" She tosses a glance at Prince. "Don't fuck this one without a bodysuit condom. She probably has AIDS and every strain of hepatitis known to man."

I smile and point, "The stairs are that way." A sudden breeze surprises me. When I turn my head back, I see Prince rushing toward Elizabeth to pull her away from me.

"Let me go!" she screams. "*She* does *not* talk to *me* like *that!*"

Prince wrestles her down the stairs.

I want to tell him to throw her over the railing. It's like a forty foot drop to the fog floating on the bottom floor. He doesn't, but he forces her down to the next level. She immediately starts arguing with him. They're far enough away, I can't hear what they're saying.

I sigh and wait, already knowing where this is going. Prince is going to talk to Elizabeth at length while she manipulates him into ignoring me by arguing and arguing until he completely forgets I'm here. They'll end up fucking in a dungeon corridor somewhere, and I'll regret I didn't go trick-or-treating with Mimi back in the Convent. I don't even know if that's a thing, but I'd rather be doing that than this.

Elizabeth's voice cuts above the music and I hear her saying, "...just because you're the youngest ever magister of the Ivory Tower, you think you can date whoever you want?! A dirty work-study slut?!"

Prince responds, but he's facing away and I can't hear what he says except for, "...of your business!" He's pissed.

Then I remember. Elizabeth, erm, Azzie, isn't talking about just any ivory tower. She's talking about *the* Ivory Tower, the one Azzie, erm, her pointed out to me my first day here. The one that looms over the entire academy like a brooding monolith. The secret society Ivory Tower. Is Prince in that? What's a magister? Is that a magician? Or just some snooty title for the president of the club or whatever? I don't know, but it sounds like Prince is the shit there and everywhere else.

Elizabeth is still bickering with Prince and I hear her grumbling, "...see what the Golden Circle has to say about that! Oh wait, let me guess. The Hidden Eye already knows, don't they?! They're just waiting for you to—"

"STOP TALKING AND GO!" Prince shouts loud enough you can't miss it, even with the loud dance music. He points past Elizabeth like he's sending her to the penitentiary.

She glares, "You're going to regret this, Prince! I'll make damn sure!" She shakes both her fists like a little baby, which shakes her boobs. I expect her to cover herself, but she doesn't. She spins around and marches off in a heavenly huff, barging past the knight in shimmering armor I saw earlier, who is up here for some reason.

Prince heaves himself back up the stairs like he's carrying a very heavy load. "Sorry about that," he says when he's back in the private box with me.

"Do you need to go after her?"

"I'm not falling for that trick. It would've worked when we were together, but I'm done with her."

"Are you sure?"

He reaches up to brush his thumb across my cheek. "Completely. This is our night, strumpet. No one else's."

When he touches me, I start to float. The butterflies inside me are lifting me up. At least it feels like it as Prince glides me over to sit down.

For the next hour, Prince has me on the edge of my seat and laughing. He has countless surfing stories from around the world, some exciting and hair-raising, others hilarious and side-splitting. Whoever dreamt up the story of Prince Charming clearly had Prince Lancaster in mind when they wrote it.

At some point, I realize I have been holding Prince's hand for quite some time. He's been stroking mine with his and it's the hottest, most erotic thing I've ever done, I swear. His hand is quite rugged for someone so refined. I can't get enough of touching him.

There's no denying it. I am in very, *very* heavy like with Prince. I've completely forgotten every bit of bad behavior I've seen from him since I got to the academy.

This is the real Prince.

This is the person I knew I'd find underneath, the diamond in the rough, the treasure in the tyrant.

"The look on Brawny's face was priceless," Prince laughs after hearkening back to our jailbreak from the Convent earlier tonight.

I laugh, "You wouldn't *really* ship her off to Antarctica, would you?"

"Never. Brawny is an institution at Castle Hill. Nothing would ever get cleaned if I did." He lowers his lids over his piercing blue eyes, sharpening them to a crystal blue clarity that pierces my heart. Or that might just be the black light.

Either way, I'm smitten.

He purrs, "You on the other hand…"

"Me what?" I sigh, slightly mesmerized by the moment. "You want to ship me off to live with the penguins?"

"No," he chuckles. "I was thinking we need to get you out of the Convent."

"We are out."

"I mean permanently. You deserve to live someplace better than that hovel. What do you think about living in the East Wing in your own private suite?"

I crinkle my nose, "Then I'd have to see those Fundy bitches more than I already do. No thank you."

"How about my suite?"

"You can do that?" I'm not seriously considering his offer, but I do toy with the idea briefly. "What would Ms. Skelter say? Is something like that even allowed?"

"How many times do I have to tell you, strumpet? I can do anything I want." He reaches up and brushes my chin. His other hand holding mine has come to lay dangerously high on my thigh.

I don't even know how it got there. All I can do is giggle. A swirling sensation surges through me and I'm squirming in my seat. When that masculine sandalwood and cinnamon scent of his tickles my fancy, I just about melt. Thank goodness I'm wearing jeans instead of a skirt. Who knows what I might let him do.

Prince is inches away.

Part of me wants to throw myself at him. The other part refuses to move.

Not to worry.

Prince swoops in for the kiss.

My eyes are locked on his luscious lips.

When his touch mine, I melt into him and his tongue plunges in.

Oh my god.

I get lost in the kiss, swimming in it.

Prince shifts his weight onto his hand holding mine, pushing it down between my legs. The seat cushion creaks audibly as he leans into me, pressing his chest into mine. I'm trapped against the cushions as he attacks me.

This isn't my first kiss.

But it's the first like this.

Complete and total bliss.

Our tongues dance for quite some time. Hours, minutes, days, weeks, I don't even know, but I never want it to end.

As unbridled as his desire is, there's a slight and respectful restraint. I want to tell Prince to let go of the reins and see where the wild horses bucking between our legs take us, but I can't. My tongue is too busy kissing.

Right when I'm ready to push him away or pull him into me, I can't decide which, he breaks the kiss and sits back down, sliding off me. This time, instead of leaving a respectful several inches between us, he's sitting against my side, pulling me gently against his heat. I mean his hip. Either way, I'm burning up.

I've never been so turned on in my life and we hardly did anything.

Doesn't matter.

This is far and away the best kiss I've ever had.

The best anything.

Who knew it could be like this?

Not me!

"Strumpet, I..." Prince trails off and heaves a sigh that becomes a deep-throated chuckle. "That was... What the fuck was that?" He laughs.

I laugh too. There aren't enough words in the English language to do this moment justice. If only Elizabeth or Azzie or whatever her name is wasn't sitting in the elevated box just opposite the sash dancer from us, and watching us with her arms folded angrily across her breasts. There's glaring daggers and there's glaring thermonuclear missiles. Elizabeth is definitely launching the latter.

Way to ruin my moment.

And I have to room with her, aka Azzie?

Please, please, *please* don't let her be in our room when I get back to the Convent.

Hmm. Would it be *completely* crazy to take Prince up on his offer of moving in with him?

Chapter 27

"Please tell me there's a ladies room around here," I say an hour later.

"I'll lead you to it," Prince says.

We walk down the various staircases that connect all the private boxes, then down to the maze on the main floor, where we turn about fifty corridor corners until we find a bathroom. I go in alone. Not quite what I was expecting after the dreamworld outside. There's one toilet and one sink crammed into the rough rock walls with a dim light bulb over the bowl. While I'm hovering over it to pee, the light flickers off.

"Can't you wait until I finish?" I growl at it.

It flickers back on.

"Thank you."

Then it flicks off.

Ugh.

At least I know where everything is. I finish my toilet time by Braille and walk out the short tunnel to where Prince was waiting.

I say, "Somebody needs to replace the lightbulb in the bath—"

No Prince anywhere to be seen.

Where did he go?

I look both ways.

Which way did we come in?

I was so obsessed with Prince's mesmerizing eyes, I wasn't keeping track of direction on our way here. No worries, I can figure it out. Follow the sound.

The bass beat thuds through the stone tunnel.

I turn a few corners and slam nose first into a stone wall. Erm, stone abs. I look up into the eyes of—

"Chase!" I gasp.

"Mugshot," he smirks. "What're you doing all by your lonesome self down here?"

"Prince took me to the bathroom. He was here a second ago." That's a hint. I glance over my shoulder. "Did you see him? He must be right here."

"All I see is you, mugshot." Chase's topaz eyes are smoldering, brightened by his pirate eyeshadow.

The next thing I know, he's backed me into a stone wall. "What're you doing, Chase?"

"Claiming my prize." He grabs my chainmail skirt piece and pulls me toward him.

I gasp as I crash into his abs, my hands up, pressing against his chest. I look up into his eyes.

"When are we gonna have some fun, mugshot?"

"When you stop calling me that," I smirk.

"Anything you say, Mary." His eyes are alight with desire.

I have never kissed two boys in one night, let alone in one hour, but I'm seriously considering it. Chase's luscious model lips are begging for it. But I can't do that. I'm no slut.

The next thing I know, Chase is pressing his hips into mine. He plants his pirate hands on either side of my head, pinning me in place.

"Why can't I stop thinking about you, Mary?"

"Because I haven't given it up for you yet. You'll forgot me as soon as I do. I know guys like you. You're a manwhore, Chase."

"That I am," he says with pride. "Can you blame me? Women throw themselves at me. Who am I to stop them?"

I snort, "You are so full of yourself."

"But you aren't."

"Please," I groan, feigning disgust at his innuendo.

"What say we change that?" He leans into me for emphasis, his hips just brushing against mine.

I am going to melt. This moment is *that* hot because Chase is *that* hot. There's a fire growing in my belly that wants desperately to be quenched.

"Say the word, Mary, and I'll make you mine."

"For how long?" I manage to mutter with less attitude than I'd like. It comes out more as a desperate question than an insightful indictment.

"As long as you like, Mary." He is purring my name every time he says it, now whispering it in my ear, his musky scent caressing my mind with slick wet touches of lust.

I'm falling for it. Oh, boy, am I ever falling for it. But I just kissed Prince! I whisper-whine, "No-a, Chase! I can't!"

"But you want to. It's all over your face."

He's right about that. I look into his eyes and bite my lower lip.

That cocky grin of his eases onto his face. He fingers the belt below my breasts, tugging on the buckle. "How many belts do you have, Mary?"

"Enough," I gasp, knowing it's not enough to keep him out for long.

"How about I start with this one and you tell me when to stop?"

I can't even speak as he undoes the first one. We haven't even kissed. This is possibly the dirtiest thing I've ever done, and we haven't done *anything*, but I swear I'm about to come unglued all over him.

"Say when, Mary." He undoes the next belt, his lips tickling my ear.

I am shivering with desire right now. "Chase…"

"Do you want me to stop?"

"Please…"

"Please stop or please keep going?"

I don't even know myself. All I can manage is a muttered, "Unh."

Another buckle comes undone.

He leans into me.

Something hard presses into me.

I reach down and grab the first thing I find.

I gasp, thinking it's his—

It's the hilt of his pistol jutting from his belt. His flintlock pirate's pistol. Or so I tell myself. I give it a tug, pulling him toward me.

"Do it," I hiss.

He obliges me and his lips pillage mine, his tongue invading my welcoming mouth and swashbuckling with mine.

Chase sure knows how to kiss.

Oh, does he know.

Unlike Prince, who was persistent and demanding and almost overwhelming in a good way, Chase is unbridled desire and full of surprise. It doesn't hurt he's pressing his pistol into me with his abs. If it wasn't for that, I'd be slumped to the floor between his legs. But I'm not. As long as I'm standing up, I could go on kissing Chase forever.

Sudden sounds echo from the end of the stone corridor and Chase pulls away.

"There you are, Mary," Prince says as he turns the corner. "Oh, hey Chase."

Chase tips his pirate hat, "Lancaster."

Prince tips a quick nod and says to me, "Sorry about that, strumpet. I had an issue to deal with that couldn't wait. Everything okay?"

I'm biting my lower lip guiltily, feeling like a very dirty girl. *Very* dirty. I have to wonder, can Prince see the gigantic flashing billboard over my head that shows me and Chase doing nasty things right under his nose? Or is that just me? I don't know, but I need a distraction.

"No," I shake my head.

Before I can correct myself and say yes, Prince frowns, "Did something bad happen?" He glances warily at Chase.

Chase looks like something really good just happened.

Not wanting to throw him under the bus, I blurt, "The bathroom light is out. It's like pitch black in there. I almost peed on the floor *and* my feet."

Prince grimaces, "That's not good. I'll make sure someone takes care of it. Chase? Can we talk for a minute?" He offers the nicest smile I've ever seen. On Prince's face it looks wrong. Frightening and hateful and bristling with cruelty.

"Sure," Chase says and Prince leads him around the corner.

I peer after them.

Prince glances at me, "Give us a minute, Mary."

"Okay," I nod and fade back behind the stone wall.

I can't hear them talking over the music. I wait. Two minutes later, Prince hasn't returned. Why do I feel like I'm in trouble? Because one boy asked me out, kissed me, and I kissed another boy right after? Okay, not boys. Men. Neither of them are the least bit boyish. But I feel like a bad little girl all the same.

Getting impatient, I lean around the corner.

They're arguing. Their voices aren't loud but their gestures are. I roll my eyes and wait.

Fifteen minutes later, they're still going at it.

I'd step in and say something, but I don't know what they're arguing about. They *might* be arguing about me. If they're not, it's not like I want to announce my indiscretion. For all I know, they're arguing about the Ivory Tower or some other piece of secret Fundy business that is none of mine.

Tired of waiting, I heave a sigh and look for an alternate escape route. Good thing the stone corridor has two directions. I go the other way and leave them to argue it out.

What a mistake that will turn out to be.

When I turn a corner, I see Darth Vader sitting alone on a stone bench carved into the wall, helmet off and cape draped around him. It's Duke. He sits slumped in the stone alcove looking pathetic and forlorn.

I had assumed he was back together with Victoria after seeing them together earlier, but you never know with those two.

Hoping to avoid a confrontation, I almost go back the way I came, but it took me forever to find my way back to the party in this dungeon maze, and I can see the dazzling lights and hear the eerie music just past him around the next corner.

Forward it is.

I stay close to the side of the rough-hewn tunnel, eyes on the floor, hoping he won't recognize me in my costume.

"Hey, peon," Duke sighs sadly and without a hint of menace as I pass. Not what I was expecting.

"Hey, Duke," I mutter without stopping.

"Can I ask you something?"

I don't slow.

"Please?" On him, saying please somehow sounds like abject begging.

I stop and heave a sigh. "Sure."

"Nice costume, by the way. Furiosa, right?"

"Yeah." I'm thinking, Can I go now? Was that your question? Please say yes.

"I loved that movie."

"Me too."

"That scene where she tackled Max and knocked him flat on his ass with one hand and stole his shotgun? Or when she head-butts that dude on the rig at the end? Totally badass."

"Right?" I grin because we're suddenly having a normal conversation *and* Duke is crushing on a strong female heroine instead of bromancing on the male hero. Not at all what I'd expect from someone like him for whatever reason. Duke always struck me as someone who wanted a wilting lily for a woman, and we all know wilting isn't my thing.

He picks his Vader helmet up off the bench and motions at the stone. "Have a seat."

My first instinct is to say no. The last thing I want is Victoria catching me sitting on what amounts to a carved stone loveseat with her boyfriend, I mean her effing fiancé.

"Siddown, Charlize." He curls a cocky grin that is simply irresistible.

Okay, if he had called me peon, I would've told him to F the F off and walked away. He didn't so I don't. In case you're wondering, I look nothing like Charlize Theron, not even in bad lighting and Halloween fog. But I can't resist the compliment and sit down on the edge of the stone bench as far from him as possible. Glance at him sidelong because I'm afraid to fall into his dark and brooding eyes if I look too close.

"Your nose job is impeccable," he says, examining my profile.

"Nose job?" I snort. "I never had any nose jobs."

"Really?" Duke asks sincerely.

I smirk at him, "Do I look like I have that kind of money?"

"Your nose does," he grins the compliment.

I roll my eyes, "It's the one I was born with, okay? What, do all the women in your world get plastic surgery when they're teenagers?"

"Men too."

"Why do I believe you?" I snort. "Have you?"

"Not me, but I know plenty of dudes who do, half of them at this school."

I shrug. I don't know if I believe *he* hasn't had any looks-maxing plastic surgery because he really is gorgeous, but I definitely believe his peers have. They're too damn perfect looking.

Duke's eyes are roaming over me.

I can feel them and it's making me nervous because I like it. Not wanting to make a mistake I'll definitely regret, I blurt, "What was your question? Oh, wait. Let me guess. It's about us kissing, right?"

"Is that an offer?" he chuckles casually.

I giggle, "Wait, that came out wrong."

"Did it?" His voice carries its usual low, dark menace that is surprisingly enticing, especially under the circumstances. It's just a little bit romantic here in the stone love seat. I mean bench. Stone bench. Nothing romantic about it at all.

"I meant, is your question about Chloe or whoever lying about you and me kissing the other day?"

"I heard about that," he smirks in disgust. "Vicious bitches and their stupid rumors. It's amazing the lies people'll believe."

"Yeah," I mutter, thinking about the lies he believes about Victoria *not* kissing Skill my first day here, and her doing it in front of everyone. How did the truth not get back to him? For all I know, it did, and he doesn't want to believe it. I'm not setting him straight, that's for sure. "What was your question?"

He leans his head back against the stone and sighs, staring at the ceiling. "Do you think I'm making a mistake marrying Victoria?"

It's nearly impossible for me not to laugh. A snippet sneaks out, but I clamp it down before it turns into rolling on the floor belly laughs.

"Do you?" He pins me with pleading eyes.

"You guys *are* rather young. You said you're seventeen, right?"

He nods. He barely looks that young. He's one of those boys who will always look older than he is, even though his skin is flawless. The light may be low here in the stone tunnel, but it hits him at an angle, and you can see he doesn't have a single zit. He literally glows with youthful but manly vitality.

I want to ask him what his skin care routine is, but I'm sure it costs a fortune and involves an army of skin care technicians to assist him at the day spa or whatever. I'm dying to ask but I almost don't want to know.

He frowns to himself, clenching his hands into fists and muttering, "Our parents think it's a good idea."

"What, that you and Victoria get married?"

He nods. "Vee and me grew up together since we were like two. We were best friends from day one. I think our parents are in love with the idea that we were meant to be, Vee and me. Like, I don't know, destined or some shit like that." He offers a look that asks for a denial.

I don't want to make his decisions for him. I shrug.

He shakes his head in disgust, "She was great until middle school. Me and her really were best friends. You wouldn't know it, but she used to be huge into sports and she was damn good. We played on the same soccer team as kids. Then she got breasts and that was it."

I crinkle my nose, "You mean her parents bought them?"

"No," he snickers. "She grew them. That's when she changed. She didn't want to hang out as much and started noticing other guys."

"Oh." I know where this is going.

"Long story short, we've been off and on ever since. We always fight. *Always*."

"That's not good."

He smirks, "The makeup sex is. Sometimes I think it's the only reason she comes back."

"You can't build a marriage on that." I have no idea how to build a marriage, but I know my parents rarely fought. If they did, they did it in private. I never once saw them mad at each other. Frustrated sometimes, but never outright mad. What I did see was them being very loving. Like, constantly. Almost too much, but it was genuine. Looking back, I can imagine it would've been embarrassing if I'd seen them doing it when I was a little bit older, like thirteen or whatever, because they were so damn smoochy all the time, but they defs loved each other. I sniff back a tear thinking about it. God, I miss them so much it hurts, even after all these years.

"You can't, can you?" Duke says.

"Can't what? Sorry, I was thinking about my—" I stop myself. I never tell anyone about my parents. For whatever reason the truth slips out, "—my parents." My breath hitches. Why did I say that? Too late to take it back now. I sigh, "I don't remember them fighting at all."

"They still married?"

I cringe. "Can we not talk about them? It's kind of a sore subject."

"Sure. Sorry." He examines his hands.

Shifting topics, I say, "Do your parents know? I mean, that you and Victoria are so shaky?"

"Yeah." He snorts and rolls his eyes, "They're in denial about it being a real problem. They call it growing pains. They say it's because we're still teenagers. They say everything'll be fine in a few years. They say we're the original high school sweethearts." Duke offers me the saddest eyes I've ever seen, like *he* wants it to be true but he knows it's not. "Total joke, right?"

Sadly, it is.

I can picture Victoria kissing Skill in front of the theater, then her waiting for him to finish kissing Jacqueline so she can kiss him more, then her lying in Duke's face and saying she wasn't kissing Skill, *then* her in the locker room blaming me for her problems and denying she's a cheater.

There is literally nothing true I can tell Duke about Victoria that can possibly help or make him feel better. Everything about her says she's a terrible person and will be a curse on whoever she marries.

"I don't know what to say, Duke." Honestly, I feel bad for him.

"No one does," he grunts. "Sometimes I think the only way to get my parents off my back is to find someone to replace her." His eyes meet mine.

I glance to the side. Immediately sense his eyes land on my lips. I can take a hint. I immediately turn my head away.

No way I'm replacing Victoria. That is a minefield waiting to happen, no matter how hot Duke is, or how bad I feel for him right now. I'm not his solution. He needs less drama in his life, not more. Same goes for me. I *just* kissed two boys the same night. Kissing Duke would be a *huge* mistake. Can you imagine how Prince would feel about that? Or Chase? Or Duke if he found out I'd kissed the other two right before kissing him? He'd think I was just another Victoria and he'd pretty much be right. I *so* don't want to be her.

I shoot to my feet. "I have to go!"

"Wait!" Duke blurts. "I'm sorry! I didn't mean to—!"

I don't hear his last words because I'm running straight for the party as fast as I can.

When I reach the main party, I see topless Elizabeth-Azzie heading my direction with Katniss Everdeen Victoria and Jacqueline, who's dressed as Black Widow from the Marvel movies.

I don't think they saw me with Duke because the three of them are giggling about something or other and look way too happy.

I certainly don't want them seeing Duke coming out of the same tunnel as me. They already have the wrong idea about me and him, which would've been the right idea if I hadn't averted disaster by running out of that tunnel.

Assuming Duke is right behind me and about to make my behavior glaringly suspicious if I'm seen with him, I hurry across the foggy party floor, pushing through people in costume, which pisses them off. I keep going until I find a side corridor and cut down that.

A few turns later, I emerge in a huge dank room. It's practically pitch black, but I can feel the air is bigger and my boots scraping off the floor echo bigger too. I can also feel something ominous, something oppressive.

I'm not big on ghosts, but have you ever walked into a place that you maybe thought was haunted? Places like that feel a certain way. There's the chill of sorrow in the air. It's unmistakable. This place has been here since the Civil War. I'm sure at least someone died a tragic death in here. Haunting is not out of the question. Since hunky Zak Bagans isn't here to help me fight off any ghosts, maybe I better turn around.

"Gutter slut."

I nearly gasp my heart out my nose when I see the three of them.

In the near dark, they're like three female demons, big hair, black eyes, long claws.

"I thought I saw you go down to the torture chamber," says Azielbeth, or whatever her name is. She and the other two Silicones lift their phones under their faces. The flashlights shine upward, making their faces even creepier than usual.

"This is her lair," Vicious sneers.

"Where she eats babies to stay young," Jackess says.

That's ridiculous. I push past them.

"Not so fast, gutter slut," Azielbeth grabs me with the help of the other two. "We've had enough trouble from you."

"Always trying to steal our men," Vicious sneers.

"Who *haven't* you fucked at this point, gutter slut?" Azielbeth smirks.

"I haven't fucked anybody!" I protest. Good thing they didn't ask who I've kissed. I yank on my arm, trying to break free. It doesn't work. "Let go!"

"Or what?" Azielbeth snickers. "You'll fight us?"

"If that's what you want," I growl. "I can handle you thr—!"

Lightning fast, Jackess kicks the side of my leg with her Black Widow boot.

My knee explodes with pain and I crumple to the cold stone floor, clutching it in both hands.

"Daddy made me take Krav Maga," Jackess smirks. "I always wanted to see if it works."

Azielbeth stands over me saying, "They used to torture traitors down here. Did you know that, gutter slut?"

All I can do is groan as shards of glass stab my knee from every direction. Whatever Jackess did was right on the money. I don't know if I'll be able to stand up let alone walk after this. How am I going to keep cleaning if I can't walk? Will I get kicked out of school if I don't? Will Ms. Skelter make an allowance for my injuries? Or is this it? Is this the moment when everything comes crumbling down and I end up in prison?

"Who wants to get hit in the face?" Azielbeth asks.

"Not me," Victoria snorts.

"I'm not doing it," Jackess says.

"*Someone* has to get hit in the face," Azielbeth insists. "It's the only way we'll get her kicked out for sure. We say she attacked us, we defended ourselves after, and Ms. Skelter boots her back to jail. One of you has to get hit."

"No!" Victoria and Jackess say in unison.

Azielbeth sighs in annoyance.

Victoria says, "Why can't we just *say* she attacked us?"

"Because Prince will defend her," Azielbeth says like I'm the enemy. "We need proof."

"You're not hitting me in the face," Victoria snorts. "Duke would kill me if I got a black eye or whatever."

I'm just aware enough to wonder how that makes any possible sense.

"I'm not paying for *another* nose job," Jackess groans.

"Fine," Azielbeth sighs. "One of you prissy bitches hit me. But not too hard."

"You know what?" Jacqueline says. "I have a better idea. Why don't we lock cancer cunt in here?" Metal squeaks but I'm in too much pain to look at whatever Jackess is referring to. She continues, "They'll never find her in here. No one can hear you scream down this far anyway."

"How would you know?" Victoria asks.

"Because I've fucked enough times down here to know. You know what else I know?"

The agony in my knee has subsided just enough I can sense her hovering over me.

"Cancer cunt is afraid of the dark, aren't you, you sniveling little bitch?"

((((pitch black))))

(((pitch black)))

((pitch black))

(pitch black)

The horrid memories push their way to the surface, but I fight them back. If I don't, they'll paralyze me. My busted knee is doing a pretty good job, but if those memories take hold, I'll go full blown panic attack.

Victoria titters, "What kind of baby bitch is afraid of the fucking dark?"

((((pain))))

(((pain)))

((pain))

(pain)

No! Not now! Please not now!

"This one," Jacqueline says. "I read it in her case file."

((((it hurts!))))

(((it hurts!)))

((it hurts!))

(it hurts!)

I fight the memories back as hard as I can.

"What case file?" Azielbeth asks.

((((please not again!))))

(((please not again!)))

((please not again!))

(please not again!)

"The one I hacked out of Child Protective Services."

"And?"

"And, her first foster mom was some creepy crank who locked her in a closet whenever she was bad."

Gladys.

She looked like a kindly grandma on the outside.

On the inside, Gladys was a monster.

Nothing about her was glad.

(You stupid retard no good for nothing lousy sack of pig shit! Look what you did to my table! You roont it! Roont!)

(It's just milk! I spilled! I'm sorry!)

(WHACK! It wouldn't be the last time with the wooden spoon.)

(Please don't hit me! Ow! I didn't do anything!)

(Did too, dummy! Did! WHACK! Too! WHACK!)

(Leave me alone! Somebody help me! Help! Please!)

(You get back here, pig shit! WHACK! Stand still and take it like a lady! WHACK!)

(Please don't! OW! Puh-puh-puh-please!)

(Stop crying and clean that up now, you clumsy little pig shit! Clean it up! Clean it! Clean it clean it CLEAN IT!)

"She'd leave her there for days—"

(pitch black)

"—with her wrists tied behind her back,"

(pain)

"not feeding her, not even giving her water."

(it hurts!)

(my stomach hurts so bad! please feed me! please!)

(Not till you learnt your lesson, pig shit!)

(i'm dying of thirst! please!)

(Shut up, pig shit! Just you shut up!)

"When CPS found her crying and dirty after like the tenth time,"

(please not again!)

"—she had shit and pissed herself and was sitting in it like a fucking sewer," Jacqueline laughs.

It's all true. I'm lying here paralyzed by the painful memories.

"Sounds like a dirty little gutter slut to me," Azielbeth says. "We should do it again."

"Put her in the iron maiden," Jacqueline says.

"The what?"

"This thing." More squeaking metal. "It's an old torture thing. They used to use them for killing witches. I don't know why they have one here, but I know I fucked in it once."

"Put her in it," Victoria sneers.

"Does it have a lock on it?" Azielbeth asks.

"I think so."

No, no, no. They're not locking me inside anything! I push myself up on my hands and one good knee, ready to crawl out of here.

A hammer slams into my ribs when one of the Silicones kicks me. I drop to the stone, my breath stabbed out of my lungs. Next thing I know, they're dragging me across the floor.

I hear a rusty squeal.

I know what an iron maiden is. I learned about them in world history. A standing metal coffin with spikes inside. When they slam the door, you bleed out the gutters in the bottom. You die standing up, held up by spikes.

I'm thrown forward with the expectation that my hands will be pierced by the spikes. They hit flat metal. The iron door slams behind me with a rusty high-pitched scream, followed by a dreadful clanking and grinding sound. No spikes slice into me, but I'm locked inside.

Evil girlish laughter cackles from the Silicones outside.

"Have fun, gutter slut!" Azielbeth taunts.

"You can't steal our men from in there, can you, Chemo?" Vicious adds.

"Stupid bitch," Jackess titters.

Azielbeth says, "Let's go, girls. It'll be a few weeks until she rots."

Chapter 28

Pitch black.

I don't know how long I've been in here. Hours? Days? Weeks? Forever?

Pain.

My overwhelming panic attack stings me repeatedly like a swarm of hornets. The glass shards in my knee add insult to injury.

It hurts.

You have no idea how much it hurts. The pain, both emotional and physical, is humiliating, debilitating. My frantic clawing at the rusty metal has left my fingernails bleeding but done nothing to get me out of my iron prison.

Please not again.

I scream for help until my voice becomes tattered scratches, barely a whisper. My mind unwinds faster than I would've thought possible. The iron maiden is an oven. Simple drips of sweat down my brow make me think carnivorous cockroaches are crawling all over me. Or my flesh is dribbling off in bloody runners. That doesn't last because I cry my eyes out and sweat my last drop of sweat in no time, until I'm dried out and dehydrated.

I can't last like this.

I can't.

Someone let me out.

Someone!

Anybody!

Let!

Me!

"Get her out of there!" someone shouts outside.

Rusty squeals, bangs, and screams as the door rips open.

Light blinds me.

A literal knight in shining armor pulls me out of my cast-iron casket.

"Mary! Are you okay?!" Rob, bless his heart, is looking at me from inside a metal knight's helmet, the visor propped open.

"You're him," I gasp.

"Huh?"

"The knight in shimmering armor. How long have you been here?" I can't decide if I'm hallucinating or not.

"We need to get you out of here," he grunts, swooping me off my feet and cradling me in his arms. Behind him are a handful of Fundies in their fancy costumes gawking at me and gossiping. Rob barks at them, "Move the fuck out my way!"

I'm barely conscious of anything as we make our way out of the dark dungeon. I'm pretty sure I fade in and out of consciousness as we pass through the party and the crowds and the electronic fog of music and merriment. That fades back until I think we're in the very same tunnel Prince and I took to get in here. Once again, it's quiet.

"WHERE THE FUCK DO YOU THINK YOU'RE GOING?!" Prince roars not far behind Rob.

We jolt to a stop in a dark tunnel.

"PUT HER DOWN NOW!" Prince commands.

Rob seethes, "Get your fucking hand off me or I will break every bone in your body." He doesn't even turn around. His voice is low, guttural and cutting.

It's so damn scary even I'm afraid.

I'm just conscious enough to peer over Rob's armored shoulder.

Prince stands there, eyes wild with hate, his hand clamped on Rob's shoulder plate. In this moment, Prince's beast costume no longer enhances his animalistic appeal. It's corny, a pathetic joke. A cartoon of a real beast compared to Rob.

Prince's Adam's apple bobs as he swallows hard.

Rob cuts, "You never should've brought her to your party, you dumb fucking trust fund piece of shit."

Even I understand the significance of this moment, of Rob's open and hateful defiance of Prince's orders, Rob's willingness to risk everything he has for me with no concern for the consequences.

Prince's hand slips off Rob's shoulder plate.

Rob adds, "What did you think would happen when your *friends* got a hold of her?" He says the word "friends" like he means demons.

Prince doesn't answer.

Rob starts marching.

Minutes later, we're outside by Prince's Bugatti. Tucker and Jonah are there and both rush over.

"What the fuck happened?" Tucker demands.

"Is she okay?" Jonah asks, clearly concerned.

"She's fine," Rob grunts.

"What happened, man?" Tucker says, pulling on Rob to slow him down.

"BACK! THE FUCK! OFF!" Rob roars.

Tucker lets go.

Rob is a machine as he marches me back to a familiar building. The Monastery. I've never been inside. Work-study girls are forbidden from entering the monastery for obvious reasons. Aka, the work-study boys live there.

Rob opens the old oak door clumsily, holding me with one hand. Kicks it open with a bang. Marches inside and carries me down the corridor. Instead of stucco like the Convent, it's carefully stacked stone, but still old.

There comes a clacking from behind, followed by agitated clanking. A side door opens. "What do you think you're doing, Fletcher?!"

I don't recognize the voice.

Rob completely ignores it.

Candle flames flicker off the corridor walls as the man chases after us.

"Get your ass back here!" The man calls out.

"Not now!" Rob shouts.

"Now fucking now, Fletcher! I order you to stop!"

"I order you to shut the fuck up!" Rob yells, but not in rage like he did with Prince. More in frustration.

"You got a girl? Is that a girl, Fletcher? You know the rules! No women in the monastery! You want to get your ass thrown outta here?"

Rob comes to a stop and growls, completely exasperated. I sense he has some respect for whoever this guy is trying to call the shots.

"If anyone finds out," the man says compassionately, "they'll kick you out. I won't have any say in the matter."

"Cover for me, Guerrero. Can you do that? Just fucking cover for me for one fucking night. This is important."

"Important enough to go back to jail over?"

"Yes," Rob barks without hesitation. "She was attacked."

"By who?" Guerrero asks, concerned.

"Fucking Fundies," Rob seethes.

Everybody knows what that means. Fundies get away with whatever they want and we suffer for it.

There's a long sigh from Guerrero, then, "Okay. Go. Get in your room. But I want her out of here before the sun comes up. You hear me, Fletcher?"

"Yes, sir, I hear you."

Guerrero grunts and he's gone.

Rob closes the door to his room behind him.

The room is half the size of mine and equally ascetic. One bed, one desk, one wardrobe, all made of simple wood. A similar prison window with a cross bar.

Rob flips a switch on his desk lamp.

A soothing glow butters the walls.

Rob lowers me onto the bed gently.

"I'll be right back. I need to take my armor off."

I nod.

A half hour later, he returns wearing boots, jeans and a black T-shirt, and holding a pitcher of water, bowl and cup. He pours water splashing into the cup.

I'm parched, my throat a desert sand storm of scratches. The water hurts going down but I need it, swallowing it down with avid gasps. He pours two more. When I finish, I fall back onto the bed. I'm exhausted from my futile fight to escape that vicious iron maiden.

Rob grabs a washcloth from his wardrobe, wets it, and sponges my face with gentle tenderness. Then he cleans my bloody fingers with a surprising degree of delicacy for a man so savage. I nearly clawed my fingernails off trying to escape that thing.

As I get my energy back, I try to sit up.

"Ow, shit!" I hiss.

"What?"

"My knee."

"Did you hurt it in the iron maiden?"

"No, Jackess kicked it."

"Who?"

"Jacqueline. That bitch is quick."

Rob helps me to sitting.

I wince in pain. "Fuck that hurts!"

"Take your pants off," he orders.

"What?! Rob! Not now! I am in *excruciating* pain here!" Any other time, I might actually do what he says.

He grumbles, "I need to look at your knee. Make sure it's okay. Your pants are too tight to pull up."

"Oh."

He's already unlacing my boot carefully. He pulls it off softly and sets it on the floor. Undoes my other boot, tugging the laces like he's tugging on my heart strings. There's an intimacy to his movements that's oddly nurturing. Nothing like bloody-faced Alpha the night I met him and his friends.

He sets my other boot on the floor.

I'm propped up on my elbows on his thin mattress.

"Well?" he prompts, tugging on the cuff of my jeans.

"Um..."

"Do you want me to take them off?"

"Could you?" This is the first time in my life I am *asking* a man on the same bed as me to take my pants off for me. Usually it's me asking them to stop trying so hard to do it. You know how it is.

He examines my many belts.

"It's the one on the bottom."

"I see it," he nods.

I swear, it takes an hour for him to unbuckle my belt. At least it seems like it, because my every nerve is on fire in anticipation. Of what, I don't know. But this handsome man is taking off my effing pants like he's done it a hundred times before. Not like he's taken some *other* women's pants off hundreds of times, no, I mean mine. Like, he has *actually* done this before. To me. It's the weirdest sensation. It's totally insane and it's fleeting, but I feel it. Then it's gone.

When he starts to tug on my unbuttoned jeans, I push my butt up to help him scootch my pants down. Big mistake. That causes the knife in my knee to turn a screw or two.

"Ow, shit!" I gasp.

"Relax, Mary. I'll do it." He inches my jeans down past my knees and leaves them binding my ankles.

I should feel trapped, like I've got shackles on my feet, but I don't. I'm fine right here with him hovering over me with my pants down.

Is it odd to say I'm *really* glad I shaved my legs just yesterday?

Rob doesn't seem to notice. He's inspecting my knees. "It's this one, right?"

"Yeah," I nod.

His hands are careful and precise as he touches and tests. "Where'd she kick you?"

"On the side."

"Nothing feels torn or sprained. There's no swelling. She might have hit a nerve."

"Literally," I snort, feeling much better with Rob by my side.

"Yes, literally. My guess is you'll be better in a few days at the most, once the nerve starts to heal."

"I hope so. Someone kicked my ribs too." I grimace when I touch my side.

"How bad is it?"

"Not as bad as my knee, luckily. I'll live. I've had worse." I lay back on the bed and smile.

He nods. His eyes flick down to my legs. He looks away like he's embarrassed I caught him looking.

"Don't peek," I joke. "I'm totally at your mercy right now. Peeking is not cool."

He smirks to himself, eyes on the ceiling.

I'm disappointed. I like him looking.

"You should sleep," he says. "Do you need to take a leak or anything?"

"Maybe later."

"Okay. Wake me if you need to go. We'll have to sneak you into the bathroom."

"Oh. Erm, where are you going to be?"

"Right next to you." He peels his T-shirt off. Then his boots and jeans. Folds them into a neat pile on the floor.

I am transfixed.

His body is godly.

Black boxers and muscles never looked so good. Even with his tattoos, his skin is flawless. His ink only enhances the hard lines of his physique.

I am aching in anticipation of what happens next.

The hottest man I've ever seen is about to climb into bed with me. Not a boy. Man, man, man. Manly perfection.

I am speechless, but the answer is yes, he's welcome in this bed.

He opens the wardrobe and pulls out a rolled blanket. Whips it out unfurling on the floor. His blanket, not his... you know. He sits down cross-legged and positions his shirt and jeans, using them as a thin pillow. He lies down.

I giggle, "What're you doing down there?"

"The bed's kinda small."

"Oh. We can share if you want."

"Nah. This is fine. I'm good here."

I'm not good with him there. "Are you sure? I mean, I am pretty traumatized from what happened." I try to sound jokey. After all these years, I've gotten pretty good at—

((((it hurts!))))

((((please not again!))))

—blocking out pain.

He nods. Stands. Picks me up and slides me against the wall. Lies down next to me. Pulls the blanket up over both of us.

He is huge.

I've never been with a man so big.

It's only *somewhat* intoxicating.

What would happen if I were to touch his...

I can't do it.

My knee is killing me. So are my ribs. Now is not the time.

But I'm dying to kiss him.

"You got enough room?" he asks like a brother or something similarly innocent. His muscled arm lies between us like a wall.

"Um, not really?"

"Do you want me to move my arm?"

"Could you?"

He lifts it, offering his side.

I'd be an idiot not to snuggle with him. I slide right in.

He tenses when I touch him.

"Sorry."

"It's fine," he hisses.

"Is something wrong?" This is so weird. In reality, I barely know Rob. We're almost complete strangers. Yet here I am, little old me in his private bedroom, snuggling up in his private bed.

"No, it's just, pardon me." He reaches down and tugs at his boxers under the blanket.

"What're you doing?!" I laugh, totally not afraid.

"Adjusting," he grunts.

"Oh. Oh! Sorry. It's that thing where boys get all, you know, at night. And in the morning when they wake up?"

"Something like that," he says stiffly.

Is he lying? Or being honest?

I'm not a hundred percent sure.

But I am a million percent sure I've never felt safer than I do right now. Sleeping in foster care was never simple. I always needed a locked door and an empty room, which I didn't always get, and I still slept with one eye open even when I did. After Gladys, a lock was mandatory. There were some nights in new homes when I'd put a chair under the doorknob or even push a dresser in front of the door if I could. Rooming with Mimi in the Convent made sleeping suddenly way easier than I can remember. I never had a BFF in foster care, but Mimi definitely qualifies, and I slept soundly in her room for the first time since losing my parents. Rooming with Azzie wasn't as easy as Mimi, but I did sleep in her room, probably because she was gaslighting me into thinking she was a wimpy little mouse. If only I'd known what a bitch she is. I need to forget about her. Anyway, neither Mimi nor Azzie compares to this. This I could get used to. Rob's arms are the bedtime armor I've always dreamed of.

The next thing I know, I slip into sleep.

And dream about Rob.

My knight in shining armor.

There's a castle, I'm locked in a tall tower, and this time I'm wearing a fabulous princess gown. He comes to save me, riding in on a white charger before battling his way up the spiral tower staircase, sword-fighting the king's guards or whatever. This time, when he bursts through the door, it's an actual dream come true.

Chapter 29

Do I march into Ms. Skelter's office first thing Monday morning to tell her I was locked in an iron maiden by three Fundies because I broke curfew and snuck out of the Convent against Ms. Braunschott's explicit orders?

I'll give you one guess who would be the one in trouble in that rosy scenario.

Anyway, after Halloween, the castle quickly becomes a battleground everywhere I venture. The Fundies and their lackeys hound my heels at every turn. Even in the hallowed halls of the Convent, my one sanctuary from their savage harassment, they attack me without mercy.

I nearly have a heart attack the morning I open my room door and find the iron maiden blocking my way. Being that it's dark out, and the Convent corridors are so dim, it takes me a moment to figure out that I'm not in the middle of a nightmare. My screams start the instant after, waking the work-study girls. Even Ms. Braunschott comes running, fireplace poker in hand.

As much as I'd love, I mean *like* to sleep with Rob every night for this exact reason, and I mean *sleep* sleep, because he makes me feel so safe, Mr. Guerrero won't allow it. Neither will Ms. Braunschott. So I'm stuck in the Convent. I beg Brawny to let me sleep in Mimi's room, but the answer is a hard no.

Each night I huddle under my covers in the room I share with Azzie or Elizabeth or whoever the hell she really is. Ms. Skelter's creepy creation? Like, Azielbeth is a demonic doll that Skelter brought to life one night while hovering over her witch's kettle and chanting Satanic magical spells? Or, for all I know, Skelter has some magic evil ring that makes her young, and she puts it on and becomes Azzie *or* Elizabeth at will? I mean, I've never seen *any* of those three anywhere at the same time! Okay, ridic. Nobody has any magic rings.

But Azzie aka Elizabeth?

You *know* it's a gaslight.

Not that it matters. I never see "either" of them. I guess she's done spying on me and would rather sleep in the East Wing where it's not so drafty. Now that it's November, there's a chill in the night air that leaves me shivering under my thin wool blankets. I also use the ones from Azzie's bed, but it isn't enough to cut the cold. Did I mention there's no heating in the Convent? Having Rob by my side would defs keep me warm, but rules are rules.

As for my work-study duties, cleaning the West Wing is quickly becoming a deplorable chore. Those entitled Fundy boys constantly trash their rooms, leaving unnecessary messes every chance they get. I consider taking my revenge on their possessions in various ways, like dropping their stuff in their toilets or accidentally dropping things like watches or phones in the trash (Oops!) but I know where that will get me.

During school hours, the taunts and verbal jabs continue. Now they call me Witch Trial or Bloody Mary.

I ignore it and suck it up and collect my stipend checks while trying to keep my grades up.

The real kicker is the night I come home to my Convent room and find a lifesize photo of Gladys from her actual mugshot photo taped over my headboard like her insane eyes are watching over me. In scratchy black letters, a speech bubble says, "I'm coming for you, Mary!"

I'm surprised they didn't call me pig shit, but I don't think that's in my file. Who knows. But I do know I have Jackess to thank for the photo, and probably Elizazzielbeth for giving her access to my Convent room.

The next morning, on my way to clean the classrooms at 5:00am, I find pictures of Gladys taped up all over campus. Thousands of them staring at me like I'm trapped inside some freaky carnival hall of mirrors. It would be terrifying if they were lit up with ghoulish lighting and laughing maniacally, but they're not. It's just printed paper, and it's still dark out.

It must've taken an army of Fundy goblin lackeys or whoever to put them up during the night without anyone noticing. There's too many for a few Fundy girls to do it in one night. Later that morning, I find my locker has been papered with Gladys photos inside and out. Whatever. I ignore them.

Guess who cleans them all up?

All thousands of them?

Me and the work-study kids. Every last one of us, boys and girls, is forced to spend three hours that night tearing them down and bagging them up in hundreds of black trash bags. It's a serious chore, and the entire time the work-study kids grumble about getting revenge. Thankfully, they don't mean on me. They know the Fundies are to blame. At least the work-study kids are on my team. I don't know what I'd do if they turned on me too. Being hated by half the school is bad enough.

Prince has tried apologizing a hundred times since Halloween. I turn my back on him whenever he does. Rob was right to say Prince never should've invited me to the All Hallows' Ball. I was so wrong for going.

I should've known!

Live and learn.

I know it's getting old to say it, but at least this isn't prison. It's not like they locked me inside a *functional* iron maiden. Mine didn't even have any spikes.

Can I get a sarcastic ha-ha-ha?

No?

Not even a mildly sympathetic and minimally indignant one? Not that either?

I hear you, sister.

This place *is* jail.

At least no one's tried to shank me.

That *does* deserve a ha-ha-ha.

How many more years do I have left to go?

I never tell Mimi about kissing Chase.

I haven't yet lost a girlfriend over a boyfriend and I'm not about to start, not that I've ever had a girlfriend as close to me as Meems. I'm grateful for her like you have no idea.

After being here nearly two months, it's clear she has a thing for Chase and I'd much rather have her friendship over his boyfriendship. Though something tells me he's not the type to settle down. I'm more than happy to savor the hint of shipping between him and Meems from a distance. Not that they have anything going, at least, not that Mimi's told me. They *might* be hooking up, but there's no obvious signals she's showing.

I don't tell her about kissing Prince either because I'm embarrassed I did. I know the iron maiden thing wasn't his fault, and I should maybe forgive him. Or not. If I wanted, I *could* craft some convoluted chain of logic blaming him for taking me to the bathroom at Halloween and leaving me there to kiss Chase which led to Prince arguing with him which led me to walking away which led to the Silicones cornering me in the torture chamber. That's not Prince's fault. It's theirs. But he *did* invite me into the viper pit in the first place. Maybe I'll forgive him *some* day. Like when he offers to buy my freedom out of here. Like that'll ever happen.

As for Duke, I did avoid any impropriety thus far, both times when he cornered me with those smoldering coals he calls eyes. I swear, when he looks at you, it's like he's trying to burn a hole through the armor around your heart so he can take it and claim it. Under other circumstances, I might consider it. Not here at the academy, not while

Victoria is still alive. As much as she disrespects him, she considers him hers. I'm keeping my distance.

Anyway, I'm done with the Rich Boys.

I don't care how hot they are.

They aren't worth the trouble from the Rich Girls.

Best to keep to my own kind.

That leaves me with Rob, Tucker, Skill, and Jonah to choose from.

I can work with that.

Not that I've made a choice, and not that any of them are making any overt signals. It's like they're too busy. I don't see them much around campus these days.

When Thanksgiving break rolls around, I decide it's time to get busy with at least one of the four Poor Boys at my first opportunity.

"No way!" I grouse. "We'll get kicked out of Castle Hill if we sneak out to see some dumb band!"

"It's just sneaking off campus down to town," Mimi pleads. "No one's going to know we're gone. We'll be back before Brawny notices."

"I should be studying," I sigh.

"That's what we've been doing all day!"

We're in Mimi's Convent room with books and papers spread out on both beds.

I sigh, "My grades *have* been slipping, in case I haven't mentioned it a *hundred* times in the past two weeks. You know I didn't do as well on midterms as I hoped. If I don't pull my grades back up to a 3.5 by the end of the term, I'll be going back you know where."

"I know, and you will, but you won't get your grades up if you burn yourself out."

"True."

"That's why you need a night off, Mare Bear."

"We've had the whole day off," I offer. Since it's Thanksgiving weekend, we didn't have to clean the Palace dorms on a Saturday because most of the Fundies have left the academy to visit their families.

Surprise, we work-study kids are trapped here and aren't allowed to leave or have family visits. Only tuition-paying families, aka Fundy families, are allowed on school grounds. It's classist bullshit, but it's the rules, which is actually worse than jail. Jail allows visitors nearly every day of the week.

What can I say? It's not like I have anyone to come visit me, but I'm sure some of the other work-study kids have families. I know we aren't all foster kids. Again, them's the rules. Whatever.

Anyway, Meems and I *have* been studying since sunup.

"Live a little," Mimi says. "You need a recharge. It's Saturday night. We don't have to work tomorrow. You can study then."

"Okay, what's this dumb band worth risking our enrollment over? Because we'll be sneaking out, right?"

"Yup."

"Past the electric fences and the Fundy hunt?"

"The what?!" she laughs.

"Never mind. How do we get past the fences?"

Mimi flashes an impish grin. "Don't worry about that. I've got it taken care of. Anyway, it's not just *any* band."

"It better be effing Beyonce or Taylor effing Swift. No, the effing Donnas *and* the Muffs *and* the Runaways having a secret popup reunion show tonight. If it's not girl punk band paradise when we get there, I'm seriously turning around and going home," I giggle.

"It's better than that," Mimi grins.

"What could be better than that?"

"You'll see."

We hitch a ride with some work-study boys from Plant Services who have access to a school van, which they're no doubt not supposed to use to drive to downtown Castle Hill with a bunch of work-study girls on a Saturday night, but they get us there without getting caught by Brawny or anyone else.

I'm wearing jeans, my Docs, a classic Ramones band shirt I got from Hot Topic forever ago, and my leather jacket. My hair has grown out to about an inch and a half, which I can semi-style with a boyish part on the side, but I don't have any product to give it lift, so I just stuff it under the Castle Hill beanie Jonah gave me. It'll keep my head warm in this brisk winter weather we've been having.

Mimi is decked out in her own rocker attire and looks like a glittery rockstar girlfriend with her overdone makeup, but not *too* overdone. Somehow, she strikes the perfect balance.

She insisted on doing my face, so I'm made up too. Mimi definitely knows her way around makeup brushes and eyeliner pencils. She even tweezed my eyebrows. I admit it, I don't look half bad.

Downtown Castle Hill is a picture postcard of a quaint little town with its chic shops, cute boutiques and pastry bakeries on the main street. Most of them are closed this late, but a bar is lit up and thumping with live music. You can tell from a distance it's some kind of hard rock band. That'll work.

There's no line to get in because everyone's already inside.

They don't card us because they aren't serving liquor. Mimi pays our cover before I have a chance to offer and we follow the work-study boys inside. The place is packed and you can't see the stage from the entrance. We squeeze through the crowd until we get to the side where we can see the corner of the stage around the huge PA speakers. I'm already nodding my head to the beat. You know it's a good band when you've never heard a single song and they sound great live. Singer's got a great voice, too.

I have to lean between shoulders and tiptoe to get a view of the stage.

When I see the lead singer, I laugh, "No effing way!" I grin at Mimi. "Are you serious?!"

She's grinning from ear to ear. She yells over the load music, "I told you it'd be worth it!"

On stage are Rob tearing up the lead vocals, Skill shredding on guitar, Jonah banging away at his bass, and Tucker smashing up the drums. No wonder they've been so busy and I never see them at the academy. They've probably been rehearsing every single night to sound this good.

They all wear jeans and boots instead of their customary coveralls. No shirts. And do they ever have the bodies for it. Jonah is humongous, all muscles, but very defined. Rob and Skill are even more cut and rugged, but not as huge as Jonah. For accessories, I see bracelets, chains, black eyeliner, and more tattoos than usual. Behind the drum kit, Tucker wears only shorts and shoes, and oh my, is his body divine. I notice his bass drum head says Outlaw Merriment and the big banner hanging behind the band also says Outlaw Merriment in the same savage font.

Rob's legs are thrust apart and he leans into the mic, singing:

"Lost in your lightning eyes,

"Dreaming of your tightened thighs,

"Dying for another try,

"Rip my heart you say goodbye!"

Can Rob sing?

Ohmygod, can he. His voice is a velvet glove caressing your chest. The loud PA speakers help with the sensual feeling of total vocal invasion, like he's sliding inside me with every thrusting note he sings.

Jonah and Skill join in to harmonize the chorus.

"Forrrrr evvvvv-er one!

"Liiiiife oooon the run!"

Mimi pushes me forward until I'm front of her and she screams over my shoulder, "Sing it, Rob!"

He turns and sees me, pointing at me as he finishes the chorus.

"Forrrrr evvvvv-er one!

"With-ouuut you I'm done!"

When the chorus finishes, Skill, Jonah and Tucker continue playing. Rob nods his head in time with the beat for half a bar before growling into the mic and improvising, "Without you I'm done, Mary!" Rob tosses me a wink before kicking the air for emphasis.

Mimi squeals beside me, grabbing me and jumping me up and down with her while hugging me and cheering, "Did you hear that?! He just *sang* to you, Mary!"

It's not like it's the Ramones or Sex Pistols singing at me but I'm laughing giddily anyway as we bounce off the surrounding crowd. I can't say I've had the honor of having a boy write a song for me, but this is the next best thing.

For the next forty-five minutes, Rob teases me, singing my name from time to time from the stage, always mixing it into the lyrics. I get plenty of attention from Skill and Jonah too whenever they're on my side of the stage. During a guitar solo, Skill has his guitar jammed between his legs with the headstock jutting out over the crowd like he wants me to grab it. I would if I could reach it, but I'm not tall enough. Mimi is and she does, tugging on the guitar neck flirtatiously and flicking her tongue at him suggestively. I snort in disgust. Skill of course pretends to come when she does it. I laugh at that. Tucker doesn't get up from behind his drum kit during the show, but he frequently catches my eye and flashes smiles my way, letting me know he sees me seeing him.

Did I mention *every* female in the audience is drooling over the band? More than a few notice Rob fawning over me and flash jealous smiles, some appreciative, others hateful. I don't care. I've never had so much fun watching a band ever, and I've been to quite a few shows since turning old enough for the all ages venues.

When it's over, I'm spent. Meems and I cheered our hearts out the whole time.

I'm so glad I snuck out with her.

Hopefully we can sneak back on campus without getting caught.

Chapter 30

"We have to go to the after party," Mimi demands outside. The crowds are heading to their cars and driving into the night.

I ask, "Shouldn't we be getting back to campus before Brawny realizes we're gone?"

"No! After party, bitch!" Mimi laughs.

"Who's hosting?"

"The band, obvi," Mimi grins.

How can I say no?

Since the Halloween party, I haven't had a chance to talk to Rob for more than brief hellos when we cross paths on campus. Can I tell you how annoying that is? It's not like he's ghosting me. He always has a warm smile when we see each other, and always says something encouraging, but he always has something else he needs to go do, like he's the busiest man on the planet.

I guess after tonight I know why. If I had my own damn band, I'd be pretty damn busy too. Does it make me like Rob that much more? Of course it does. Maybe I can catch him alone tonight and figure out where we stand. I mean, I slept in his effing bed! I would very much like to continue from where we left off, aka me spending *more* nights with him. If that's not what he wants, I at least want him to say so.

Meems and I pile into the Plant Services van with the work-study boys, and several work-study girls I recognize. They immediately start flirting with the boys while we drive down dark twisty mountain roads. I have no idea where we are.

We end up in a dirt parking lot hidden deep in the trees. It's already full of cars and people are migrating into the forest. The work-study boys who took us here unload kegs from the back of the van. I should've noticed but they were hidden under moving blankets until now. The boys roll them on dollies into the woods. It's a short walk to a bunch of picnic tables and several huge campfires burning in rock pits. Music plays on a portable set of big PA speakers hooked up to someone's phone. The songs are Outlaw Merriment. I recognize Rob's voice and the choruses.

There's lots of kids here partying I don't recognize. Kids from Castle Hill the town maybe? I don't know.

Mimi and I chitchat with a bunch of the work-study kids. Luna from the Castle Hill salon is there, and several other girls I've gotten to know. I toss caution to the wind and drink beer from the red plastic SOLO cup

Mimi hands me. Feels so familiar I can't resist. I pace myself so I don't end up drunk, but it's not like we're driving back. I keep an eye on our drivers. One tells me he's designated, but I watch him anyway. True to his word, he doesn't drink a drop.

Finally, the band arrives.

Rob and the Poor Boys.

Or should I say, Outlaw Merriment.

The kids cheer when they stroll into the orange light of the campfires. I can't even get close to them. Mimi and I hang back while they soak up the spotlight. Eventually, Skill makes his way over to me and Meems at the edge of the crowd.

He says to her, "You sure know how to work my headstock."

"You're bad," Mimi laughs and slaps his muscled shoulder before sipping her beer to hide her blushing.

Skill gives me his grin, "Why didn't you grab my headstock, War Paint?"

"I couldn't reach," I snicker.

"You can now," he says, hooking his thumbs in his belt and thrusting his hips toward me.

"I am not giving you a handjob," I laugh. "That costs extra, remember?"

"I told you before, name a price, War Paint, and I'll pay."

"Pay for what?" Rob says, interjecting himself into the conversation when he walks up.

"Hey, you!" I smile.

Rob picks me up in a hug and spins me around, nearly knocking Skill out of the way with my spinning boots.

Skill frowns in irritation.

"How you been, Mouth?" Rob asks, sounding like my older brother or something.

"Mouth?" Skill chuckles. "You call her Mouth? Show some respect, Rob!"

"Look who's talking, handjob. I heard what you said to her," Rob gives Skill a friendly shove.

Skill stumbles back and laughs, "Take it easy on the talent." His voice is a mixture of deference and irritation, like he wants to bite back but doesn't.

Rob rolls his eyes and says to me, "How'd you like the show?"

Mimi butts in, "It was fucking awesome! You guys seriously fucking rock!"

"Thanks," Rob smiles but he's embarrassed by the compliment. "What'd you think, Mouth?"

"Mmm," I shrug. "I've seen better."

"Bullshit," Skill laughs. "Nobody can rip a solo like I can."

"It's true," Rob says supportively.

I crinkle my nose, "Erm, pretty sure you guys were out of tune half the time." I'm lying for effect.

"Now that *is* bullshit," Skill laughs.

Rob grins, "He has perfect pitch. We're never out of tune."

"Maybe *he* isn't," I smirk, "but you were."

Skill snickers.

Rob is chuckling, but there's a vulnerability to it, like *maybe* he thinks I'm right. It's a side of Rob I never imagined might be there. A side that isn't one thousand percent confident in everything he does, or walking out of the woods with black blood up to your forearms like it's business as usual. This Rob is different.

Feeling bad for him, I say, "You sounded perfect on stage. You guys are really good."

Rob looks relieved.

"There she is!" Tucker walks up with Jonah in tow.

"Hey, kid," Jonah smiles at me. "Still workin' the beanie."

"You know it!" I laugh. Before I know what's happening, Tucker sweeps me off my feet and lays me out like a ballroom dance move, except he's actually holding me up off the ground by my shoulders and ass with me floating on my back and my ankles dangling in the dirt. His nose hovers an inch from mine. The world disappears and all I see are his mesmerizing eyes.

"Kiss me, hotness," he says softly.

"Hotness?" I giggle. Before I can say more, he kisses me.

His insistence is impossible to resist. His tongue strains inside my mouth: hot, hard, and filling me with his throbbing need. This man is overwhelming.

I clutch his T-shirt and moan, kissing back.

"Give her room to breathe, Tuck," Rob chuckles, irritated.

Tucker pulls out of my mouth and lifts me to standing, his wicked eyes shining with feral desire. He clearly wasn't done and glares at Rob like he's angry for the interruption.

Rob arches an eyebrow in challenge.

Tucker starts to snarl, his face flickering fury.

It wasn't that long ago that Tucker and Prince were fighting over me before the All Hallows' Ball. Here Tucker is doing it again, and with his friend, no less. How is that possible? Especially now. Mimi is standing *right* next to me, and she is so obviously hot enough to fight over. But me? Not so much. I don't get it. The main thing is, I really don't want

Rob and his friends *actually* fighting each other over me or anybody else. Friends shouldn't ever fight each other. There's more than enough enemies in the world to fight, you don't go fighting your friends. That's why you have them.

"Wow, what was that, Tucker?!" I laugh, trying to play it down. I'm totally kidding, pretending I didn't like it so nobody gets mad.

"Yeah, Tucker," Mimi snickers. "You attacked her."

"You're next," he grunts, eyes all over her.

"Ew!" Mimi giggles, obviously liking the idea because she's totally blushing but pretending not to.

Tucker looks ready to ravish her like he did me.

"Anyway," I say, trying to cut the sexual tension, "You guys were amazing tonight. How come you never told me you have a band?" I flick my eyes between the four of them.

Skill winks, "We're mysterious like that."

"I'll say," I grin. "What other secrets are you guys hiding?"

The four Poor Boys exchange a strange look.

Skill says, "Mimi, you mind giving us a minute? We need to talk business."

"Sure," she shrugs. "Come on, Mare Bear. The boys need to be mysterious, per usual." She grabs my hand to lead me back to the rest of the crowd.

"Mary stays," Rob says.

"What?" Mimi asks over her shoulder.

"We want to talk to her."

I look at Mimi.

She shrugs. "You'll be safe with them. I'll be over by the kegs."

"Okay, see ya." I put my hands in my jeans pockets and look at the four Poor Boys. "What's the mystery?"

"Have a seat," Rob says, motioning to a picnic bench.

I sit down on the table top with my boots on the bench and the four of them surrounding me. I can't say as I've ever had four gorgeous men crowd around me like this, prying at me with their penetrating eyes. It's a trifle frightening but mostly it makes me giddy. They're as dangerously dashing as the night I met them at the cannibals' GTO, the night I ran away. In the dim light of the campfires now, I see in them the same sharp edges I saw that night two months ago. So much has happened since then. The biggest surprise is these four seem to be a permanent part of my new life. I can't complain.

"What's the mystery?" I ask.

Jonah says, "We heard about what happened on Halloween."

"Who didn't?" I try not to cringe as I fight back the horrid memory of that night. Scowling, I say, "Those silicone bitches made sure everyone on campus knows. You saw the pictures of Gladys. Ugh. Why did they have to single *me* out?"

Skill says, "Because they're heartless bitches who don't give a shit about anyone other than themselves."

Jonah says somberly, "They like hurting people. They get off on it. It's all a game to them."

"That's an understatement," I snort.

Tucker tips his chin and practically snarls, "Wanna fuck them over?"

"What?!" I snort a laugh.

"You wanna help us fuck them over?"

"Uh, *yeah*," I snicker. "If only there was a way to do it without *us* getting in trouble. You know they'll find a way to turn it around back on us and get us busted with Ms. Skelter or whoever."

Rob shakes his head, "That's where we come in."

"Sounds like you already have a plan?" I glance between the four of them.

"You could say that," Skill grins.

"Mind sharing?" I ask.

Rob says, "If we let you in on this, there's no going back."

"In on what? You guys sound really creepy all of a sudden."

Jonah jokes, "That's just Rob. He always sounds creepy." Jonah always sets me at ease.

I grin, "So what is it then? What's the big mystery?"

Rob says, "Have you heard of the Ivory Tower?"

I say, "The secret society on campus? The one Prince belongs to?"

Rob frowns, "How do you know about that?"

"I overheard Azielbeth talking to him about it at the All Hallows' Ball. She said he's the youngest ever magister or something like that."

"Who said?" Skill asks.

"Oh," I titter. "I meant Eliza-bitch Morgan-*Hearse* with an e. Because she's like the Angel of Death or whatever. She said Prince is the magister of The Ivory Tower."

Rob nods, "He is. How would you like to get back at her and her friends for what they did to you?"

I sneer, "Are we locking them in their own iron maidens in the dungeon? Elizabeth, Victoria, and Jacqueline?"

"Nothing so prosaic as that," Skill says.

"What then? Get them kicked out of Castle Hill Academy permanently?" I grin. "Something like that? I'm totally up for doing that."

Rob says ominously, "No, we want to take down their entire

families."

"What do you mean by take down?" I ask shrewdly.

"Use your imagination," Rob says cryptically.

"Kill them?" I ask carefully.

"Nothing so extreme."

"What, like bankrupt them?" I titter.

"For starters."

"Hmm. Their *whole* families?"

Rob nods.

"How many people is that?" I ask.

"Dozens. If you count extended family for all three girls, Elizabeth, Victoria, and Jacqueline, and you include anyone on the family inheritance lists, well over a hundred people get affected."

"Um, what if, I don't know, what if Grandma Morgan-Hearst is a kindly old lady or something, and all she does is donate money to charities and feed her thousand cats gourmet organic cat food? She doesn't deserve anything bad, does she?"

Rob says flatly, "What if I told you that forty years ago, Grandma Morgan-Hearst personally saw to it that a bunch of sweatshop factories, and tobacco and tea farms the Morgan-Hearsts own overseas, started forcing children to work sixteen hour days in dangerous conditions for close to no money so the Morgan-Hearst companies continued to turn a profit every year?"

"Is that true?" I gasp.

Jonah scowls, "Disgusting but true."

Tucker hisses to himself, "Fucking ruthless bitch."

Skill muses sarcastically, "Why hire adults who demand a living wage when you can enslave orphans who're too young to understand? We're talking kids five, six and seven years old without any families to protect them."

Being a foster kid for so many years, what they're saying is a hundred knives to the gut. I know what it's like to have no one watching out for you, and what can happen when—

((((pitch black))))

((((pain))))

((((it hurts!))))

((((please not again!))))

—you fall into the hands of evil people. People like Gladys. I look to Rob for confirmation.

He says, "In one case, the kids managed to escape from their dorms —"

"Shitholes," Tucker says. "Dorms makes it sound nice. They made them live in dirty little shitholes. Rats, garbage everywhere, dirt floors, no medical attention, shitty food, not even running fucking water. They had to drink from the fucking *river*. You have any idea the amount of human *shit* that goes into that river?"

Skill says somberly, "If the malaria didn't kill the kids, the dysentery did."

"When was this?" I ask, horrified.

"Back when Grandma Morgan-Hearst ran things," Rob says. "Back in the sixties and seventies, when a bunch of the kids escaped and went to the local village for help, and the villagers took the kids in and fed them, kindly old Grandma Morgan-Hearst hired a bunch of local armed men with jeeps and assault rifles to round up the kids at gunpoint. Jammed them into the backs of old military trucks and drove them right back to the factory and forced them to keep working."

I'm flabbergasted. "Are you guys serious?"

"As a fucking stroke," Tucker growls, looking ready to bite someone's face off. "Hundreds of kids died in *one* fucking factory because Grandma Morgan-Hearst didn't think they needed clean fucking water. It was cheaper to snatch up more local orphans than the millions it would've cost to clean up a polluted river. Or do something as simple as truck in fucking clean water. Fucking heartless penny-pinching bitch."

Skill adds, "And that's just the tip of their vile iceberg empire."

I gasp trepidatiously, "How do you guys know all this?"

Rob's face is dead set and painfully grim when he says, "Let's just say we've been studying the business empires of the Morgan-Hearsts and the Hanover-Wessexes and the Stanford-Cornwalls for a long, *long* time."

"Who're they again?"

"Elizabeth, Victoria and Jacqueline's families."

Tucker grunts, "Don't forget the fucking Lancasters."

"Prince's family?" I blurt.

"They're as shitty as the rest of them," Tucker grumbles.

Skill says, "So are the Montfortes and the Wendinghams and a dozen others at the academy."

"Duke's family?" I ask.

Rob nods, "Among other things, the Montfortes are one of the biggest builders of private prisons in America. The more people who get locked up, the more money the Montfortes make."

"Who're the Wendinghams again?" I ask. "I've heard that name." My eyes light up and I snap my fingers. "Chase! That's Chase's family, right? Him too?"

Skill scowls, "They're no better than the rest."

It takes a moment for me to process what they're telling me. "So, what, you're saying Prince and Duke and Chase are as bad as Eliza-bitch and her silicone friends?"

"Afraid so," Jonah says. "Rich and powerful people don't get that way being nice and generous."

"They fuck everyone over," Tucker barks. "Even kids. Every one of those fuckers deserves to rot in fucking hell for what they do. Fucking kids!" Tucker looks at me wide-eyed like the world has turned upside down and nobody is saying anything about it except him.

No, that's not true.

They're *all* looking at me like that.

"What do you say, Mary?" Rob asks. "You want to help us take them down?"

"Umm... how?" I ask nervously.

"For starters, we, or should I say you, infiltrate The Ivory Tower."

"How am I supposed to do that?"

"By getting close to Prince. Very close."

Not sure if I like the sound of that, I titter, "What exactly does that mean?"

Rob's face darkens and he opens his mouth to reply when there's a commotion in the campfire crowd and everybody looks in the direction of the parking lot beyond the flickering flames.

"What is it?" I ask.

Tucker grumbles, "The fuck are they doing here crashing our shit?"

"Who's crashing?" I whisper because I can't see over Rob and the rest of them.

"The fucking Fundies," Tucker grouses.

"Which ones?"

"All of them."

"That can't be good," I grimace.

Skill says, "Nothing about them ever is."

Tucker grunts, "They wanna fight a fucking war? Bring it fucking on."

Let the drama begin.

Every single one of us work-study kids are breaking the rules being here. Not only is it way past curfew, we're nowhere close to being on campus. And we've got kegs, meaning underage drinking aplenty.

I immediately dump my SOLO cup of beer in the dirt and throw the cup under the table, already eying an escape route that will take me to Mimi, and the both of us safely away so we can sneak several miles through the forest and back into our rooms without getting caught. What're the chances of making that happen?

Zero?

Less than zero, obvi.
We never should've done this.

Chapter 31

Prince says, "You threw a keg party without inviting us? I'm hurt, Fletcher. I thought we had an understanding."

Prince strolls up to the campfires flanked by Duke and Chase and two dozen other Fundy boys I recognize from Castle Hill. They all wear suits. Not academy uniforms. Regular blazers and slacks and dress shoes that shimmer darkly, like you'd expect if they were going out clubbing.

Rob faces them, backed by Skill, Tucker, and Jonah, and a huge crowd of work-study kids.

Mimi and I are moving through the shadows behind some trees, heading for the parking lot and the road beyond. When I realize no one is running for the cars, not the Castle Hill townie kids nor the work-study kids, Mimi and I stop to watch the confrontation.

"Get the fuck outta here!" Tucker barks at Prince.

"Dial it down," Rob grumbles at Tucker before stepping up to Prince.

Prince says, "Care to kiss my shoe, Fletcher?"

"How about you kiss mine?" Rob folds his muscled arms across his chest and his big biceps bulge with menace.

"Hmph," Prince sniffs like he's above it all when he's obviously not.

I suddenly realize things are very different off campus. Rob isn't acting so beholden. He's standing his ground and daring Prince to cross over the invisible line drawn in the dirt between them.

Prince clearly has no intention of crossing it.

Rob says, "Shouldn't you be in Fiji surfing or some shit?"

"Not until winter break," Prince grins. "Aren't you going to play the good host and offer us beers?"

"You're not welcome here," Rob says flatly.

The crowd of work-study boys behind Rob rumble their agreement.

Prince says, "That may be true, but I believe you aren't either. The park closes at sundown. What would the sheriff say if I call him and tell him about all the underage drinking going on?"

"We'll be long gone before anyone gets here."

Skill says, "He probably called them already."

"Now, now," Prince clucks. "We came to enjoy ourselves."

"Slumming for sluts," Chase chuckles lustily, eying several cute Castle Hill townie girls I don't recognize. They giggle and welcome his plundering eyes.

Mimi rolls hers in disgust.

Is she into him? I never can tell for sure, but she's acting like it now.

The townie girls are also tossing flirty looks at Prince, Duke, and the other Fundy boys, many of whom are pretty cute. You can't miss the Fundies' expensive cars parked in the dirt parking lot. I don't see Prince's Bugatti, but I do see plenty of Porsches, Land Rovers, and a Ferrari. I guess they took the cheap cars out for tonight. I can tell the townie girls are wondering what it'd be like to go for a ride with these boys in those cars. If they only knew what dicks they are.

"Get the fuck outta here," Tucker says to Prince and his friends. "Before I fuck up all you fucking Fundies." He looks ready to fight every last Fundy boy on his own, and he looks like he might just win. Not that he needs to. He has plenty of help.

Prince frowns at Rob, "Do us a favor and muzzle this mongrel." He's referring to Tucker.

Rob quips, "I'll let you do the honors."

Tucker jams a fist into his palm, cracking his knuckles. Then he cracks the other. "Go for it, princess. Try and muzzle me. You don't get a free shot tonight."

Prince looks down his nose at Tucker for a moment before lowering his eyelids sleepily and turning to Rob, "What do you think Ms. Skelter will say if I call her and tell her half her work-study staff are breaking curfew and partying off campus?" Prince waits for a response. When he doesn't get one, he says, "I think Ms. Skelter might decide it's time to send you all back where you belong." He obviously means prison.

Tucker barks, "No, she'd tell you soft as fuck shitheads to get over it."

Skill says, "He's right. Skelter can't afford to lose half her staff. Who'll clean your rooms and wipe your asses if we get kicked out?"

Prince grins, "I'm sure we can replace you with a fresh batch of delinquents." He's clearly enjoying his authority and power.

"Never gonna happen," Tucker snorts. "Like Skill said, you rich shitheads don't even know how to wipe your own asses. If it wasn't for paying someone else to do it for you, you'd be sitting in shit like a bunch of babies." You have to give Tucker credit. For a seemingly short-fused hot head, he's quite clever and thinks fast under pressure.

Rob chuckles dismissively, "Skill and Tucker are right. Replacing us would take weeks if not months and you know it, *Prince*. Unless you plan on making your own beds, cleaning your own bathrooms, and cooking your own meals for the next couple months, you need us."

Prince says, "We'll hire temporary staff. Bonded, so they won't steal." He's implying we have done just that.

I can tell you I've never stolen a single thing. It's not worth the risk.

Mimi barks loud enough for everyone to hear, "We don't steal any of your stuff and you know it!"

Prince turns to look.

Mimi steps into the light, pulling me with her, and says with disgust, "We don't *want* your stupid stuff. Tell him, Mary."

"Erm, she's right," I say.

"Strumpet," Prince says affectionately.

"Don't call her that," Rob growls and surges toward Prince without hesitation. "Use her fucking name or I'll rip your tongue out where you stand."

Tucker is right beside Rob and scowling at Prince, "I'll fucking bite it off his rich boy mouth, spit it in his face and feed it to him."

Duke lunges to Prince's side, hands fisting at his sides. He warns Tucker, "Over my dead fucking body!"

Jonah steps up beside Rob and towers over Duke. "It would be my pleasure."

Chase says, "You'll have to go through both of us."

Skill saunters up and says, "I'll go through all three of you." Having seen Skill fight, I think he probably could.

The other Fundy boys loom forward, forming a phalanx of fists behind Prince, Duke, and Chase.

Behind Rob, dozens of work-study boys step up to bat. They outnumber the Fundies four to one, and that's not counting the work-study girls, and townie boys and girls. Not that I expect the townies to fight, or the work-study girls, but maybe the townie boys would. They seem to like Rob and the Poor Boys just fine.

For tense seconds, it seems certain a brawl will break out.

"People, please!" Prince laughs loud. "We came to party, not to fight." He reaches into his suit jacket to pull something out.

"He's got a gun," Skill hisses.

Rob and crew surge forward.

"Relax!" Prince chuckles loudly. "I'm not armed." He holds a car remote aloft. In the parking lot, the lights on a Range Rover flash and the back gate opens automatically. "Who wants edibles?"

Two Fundy boys carry over a large cooler and set it down, opening it in front of everyone. It's like a bakery inside. Obviously marijuana-laden baked goods.

"Who wants some?" Prince asks the crowd. "There's more than enough to go around."

The townies rush forward muttering joyfully amongst themselves as they start taking handouts.

When some of the work-study kids step forward to get theirs, Rob holds up a halting hand. He doesn't even look at them, but they stop like he's the effing general of the work-study army. Maybe he is. I don't know. But they stop like Rob is Russell Crowe in Gladiator shouting "Hold the line!" or Mel Gibson in Braveheart shouting, "They can offer us pot, but they'll never take our freedom!"

The work-study kids aren't going to touch the drugs because Rob said so.

With a single hand gesture.

I blurt a laugh in complete disbelief.

Rob isn't afraid to stand up to Prince and the Fundies after all. To think I was once embarrassed for Rob when he kissed Prince's shoe my first day at Castle Hill. I'd thought Rob was a nothing-burger for doing something so demeaning. Yes, I quickly realized he was only bowing and scarping for Prince to protect me from being demeaned, but I never would've imagined this.

Rob is the freaking king.

Ohmygod, it is so effing hot.

What are the chances I'll end up in his bed later tonight? Sleeping only, of course. Ahem.

To my immense disappointment, Rob spends the rest of the party basically chaperoning all the work-study kids, making sure none of them sneak any edibles or get too drunk. He keeps reminding them they need to be back on campus soon and be sober when they get there. The work-study kids aren't too worried about drinking because alcohol doesn't stay in your system too long, and it's easy to act sober if you try hard enough and don't get too hammered (I've had practice), but we all know we could get drug-tested randomly later in the week or whenever. Yet another thing in the student handbook Mimi told me about that I never bothered to read. Anyway, if you fail a drug test, you get kicked out of the academy, obvi. Drinking is slightly risky, but tonight some of us don't seem to care. Sometimes, you just have to say fuck it and cut loose.

When it comes to the townie kids, the readily available edibles make up for the fact that Prince and the Fundies crashed the party. The townies are down. The girls in particular are all over the Fundies. Chase is the standout star. I lose count of how many girls I see hanging off him. Mimi doesn't. She keeps close count and keeps reminding me he's a manwhore.

Prince tries to get close to me several times during the night, but I swear Rob beelines over every time Prince gets close. It gets a little frustrating.

"I just want to apologize to her," Prince groans on his fifth try.

Rob growls, "You lost your chance on Halloween. Talk to somebody else. There's plenty of other girls here."

Prince glances absently at some of the townie girls, many of whom are now ridiculously high on the edibles. "I don't want them," Prince hisses to himself. "I want to talk to Mary."

"Find somebody else," Rob says, standing between me and Prince.

"I can't even apologize?" Prince sighs.

"You can kiss her shoe," Rob smirks.

"If I kiss her shoe can I talk to her?" Prince is practically begging.

Rob relents and looks at me. "Do you want him to kiss your shoe?"

"Erm," I giggle. "Maybe?"

Prince drops to his knees in the dirt, giving no thought to his super expensive clubbing suit. He holds his arms out wide. "Let me kiss your shoe, princess. It's the least you deserve after how I've treated you."

I offer Rob a guilty grin that says, "What am I supposed to say? No?"

Rob grits his teeth and his jaw ticks, clearly saying, "Don't fucking talk to this piece of shit." But he doesn't say it. He says to Prince, "I've got my eye on you. Don't try anything. I'll be back in five minutes."

"Yes, dad," Prince chuckles.

Rob gets right in his face, "Don't fuck with me, Lancaster. You know out here I'll be more than happy to put you in the hospital if you piss me off."

"Yes, sir." Prince offers a mocking military salute.

"I'm serious, turd. This is not your turf."

"Funny, last time I checked, the land deed is in the Lancaster name."

"Bullshit," Rob laughs. "The Morgan-Hearsts own it. Check the county records." Why does he even know that?

"True," Prince chuckles. "Be that as it may, I'm sure I can call in a favor with Elizabeth if need be. She would be more than happy to have the sheriff escort you off her land."

"Fuck off, Lancaster. You've got five minutes." Rob walks away, glancing back at me. "Call me if you need me, Mary."

"Sure," I nod, suddenly wondering if Rob is leaving because of what he said earlier, that he wants me to get close to Prince to help take his family and the other Fundy families down. I never agreed to anything. Is that supposed to start now?

"Princess," Prince leans down, fingers pressing in the dark dirt. "I will now kiss your shoe."

"You don't have to do that," I snicker.

"No, I owe you. It's the least I can do after everything." He loudly smacks the toe of my Docs with his lips. "Mmm, leather," he chuckles and stands up, dusting off his knees.

"Sorry about your slacks," I say. "They look really expensive."

"They are," he says with customary nonchalance. "But you're worth it."

"I only get one kiss?"

He offers a sly grin, "I thought you'd never ask." He leans in for an actual kiss.

"No," I giggle, "I meant my other shoe. You only kissed one."

He drops down and kisses my other Doc. Lifts his head to look at me. His face is disturbingly close to my crotch. Good thing I'm wearing jeans. "What else would you like me to kiss, strumpet?" He flicks his eyes between my legs.

"Would you stop?!" I laugh. "Stand up already. Before Rob sees."

Prince stands and grumbles, "Are you and he seeing each other now?" His disappointment is unmistakable.

"No-a! I mean, I don't know." I shrug. "He's busy."

"I'm never too busy for you, Mary." He's being sincere. "But that's not why I'm here. I'm here to apologize. I was hoping to make a peace offering."

"It definitely worked." I assume he means the drugs, which is the exact kind of extra that gets a party going. I glance around at the kids having fun around us, the dancing, the drinking, the loud music. It really is an epic event for something thrown together last minute in the woods.

"I meant you, princess. I've been extending the olive branch to you for a month, but you refuse to take it."

"Can you blame me?" I laugh nervously.

"No I cannot. What they did to you was ruthless and undeserved. But you have to understand, I had no part in that. Had I known, I would've put a stop to it. I think Elizabeth came up with the idea on the spot, committing a crime of opportunity, otherwise it never would've happened. Had I been by your side like a gentleman, you would've been safe."

We all know why he wasn't. Because I kissed Chase mere minutes after kissing him and they argued about it after.

Now, Prince's anger is building. He's probably thinking about it too.

I'm afraid to say anything.

Prince blows a heavy sigh, "Forget about the past. What's done is done."

"I can't forget." I force an irritated smile. "Halloween was just a little bit traumatic, in case you didn't get the memo."

"I did, and I'm so sorry for that, princess. I really am. If I could take back the past, I would. Let me make it up to you. It'll take time and effort on my part, but I'm confident I can make up for my failing. Eventually you'll realize I wouldn't ever do anything to hurt you."

Now that he's opened up this old wound, I'm getting uncomfortable thinking about it. "You didn't hurt me. They did. You don't owe me anything, Prince. It's fine. I appreciate it, but you don't have to do anything for me. I'm over it."

"Are you?" He looks right in my eyes.

"Yes!" I huff and look away, watching the party.

For a moment, he does too, then says casually, "How is life in the Convent treating you?"

"Good, I guess. It's a bit drafty now that it's cold out, but I can deal."

"My offer still stands."

"Which offer?"

"You living in my suite in the West Wing. There are no drafts, I assure you."

"Oh, erm," I wince. "I couldn't. I like having my own space."

"Then I'll get you your own private suite next to mine."

"You can't do that! That's the boys' building!"

"How many times do I have to tell you, princess? I can do anything I want. I can have the administration clear out the entire top floor of the West Wing and dedicate it to our exclusive use. How does that sound?"

"Are you serious?" I laugh.

"If that's what you want, that's what you get. Anything for you, princess."

"Why are you doing this, Prince?"

"Isn't it obvious?" He takes my hand in his. "I like you, princess."

"Do you have to call me that? It's weird."

Prince and his Princess sounds a wee bit creepy. I'm a person, not a title. It's not just that. His sincerity is making me uncomfortable. It's almost too good to be true. Doesn't mean I don't want it to be. Worse, I've completely forgotten anything Rob said and I'm fully focused on the fact that Prince is surfer hot, rich as sin, and he seems genuinely interested in me, which makes absolutely no sense whatsoever.

"I can call you Mary if you prefer. What's your middle name?"

"Anne."

"How about I call you Marianne. It's much more dignified than simply Mary."

"Nobody ever calls me that," I say. I remember my mom calling me "Mary Anne Angerman!" whenever I was in big trouble, but that's the only time. No boy ever called me that, but I have to admit, it's much better than strumpet or princess.

"Marianne it is," Prince smiles. His blue eyes fire with obvious desire.

I feel an instant thrill fill me from head to toe.

He looks like he's angling for a kiss.

I'd let it happen if it wasn't for Rob tossing irritated looks in our direction every two seconds. With him as tall as he is, he can easily see me and Prince over everyone's heads. He would definitely see if me and Prince kissed. Don't want that.

Trying not to blush and hoping to distract, I say, "What's *your* middle name, Prince? J-something, right?"

"John. Prince John Lancaster the third."

"Why do you go by Prince? It's so, I don't know, so effing presumptuous," I laugh.

"Blame my parents. Who am I to argue with those two paragons of propriety?" His voice betrays a hint of irritation and his icy smile makes it abundantly clear he's not exactly best friends with them.

"Oh."

"Forget about them. Let's talk about you, Marianne. Where are you going to live moving forward? In a drafty old convent with Popeye watching over you, or—"

"You mean Brawny?" I titter.

"Who else?" he chuckles. "You can live with her breathing down your neck, or move into a penthouse suite in the West Wing next to mine, which might take a few days to arrange, or you can move into the guest bedroom in my suite immediately. Have it all to yourself."

"Your *dorm* room has a guest room?"

"Complete with an en suite."

"A what?" I ask.

"It's own full bathroom."

"Oh, right. Does the shower have an mp3 player like the other Fundies have?" I laugh.

"Of course it does. My guest room is yours if you want. Just say the word."

"Time's up," Rob barks, barging in all of a sudden. He grabs Prince by the arm and pulls him along.

"Relax, Fletcher," Prince chuckles. "I know when I'm not wanted." Walking away, he hollers, "Let me know what you decide, princess, and I'll make it happen!"

"Okay," I laugh, shaking my head. With them gone, I look around for Mimi. I have to tell her about this ridiculousness. Can you believe it? Me living with Prince? How crazy would that be?

Before I can find her, Rob finds me. He's alone.

"Say yes," he says without explanation.

"What?" I laugh.

"Move in with him."

"With Prince?"

Rob nods.

I don't know what to say. Here I was expecting Rob might ask me to move in with him. Or at least sleep in his bed tonight, for at least *one* night. Maybe two. He doesn't even give me that. What is up with him? I search his mahogany eyes for a clue, but they're dark mirrors.

"What about..." I trail off. I wanted to ask him, what about us. But he's making it pretty damn clear where we stand. Nowhere. Suddenly angry, I blurt, "Fine. I'll move in with effing Prince! I hope you're happy!"

Rob's face is a stone mask. The same dark gargoyle I saw in the backseat of Mr. Ralston's Mercedes the day we met.

I'd like at least a tiny bit of resistance from Rob.

He doesn't offer any.

"Is that what you want?" I huff. "Me living with Prince?"

"Yes," Rob grunts.

"You don't mind me sleeping in his bed?" I'm making the guest bedroom situation sound like more than it is.

"He said his guest bedroom," Rob says tensely.

"You're okay with that? Me living in Prince's guest bedroom?" I'm trying to get Rob to say no, he doesn't want me living with Prince, he wants me living with him in the Monastery. I arch an eyebrow, hoping for the answer I want to hear.

Rob's lips are dancing like they want to snarl but he doesn't. "If that's what it takes, yes."

"If that's what what takes?" I snort.

"We went over this before." Rob's eyes blaze with rage. "Are you in or out, Mouth?"

"Whatever you say, *Rob*," I sneer irritation.

So much for sleeping with Rob tonight.

I'm suddenly not in the mood.

When we get back to campus, Ms. Braunschott and Mr. Guerrero are waiting for the work-study kids looking pissed. Having *that* many kids sneak out doesn't go unnoticed. I guess we're busted? No, because Prince steps up for everyone and explains that he needed our services for the evening, his words. Brawny and Mr. Guerrero can only harrumph as we stroll past and filter back to our rooms without any consequences.

Being friends with rich royalty does have its privileges.

Chapter 32

"Will this work?" Prince asks.

"Oh my God," I laugh, standing just inside the double doors in his private penthouse suite at the top of the West Wing. It's *better* than an ultra-exclusive high-rise penthouse loft in New York City or wherever. I've got all my stuff, which wasn't much. Prince is carrying my school books, which I couldn't manage on top of my work clothes, school uniform and several spare uniform shirts, all of which are on hangers. I sigh, "This is insane. How come I've never been up here?"

"Only the most trusted college-age work-study maids are allowed up here."

I roll my eyes, "Is it possible for you to *not* sound snooty *all* the time?"

"No," he chuckles.

"I can't believe Brawny agreed to this." I was there in her office watching him talk her into this not ten minutes ago. I still can't quite believe he convinced her.

"I can."

"You're so full of yourself."

"Would you have it any other way?"

"Yes," I laugh. "Can you be normal for like, five minutes?"

"Normal is boring."

"How about not arrogant? Can you do that?"

He sniffs, "It'll be an effort, but I'll try. After you, Marianne."

"You don't have to call me that," I blush.

"I like to."

"Okay then," I smile. "How far is it to the guest room? Should we walk or take a golf cart or whatever?" The suite is *that* big. It's like the inside of a luxury warehouse, not a dorm room.

Prince checks his watch, the Bugatti one. "The next horse and carriage will be here any minute."

"Stop," I laugh and start walking. The main area is a living room with high ceilings and a two-story tall wall of windows and enough couches for like twenty people to sit around and enjoy the view when the sun's out. At the moment it's dark out, and the elaborate light fixtures, which look like floating stars, reflect off the glass.

Prince slides out of his suit jacket and lays it across the couch like he assumes someone else will pick it up for him, because of course they probably do, and have been doing since the day Prince was born. I know it's not just him. Since being a maid here, I've picked up more than my fair share of Fundy boys' clothes laying around their rooms. Whatever. If Prince thinks I'm picking up his clothes, he can suck it.

A gravity-defying spiral staircase in the middle of the living room leads up to the loft level. By loft I mean second story of this warehouse mansion. Up there, I see several doors along the balcony and a hallway leading to the back with more doors.

I snort, "How many effing rooms does this place have?"

"More than I need," he grins.

Downstairs to the side is a full-size kitchen and dining area with a classy minimalist table for eight. It's covered in expensive place settings and a center piece exploding with fragrant flowers.

I say, "Are those flowers from the shop on campus?" Every day on my way to class I pass the Castle Hill Academy Florist shop. Yes, the school has its own florist. I never go in. What do I need flowers for? I can't afford them. But I do see Fundy boys buying bouquets all the time for Fundy girls. Must be nice to have money to burn.

"They are," Prince nods. "They bring them up every morning."

"No way! What's that cost?"

"A small fortune."

"Do you really need fresh flowers *daily?* I mean, isn't that a bit excessive?"

"I never really thought about it."

"Maybe you should. Some people can't even afford fresh water."

"You have a point," he nods. "From this day forward I'll have the staff replace the fresh flowers with something permanent, and I'll donate the funds for the flowers to the charity of your choosing."

"Are you serious?" I drawl.

"Very. Name a charity."

"Um," I hesitate. "I don't know. How about Save The Children?" It's the only one I know off the top of my head. "They're all about bringing clean water to whoever doesn't have it."

"Done. Anything else?"

"I'm accepting donations." I wink and hold out my hand.

"How much do you need?"

"Totally kidding!" I drop my hand and laugh guiltily because I'm sort of not kidding, but I would never take Prince's money even if he offered.

"I'm not," Prince grins. He's serious. "How much money do you need?"

"Um, thanks, really, but I'll be happy if you just show me my room. It's getting super late and I can barely keep my eyes open." I yawn for real as I say it.

"This way," Prince says.

Did I mention this is insane? I'm moving in with the hottest surfer stud I've ever met, and he's rich as sin! It really is crazy, but here I am.

We turn a corner downstairs and go down a short hallway.

Prince opens the glass-and-wood door, "It's all yours."

"Wow," I laugh when I see the fully furnished bedroom. It has a plush queen-size bed, stylish furniture including two chairs and low table in front of the entertainment center, bookcases with antique books and artful shelf nicknacks, and big windows that probably have a great view during the day.

Prince sets my books on the table and takes my clothes. He walks through another door in the room. I follow him into a walk-in closet. He turns on recessed ceiling lights, which are like tiny spotlights, and hangs my two outfits and shirts on the empty racks.

"We'll need to fill this out," he says, referring to the empty racks.

"Huh?"

"You need more than two sets of clothes in your wardrobe."

"I have more." I hold up my arms, meaning the leather jacket and band shirt I'm wearing. "See? Three outfits."

"I mean more *nice* clothes."

I roll my eyes. "I thought you said you wouldn't be snooty for at least five minutes."

"It's been six," he winks.

"You're terrible," I smirk and suddenly yawn again. "Sure is getting late." I walk out of the walk-in, hoping he'll take the hint and follow.

He does. "If you need anything, just whistle."

I expect him to linger but he closes the door on his way out.

It doesn't take long for me to get ready for bed. I know my way around the fancy shower fixture because it's similar to the ones in the rest of the West Wing dorms, only with more nozzles. After rinsing off, I slip into bed and lay there with the bedside lamp still on. I sort of want to enjoy the view of my room a few more minutes before going to sleep. I really can't believe I'm here. I've never slept any place this nice, not ever. With a contented sigh, I pull the covers up to my chin and snuggle in to enjoy the view.

Do I feel guilty I'm up here in the lap of luxury while Mimi, Luna, and the other work-study girls are stuck down in the drafty Convent?

You better believe it.

It's totally not fair.

I'm honestly not sure how long I can do this. Tonight, sure. But after tonight? I'll have to seriously reconsider going back to my old room where I belong.

A soft knock on my door startles me.

"It's Prince," he mutters, his voice a gentle rumble in the quiet of the silent suite. The door has a pane of floor-length smoky glass set in the frame, but I can see his silhouette backlit by the light in the hallway.

"What?"

The door unlatches and he leans in. He's wearing lightweight pajama pants and nothing else.

Oh.

My.

Gabs.

I mean abs.

They're perfect. All of him is perfect. Sweet heat ripples through my body in sensuous waves.

"You warm enough?" he asks softly.

"What?!" I giggle, burning with blush.

"The thermostat. I turned it up a tad so you won't be cold."

"Oh, erm, sure. It's fine." I'm boiling, but it isn't because of the thermostat. Gabs! I don't know how I'll ever get to sleep now.

"If you get too hot—" he trails off suggestively.

I'm ready to boil over, but I'm not telling him that. That might lead to me doing something I shouldn't.

"—just whistle and I'll *come* running," he finishes, his voice dripping with sexual innuendo.

"Go away!" I giggle and throw a pillow at him.

"Just whistle," he chuckles and closes the door.

I turn off my bedside lamp and lay there thrumming in frustration for over an hour. Sleep doesn't come until my fingers get the job done.

<(—)>

"Rise and shine." It's Prince outside my room.

"Shine?" I groan from the lonely bed. "It's pitch black out! Would you go away so I can sleep?!"

"It's almost ten."

"At night? How long did I sleep?"

"No, in the morning. You want me to come back in an hour?"

"Don't come back until the sun's up!" I moan.

"It is up," he chuckles through the door. "The blinds are blocking it out."

"What blinds? I don't remember any blinds."

"I'll fade them back."

"Huh?"

A second later, the windows facing outside lighten slowly. So does the bedroom door. Now I can see Prince's silhouette in the hallway. Outside the window, I see the roofs of the campus buildings below and the surrounding hillside, but it's dark like sunglasses.

"How'd you do that?" I marvel, getting out of bed to go look out the window.

"With my phone."

"Why is it still so dark?"

"I set it at fifty percent on a ten second fade. It'll go to a hundred percent after a few minutes. I didn't want to blind you. Give your eyes time to adjust. Mind if I come in?"

"Sure."

When he opens the door, bright light floods in.

I crinkle my eyes and hold up my hand to fend off the glare.

"Sorry," he says and quickly closes the door, returning my room back to a soft ambiance. He's holding a breakfast tray in one hand, his phone in the other, and he's wearing his pajama pants again and nothing else. Gabs!

"What's that?" I beam, looking at the tray of food.

"Breakfast in bed," he grins.

"Awww. Did you make it for me?"

He smirks, "I *arranged* to have it made. If you get back in bed, I'll bring it to you."

How can I resist? Giggling, I dash back into bed and pull up the covers sitting up.

He carries the tray over and sets it over my legs. "Hot buttered croissants made fresh this morning, a selection of muffins including blueberry, blackberry and boysenberry, vegetarian omelette with shiitake mushrooms, and fresh strawberries flown in this morning from Argentina since they're out of season here."

"Uh uh," I laugh. "You did not order those for me."

He chuckles guiltily, "I had them ordered for me yesterday morning for today. This was supposed to be my breakfast. I already ordered a second breakfast for myself, and it's on its way, but I thought you might like this while everything's fresh."

"How generous," I snicker. "You're too much, you know that?"

"Too much for you?"

"Erm…" I laugh and look at my food. My mouth is watering looking at the food. "Can I eat?"

"Dig in."

"Have a seat." I motion toward the edge of the bed.

He sits. In broad daylight, which is now streaming brightly through the windows, his tan skin is flawless and caramel smooth. The muscles underneath are equally sweet. Gabs!

I savor his body with my eyes while my mouth savors breakfast.

He watches me closely while I chew.

"What?" I titter nervously.

"Enjoying the view," he grins, his blue eyes on mine.

"Whatever," I laugh and bite down on sweet strawberries.

It took Prince maybe eight hours to make me feel completely spoiled. No, I'm not *completely* spoiled. You're only completely spoiled if you get used to it like it's normal.

I don't think I'll ever get used to living like this.

Chapter 33

The first Friday in December rolls in, bringing with it a blizzard of icy stares and glares from every Fundy girl I pass on campus. I swear, the tea about me living with Prince made the rounds faster than the Black Plague blanketed Europe in the 14th century.

Now everybody knows I'm a dirty witch living in sin. Next they'll be dunking me underwater to see if I drown or not, or slapping a scarlet A on my chest and throwing rotten tomatoes and old eggs at me wherever I go.

And I'm like, "Hello, twenty-first century! We're just roommates!"

To me, it's not even a big deal. I've lived with tons of hot guys in foster care over the years. Grayson, Kade, and so many others. Here, it's like some kind of divine revelation. Gasp! A boy living with a girl! How could they?! Surely, this signals the coming of the apocalypse and the fiery end of human propriety!

From the work-study girls, I get a lot of "You go, girl!" At least they're grounded in reality.

From the Fundy girls, I get nothing but hate and petty jealousy. You'd think I stole *their* boyfriend.

Last time I checked, Prince wasn't dating any of them, at least not according to the gossip I've heard since getting here. According to the rumors, Prince is a manwhore. I already knew that. But he isn't dating anyone currently. Now I live with him. We're not hooking up. And the problem is…?

It's not like the faculty cares.

Every time I pass Ms. Skelter on campus, she smiles politely and says things like, "How are your studies coming along, Mizz Angerman?"

I always say, "Great."

When I report in with Ms. Braunschott about my maid duties, she never mentions anything about my living situation. She's all business, and I guess me living with Prince isn't any of hers.

The teachers don't say anything at all.

Anyway, I guess the Fundy girls are just jealous I landed the hottest man on campus.

Okay, maybe I'm exaggerating, because there hasn't been any landing, ahem, and there are other hot men on campus I sort of have my eye on.

Men like Rob.

Honestly, I don't know what's up with him. We haven't talked since his band's campfire after party.

Did I piss him off moving in with Prince? Was Rob testing me when he told me to say yes? Did he really want me to say no? I can never tell with Rob. He takes mysterious to a whole other level.

"I need you to do something for me," Rob blurts in my ear a week later when he catches me on my way to US History after the morning break. He falls into step beside me as I walk.

I gasp in surprise, "Geez! You scared the crap out of me!"

"My bad."

"You sure know how to sneak up on a person."

"Old habits."

"Huh?"

"Never mind. I need a favor."

"Nice to see you too," I sneer.

He grunts and rolls his eyes. "Can you help me out or not?"

I stop and search his eyes.

They're the mahogany mirrors I remember from the band after party, and I have no idea what he's thinking.

I tease, "Aren't you going to ask me about living with Prince? It's the talk of the town these days."

"No," he snaps. "I don't want to hear about it."

"Sor-*ry*," I snark.

"Can you meet me at the lacrosse field after your last class so we can talk?"

"Can't you tell me now?" I groan. "I have a ton of homework."

"No. We'll talk later." His eyes dart around suspiciously.

"Erm, okay?" I crinkle my nose and shake my head, "Why're you acting like such a creeper all of a sudden? Is it because—"

"Shh. Not here."

"Cameras, right?" I smirk.

He nods, "Meet me at the field after your last class." He spins around and walks off before I can say anything else.

Whatever.

I continue to History class and sit through that, taking copious notes about the framing of the US Constitution with my fountain pen. I've never done so much elaborate handwriting in my life as I have since getting here, and I'm getting a lot better at it. When I started, my personal notes were all printed, but now my leather bound Castle Hill notebooks are bursting with cursive. I kind of enjoy it, actually.

Something about writing in looping script helps me focus better. Who knew?

On my way out the door to my next class, AP English, someone snarks in my ear:

"Hey, gutter slut." It's Elizabeth. She came out of nowhere. "Does Prince know you're two-timing him with Rob?"

"What are you talking about?" I titter.

"I saw you talking to Rob before third period."

If I didn't know better, I might say Azielbeth here might have a thing for Rob? Or is it just her thing for Prince? I'm not sure. I glare at her, "Are you following me again, *Azzie?*"

She ignores my question. "If Prince finds out you're meeting up with Rob, he'll kick you out of his penthouse."

"Who says I'm meeting with Rob?"

"I heard you talking to him."

"Stalker much?" I grumble.

"Doesn't change the truth. Prince won't be happy when he finds out."

I scowl, "What, are you going to tell him?"

"If you piss me off," she shrugs a superior smile and examines her nails, which I notice are freshly manicured. The style is classic French, but the usual white free edge at the end of the nail is shiny gold, and there's a precise silver loop circling around the back of the nail near the cuticle, leaving the center of the nail a perfectly natural pink. Very classy.

Did Azzie have a manicure? Crap. I don't remember. I never looked that close. That would've been proof Azzie is Elizabeth. Eh, it doesn't matter. It's obvious to anyone with eyes that Elizabeth here *is* Azzie.

Elizabeth yawns, "You know, the more you fuck Prince, the more he'll fuck you over in the end."

"Is that what he did to you?"

She hmphs.

I want to tell her the truth hurts, but I'm not a bitch, so I walk around her and never look back.

When my seventh period drama class ends, I make my way to the fields. I'm not sure which one is for lacrosse until I see it's the one *without* the football team on it. A bunch of Fundy boys are wearing helmets and pads on that field, and running plays. In one, I see an offensive player with the ball. He's already in the process of getting tackled by a defense guy when he suddenly gets speared out of nowhere by a *second* defense guy. The second hit sends the poor offensive player flying. You can hear the smashing of the savage tackle from a distance.

I can't help but cringe.

Whoever did the tackle is an animal.

Mr. Perkins, the PE teacher who made me run laps, rushes over and blows his whistle and shouts in the face of the second defense man who's still standing over the downed offensive player. "That was a late hit, Montforte! I don't wanna see that shit during practice, you understand! You trying to kill your own teammates?!"

Montforte? Does he mean Duke?

"Are you listening to me, Montforte?!" Mr. Perkins shouts.

Montforte says something, but I can't hear it from here.

"What did you just say?!" Mr. Perkins bellows.

Another inaudible response from Montforte.

Mr. Perkins explodes, "Showers! Now! I will not have that attitude on my field, Montforte! Move it! Move! MOVE!!"

Montforte marches off the field, his slow walk the only sign of defiance. He takes his helmet off and lets it dangle from his hand. It is Duke, his dark hair sweaty and disheveled, his face a hateful mask.

Not wanting him to see me, I head to the other field. I see what looks like Rob, Jonah, and Skill sitting on the lacrosse bleachers. They're tiny at this distance, but you can't miss Skill's scarlet hair, and I can make out Jonah from his giant form. No one on campus is as big as him.

When they see me, they amble off the bleachers and walk behind them.

I roll my eyes and follow.

The three of them stand there by the chainlink fence covering the bleacher backs wearing coveralls and muttering to each other.

I ask, "Why couldn't we talk on the bleachers?"

"Too many watching eyes," Rob says.

"Whatever," I grumble. I fold my arms across my chest. "Where's Tucker? Shouldn't he be here too?"

Jonah says, "He's in the kitchen. They're prepping dinner for the Fundies."

I nod, not caring. "Soooo, what's this about?" With the other two here, it's obviously not about me and Rob and whatever thing he and I do or don't have going.

Skill says, "We need you to put cameras in Prince's penthouse suite."

"Cameras?" I scoff. "For what?"

"For collecting evidence," Rob says.

"What kind of evidence?"

"Any kind we can get."

Skill lifts up a leather Castle Hill book bag that matches mine. He opens it. "These wifi cameras are battery powered, and voice and motion activated." He pulls out a handful to show. The cameras are tiny black cubes the size of gambling dice, but without the pips. Instead, they have a single little lens. "We need you to hide them wherever you can in Prince's suite. Try to put them where they'll see Prince's face the most."

"His face?"

"Yeah," Skill nods.

"Why?" I'm not liking the sound of this.

Rob says, "Remember what we said about taking his family down?"

I sigh, "I thought you wanted to take down the Silicones' families."

"Who?" Skill asks.

"Elizabeth, Jacqueline, and Victoria."

"We're working on them," Rob says. "We need *you* to get intel on Prince."

"Intel?"

The trio of rough and ready Poor Boys all nod, sporting hopeful looks.

"Fine," I sigh. "What else?"

Skill pulls out a wireless router. The same one I've seen in the Fundy dorm rooms. "Replace Prince's router with this one."

"How do I do that?"

"Unplug his and plug this one in."

"Won't he know it's different? Like, it'll have a different password or network name or whatever?"

"That's all taken care of," Skill says. "Just switch them out. He'll never know."

"What's it do?"

"It's a normal router, but I programmed it to capture data from the cameras. And other stuff."

"Whatever. What do I do with his old router after I switch it out with yours? Keep it, or…?"

"Give it to me over at IT. Tell Arthur or whoever one of the Fundy boys said it was broken."

"But it's not, is it?"

Skill smirks, "Those Fundies are always saying things are broken when they're a day old. You know how it is, if it needs dusting, it's broken, and they're like, gimme a new one," he snivels for effect, imitating every Fundy goblin boy ever.

"Yeah," I grin.

"Anything else?" he asks.

"How long do the camera batteries last? Just curious."

"A week or two, depending on how active they are. I'll make sure you have a new batch of cameras to switch out the old ones then."

"How many times do I have to do that?"

"As many as it takes."

I groan, "I have to hide cameras in Prince's suite every week or two until forever?"

Rob asks, "Do you not want to do this?"

"Kind of no," I say.

Jonah says, "This isn't for us, Mary. Remember what Tucker said about the kids who got screwed over by Grandma Morgan-Hearst?"

"Yes," I groan. "I've had nightmares about them." It's true. Not every night, but I did once, and *I* was one of the kids slaving away at gunpoint in a factory somewhere, sweating my ass off and hating life like you wouldn't believe. Guess who my nightmare guard was? Gladys with a gun. Wearing some kind of military uniform. It was almost too real. Probably PTSD, like Rob said back when, only made worse by my time locked in that stupid iron maiden.

"Remember, Mary," Jonah says, "Prince's family isn't any better than Elizabeth's."

"Fine," I sigh. "I'll do it. Is that it? Or can I go?"

"That's it," Rob says. "Anything to report on your end?"

"Report?" I scoff. "What, are we soldiers now?"

"No," Rob smirks grimly. "Soldiers follow orders. We don't." He lets that sink in. "Like I said, anything to report?"

I think for a moment and smirk, "Elizabeth saw me and you talking earlier and overheard you say we should meet up today."

Rob's eyes goggle, "Did she follow you?"

I cringe, "Erm, I kind of forgot until just now."

"Shit," Rob hisses. He, Jonah, and Skill scatter in two different directions, crouching low and running toward the front of the bleachers.

"Where are you going?!" I whine, annoyed I'm now stuck in their drama.

"Stay there!" Rob snips before turning a corner.

"Fine," I grumble to myself and wait.

A few minutes later, the three of them return, looking irritated.

"Was she there spying?" I tease.

"We're clear," Jonah says ominously.

Rob says, "Mary, you have to tell us immediately if *anything* like that happens again. It's mission critical. No one can know what we're doing. This is serious shit. If we get caught, we get kicked out. You know what that means. Prison. Do you understand?"

"Yes! I'm not an idiot!" Honestly, I hadn't considered it until now, but *obviously* spying on a Fundy is not approved behavior in the Castle Hill student handbook.

Rob nods. "Did Elizabeth say anything about you and me?"

"She threatened to tell Prince."

"Tell him what?"

I roll my eyes, "That we have a thing. You and me."

"What kind of thing?"

"I don't know," I grouse. "I assume she meant we're hooking up."

Skill and Jonah both goggle at that.

"You dirty fucking dog!" Skill laughs, elbowing Rob's muscled arm. "You and War Paint hook up and you don't tell us?!"

"We didn't hook up," Rob barks, glaring at me like he's disgusted by the idea of us being together and he's only talking about it because I brought it up.

"And we won't be either," I say for the benefit of Skill and Jonah, and to piss off Rob.

Skill grins, "If you aren't hooking up with Rob, maybe we should be hooking up."

Jonah barks, "Not now, Skill."

Rob glares at Skill but says nothing.

I want to tell Rob I'd be disgusted if we *had* hooked up. I never should've let him take me to his room on Halloween night to cuddle. What was I thinking?! He's not into me. He never was. He's like, I don't know, my annoyingly overprotective asshat of a big brother or something. Like I need one of those. I've already got Jonah for that, and he's not one-tenth as infuriating as Rob. Jonah is like the perfect big brother every girl wishes she had. Rob is just a perfect ass.

"Can I go now?" I whine.

Skill holds up the book bag with the cameras and says, "Give me yours."

"My bag?"

"Yeah."

"Why? Can't I just keep my book bag and put your cameras in?"

"Not with the router," he says insistently. "Just give it."

"Fine," I sigh and make the switch. "When do I get *my* bag back? It has my notebook and stuff."

"I'll put it in your locker."

"You don't have my combo."

"I'll get it," Skill says suspiciously.

"You can do that?" I ask.

"We can do anything we damn well please," he grins with smarmy confidence.

What am I getting myself into?

Skill says, "Make sure you spread the cameras around Prince's suite. We want maximum coverage. Focus on his face."

"Fine."

Rob says, "Hide them where Prince won't find them."

"I know!" I groan and walk away slowly.

Why do I not like whatever it is I've agreed to do? Is it because I really have no idea what Rob and crew plan to do? Or is it because Prince has been nothing but nice to me and now I'm betraying his trust? Time will tell, but I'm starting to worry this won't end well for anybody.

The funny thing about disasters is, nobody ever sees them coming, do they?

Chapter 34

The only place on campus with internet access is the school library. Unlike the living and dining areas on campus, where the work-study kids are segregated from the Fundies, the library is for everyone.

The Evelyn Morgan-Hearst library.

As I march past the sign and up the steps toward the imposing stone building, I have to wonder if Evelyn is mean old Grandma Morgan-Hearst the child slave lord Jonah and Tucker mentioned, or some other older Morgan-Hearst matron who owned actual slaves back in the Civil War?

I hate to think.

More importantly, I'd like to find out what sort of shenanigans the Lancaster family have or have not gotten themselves into. Is Prince's family as bad as Rob and the Poor Boys suggest? If I can find proof, it might make me feel better about spying on him. If not, I may have to rethink my agreement and return these cameras to Skill or whoever.

I have to wait for a computer because every one is taken by a work-study kid because we aren't allowed to own a computer. Obviously, Fundies have their own laptops and use wifi. I pencil my name onto the waiting list, check out a calculator from the librarian, find an empty study carrel, and start on my trig homework, busying myself computing vectors and graphing a bunch of different trigonometric functions.

When it's my turn for the computer, my curiosity gets the best of me and I Google "Morgan-Hearst" first. I'm horrified but not surprised by what I find. There's no photos of over-worked kids in sweatshops because it was way back in the 1970s, I guess, but I do find a few grainy black-and-white photos of Evelyn Morgan-Hearst on the socialite pages of the New York papers from back then.

In them, Evelyn wears a variety of frumpy dresses, always with pearls, with her hair up and surrounded by dashing men in tuxedos who have bushy mustaches, sideburns, shaggy long hair, and less than perfect teeth. Definitely the 70s.

Evelyn is blonde and beautiful and the spitting image of Elizabeth aka Azzie. Heck, she could *be* her, but I don't think time travel is a thing, and I don't think Evelyn found the fountain of youth to keep herself young. Unless she eats babies or puppies or kittens or whatever witches like to suck the youth out of.

Nah.

The other thing I find is a scan of an old article from the New York

Times that paints a pretty dark picture of the Morgan-Hearst business empire, naming Evelyn as Chairman of Morgan-Hearst Industries and pinning the blame on her for a range of dubious business practices, especially overseas. The article ends by suggesting the Morgan-Hearst empire is under ongoing federal investigation for several unnamed humanitarian violations. Everyone knows what that means. Treating people worse than dirt.

I grimace a sigh. I guess Rob and the Poor Boys weren't exaggerating.

"Mugshot," someone purrs in my ear, kissing my skin with a scent of minty musk.

"Chase," I smirk and I turn to face him sitting next to me. I glare at him, "Do you mind? I'm trying to study."

"What're you studying?" He looks at the screen.

I hastily X out of the browser window with the New York Times article and smirk, "I was looking up recipes for man repellant."

"Whatever it is, it isn't working." He slides his hand up my stocking-covered thigh toward the entrance of my school skirt.

"Would you stop?!" I slap his hand away laughing in disbelief. "We're in the library!"

Some of the nearby kids in carrels glance our direction before going back to studying.

Chase says, "We should go somewhere else then."

My jaw drops and I whisper, "No-a! What is wrong with you?!" If Chase wasn't so freakishly gorgeous, I would've punched him in the face months ago and every day since. But he *is* that hot. A tad handsy, but it's hard to hold it against him and his smoky topaz eyes. Every time I see them, a bonfire of hope lights in my breasts, hope that he's sincere instead of an opportunist, hope that our kiss at the All Hallows' Ball was more than a passing thing.

"The only thing wrong with me," he says, "is you, mugshot."

"Not my problem," I smirk.

"You're mine. I can't get you out of my head. Ever since you moved in with Prince, I keep asking myself where I went wrong."

"You're pathetically predictable, Chase. You just want what you can't have. Whatever happened to that blonde you screwed in drama class, the one in the theater box?"

"She came," he grins. "Several times."

I laugh in disgust, "Do you hear yourself?"

"No, but I heard her," he chuckles, eyes faraway like he's remembering. "So did everybody, if I remember."

"I've known plenty of boys like you, Chase. You're all sluts."

"How well?"

"How well have I known them?" I ask in surprise.

He nods, his eyes smoking with lust.

"That's none of your business!" I hiss. "Would you go! I'm busy!" I give him a shove.

"Go to the winter formal with me."

"Work-study girls aren't allowed." Ever since Thanksgiving, I've been hearing the work-study girls grumbling about the winter formal because they're not allowed to go. Are they jealous the Fundy girls get to go and we don't? Of course they are. Nobody likes living on the bottom rung of a classist society run by elitist assholes. Me, I've tried to tune it out and not worry about it. Who needs to go to a stupid dance with snooty Fundies? Knowing them, it would be a repeat of Halloween, except the iron maiden would have spikes this time to actually stab me.

"If you're my date, it won't be a problem getting you in. Go with me."

"No-a! You know what happened Halloween."

He smirks, "I kissed the fuck out of you."

"Not that, ass! The thing! With the—!" I don't want to say iron maiden. "With me getting assaulted! Locked in the stabby-stabbing cage?! Duh! Remember? I don't want that happening again! No stupid dance is worth that!"

"If we're joined at the hip the whole night," he says it like he's implying a long lusty night of sex, "there is zero chance of that happening. I'll protect you, mugshot. I won't let those bitches get you down. But I will be more than glad to go down all damn night, if that's what it takes." He offers a sly grin. "Go with me, mugshot. I'll make it worth your while."

On paper, Chase's manwhoring words make him sound like a complete prick. Looking at him, it's like, honestly, it's like he's effing *mesmerizing*, okay? Men don't get any hotter than this one.

"Go with me," he says gently.

I sigh, "Is that how you ask?" I purse my lips and fold my arms across my school jacket.

"Is that how you say yes?" He glimmers a grin.

"No-a!" I laugh.

"Your laugh says yes."

He's right about that, but I am not going to get myself caught up in more drama. I've had too much already. If I wasn't living with Prince, who has not mentioned any winter formal and certainly not asked me to go, I would definitely say yes to Chase. It's just a dance. Not a wedding proposal. What's wrong with going to a dance? But I *am* living with Prince, and now I'm embroiled in Rob's spying drama. Going with

Chase sounds like a terrible idea.

I sigh, "No, Chase. I can't go. I need to focus on studying and my job, not some stupid dance."

His disappointed eyes search mine. He sighs and sits back in his chair. Runs his hand through his hair. He slides out of his chair onto one knee, takes my hand in his, and says, "Mary, will you please go to the winter formal with me? I'd be honored if you said yes."

I giggle gleefully. All of a sudden, it *is* like an effing wedding proposal. Nobody has ever gotten down on one knee for me for any reason. Okay, Prince kissed my shoes the other night, but he owed me for that. For what he did. That was payback. This is, it's magical.

Whispers and tittering erupt around us.

I distinctly hear work-study girls gushing about Chase, saying he's never done anything like this. I wouldn't know, but I suspect they're correct. Chase never bows to anybody that I've seen, least of all women.

Maybe I *should* say yes.

He's asking so nicely.

Then I remember Mimi.

I've known her long enough to know she's always talking about Chase. Always. It's still unclear if they've ever hooked up, or if he's interested in her or not. No, he *has* to be. She's way better looking than I'll ever be. He must've noticed her at the very least. She would kill me if I said yes to him. I would never do that to her. Chase is her thing, not mine.

I sigh, "Forget it, Chase. Dances aren't my thing. Sorry."

There are gasps from the surrounding work-study kids. I forgot we had an audience. They're mumbling about Chase getting shot down. Some of the girls are catty about it, like they're glad I said no because Chase is getting what he deserves. Others sound hopeful he'll ask *them* out.

Chase hears them, but he's ignoring them, his topaz eyes locked on mine.

I say, "Why don't you ask Mimi? I'm sure she'd love to go with you."

Chase's face is blank. He's completely unreadable. He stands up and arches a thoughtful eyebrow. "Your loss, mugshot." He suddenly turns and goes, hands stuffed in the pockets of his slacks.

Did I piss him off?

Or hurt his feelings?

Hard to say either way.

We did kiss.

Then again, he kisses everybody.

I'm not going to worry about it. I have bigger fish to spy. I mean fry.

No, both.

I open a browser window and search online for dirt on Prince's family.

Surprise, surprise.

Prince J. Lancaster II, aka Prince's dad because duh, how many can there possibly be, is named in a number of criminal cases for white collar crimes in the 80s and 90s. Securities & Exchange Commission violations. Insider trading on the stock market. Business fraud. He sure was a busy little thief.

According to the article in The Wall Street Journal, the biggest case was about Dad Lancaster getting insider information from his mistress, a woman married to some oil executive whose petroleum company was about to go belly up. Dad Lancaster used this information to sell a shit-ton of oil shares before the stock price collapsed, saving himself from losing tens of millions of dollars back in the day.

The SEC didn't like that and took civil action against Dad Lancaster. His team of lawyers negotiated a sweetheart deal of six months in a country club jail, but they slapped him with a hefty fine of $2.5 million dollars, which must've been a ton of money back then. I mean, it's a ton of money now, I can't imagine having that much, but it was more then.

Anyway, six months later, Dad Lancaster walked out of prison a free man and married his mistress. Her husband, the old oil tycoon, had died of a stroke immediately after his oil company went bust, which was long before Dad Lancaster even went to trial.

Shortly after being set free, Dad Lancaster started a family. They had four kids.

Gosh, does that mean Prince's mom is a cheater?

An ex-mistress?

That's weird.

It's also completely normal.

People cheat. What else is new?

After another hour of searching, it's time for me to get changed and head over to the West Wing to clean rooms.

I couldn't find anything worse about the Lancaster family than cheating the system and cheating on husbands. They aren't half as bad as the Morgan-Hearsts, but they aren't exactly model citizens. I'm not sure what Rob has planned with all these cameras I'm supposed to plant on Prince. Maybe it has something to do with money?

Who knows.

If I had more time, I'd search for dirt on Chase's family, and Duke's, and Victoria and Jacqueline's, but I don't. I'm sure they're terrible and I have toilets to scrub.

<(—)>

That night, I'm studying in Prince's guest bedroom by myself when he knocks on the open door frame.

"Hey, Marianne," he says. "I'm going out for a few hours."

"Oh?" I look up from my books. "Where to?"

"To a meeting."

"What kind of meeting?"

He forces a smile. "I can't say."

"Erm, okay." I shouldn't have asked. I wonder if he's going to a meeting at The Ivory Tower. I can't say decisively that he doesn't have some weird magister's cult leader uniform hidden under the suit he's wearing, and a creepy hood hidden in his jacket pocket, but he might.

"I'll be back in a few hours. Will you be okay here?"

"Of course," I smile.

Fifteen minutes after Prince leaves, when I'm confident he hasn't forgotten anything and won't make a surprise return, I switch out the wifi router in Prince's office upstairs with the one Skill gave me.

Did I mention Prince has the best office ever? It's like a stylish executive's corner office with windows on two corner walls and a terrific view, like he's already practicing being a CEO.

I plant Skill's little cameras throughout the penthouse, hiding them on shelves behind sculptures or in bookcases on top of dusty books that haven't been moved (they look like decorations nobody ever bothers to read), or wherever I can put them that's inconspicuous, except in my bedroom. I don't put any there. I like my privacy. I don't want Rob and the Poor Boys spying on me. Call me hypocritical. I don't care. I'm not helping them make any pervy videos of me in bed or whatever.

I don't think they'll be making any sex tapes of Prince either. There's nothing to tape. It's not like he's sneaking women into his bedroom at night. I'd hear. All he does is sleep. You can't make a sex tape without any sex.

I ignore my misgivings about this process and place more cameras throughout the penthouse. Surprisingly, it takes over an hour. The whole time, I cringe every time I hear the slightest creak, thinking Prince came back early, but he never does.

When I'm done, I make myself some tea in the kitchen to relax for a moment before I go back to studying.

I sure hope spying on Prince won't come back to haunt me. Nobody likes a spy.

<(—)>

Nearly every evening that week, Prince and I spend time studying together. Usually it's after dinner or later because he's got so many extra-curricular activities in his life, but he does have to study, and he hits the books hard each night, same as me.

When I admit I've been struggling with physics and trig, he is happy to help explain things. Turns out he's a bit of a math whiz and he took trig last year. Now he's in calculus, a year ahead of me and most kids at the academy.

Somehow, he makes math enjoyable. Normally, I just slog through it and hope for the best, but Prince makes it a game, turning every problem into a fun puzzle.

Does it hurt that he's so handsome?

Not one bit.

Every girl should have a hot surfer for a tutor.

The only thing stopping us from fooling around each night after studying is both our grades. I need to keep mine up to stay at the academy, and he needs to keep his up to stay competitive, or so he says.

"What do *your* grades matter?" I ask one evening. We're both lying on my bed in the guest bedroom with our books spread out between us. I always make sure we have books between us. If I didn't, I'm pretty sure we'd never get any studying done. "It's not like you need to be *more* successful. You already have everything you want in life."

"Not everything." He tosses me a sexy smirk, leaning on one elbow. "Some things take work." He gives me a pointed look.

I roll my eyes, pretty sure he means me. I'm not sure what he's working up to, but I am flattered. One good thing about Prince I can't say enough is, no matter how bold and brash and arrogant and entitled he may be, he never pressures me for anything. Especially not sex. I mean, he's been a saint since I moved in with him. He teases the crap out of me, sure, always flashing his abs, but he never pressures me.

He really is the perfect gentleman.

Which makes me feel like a total and complete ass for helping Rob spy on him. I never should've agreed to hide all those cameras. I have a sudden urge to walk around the penthouse giving every camera a one-finger salute, which I know Rob and company will see me doing. Good thing there aren't any in my bedroom, otherwise I might do it now, and Prince would ask questions about why I'm flipping off nothing. Don't want that.

"Something bothering you?" Prince asks.

"No," I lie. "Just tired."

"We should go to bed."

I blush brightly.

"You know what I mean," he chuckles, standing up from the bed. He picks up his books and notebooks. "Sleep tight, princess." He closes the door gently on his way out.

He really is perfect.

And I'm a perfect liar.

I don't know how long I can keep living like this. Sooner or later, the truth is going to rear its ugly head and take a bite out of my criminal activities.

That weekend, Prince disappears without explanation.

When I realize he isn't coming home Saturday night, I start to worry, which is stupid. He's probably doing some secret Ivory Tower thing, which is totally none of my business.

Unless he has a secret girlfriend here on campus?

I know he and Elizabeth, or Azzie or whatever she's calling herself today, used to be a thing, but I thought that stopped on Halloween. No, sooner. He said like a year ago. I mean, he didn't get back together with her, did he?

Not that I care.

I mean, I *really* don't care.

It's not like Prince and I are a thing. I'm his guest, not his girlfriend. And I'm spying on him! I'm sure he'd love to know that. Then I'd never be his girlfriend. Not that I want to.

Anyway, I'm sure it's nothing.

I'm sure he's not on some surfing getaway in Fiji or wherever and sleeping with every beach bunny he sees lounging on white sand beaches in their bikinis. He'd never be interested in that.

What I'm *not* sure about is whether or not he has a secret girlfriend in Fiji. And another in Australia. And Maui. And ten other countries I haven't thought of.

I tell myself I'm worrying over nothing.

We aren't even dating!

Not that I want to.

Nope.

I titter nervously to myself.

I hope he comes home soon.

Chapter 35

"What should I do about my hair?" I ask Mimi.

We're in her drafty Convent room studying one night after work. To help keep the cold out, she has stuffed the tiny open window with a pillow. It's actually a Fundy pillow she stole from the laundry room. Technically, she's not supposed to have it. Whenever Brawny Braunschott comes by, Mimi has to hide the pillow in the closet until she's gone.

My hair has grown out to almost two inches.

I say, "I was thinking I could bleach it, shave the sides, and spike the top."

Mimi rolls her eyes, "And violate hair policy in the student handbook. Ms. Skelter would never allow it."

I groan, "This place! It's like 1984 around here!"

"You mean the George Orwell book?"

"Yeah," I nod in disgust. "It's like they've criminalized happiness and any form of personal expression."

"Not if you're a rich kid."

"Don't remind me," I scowl.

"Too bad it's not The Hunger Games."

"Right? Give me a bow and some arrows and I'll go Fundy hunting."

"Two bows," she laughs. "We'll go hunting together. We'll hang the Silicones' heads over our beds like taxidermy trophies."

"Wouldn't that be nice," I sigh in defeat and run my fingers through my hair. "I should shave it all off again. At least then I'm unique, and that's allowed."

"Uh uh," she shakes her head. "Check the handbook. No shaved heads."

"I thought that's for boys."

"No, I think it's for everyone. Ms. Skelter probably let it slide for you when you got here because she didn't have a choice. Now you'll piss her off if you shave it again. Best thing to do is let it grow out."

"Whatever."

We go back to studying.

A short while later, Mimi says sarcastically, "Have you picked out your dress for the winter formal?"

My thoughts go to Chase asking me in the library and not her. If he has, she never mentioned it. You better believe I'm not mentioning Chase asking me! My eyes saucer but I try to hide it by focusing on my homework.

"I heard Chase asked you to go," Mimi says, her voice tense.

I'm not surprised she knows, but I cringe anyway. "Sorry, he snuck up and sprung it on me. I totally said no. I told him he should ask you. Did he?"

"You know how he is." Her face is tight and slightly irritated.

"Erm, I thought I did. Did he or didn't he? Ask you, I mean."

She relaxes into a giddy smile, "He totally did!"

"That's fantastic, Meems!" I jump off my bed and grab her in a laughing hug.

"I know, right? I never thought he would!" She's ecstatic.

I congratulate her for awhile until our excitement dies down into sighs, then I go back to my old bed to resume studying.

She says, "What about Prince?"

"What about him?"

"Have you two hooked up yet?" Her innocent question is so obviously not.

"No-a!" I throw the thin pillow off my bed at her. She throws it back. It hits me in the face, but I barely notice. "I forgot how thin these are."

"Already?" Mimi says, slightly jealous. She knows how plush the pillows are in the West Wing from cleaning and fluffing them. "How many does your bed have? Four?" It's the standard number for Fundy boy beds.

"Eight," I say, embarrassed.

"He pulled you right out of the slums, didn't he, Cinderella?"

"I can't help it!" I whine, feeling bad.

"You could've invited me," she sniffs. "This place is frigid." She glances at the pillow stuffed in her window. "Any chance I can room with you?"

My eyes light up. "You totally should! There's more than enough room in my bed! I mean, if you don't mind sharing."

"Sharing your bed or… sharing Prince?" She bites her lower lip and blushes.

"I told you already! I'm not sleeping with him, okay?!" I laugh. "Gosh! How many times do I have to tell you?!"

"I would be."

"Sleeping with him?"

"Prince is a stud. Who *wouldn't* sleep with him?"

"Brawny," I snort. "She'd be afraid of breaking him. She's *that* brawny."

"Totally," Mimi laughs. "I heard, back in Germany, she used to be married to a bear."

"An *actual* bear?" I frown doubtfully.

"Uh huh," she nods sincerely. "A grizzly, I think."

"They don't have grizzly bears in Germany."

"He's from Canada. He has dual citizenship. Canadian and German. He moved over for her."

"Did not," I snicker, picturing a bear wearing a red and white maple leaf ice hockey jersey and no pants. I throw my pillow at her again.

This time she hordes it and says, "Has Prince asked anyone?"

"Not that I know of."

"Who do you think he'll ask? Elizabeth?"

"I hope not."

"You? Has he asked you?"

"No."

"Are you disappointed?"

"Conflicted. I can't figure out what's up with Rob." I haven't told Mimi about my spying and I'm not going to, but she knows all about my Halloween cuddling after Rob saved me from the torture chamber. Meems and I had both thought it was the start of something serious until Rob basically ghosted me.

"Forget Rob. He's been ignoring you since Halloween."

I shrug. I can't tell her the truth. I promised I wouldn't and it's way too complicated anyway.

"You should ask Prince, Mare Bear. If you do, we can go to together."

"You and Chase and us?"

"Mmm-hmm," she nods. "I'll make sure those Fundy bitches don't try anything funny. If they do, I'll fuck all their boyfriends." She giggles with mischievous confidence. "See how they like that."

"You know," I muse, "so many of them are hot, that's not exactly a heinous idea."

"Right?" she grins guiltily.

"I mean, not that I'd want to—"

"Me neither."

"—but you could totally pull it off." I know Mimi could have any guy at Castle Hill she wants. All she has to do is take them up on their constant offers. Whenever she walks by groups of Fundy boys, the innuendos flood from them like it's hurricane season in the midwestern state of Sexual Harassment.

"Those Fundy bitches already think we're sluts, so why not?"

"Right?" I add.

"Not that I would."

"But you could."

She shrugs, "I'd rather have Chase."

"If things go haywire, we can both cut us some bitches. We'll get knives from the kitchen."

"How?"

"Tucker. I'm sure he'll steal some for us if we ask."

"Wow, Mary, listen to you." Mimi marvels. "When did you get so deadly?"

"What? I always carry a knife. It's only since I've been here and Mr. Ralston took mine away that I've been playing nice. Halloween wouldn't have happened if I'd had Grayson's knife." I've told Mimi about Grayson and Kade and all the other boys I've known a hundred times since I got here. We're always talking about boys. I'm surprised we ever get any studying done.

"Can you get us some big butcher knives? So we can butcher those bitches if they try anything? We'll go slasher movie on their asses. Ree! Ree! Ree!" She mimes a stabbing motion.

I titter snickery laughs. "Totally. Except, butcher knives might be hard to hide under our dresses. Maybe some paring knives or something small like that?"

"That'll work. All you have to do now is ask Prince to take you to the winter formal."

"I can't do that! He has to ask!"

"I don't mean *ask* ask. Hint. A lot. You know how to hint, don't you?"

"Have you ever been to the winter formal?" I ask nonchalantly over dinner with Prince.

"I have," Prince says after swallowing and blotting his mouth with his linen napkin.

We're in his kitchen, sitting at the bar on barstools, eating the food he ordered from room service. He doesn't eat with me every night, so this is nice. Most nights, he eats in the Palace Dining Hall without me. I'm not allowed in there. That's one rule Prince hasn't broken for my sake. Not that I notice. I'm always cleaning the West Wing while he's eating. When we do eat together, like tonight, we eat after I get back from work, and he always has dinner waiting for me. It feels eerily like we're a couple, which we're not, not that I know of.

I say, "Is it any fun? The winter formal?"

He shrugs, "If you like formal functions."

"What's it like?"

"Formal," he smirks and forks up more food.

I detect he doesn't want to talk about it. That's fine. I'll just hint. "I've heard it's lots of fun. Everybody's been talking about it. Does it live up to the hype or...?"

"Nothing ever does."

"Okay, granted, but it can't be terrible, can it?"

"Depends who you ask."

"Mmm," I nod. Why is he being so effing dodgy? Am I not supposed to ask? I mean, it's not like I'm asking him to ask me to go. I'm effing hinting. Take a hint, Prince! But seriously, I'm just making conversation and asking about a stupid dance. What's wrong with that?

He takes another bite and chews.

"Would you believe I've never been to a single high school dance?" It's true. I have been asked, but I've never gone because usually I'm in trouble with the vice principal, or I change schools before I can go to one, or I can't afford a nice dress for the more formal dances.

"Yes, I would believe it," Prince says and resumes chewing.

What kind of an effing answer is that?! Can this man not take an effing hint? Is he playing dumb? Or just plain dumb? I don't know, but my frustration kicks in like a rabid mule.

I suddenly blurt, "Ask me to the fricking winter formal already!"

Prince continues chewing like I'm not even there. Swallows. Blots his lips with the linen napkin. Folds it neatly and lays it beside his plate. Turns to me with a wicked grin. "I'm sorry. I simply can't resist watching you squirm."

"Ass!" I slap his muscled shoulder, which is currently covered in a thousand dollar dress shirt. I know it cost that much because he mentioned the price in one of his snootier moods.

He laughs. "Marianne, would you do me the honor of accompanying me to this year's winter formal?"

"No!" I jump up from my bar stool. "I have too much homework and too much work. You snooze, you lose!" I march back to the guest room and slam the door. Sit on the edge of the bed waiting.

Footsteps.

A knock at the door.

"Yes?" I titter.

He opens the door a crack and asks, "Do you want to hear begging?"

"A little," I giggle guiltily. "But only because you're such an ass."

Prince opens the door all the way. Unknots his tie with methodical confidence. Hangs it on the doorknob. Unbuttons his shirt while staring me down with burning blue eyes. Strips it off and tosses it over his shoulder. Plants his hands on his trim hips and flexes his abs. Smirks at me.

Gabs.

I snicker, "Is that supposed to be you begging?"

"Me beg?" he chuckles. "I never beg. I meant you."

I gawk at him, my mouth in an O.

"Wider," he says.

"What?" I frown.

"You'll need to open your mouth a little wider if you want to fit it all in."

I know exactly which it he means. "Get out!" I shoot to my feet, pointing over his shoulder. "Now! Out, out, out! I am never going to any dance with you ever, Prince John Lancaster the Turd!" Expecting him to back down I march forward.

He doesn't move. He just chuckles with cocky confidence.

I have no choice but to stop short. I'm afraid to touch him when he's shirtless. Not afraid to do it. Afraid of the consequences. It might quickly lead to us doing *things*. Ahem.

I whip my finger for emphasis and point. "Out of my room!"

"Or what?"

"Or I'll make you leave! Go, Prince!"

"Please make me," he chuckles.

I'm getting fucking flustered for exquisitely obvious reasons. "Leave! Please! Or put a shirt on! Anything!" Gabs!

"Are you begging, strumpet?"

"No-a! *You're* supposed to be begging!" We're inches apart and I'm a slick quivering mass of feminine flesh. He's a hard mountain of slabs of abs and tan surfing muscles.

"I told you, begging isn't my style. On you, I find it quite enticing."

I'm dying for him to kiss me right now. I don't care what happens. He can throw me on the bed behind me for all I care.

He says, "Do me the honor of going to the winter formal. Then we'll see about doing you."

I almost gawk and drop my jaw into another O, but I don't want to give him any ideas.

"Yes or no?" he asks.

"Fine! I'll go to the stupid dance!" Now kiss me already! I refuse to actually say it, but I'm dying for him to do it.

He caresses my chin with a single finger and plants a sensual kiss on my lips. My knees practically buckle from the sensation. I'd fall over but I think I'm floating. I open myself to let him slide all the way in and his tongue teases the tip of mine. I swear, it's the most erotic kiss I've ever had, like we're flying, I can't even describe it. Also, it's the first kiss we've shared since Halloween. I was starting to think he'd lost interest. Obviously not.

I moan, ready to let him deepen it.

Something suddenly chimes.

Prince's phone. In his pocket. He grunts and pulls away like he's in pain.

"I have to go," he hisses.

"Now?" I whine.

"A meeting."

"What?"

"I have an important meeting. I can't be late." He's already picking up his shirt and buttoning it back on. Gabs.

"Is this an Ivory Tower thing?"

He frowns. "How do you know about that?"

"Please. Everyone knows about that. You can see the tower from anywhere on campus."

"I know that," he nods in irritation, "but why would you ask if I was going to one of their meetings?"

"Duh! I heard you fighting with Elizabeth about it at Halloween. She said you're the magister or whatever."

Prince grimaces, "That woman cannot keep her mouth shut."

"So what? It's just some stupid club."

He slaps me with an angry glare.

I feel it like a physical thing. "Fine! Go to your stupid meeting! I'm sure it's more important than me anyway," I pout. Why am I acting like this? We're not even dating! I'm just his effing roommate! "Sorry. That came out wrong. Go to your meeting. I'm sure it's important. We don't have to go to any dance. You have your life, I have mine."

"What are you saying?" he says gently.

"I'm saying I should just move back into the Convent so I'm not in your way."

"You can't do that," he says with concern. "That place is horrendous."

"You think?" I snort. "How do you think Mimi and the other work-study girls feel about it? It's freezing over there! I shouldn't be living here! I don't deserve better than them! I feel like an ass for being here!"

"You shouldn't."

"Yes I should. I'm a work-study girl, Prince. Not a Fundy like you. Between my job and my homework, I don't have time for fancy dances."

"You would if you didn't have to work."

"I don't have any choice. It's part of the deal for not going to prison. I'm sure you know about that."

He shakes his head in frustration, "I don't care what the rules are. You don't have to work as a maid, Marianne. You have other options."

"No I don't!"

"You do if I make the arrangements. One phone call and I'll see to it you never have to work again while you're here at Castle Hill."

"I can't do that," I laugh. "What would Mimi and the other work-study kids think if all of a sudden I got special privileges none of them get?"

"They'd think they wished they were you."

"No, they'd hate me! Add that to the Fundies who already do, and that makes everyone in the school hating me, Prince!"

"I don't hate you," he mutters, head lowered, almost embarrassed. He lifts his jeweled blue eyes to mine and whispers, "Marianne, I, I think I, I..."

Suddenly, I'm on the edge of my toes wondering if he's suddenly going to drop the L-bomb.

"Marianne, the last couple weeks of you living here have been, I can't explain it. It's been the best two weeks of my life."

"It has?"

"I've never had so much fun."

"What do you mean? We barely see each other. Whenever we're here, all we do is study."

"True, but we have fun. You know that. Before you, I hated this place. I'd rather be surfing anywhere but here. Now all I want to do is be here with you. I don't even care about the surfing."

"What?!" I laugh. "You're always telling surfing stories like it's the best thing in the world."

"It is."

"But I'm not in them."

"You could be. Fly with me to Fiji over winter break."

"Um, I don't think Ms. Skelter would allow it." I already know from talking to Mimi that the work-study kids don't get to leave campus over winter break. Same as Thanksgiving weekend, we're stuck here.

"Princess, what have I told you about the rules?"

"They don't apply?"

"Exactly."

"I can't go to Fiji, Prince. For the same reason I can't live here. I'm going to alienate my friends. Unless you plan on taking *all* the work-study girls to Fiji."

He grows thoughtful. "It could be arranged. We'd have to charter several jumbo jets to get the lot of you over to Fiji. That many passports might be a problem. What about Maui? We could do that. It'll be rainy, and the surfing might be too intense for beginners, but we could at least get everyone there."

"Are you serious?" I laugh. "You would fly every work-study kid to Maui? For me?"

"Only the girls."

"Not the boys?" I laugh.

"What would be the point in that?" he grins.

"Can you, I don't know, move all the Fundies out of the East and West Wings, and move the work-study kids in? Put the Fundies in the Convent and the Monastery?"

He grins, "There would be campus-wide riots if that happened. Let's focus on getting you and the girls to Maui."

"How much would that even cost? There's a lot of us work-study girls. It has to cost hundreds of thousands of dollars. Maybe millions."

"Pocket change."

"You're too much," I laugh.

"That's what they've been saying my entire life," he grins. "Listen, princess, let's not worry about this now. I have my meeting. We can talk about Maui later. But I would very much like it if you continued living with me, and I *am* taking you to the winter formal."

"Is that an order?" I smirk.

He takes my hand in his. "It's a request. Will you go with me?"

"I guess," I sigh.

He smiles, "It's a date. I'll have dresses sent up the day before so you can pick one out."

"What?! No-a! You can't do that! Stop buying things for me already!"

"As much as I'd like you to accompany me with you wearing one of your French maid outfits from work," he slips a sly wink, "they won't let you into the dance in something so slutty. You need a proper dress."

"Okay then. I guess I'll pick one out."

On his way out the front door, I follow him and he gives me a quick peck on the lips.

"We'll talk later. You won't regret this. Goodnight, Marianne."

"G'night!" I'm grinning from ear to ear as I shut the door. Now it really does feel like we're a couple living together.

When Prince is gone, I suddenly remember the spy cameras and Skill's wifi router. Here Prince is laying it on the line for me, and I'm spying on him!

I can't do it.

I rush from room to room gathering up the spy cameras. I'd switch out the router if I could, but I don't have the old one. I gave it back last week, like Skill said. At least the cameras are now buried in my book bag.

First thing tomorrow, Rob and I are going to have a little talk.

<(—)>

"No more spying, Rob," I say bluntly and drop the spy cameras into his open palm.

I've been carrying the cameras around in my book bag all day. It took forever to find him. I even told Mimi to find me and tell me if she found him first. Turns out I found him here mopping the floor in the math building. I can see the half-mopped puddle where some absent-minded Fundy no doubt spilled an entire mug of creamy Castle Hill cappuccino all over the tiles. I say Fundy because guess who isn't allowed to buy coffee at the Castle Hill Cafe? The work-study kids. So much for me ever buying Luna a coffee like I promised.

Rob stands here beside his rolling yellow mop bucket resting the mop on the floor. He quickly jams the handful of cameras I gave him into the pocket of his navy coveralls, looking around suspiciously as he does it.

I say, "I need the old router back."

"Shh. Not here." He grabs my elbow and drags me past classrooms and into a broom closet around the corner and off the corridor. A very small broom closet.

It's just me and him in this very dimly lit and intimate space. His masculine presence is nearly overwhelming. His leathery motor oil scent triggers memories of the night we met with the black racing motorcycles and black blood on his hands, him saving me from the iron maiden on Halloween, lying in his bed after, pressed tight against his muscled thighs like he would never ever let go. Too bad he did.

He frowns in disbelief. "What happened? Why the change of heart?"

I smirk, "It's complicated." In other words, you ghosted me and I'm done with you and your spy games. It takes everything I have not to ask for an explanation. Rob had his chance. Now it's Prince's turn. I sigh, "When can I get the old router back?"

Rob looks dumbfounded.

"Forget it," I say. "I'll ask Skill myself."

I open the door an inch.

Light from the hallway pours in and I listen for footsteps. The last thing I want is anyone seeing me coming out of a dark broom closet with Rob. Knowing this rumor mill, Prince would hear about it within the hour. I definitely don't want that happening.

When I don't hear anyone coming, I open the door and slip out. I gasp when someone turns the corner. A work-study girl with their sneaky flat-soled shoes! If it'd been a Fundy, I would've heard clacking high heels, but I didn't! Obviously, work-study girls are perfectly capable of spilling the tea, even when it involves one of their own, meaning me. I'm about to jump back into the closet and slam the door shut when I realize Rob is coming out after me. He's way too big to shove back in. Now we're caught!

I'm about to have a heart attack when I see it's Mimi.

"What're you doing?" she whispers, eying Rob. "Were you two just —"

"Talking," I say sourly. "Just talking. Nothing happened." Maybe it would have if Rob hadn't lured me into his lying lair before ghosting me, who knows. But he did. "Believe me, nothing happened."

"Too bad," Mimi pouts. She knows how I feel about Rob.

Rob shakes his head and grunts, "I have a floor to mop." He shoulders past us.

"Nice to see you too," Mimi says sarcastically, shaking her head when he turns the corner. When he's gone, she mutters, "Ass. You okay, Mare Bear?"

"I'm fine," I sigh.

I really am. Now that the weight of spying on Prince is off my shoulders, I feel a million times better. I have only one little thing left to do to undo what I started.

The next morning, I go to Prince's suite during lunch while he's eating in the Palace Dining Hall, disconnect the hacked router, drop it on the floor, cracking it, and take it to Arthur Hovarth in IT. He gives me a new one without question when I tell him it's Prince's. Skill is there in the office and he gives me a dirty look. I give him two in return. He can suck it because I'm nobody's sucker.

Let the Poor Boys do their own spying.

Chapter 36

Ever since Mimi told me Chase asked her to the winter formal, I've been making her clean his room. I don't want him getting any ideas or making any moves on me if I'm alone and he walks into his room. Consequently, I now clean Duke's room every dinner time instead. He lives on the same floor as Chase. Not that it matters, they're rarely in their rooms. Too busy networking in the Dining Hall, which I hear is practically a meet-and-greet for the Fundies.

Like I always do, I knock on Duke's door before entering. "Housekeeping?" I ask in a shrill comic voice. It's a running joke between me and Meems.

When no one answers, I push into the dark room with my bucket of stuff. I hear a noise like someone left their music on, but it's really quiet, like insects chittering away, so maybe headphones sitting on a table or whatever and playing music? It's kind of creepy. I say, "Lights."

They don't turn on.

Usually a voice command is enough. It's not like the light switches require a password. I fumble for the touchpad on the wall.

"I broke it," a masculine voice says from the shadows.

I jump out of my shoes before I realize it's Duke.

He's lying on his bed in the shadows, hands behind his head, wearing his uniform slacks, no socks, and his dress shirt is unbuttoned, showing a sliver of his savage gabs. I mean abs.

I try to laugh off my fright, "You scared me."

"Sorry. I didn't hear you come in."

"Shouldn't you be at dinner?"

"I'm not in the mood," he grumbles.

"I can relate." I glance over my shoulder at the open door. It means I have an escape route if necessary, but it also means anyone could walk by, look in, and see us together. I wouldn't want word getting back to Victoria. It'll just cause more trouble for Duke that he doesn't deserve. Then again, it is dinner time, and all the Fundies are eating in the Dining Hall. I'm safe for now. I can tell from the brooding mood pervading the room that Duke needs a little cheering up. "What're you doing sitting here in the dark? Catching up on sleep or something? I know your guys's football practices are exhausting."

"I skipped practice today."

"Why?"

"Didn't feel like it."

"So you came here to listen to music or whatever?"

"Yup."

"What're you listening to, if you don't mind me asking?"

"Five Finger Death Punch."

"The metal band?"

"You know them?"

"Who doesn't?" I laugh.

"Everyone here."

"What, Fundies don't like metal?"

"Metal is for angry people. Fundies are too rich to be angry. Or too high on prescription meds."

"Oh. I guess that means you're not on meds?"

"You could say that."

"Why're you angry?"

"Vee's cheating on me again," Duke says.

"What?" I gasp, even though I'm not surprised.

"I caught them fucking," Duke growls, his eyes burning with hate. "Her and Skill."

My face sags in disgust. Why am I not surprised? From day one, I could tell Skill was a professional player. Manwhore to the max. I sit down on the couch opposite his bed because Duke obviously needs to talk. I sigh, "Was it the first time?"

"What, that I caught her?" He says it with acidic loathing.

I nod.

"No," he grumbles. "But it's the first time she ever said she'd never marry a dumbfuck jock like me."

"She said that?" I cringe.

"And worse," he scowls.

"Do I want to know?"

"Fuck no," he grunts and jumps up from the bed. He starts pacing in front of me. "Fuck her," he spits, then goes on a rant for five minutes straight.

I just listen.

Eventually, he drops onto the couch beside me and leans his hands on his muscled thighs like he's ready to throw up all over the floor. "Why does she have to be like this, you know? I just don't get it!" He's practically pulling his jet black hair out of his skull in frustration.

From the side, I see his face shake like it's ready to crumble under the weight of the ocean of tears pressing behind his eyes.

He turns to me for sympathy. "Just fuck that fucking bitch! I don't need that shit!"

"No," I shake my head for emphasis. "You deserve better." I reach over and squeeze his hand.

"Do I?" He sniffs and gives me this puppy dog look with his dark puppy dog eyes. On his handsome face it's heart-breaking, like a man this tough and rugged should never be this vulnerable. It's not a look I ever expected to see cross Duke's face, but here it is.

My heart swells with compassion and I grab his hand. "Of course you do! Nobody deserves to be cheated on, let alone talked to like that! How could she say that?! It's awful."

"Yeah," he mutters and hooks his thumb around my fingers, which are resting on top of his hand. His eyes swim with tears. "My dad is always calling me a dumbfuck jock. He says I spend too much time worrying about sports and not enough thinking about the family business. Vee knows Dad calls me that. That's why she said it."

"What?!" I blurt. "How could she?!"

"I don't think she wants to get married," he says with weighty disappointment.

"You shouldn't either! I never like to talk bad about other people, Duke, but I have to say this. Victoria is a bad person. She locked me in an effing stabbing cage because she thinks I'm trying to steal you from her! That's not even true! And she doesn't even *want* you?! What the F is her problem?! I'm telling you, Duke, don't waste your time on her. Tell your parents the wedding is off."

"It's not that easy."

"Yes it is! Your fiancée is *cheating* on you! She has no respect for you! None! What more do they need to know before they get their heads out of their asses?!"

"A pry bar."

"A what?"

"A pry bar, you know, to pry their heads out," he chuckles. "Or a tow truck."

I laugh at that. "You think that'll be enough?"

"Two tow trucks," he grins. "One for each of them."

"Exactly," I laugh. "Gosh, Duke, I don't know what to say. I mean, it's not like they can force you to marry her, can they?"

"Maybe not legally, but yeah, they can."

"Not once you're eighteen. Then they can't make you do anything you don't want."

He offers a cringy sneer.

"What?" I ask.

"They can disown me."

"Good. The sooner the better," I blurt.

"I mean financially."

"So?"

His face softens in thought. "Only thing is, if I did, I'd be losing out on a mountain of money."

"Who cares?!" I snort. "You can get a job. You don't need their money."

His wheels are turning. His eyes shimmer with possibility. Then they darken. He says somberly, "You've never had money, have you?"

"No. So what? Money doesn't solve everything. Money doesn't make you happy. Love makes people happy."

He frowns.

I suddenly realize Duke probably has no idea what it feels like to be loved. My heart tightens with sadness. I can't imagine what it would be like to have parents who hate you. I may have spent nearly half my life in foster care, but the first half of my life was heaven by comparison. My parents loved me like crazy. I can't imagine not having had that. Sometimes, memories of their love is the only thing that keeps me going.

"Oh, Duke," I sigh and throw my arms around him in a big hug.

At first, he's stiff, just sitting there. Then his big arms slide around my waist in an awkward side hug.

My body buzzes with compassion for this young man, like I'm trying to squeeze as much love into him as I can.

Eventually, he squeezes back, pulling me into him. I'm intimately aware that my breasts are pressing against his hard chest. I try to ignore it. I'm here for the hugs. Duke desperately needs them. It isn't easy with his hard muscles and cedar scent teasing every inch of me. I do my best to ignore it and focus on our friendly embrace. Two friends hugging. Nothing sexual about it. Nope, not turned on at all.

We hug for several minutes before he breaks away.

"Thanks, I needed that," he smirks, slightly red-faced, like maybe he's embarrassed about being vulnerable.

"Any time," I grin. "You don't need money for hugs. They're free."

"Yeah," he chuckles and takes my hand, lacing his fingers in mine, examining them, turning them over and over. His hand is warm and big, yet gentle and affectionate.

It sends a thrill through me, piercing my defenses and sending my heart fluttering.

He frowns, "You know what?"

"What?" I giggle, trying to hide my desire.

"Vee and me stopped holding hands a long time ago. I remember doing it when we were little, then it stopped."

"Why-a?" I practically sneer. "My parents always held hands. All the way until—" There I go again, telling Duke about my parents when I'd rather not.

"Until what?"

"Nothing. You were saying about you and Victoria?"

He shakes his head, mystified, "We just stopped holding hands." Then he sneers. "We kept fucking, but no hand-holding."

"What is wrong with her?!" I scowl. "She's like, I don't know. Heartless or something. Wait, does she hold Skill's hand?"

Duke flinches.

"Sorry, I shouldn't have asked that."

"It's cool," he grumbles. "I don't really know, actually. And I don't fucking care." His face flashes through a hurricane of conflicted emotions. Anger, annoyance, disgust, amusement. "She can have him."

"Good," I smirk. "Throw that bitch under the next bus."

"The next ten buses," he chuckles. "Really run her over."

"Yeah," I laugh.

He sighs, "Man, if I had someone like you in my life, I wouldn't need money."

"See?" I smile. "When you have love in your life, money doesn't matter."

His face changes.

Did I just say love? Oops. I didn't mean it like that! I meant in general! I giggle nervously.

Duke's charcoal eyes search mine.

I bite my lower lip.

We're still holding hands.

I don't know what he's doing, but there's a flood of butterflies rushing up my arm and swirling around my heart and breasts and everything else.

He leans in and—

"Duke, we shouldn't," I whisper, tipping my head down to hide my lips from his.

"Yeah," he grumbles, touching his forehead against mine. He sighs heavily.

Now is when he lets go of my hand and we sit up straight like a couple of well-behaved teenagers.

Neither of us moves.

My heart is pounding, sending out throbbing waves that make their way between my legs. My skin tingles in slippery anticipation.

This is a terrible idea.

But I can't move!

A firm hand lifts my chin.

He says earnestly, "I don't want to live a life without love, Mary."

Don't you just want to awww? I do but I don't because I feel this warm energy reach out from him and pull me forward into a kiss before I realize what's happening.

Duke's mouth welcomes mine.

Then his tongue finds its way home.

I lose all control.

Sizzling stardust erupts from our lips.

I grab his shirt and clutch it in my fist.

Duke grunts and pulls me into his lap without breaking the kiss, practically picking me up and lifting me.

I settle in and stroke his cheek with my free hand. His other hand won't let go, trapping mine in his. I pull it between my breasts and hold it close to my heart.

We're both heaving into each other as the kiss continues, exchanging breaths like we've become each other's oxygen, like our souls are intertwining inside of us, mine in him, him in me.

I'm lost in bliss until I feel him straining and rigid underneath me.

That brings reality crushing back.

What am I doing?!

I'm living with Prince and he asked me to the effing winter formal! I don't need more men in my life! One is more than enough! Yet here I am with Duke on his couch. Kissing and couches always, *always* leads to fumbling and f—

"Stop," I mumble.

Duke instantly breaks away. "Is something wrong?"

"Erm," I relax my hand.

He releases mine.

I shoot to my feet.

"What?" he asks, suddenly afraid.

"I just, I need to, I forgot, I have a—"

"Is something wrong? What'd I do?"

"It's just—" There are no words. I rush out of the room before he can stop me. I find Mimi in whichever room she's cleaning and gasp, "I need you to cover for me!"

"What's wrong?" she asks, immediately concerned.

"Mary?" Duke calls out from the hallway.

"Is that Duke?" Mimi asks, in a loud whisper.

"Yes!" I hiss.

She cringes, "Did you and he just—"

"Yes! I need to get out of here! Cover for me!"

"Mary?!" Duke calls out, just outside the room.

Mimi grabs her cleaning stuff and rushes out the door of the room, closing it behind her.

The doors to these rooms are almost completely sound proof, but if you put your ear to them, you can sort of hear. I listen to Mimi make excuses for me, telling Duke I'm not here. Eventually, their conversation stops. A minute later, Mimi opens the door and whispers, "Go! He's back in his room!"

I dash down the hallway to the elevator and take it to the penthouse floor and hide in Prince's guest bedroom.

Kissing Duke was a huge mistake.

How could I let that happen?!

He's knockout hot, that's how!

I am so stupid!

I can't be with Duke! I've got this thing with Prince! This living together thing! I need to do something about Duke. I can't for the life of me understand what he sees in me, other than I'm not heartless, but I just can't be with him!

What I need to do is distract him from me, and I know just the person who can help.

"You need to stop sleeping with Victoria so she and Duke can get back together," I say insistently to Skill. We're in his office in the IT department. Peanut-faced Arthur Hovarth is in the bathroom, thankfully.

Skill slouches into his office chair with a cocky grin, and spreads his legs invitingly. He's wearing jeans, but he's acting like he isn't wearing anything.

"Do you mind?" I sneer.

"Mind cutting things off with Victoria?"

"No-a, your legs."

"You like them?" He spreads them wider.

"Stop it, Skill! And stop seeing Victoria!"

"Why? So you can see me?"

I huff. "I'd never *see* you." It's a lie. If Skill cleaned up his act, I'd seriously consider his offer. Only his manwhoring ways stop me from sending any signals that might invite him to take things further.

"You're seeing me now. Would you like to see more?" His scarlet bangs dangle over his chocolate eyes and he lifts up his T-shirt, revealing rock-hard abs. Gabs! Worse, his jeans and boxers are riding very low at the moment. "Does this do it for you, War Paint?"

"Don't call me that," I grouse and look away reluctantly from his abs. Gabs!

"Does it?" he presses on.

"No-a! It doesn't do anything for me! You need to cut things off with Victoria. You're breaking Duke's heart."

"What do you care about his heart? He's a dick."

"I *don't* care." It's a lie. The truth is, I probably care too much. The only reason I'm here is because I'm scared that if Victoria doesn't get back together with Duke, I'll find myself getting deeper and deeper into Duke's drama, or I might accidentally let Duke get deeper and deeper into me. My heart. I mean deeper into my heart. Not anything else.

"If you don't care, why are you here?" He reaches up with a booted foot and kicks the office door closed. Suddenly, it's silent and we're all alone.

"You know Arthur is coming right back."

Skill smirks, "His morning dump takes at least twenty minutes. That should be long enough to get your motor going and the lube flowing." He is so obviously talking about sex. With him.

"Unh!" I gawk at him. Literally gawk. "What did you just say?!"

"You're not here because of Duke. You're here because of me. You don't like the idea of me hooking up with Victoria after what she did to you."

I sneer, "You're a genius, Skill. You figured out I don't like Victoria."

"No, I figured out you like me."

"Ha!" I laugh sarcastically.

"It's true," he grins.

Do I need to remind you that Skill is model hot? Now that *that's* out of the way, I snarl at him, "You are pathetic, Skill. Just because other women fall for your arrogant attitude, doesn't mean I will."

"Then why *are* you here, War Paint?"

"Do you have to keep calling me that?" Secretly, I absolutely love that nickname, but we can all see that Skill should never *ever* know that fact.

"I'm not calling you Mary," he scoffs.

"Why not? Is there something wrong with my given name?"

"It's too plain. Too soft. Mary sounds like somebody's mom offering milk and cookies after the kids run around at the playground. You're a fucking warrior. You need a warrior's name."

I force a fake smile, trying to hide the fact that Skill knows how to charm the pants off anyone, even me.

"Why'd you really come here, War Paint?"

"I told you!" I gasp in exasperation. "You need to stop seeing Victoria."

"You said that already. Why should I? What's in it for me? You?" His full lips spread into a wicked grin. "For you I'll do it."

"Erm," I giggle.

"We have a deal? Me and you?"

"No-a! Would you stop?! I'm living with Prince, in case you forgot!"

"He doesn't need to know about us," Skill smiles.

"There isn't any us, Skill!"

"There should be."

"Uch! Can you just, isn't there some other Fundy you can fuck besides Victoria?"

"There's plenty," Skill says, slouching back into his chair. "But I'd rather fuck you, *War* Paint," he says pointedly.

The office door opens and Arthur steps inside. "Why is the door closed?" He glares at Skill suspiciously.

Skill offers a shit-eating grin and says, "Mary and I needed some privacy, if you know what I mean."

Arthur blushes, "Mr. Rose! You know I don't condone that sort of behavior in the server center! This is a place of work, not a place for you to indulge in your extracurricular activities!"

"Oh, we were definitely indulging," Skill chuckles.

"Mr. Rose! Do not add insult to injury! Miss Mary, I ask that you please leave. That is, unless you have official business to attend?"

I glare at Skill and say to Mr. Hovarth, "It's already attended. Right, Skill?"

He shrugs.

I give him a silent ugh.

Why does Skill have to be so infuriatingly hot?

Why?!

I march out of there before I make a mess of things. Mr. Hovarth insists on escorting me past the stacks of computers.

He opens the outside building door for me and says quietly, "Miss Mary, I suggest you give very careful consideration to the topic of getting involved with a young man like William Rose. The more I get to know him, the more I come to understand he is nothing but trouble."

"You're telling me," I mutter.

"Were it my daughters, I would vigorously discourage them from dating a smooth operator like him, and I will do the same for you. Stay away from him, Miss Mary. Any involvement with William Rose will only lead to heartbreak."

"Thanks. Pretty much figured that out."

What I can't figure out is whether or not Skill listened to a word I said about Victoria. I hope so.

For Duke's sake.

And mine.

Have I mentioned that bad boys are an aggravating pain in the ass? I mean, absolutely aggravating? Like sponging yourself with sandpaper and saltwater?

You have been warned.

Chapter 37

"What a freaking week," I sigh as I walk into Prince's penthouse. It's Friday and I just finished seventh period. I have a few hours to study before I put my French maid's uniform on and go clean the West Wing with Mimi, per usual.

When I walk into Prince's living room, it's a bustle of activity and fashionably dressed people I've never met, and Prince is in the middle of it looking at a bunch of dress racks loaded with what have to be designer ball gowns, from glittery and glitzy to more traditional satin and silk. Afternoon sunshine pours in through the window wall, making the gowns all shimmer and shine and sparkle.

"What's going on?" I laugh.

"Princess," he grins when he sees me. "I told you the other day, you need to pick your dress for the winter formal."

"I know, but, Prince, this is ridiculous! There's like a hundred dresses here! How am I going to pick one?"

"Pick them all, I don't care," he chuckles.

"What am I going to do with a hundred dresses?" I laugh. "I can only wear one at a time."

"Go to a hundred different dances with me, of course," he says like it's a no-brainer.

I notice the other people are staring at me now, smiling expectantly like they're ready to wait on me hand and foot. It's slightly overwhelming. "Erm, who are these people?"

"The designers." Prince rattles off a list of names, some I've heard, some I haven't, and gives their pedigrees. They're either already famous (one of them has a line of clothes at bebe *and* Macy's, and another has one at Forever 21), or they're up-and-coming fashion designers from New York. I swear one of the up-and-comers is one of the past winners from Project Runway. The group of them were obviously flown in by Prince. I've never been on a plane, and I have no idea how much plane tickets to and from New York cost, but for all these people and dresses, it has to be a fortune.

"You didn't have to do this, Prince," I say. Having all this money spent on me is beyond weird.

"But I did it anyway," he grins.

I want to tell him we could've rented a gown for like a hundred bucks somewhere. I can already see the designers and their assistants scoffing at my comment without having to say it. As much as I want to, I can't tell them to pack up their dresses and go home. That would be an even bigger waste of money and totally rude. I guess I'm doing this.

"Which dress would you like to try on first?" Prince asks.

"You pick," I grin and consent to being the center of attention while trying on dresses. It's like Fashion Week came to Prince's penthouse. I'm surprised he didn't have them set up a runway for me to catwalk, and hire a bunch of photographers to document the event.

So much for doing my homework before I work tonight.

The entire time, the designers shower me with compliments. They call me "darling this" and "honey that," telling me how "simply ravishing" I am, obviously trying to convince me to pick *their* dress. It's crazy. It's one thing to have men fight over you. Who doesn't enjoy that battle? But these people? They're fighting over my money. Erm, Prince's money. And probably status. You'd think the Castle Hill Academy winter formal was the red carpet in Hollywood from the way they're jockeying to get me to pick *their* dress.

Eventually, we narrow it down to the best dress from each designer.

"I can't decide," I whine. The dresses are all beautiful, but I don't want to be the one to disappoint every other designer by telling them I didn't pick *their* dress.

"I can," Prince says. "The one you're wearing."

It's a white gold nude gown with a plunging back and sweep train. The sheer bodice and rest of the dress are embellished with beads. I titter, "I do like the beads."

"Those aren't beads," Prince says.

"Huh?"

"They're diamonds and other precious stones."

"Shut up!" I laugh guiltily. "How much does this cost?"

"I have no idea," Prince chuckles. "We'll take it." He smiles at the designer.

She smiles wide in return, and the rest of the designers hide their pouts while packing up their dress racks.

I whisper to Prince, "Erm, what time is it?"

He checks his Bugatti watch. "Just past six."

"Oh, shit!" I gasp and adrenalin rips into me. "I was supposed to be in the West Wing cleaning over an hour ago!" My comment draws scoffs from the designers and their assistants. I don't give a crap what they think. "I left Mimi hanging!" I turn to run for the guest bedroom to change, then realize I'm still in the gown. I look at the designers frantically and blurt, "Someone help me out of this!"

The losing designers snoot, while the winning designer and her team rush over to help me out of the gown so I don't destroy it.

"Calm down, Marianne," Prince soothes. "It's taken care of. I already informed Ms. Braunschott you would be unavailable this evening."

"Who did you get to replace me? To help Mimi, I mean?"

Prince's face twists into amused embarrassment.

I smirk, "You *did* find someone to help her tonight, right?"

"I *can*," he offers confidently.

I shake my head in disgust as the assistants help me out of the gown. As soon as I'm free, I rush across the floor in my bare feet, bra, and panties. Before, when I was climbing in and out of gowns, I had changed behind a fancy French dressing screen so Prince wouldn't see me in my undies. Now I don't care. I feel too awful about Mimi getting left in the lurch.

I rush into the walk-in closet in the guest room and start putting on my French maid uniform.

"Relax, fairest," Prince says, leaning into the closet to watch. He's holding his smart phone to his ear. "I'm calling Ms. Braunschott's office as we speak. I'll have her send reinforcements to help out your friend Mimi." He says it like it'll fix everything.

I'm bent over attaching my garters to my stockings. I glare at him, "That's not the point. I let Mimi down. I was supposed to be there to help her out."

"She's not answering," Prince says absently. "I guess I'll let it ring. Does she have voicemail?"

"I doubt it," I grimace, pushing down my skirt. "You do realize, getting other girls to help Mimi means *they'll* have to stay late, right? They still have to finish their regular tasks."

He frowns.

"You didn't think of that, did you?"

"I did not," Prince admits.

Annoyed, I shake my head while tying my white apron behind my back. I'm dashing out the front door while putting my head piece on. Lucky for me it's a quick elevator ride down to Mimi and my usual floor.

"Where were you?!" Mimi grumbles when she sees my trotting down the hallway. "I thought something happened!" She obviously means something bad.

"Sorry, Meems," I sigh. "I got tied up."

"By Prince? How tight did he tie you?" She titters with sinful implication.

"No-a! Not that kind of tying! I mean I was trying on gowns for the winter formal."

"Just now?"

"Uh huh. He flew in a bunch of designers and their dresses from New

York."

"What?!" she gasps.

"It was insane. Like Fashion Week. I swear it took forever. I totally had no idea what time it was. I'm really sorry, Meems."

"Did you pick out a dress?"

"I didn't. Prince did. There were so many I couldn't decide."

"Right," Mimi nods strangely, eyes narrowed.

I suddenly realize she's jealous. I know she hasn't picked out a dress yet. I don't think Chase is exactly the thoughtful kind of guy Prince is. Mimi'll probably have to actually rent one herself. I suddenly get an idea. I grab Mimi by the elbow and drag her down the hallway. "You're coming with me."

"Mary! What're you doing!" Mimi laughs, stumbling along behind me.

"We're getting you a dress," I say with determination.

"What about the rooms?! We have to clean them!"

"I'll make Prince take care of it."

We're back in his suite minutes later. I push through the door with Mimi in tow. The room is still crowded with the designers and their assistants, who are packing up dress racks. When I see Prince, I say, "Did you get a hold of Ms. Braunschott?"

"She never answered."

"She's probably busy," I say. "Do me a favor?"

"Anything for you, princess." He glances at Mimi.

"Hey," she says shyly.

"Mimi, right?" he says.

She nods.

I say, "Prince, go find Ms. Braunschott and tell her Mimi and I are running late, but we'll have everything cleaned in a minute. You got that?"

"Yes," he nods.

"As soon as we finish down there, we're coming back up here to find a dress for Mimi. Can you *arrange* for the designers to stay and help her pick a dress?" I smirk.

"I can," he grins, realizing he's off the hook. He claps his hands to catch the attention of the designers and their teams. "Everybody stop! We have one more dress to select!"

Mimi's eyes beam and she gasps, "No way!"

I smile at her, "*Way* way. Let's go finish cleaning our floor. When we're done, we'll get you a dress."

"Fabulous idea," Mimi laughs.

Chapter 38

It's eight o'clock when Mimi finishes picking out a gown. The designer has to size it for Mimi because the dresses were all sized for me. Prince got my measurements from Ms. Skelter's office before the designers flew out, but he didn't get Mimi's. They'll have to scramble to make alterations and get her dress ready for tomorrow night.

I apologize to them fifty times for making them work late.

They tell me it's their pleasure.

Prince mutters in my ear that they're being well paid.

At least there's that.

When everyone is gone, it's past nine.

My stomach grumbles audibly.

"You hungry?" Prince asks.

"You have no idea," I laugh. "I forgot to eat. I always have dinner at the Cave before Mimi and I start our shift. I never made it because you made me try on dresses!" I swat his arm in fake irritation. "You could've at least offered to order room service for me and Mimi! Now the Cave is closed! What's she going to eat?"

"I'll have room service send her dinner in the Convent. I'll call Ms. Braunschott now."

While he does, I change out of my French maid uniform. I've been wearing it the entire time. I'm so used to it, it's normal.

"You changed," Prince says when I come walking out of the guest bedroom into the living room.

"Yeah. It's getting late." I'm wearing a T-shirt and the same crappy sweat pants I've been sleeping in for years. "Can we order room service? I really need to eat before it gets any later."

"I may have made plans," he says carefully and slides his hands into his slacks. He's not wearing his uniform slacks and blazer like earlier. While I was changing, he changed into a deep teal green suit with jeweled lapels and matching pinstripe tie, a white dress shirt, black shoes, and no socks, or socks so short you can't see them. I've never seen him without slacks that cover his ankles, but they're uncovered now. Ooooh! Naked ankles! It's like a Victorian-era porno around here!

"Oh?" I say. "Dinner plans?"

"Yes," he nods.

"Erm, it's kind of late. I have to work tomorrow, remember?"

"I do. I had expected we would be leaving much sooner than we are."

"Don't blame me, you're the one who brought a million dresses for me."

"I did, but I hadn't planned on your friend Mimi—"

I interject, "Having to cover for me?"

"Yes, for that," he smiles agreeably. "As for you working tomorrow, I can *hire* someone to cover for you, if need be."

"No. You're spending way too much money on me."

"It's what I do," he smirks.

"Fine for you, but I feel like I owe you." I sound pouty, but it's true.

Prince takes my hands in his, "Fairest Marianne, you don't owe me anything. Money is in my blood. Is judging me for having money any different from someone judging you for not having any?"

"When you put it like that," I snort sarcastically, trying not to sound too offended.

"I didn't mean it like that. That came out wrong," he sighs in frustration. "What am I supposed to say? I'm rich. I was born this way. Am I not supposed to spend my money on the things that matter to me?" He obviously means me.

I look up into his sparkling blue eyes. They're so full of hope it slays me where I stand.

"If you prefer, we can have room service for dinner and you can work your Saturday morning shift like you normally do. Or, we can do what I have planned for tonight. If we hurry, we can be back in time to get you to bed like always, and you can still work your shift. Say, midnight? That's not too late, is it?"

How can I resist?

I ask, "Can I go like this?"

Prince looks at my T-shirt and sweats and tries not to smirk.

"Should I put on my leather jacket and jeans?" I ask sincerely. Those are my going-out clothes.

"I got you something for tonight."

"Another gown?" I laugh.

"Nothing so formal." He leads me back to my guest bedroom to the walk-in closet. Unzips a garment bag on the rack. "A little black dress. You can slip into it, fairly quickly, don't you think?"

"I can, but, I don't have any shoes. Just my Docs."

"All taken care of." He pulls a shoe box off the top shelf. The box looks like it's made of leather. Gucci is stamped on top in gold.

"Is that real leather?" I ask, wanting to touch it but not, out of respect.

"They said it was," he says thoughtfully. "Does it not look real to you?"

"Can I?" Curious, I reach out to touch it, but stop myself.

"They're your— sorry. Yes, you can."

I caress the velvety leather with my fingers. "Feels real to me."

"I hope so. They said the lettering is 24K gold leaf, but what do I know?"

I give him a look.

"Sorry," he chuckles. "Listen to me, right? Always talking about money."

"It's fine," I grin.

He pulls the lid off, revealing the cutest patent black leather pumps with stiletto heels.

"I don't know if I can walk in those," I say seriously.

"You don't have to wear them. Go barefoot."

"Wait, really?"

"Why not? I never wear shoes when I go surfing. I don't even bring shoes," he chuckles. "I just get on my jet barefoot and—" He sighs regretfully, "Sorry. I'm talking about money again, aren't I?"

I laugh and wave a hand, "Don't worry about it. Like you said. You were born this way, right?"

"Right. Will you at least wear the dress?"

"Sure. Why not. Is it from one of the designers from before?"

Prince opens his mouth to speak, wearing his usual snooty expression, stops himself, smirks, and says, "Walmart. I bought it at Walmart for $19.99. Went in myself. Waited in line like everyone else."

"Did not," I laugh.

"Do you want to hear the truth?"

"No," I sigh. "If anyone asks, we'll say it's from Walmart." I kick him out of the walk-in so I can change into the dress. When I walk out, I'm wearing the Gucci pumps he gave me. "What do you think?"

He's sitting on the bed. "I think I want to fuck you."

"Prince!"

"Sorry. It just slipped out," he chuckles endearingly. "You wore the shoes."

"They're not much taller than my work heels, and I have to work in those. I think I can manage in these, as long as I don't have to scrub any toilets."

"None of that, I promise. Shall we?"

We take the elevator up a single floor.

I say, "I thought you lived on the top floor."

"I do," he says as the elevator doors open onto a small concrete room lit by a fluorescent light. He opens a metal door that leads to the roof. "After you."

"Is that an effing helicopter?" I gasp.

"I believe that's what it is," he says, amused.

"Don't tell me you're going to Fifty Shades me," I laugh guiltily. I *maaaay* have read the books more than once. How many times, I'm not saying.

"Fifty shades you?"

"You know what that is, don't you?"

"Not really," he shakes his head. "Is that a thing?"

"It's a book. Fifty Shades of Grey?"

"Oh, that. I've heard of that. What's that have to do with helicopters? I thought it was some old porn story for moms or something."

"Who told you that?" I snicker.

"Probably some mom," he winks. "Do they have helicopter sex in the book or something?"

"Erm, I don't think it's safe to have sex while you're flying a helicopter."

"Strange. I thought everybody did that."

I frown, "Have sex in a helicopter while flying it?"

"You mean piloting it?"

"Yeah. Christian Grey is a helicopter pilot."

"Sucks to be him."

"Why?"

Prince smirks smarmily, "I'd rather have sex in back while someone else flies it up front."

"Have you?" I blurt in disbelief.

He winks, "Not yet. Maybe we can change that tonight."

"See ya!" Laughing, I spin on the toe of my Gucci pump and start walking toward the elevator.

"Joking," he chuckles, grabbing my elbow. "Let's go. We don't have to have sex in the helicopter unless you really want to. In other words, only if you ask me nicely."

I gasp huffily.

"Come on, strumpet. Dinner is waiting." He winks and leads me to the helicopter and gets the door for me, helping me step up into it.

We sit down and buckle in. He puts the headphones on me and says to the pilot, "Nash, please take us up."

"Yes, Mr. Lancaster," I hear the pilot say over the headphones.

"I can't believe this!" I laugh as the propellors spin faster and faster and we lift gently into the air. "I've never even been on a plane!"

"This is much more fun," he grins. "Nash, circle campus for us, if you please. I want Marianne to get a good view." He smiles at me, "This place looks amazing at night. They did a great job lighting it up for maximum effect." He isn't exaggerating.

"It's like a storybook castle," I marvel. "Straight out of a fairy tale.

There's the Convent!" I wave. "Hey, Mimi! Check us out!"

Prince chuckles and squeezes my knee, "Did I or did I not tell you how much more fun you make everything?"

"You did. Where are we going?"

"Out to sea."

"Huh?"

"You'll see," he winks.

It doesn't take long before we pass over downtown Castle Hill, then endless dark forests on our way to the ocean, then we're over black water.

"Should I be worried?"

"No," he smiles.

"Wait," I gasp. "We're not going to Maui, are we?"

"No, this bird doesn't have that kind of range."

"Oh."

"Don't worry, we're almost there."

A few minutes later and not too far from shore, we start to turn a slow circle.

"Are we landing?" I ask, searching the empty waters below us outside the window. "I don't see anything but ocean. Oh wait. Is that a yacht?! Shut up! It's gigantic! Are we landing on that?!" I practically laugh.

"We are," he grins.

"No way! Whose yacht is this?"

"My family's."

"Of course it is," I snicker.

There's a bump when we touch down.

Prince says, "We're lucky the weather is so good for December. It wouldn't be safe to land if the swells were too big."

Nash the pilot is already opening the door for us.

Prince slides out first and takes my hand to help me out. I have to be careful stepping down in my heels.

"Thanks, Nash," Prince says.

The pilot nods, "Any time, Mr. Lancaster."

Prince smiles at me, "Shall we?"

"Don't tell me this is where we're having dinner?"

"Surprise," he chuckles. "It's not too much, is it?" His sarcasm is good-natured.

I give him a good-natured smirk.

"McDonald's was closed," he jokes. "This was the only other option."

"You're too much," I smile.

The wind whips across the helicopter deck and blows my little black dress up over my panties. My ass is totally hanging out and that pilot guy is getting a free show.

Prince grabs my dress and yanks it down before I have a chance to react. "You didn't see anything, did you Nash?"

Nash grins, "No sir. Not a thing."

I grumble, "We're not eating outside, are we?"

"No," Prince says. "This way."

He leads me inside the yacht and down a fancy curving staircase with dark wood walls and a massive chandelier overhead. We go down two levels and walk along a carpeted hallway before emerging in an intimate dining room walled in by a semicircle of floor-to-ceiling glass. The recessed lights are dim enough that you can see the harbor lights in the distance.

"Wow!" I gasp. "The view is amazing!"

"It is," Prince mutters.

I turn and see him staring at me.

"Shut up," I laugh.

"You shut up," he says like a pouty teenager.

I cackle at that. Prince definitely knows how to be funny when he wants.

"Have a seat." He pulls out a chair from the little table for two.

I drop into the seat and he pushes me up to the table before sitting next to me.

A waiter wearing white gloves and a tux walks in with a bottle of wine and holds the bottle out like he's presenting it to Prince. The waiter says, "Sixty-four Chateau Lafite Rothschild, as you requested, sir."

"Very good," Prince nods.

The waiter makes an elaborate show of cutting the cap and popping the cork, which he holds under Prince's nose.

Prince sniffs and nods.

"Would the lady care to give her approval?" the waiter asks, looking at me.

"Who, me?" I giggle.

Prince nods.

"Sure, I guess. I'll sniff it."

The waiter frowns.

"Should I not have said sniff?" I ask.

"It's fine," Prince chuckles.

The waiter circles the table and wafts the cork under my nose.

"What am I sniffing for?"

"Cork taint," Prince says.

"What's that again?"

"You'll know," Prince says.

"Erm, I guess it's fine? Like I said, I'm not sure what I'm smelling for."

"Does it smell like year-old gym socks or a serial killer's basement?"

"No," I laugh. "It smells like wine."

"Then it's fine."

"Very good, sir," the waiter says and pours a half inch for Prince.

He swirls the dark red wine in the glass, inhaling before taking a sip, which he swishes around before swallowing. "Excellent."

"Very good, sir." The waiter pours glasses for me then Prince before stepping back into the shadows where he stands holding the bottle.

Prince lifts his glass. "What should we toast?"

"Erm, is it cool neither of us are old enough to drink?"

"It's fine," Prince says. "We're over international waters."

"We are?"

He leans close and whispers, "Actually, no. We're too close to shore. Don't tell anyone."

"Okay then," I smile.

"Make a toast, my fair Marianne."

I raise my glass, "Um, okay. Here's to us both acing our finals."

"You have to toast something better than that," he chuckles.

"What?! If I don't ace my finals, I don't know if I'll manage a 3.5 GPA this term. If I don't, it's back to the hoosegow for me. You know about that, right?"

"I do. I'll make sure it never happens."

"What, are you going to tell Ms. Skelter to change my grades?"

"If it comes to that," he says sincerely.

I almost protest, almost tell him he can't go around pulling strings for me every time I have the littlest problem, then I realize how I got to Castle Hill in the first place. Running away from Dwight and Shayla. Going to juvi. Fighting Queen LaQueefa. Getting charged with attempted murder because she was trying to kill me. You know what? Screw it. Let Prince rig the system for me. It's already rigged me plenty.

Then I find myself thinking about Mimi and all the other work-study kids I've gotten to know since getting here. Like me, they're good people who work their asses off every day with the guillotine of their GPAs hanging over their heads. Like me, most of them weren't doing anything too terribly bad when they got arrested. I know from talking to them. It's petty stuff. The only real crime any of us committed was having the bad luck of being born with rusty spoons in our mouths instead of silver or gold or platinum or whatever the Fundy kids are born with.

Prince says, "Are we toasting honestly earned good grades then?"

"What if someone else doesn't make a 3.5 at the end of the semester? I mean other work-study kids. What if they don't make a 3.5?"

"Do you have someone specific in mind?"

"How about all of them?"

"All?"

"Yeah. All. Do you have any idea how hard it is to work twenty hours a week doing manual labor, and take AP classes, *and* keep your grades up?"

"I don't."

"Can you do it? Help any work-study kids not get kicked out? Not just me?"

He looks around thoughtfully. "I suppose so. I mean, if they haven't done anything criminal, if it's just a matter of their GPA slipping a few tenths of a point, sure, why not? I can talk to Ms. Skelter if it comes to that."

"For everyone?"

"Yes, everyone."

"I'll toast to that," I grin.

"To GPAs," Prince says, raising his glass. "May they never lead to the expulsion of another work-study kid."

"Yeah." I clink his glass and sip my wine.

He does too. "What do you think?"

"I hope you never have to do it, but knowing you can makes me feel a lot better. For me, for Mimi, for every work-study kid."

"I meant the wine," he says.

"Oh, uh," I take another sip and grimace, "It tastes like wine?"

The waiter in the shadows gasps.

Prince arches an eyebrow.

"Sorry!" I laugh, glancing at the waiter. "I don't know wine! I'm sure it's really good! It's the best I've ever had! Puts grape juice to shame!"

"I should hope so!" the waiter scoffs. "Sorry, sir. I meant no offense."

"No worries," Prince chuckles. "It's excellent, Jules. Better than that sixty-two you gave me last time."

"Nothing is better than the sixty-two!" Jules says, offended.

"I beg to differ," Prince grins. "The finish was a trifle too spicy."

"There is no such thing!" Jules grumbles humorously.

Prince says to me in a low voice that Jules can obviously hear, "We've been arguing about wine ever since I started drinking it."

"When was that?" I ask.

"When I was eleven? Twelve? Something like that."

"He's been your waiter since you were twelve?" I whisper.

"Longer than that. Jules, how long have you been our sommelier?"

"Twenty-seven wonderful years, sir," Jules says proudly.

"Wow," I say. "That's a long time."

"He's family," Prince says casually.

"Thank you, sir," Jules says.

"Pour yourself a glass, why don't you, Jules?" Prince suggests over his shoulder.

"Never, sir. The wine is yours and the lady's to enjoy."

I say, "Have a glass, Jules. Then you can argue with Prince about the finish or whatever."

"I couldn't," Jules chuckles from the shadows.

"Pour one for yourself," Prince says.

"If you insist, sir."

"I insist."

There's some commotion while Jules fetches another wine glass and pours himself a half glass. He and Prince then argue for five minutes about how good the '64 is in comparison to the '62. I'm smiling the entire time, impressed that Prince doesn't consider himself above Jules. I can't imagine what it'd be like to have a family wine guy for my entire life, but if I did, I'd treat him like an uncle. How could you not?

Eventually, appetizers, soup, salad, and the entrees arrive. Everything is of course seafood, but it isn't fishy. It's buttery and melt-in-your-mouth deliciousness. I can't describe it, but it certainly isn't fish sticks, which is the only seafood I've ever had before this.

Dessert is chocolate cake, but not just any chocolate cake. There's nine layers with nine kinds of chocolate from light to dark, from the creamy frosting to fudge sauce to the crisp drizzle lines dried to the plate.

I eat it all. When you work as much as us work-study kids, you're always hungry.

"That was so good," I sigh, sitting back in my chair. "I'm not even full."

"Do you want seconds?"

"Oh, no. I'm good. It's already almost too much. I just meant I didn't stuff myself. Everything was so good! I couldn't stop myself!"

"I'm glad you liked it," Prince chuckles. "Would you care for a walk around the deck?"

"If it's not too windy," I say, thinking of the gust that nearly blew my dress off earlier.

"I think the wind has died down."

The main deck of the yacht is large enough for actual strolling. We do a few laps and end up at the back, which Prince says is the stern, and we lean on the railing looking at the twinkling harbor lights in the distance.

"It's so nice out here," I sigh.

"Whenever I need to relax and get away from it all, I always come out here."

"I can imagine."

He reaches into his suit jacket and pulls out a smart phone. "I got you something."

"A phone? We're not allowed to have them, you know."

"I know. It's not that," he says. His phone screen flashes an unlocking padlock.

"How'd that happen? I always have to enter my password. You didn't even touch the screen."

"Facial recognition," he says, then thumbs around the screen and pulls up some photos. "Check this out." He hands me the phone.

"What am I looking at?" I swipe through a series of photos of villagers obviously in a developing country. In each one, they're standing around this blue jug thing that stands in the dirt in front of a variety of different broken-down buildings, each jug in a different place with an entirely different set of people and foliage in the background. Two things are the same in each photo. One is the blue jug. Each one has a bunch of spouts with pull handles like on a water cooler and people are pouring glasses of water from it. The other thing the same is there's always someone wearing a blue T-shirt with a logo for Water Of Life somewhere on the shirt.

Prince says, "Remember you asked me to donate the money from my fresh flowers for clean water?"

"To Save the Children?" I say with excitement.

"I found another non-profit that only does clean water called Water Of Life. That's their specialty and they have great ratings. They go around the globe donating water purifiers to communities in need. The purifiers are called LifeStraws and they're World Health Organization approved, some of the best on the market."

I'm still swiping through photos, each one unique. "How many did you buy?"

"A hundred."

"What did that cost?" I gawk.

"Less than a year's worth of fresh flowers, though I think training was extra."

"Training?"

"You need to pay people from the non-profit to transport the purifier to the village and teach them how to use it properly."

"You paid for that too?"

"What's the point of giving them a purifier if they don't know how to use it?"

"Shut up," I laugh.

"They say the filters make enough water for a hundred people for three to five years. I already paid to make sure someone changes them out when the times comes."

My jaw drops when I get to the last photo.

Prince is in it, he's wearing a Water Of Life T-shirt and he's drinking a glass of clean water standing in front of a bunch of villagers.

"Is that you?" I gasp.

"Yeah," he nods. "I only had time to fly out and see one village. You know how busy school is."

"Is that where you went a couple weekends ago?"

"Yeah, why?"

"Oh, I," I trail off, tittering.

"What?"

"It's stupid."

"Tell me."

"Do you really want to know?"

"Of course I do."

"This is going to sound really insecure," I groan and slouch pathetically. "I thought you were in Fiji surfing or whatever." By whatever, I mean hooking up with every gorgeous girl who was interested, which with his looks, is all of them.

"Why is that insecure? Big wave surfing is dangerous. People do get killed."

"Yeah, that," I smile guiltily. I'm *so* not telling him what I was really thinking.

"Not to worry," he grins. "I was just helping set up that water purifier in Honduras."

"Is that where you were?"

"Now *that* place *is* dangerous. Everyone on the trip had to dress down so we didn't attract too much attention. Even the security detail."

"Security detail?!"

"Of course," he snorts. "I'm not going to Central America without armed guards. Do you know how many people get kidnapped abroad? Especially rich people?"

"Don't tell me that!" I slap his arm. "Now you're worrying me!"

"Don't. I'm right here. Didn't get kidnapped," he grins confidently and puts his arm around my shoulder and pulls me close.

What a perfect evening. And it's just getting started.

He says, "We should probably be getting back."

"What?!"

"You said you have to work tomorrow. I don't want to keep you up too late."

"Oh, right," I say, hiding my immense disappointment. We haven't even kissed yet! After the water purifier thing, I was thinking I'd let him do more than kiss me if he wanted. I mean, we're on an effing yacht! Who doesn't want to sleep on a yacht?! And other things that aren't sleeping?

He checks his Bugatti watch. "If we leave now, we'll be back at the penthouse before midnight, as promised."

I'm dumbfounded. Most guys I've known, if they flew you to their yacht in a helicopter and bought a hundred water purifiers for villagers for you, *and* hand delivered them, they would expect a lifetime of blowjobs and then some. Prince isn't even asking for a kiss! Can you say perfect gentleman?

I whine, "Can't we stay a few more minutes?" So we can at least kiss like crazy for an hour? I don't say that.

"Nash has to fly our helicopter somewhere tomorrow morning for a family thing. He needs to rest up for that. Pilots need their beauty sleep too," he winks.

"Oh, right."

Prince smiles, "Besides, we wouldn't want the helicopter turning into a pumpkin while we're in the air over the water, would we?"

"No," I say plainly disappointed but not wanting anything as drastic as that to happen. Then again, if the helicopter did turn into a giant pumpkin and fall out of the air and land in the water with us inside, me and Prince could carve it out and make a boat out of it and paddle to a dessert island. Yes, *Dessert* Island, a storybook island made of every kind of dessert you can imagine, including nine-layer chocolate cake mountains with chocolate waterfalls, and me and Prince would live there forever. Or we could just fly his helicopter back to the academy so I can scrub floors and toilets tomorrow. Sigh.

He says, "We should go."

"If we must," I mumble.

Shortly after midnight, I'm lying alone in the guest bedroom, completely frustrated. That settles it. If Prince wants to sleep with me after the winter formal, I'm letting him. If he doesn't ask, I'll offer.

Stupid work-study work!

Ruined a perfectly good romantic evening on a yacht!

Chapter 39

The penthouse is empty Saturday when I finish my work-study duties at noon. Hungry and not wanting to eat alone, I change out of my French maid outfit into my street clothes. Leather jacket, band shirt, jeans, Docs. So far, nobody has told me I can't dress down on weekends, so I'm always doing it.

I head to the Convent to find Mimi and see if she's gone to eat yet. If she has, I'll look for her in the Cave. When I step out of the West Wing's elevator and cross the Palace quadrangle, I see Rob in his navy coveralls wheeling a mop bucket along near the wall.

I so don't want to see him. I speed up my walk and ignore him.

Squeaking wheels speed up and aim for me.

Squeaka, squeaka, squeaka!

I drop my walk into second gear and crank the throttle on my legs, speeding toward the exit doors that lead out of the Palace proper and into campus.

"Mary, wait!" Rob calls out. There's a clack which I assume is his mop stick hitting the ground, then boots thudding, him jogging after me.

I know how fast Rob can run. I saw it the night we met. Werewolf fast. I groan and slow to a stop just inside the Palace's exit doors.

"What?" I grumble.

"I need to show you something," he says, his voice the same husky baritone that sang for me when he was onstage with Outlaw Merriment on Thanksgiving.

"Show it," I say tersely.

"It's not here. I need to take you someplace."

"Let me guess. The lacrosse bleachers. I've seen those."

"Someplace else."

"Where, Rob?" I'm still not looking at him. If I do, I'll stupidly agree to whatever dumb idea he has this time.

"Just come with me. I'll show you."

"Can I eat lunch first? I've been working my ass off since seven this morning."

He lowers his voice to a whisper, "We can get lunch on the way."

"The way?" I sneer. "You mean off—" I was going to say off campus, but he cuts me off.

"Shhh. Yes."

Do I want to sneak off campus? It's not allowed, even if it is Saturday, not for work-study kids like me. Sure, Prince can get me out of anything.

Trouble, I mean. Can Rob? He got me out of that iron maiden, but can he get me out of trouble with Brawny or Ms. Skelter or whoever else? Probably not. It's not worth it.

"No, Rob."

He squeezes my wrist gently.

"Would you let go?!" I glare at him. Big mistake. God damn, he's *so* hot. "No, Rob. I mean it."

"It's very important, Mary. I wouldn't be asking if it wasn't." He's sincere. And sincerely handsome.

Looking at him makes my heart ache. Prince is to die for. But Rob? I don't know what it is, he's just, I can't explain it. Rob has this effect on me. Chemistry or whatever. Seeing him, smelling him, being touched by him, is intoxicating.

"Okay," I sigh. "Show me your thing."

He arches an eyebrow.

I roll my eyes, "You know what I mean."

Grinning, he nods. "This way."

"Don't you need to move your mop bucket or whatever?"

"Right. Thanks." He grabs it and I follow him to a broom closet here in the Palace where he stashes it.

Outside the Palace, he says, "Meet me at the Plant Services building. You remember where that is, right?"

"Yes. Why can't we just walk there together?"

"I don't want anyone seeing us. I'll take the long way there. See you in twenty."

"Fine," I grumble and make my way across campus to Plant Services. There, I walk inside the open roll-up doors. I expect to see Jonah when I get there, but don't. It's the weekend. Things are slow.

Inside, there's pipes and I think gigantic boilers for the hot water or whatever, and big electrical boxes. There's a big flat concrete area inside with stacks of stuff on wood palettes wrapped in shipping plastic and near that, a Plant Services van.

I lean against a palette and wait.

Fifteen minutes later, Rob walks in.

"You're late," I joke.

He rolls his eyes and gets the passenger door of the van for me and says, "Get in the back and hide under the tarp."

"How romantic," I snark and climb over the seat. In the back, I slide under the tarp and lie down. My door thunks behind me. A moment later, Rob drops in the driver's seat and starts the engine. I grumble, "Why are you always sneaking and spying everywhere you go?"

"Shhh," he says. "Keep your mouth shut and your head under that tarp. If you don't, I'll have to blindfold you."

"What?!" I laugh. "Shut the fuck up. You are not blindfolding me," I say, annoyed.

"I'm not kidding, Mouth. Do what I say."

"Fine," I groan. I guess Mr. Prison Rob is back in the house? We drive for a while. "Where are we going already? This tarp stinks like mildew."

Rob doesn't answer.

Not long after, the van stops, the brakes squeaking meekly.

"You can get out," Rob says.

"I guess we're at the Batcave?" I quip.

Rob grunts and gets out.

I climb from under the tarp and out of the passenger side where Rob is holding the door. We're parked inside an automotive garage. Nobody is here except us.

I smirk, "Is this your chop shop where you break down stolen cars for parts?"

"No," Rob grunts and leads me over to a black racing motorcycle. I recognize it immediately. It's one of the ones from the night I met him and his friends. Two helmets sit on the seat. Rob kicks off his work boots and unzips his coveralls to his waist, revealing a tight black T-shirt glued to every rugged muscle underneath.

"Do I get a free show?" I titter.

He smirks and pushes his coveralls down past bulging boxers.

I blush and avert my eyes. Somewhat.

Rob pulls a dark pair of jeans off a workbench and jumps into them. Slides on a nondescript black leather jacket. Pulls on his work boots. Damn if he isn't the perfect picture of a rebel biker.

Rob grabs one helmet from the motorcycle and tosses the other to me. I catch it. "Where's mine?"

He frowns.

"My motorcycle," I smirk.

"Put your helmet on," he barks.

"Are you always this terse when you're sneaking around?"

"Yes." He puts his helmet on. "Well?"

"Well what?"

"Your helmet, Mouth. I know you know what to do with it."

"Oh yeah, how?"

"You were riding your motorcycle the night we met."

"Nope." Technically, it was Dwight's.

"Okay, you stole it."

"How do you know about that?" I never told him about getting arrested. Then again, he knew I was in jail for attempted murder.

"I know lots of things, Mouth. Helmet. Now."

"Fine," I sigh. "Do I get to drive?"

"No. We don't have time." He lunges toward me and grabs me under the armpits.

"Hey! Stop that!" Before I know it, he tosses me onto the back of the bike. I whine, "Don't man handle me!"

"Then do what I say." He takes my helmet from my hands like he's going to put it on for me.

"I can do it!" I grab it and put it on, tightening the chin strap.

Rob ninja-kicks his leg over the seat and says, "You ready?"

"Yes! Go already!"

"Hold on tight." He pulls something out of his jacket. A remote. He clicks the button and the rollup doors of the garage rattle open. "Get a good grip, Mouth. I'm not going until you do."

"Okay!" I grouse and wrap my arms around his trim waist.

"Tighter." He reaches back and pulls my hips against his until it's a snug fit with my thighs spread wide.

I gasp in surprise.

He revs the engine and we roll out of the garage.

When we hit the street, the engine screams and the acceleration nearly throws me off the back of the racing bike. I don't go though, because this isn't my first bad boy rodeo, and I know how to hold on to a man on a motorcycle.

Looking around, I quickly realize we're in downtown Castle Hill, not far from where Rob's band played. When we get to a stop sign I say loud enough for him to hear and with ample sarcasm, "Good thing you made me close my eyes on the way here. Now I know where downtown is."

The engine revs and we slide through town. The Christmas decorations are out. Glittery bows and candles and trees attached to every lamppost.

A few minutes later, we reach the outskirts of town and pass what looks like a smallish sports arena slash event hall. It's a flurry of activity, with trucks coming and going and scaffolding and workmen putting up what looks like fake snow and ice panels and whatnot on the outside.

"Any idea what that is?" I holler. "Some kind of Christmas pageant or something?"

Rob shrugs.

When we hit the open mountain roads, Rob really opens up the motorcycle. We very literally race around the snaking roads. Rob sure knows how to ride. Good thing I know how to lean into the turns with him because our knees are almost scraping pavement around every corner. I can't see the speedometer, but we're going blinding fast. If I had to guess, sometimes as fast as a hundred miles an hour.

I'm not sure how long we go that fast because my adrenalin is pumping so hard, time slows to a crawl. After what is maybe twenty or thirty minutes of hard riding, it seems like two hours or more have passed.

I'm drained when we turn onto a gravel road between trees that leads off the main road into the woods. This road we go down slow. We stop at a gate that says Private Property. Rob gets off to unlock it and we continue at least a mile until we get to a boxy building painted army green and hidden under the canopy of pine trees. It looks basically brand new and sits on a concrete pad and has a gravel ramp leading up to a rollup garage door. It also has a regular door made of steel. There's not a single window I can see anywhere on the building.

Rob turns off the racing bike and slides his leg over the seat, then takes off his helmet.

I flip up my visor and say, "Is this where you keep the bodies?"

"Yes," he smirks. "Once I drain you dry, I'll add you to the pile."

I can't decide if that was innuendo, a threat, or both. Whatever. "How come no blindfold? I saw how we got here. I can find my way back."

"Good. If you're ever in trouble, come here."

"Erm, okay."

"Let's go inside." Before I can climb off, he picks me up and swings my legs around, setting my boots down on the gravel. He unlocks the rollup and pushes the black bike inside. Three others are parked there already. I recognize them as the same ones Tucker, Jonah and Skill had the night we met. Red tool chests line the walls. It's like the inside of a motorcycle repair shop. Rob pulls down the rollup and locks it from the inside. "This way."

He leads me through a door into a single room with a concrete floor that is fairly large. It's dark, filled with racks of blinking computers and monitors, shelves loaded with all kinds of random gear, including computer parts, packaged food and bottled water. It's like an apocalypse prepper's paradise. Skill, Tucker and Jonah sit in rolling office chairs facing the computers. They don't even glance at us.

Then I realize why. They know it's us. On one of the monitors, I see video of the outside of the building. I'm guessing they have cameras everywhere? Makes sense with all the spying they do.

Rob says, "Mary, do you want some water or a snack?"

I smirk, "You have any MREs?" I'm referring to military Meals Ready-to-Eat. I've never had one, but I've heard the term in movies or whatever.

Skill spins around in his chair grinning, "Did I mention how much I like you, War Paint?"

"Hey, Skill," I say.

Tucker spins around with a lascivious grin, "I've got your MRE right here, Mary." He means the MRE in his jeans.

Rob glares at him. "Lock that shit up, Tucker."

Tucker ignores him. "Mary, you wanna get locked up? Just you and me somewhere romantic? I can make it happen. Say the word."

Rob barks, "Shut the fuck up, Tucker! I didn't bring Mary here so you could practice your game."

Tucker rolls his eyes and snickers to himself, lacing his fingers behind his head and showing off his muscled arms popping out of his tight black T-shirt.

I say to them, "Why did you bring me? What is this place anyway?"

Skill says, "Our secret fucking hideout." He points to a neon sign above the monitors that literally says Secret Fucking Hideout in red neon letters.

I laugh, "Whose idea was that?"

"Mine," Jonah says.

"Nice," I grin. Jonah is always surprising me with his quiet mystery. Sometimes, despite his gigantic size, I think he's my favorite of these four Poor Boys. "Anyway, what's the deal? Is this where you guys bring your stolen money or whatever?" They all know I know they took a million dollars in cash from the GTO cannibals, or however much it was.

"Among other things," Rob says. "Take a seat, Mary." He rolls the fourth and currently empty office chair over to me. "We need to tell you a few things about Prince Lancaster that you're not going to like."

Chapter 40

"Prince Turd is lying to you," Tucker says.

"Lying," I scoff. "About what?"

"Take a look," Skill says. He opens an image on the computer screen in front of him. It's that photo of Prince in Honduras handing out water purifiers.

"Where'd you get that?" I gasp in surprise because they must've stolen.

"From Prince's cloud account," Skill says.

"When?"

"A few days before you returned his broken router."

Rob says, "I wish you hadn't done that."

I smirk, "I wish you hadn't made me put it in his penthouse in the first place."

Rob grumbles to himself.

Skill says, "Prince stole this photo."

"What," I snort, "from himself?"

"No," Skill says. "From the charity that actually installed the purifier."

"That's ridiculous," I scoff.

Skill opens another photo. It's the exact same image as the one with Prince, except this time, Prince is replaced by some random smiling guy wearing hipster eyeglasses and a blue T-shirt with the logo Water Of Life.

"Wait, what?" I laugh. "What happened to Prince? What is this?"

"It's from the Water Of Life website," Skill says. "The same place Prince stole a hundred other photos."

"Stole?"

Skill shrugs, "He downloaded them the same day he downloaded the doctored photo I just showed you."

"How do you know?"

"It's on the data log from when you had our hacked wifi router jacked into his penthouse. About an hour after he downloaded them all, he emailed the un-doctored one to some graphic designer living in New York somewhere."

"How do you know all that?"

"Their contact email is on their website. They do design work and Photoshop work, shit like that. The next day, Prince gets an email asking for photos of him with the same lighting as in the water photo. Prince emails some local photographer not far from Castle Hill and arranges a photo shoot the next day, saying price is not an issue. The photographer quotes him a ridiculous price. Prince agrees."

That definitely sounds like Prince.

Skill continues, "Prince also contacts one of those print-on-demand T-shirt websites and has them make him a T-shirt, rush delivery. A few days later, the photographer sends Prince dozens of photos that show Prince matching the pose in the water photo, the one you saw. Prince forwards those to the graphic designer. Two days later, Prince gets the Photoshopped photos back." Skill taps the photo on the monitor. "This one."

I shake my head, "How do I know any of that's true? How do I know you guys didn't Photoshop this Water Of Life guy out of the photo, and put Prince in, just to trick me?"

Skill opens a browser window to the Water Of Life page. Clicks a tab marked "Our Work." A series of photos load. Photos I recognize from Prince's phone. Dozens of them. Including the one Prince is in, except he's *not* in the one on the website. The random guy with glasses is.

That can't be right. I blurt, "How come Prince is wearing a Water Of Life T-shirt? Did they Photoshop that in?"

Skill opens a series of photos of Prince standing in a photo studio in front of a blank green backdrop. He's wearing a blue T-shirt with the Water Of Life logo. "Guess what custom T-shirt he ordered?" Skill smirks at me. "He took the logo from the Water Of Life website and put it on the shirt he ordered."

I'm suddenly boiling hot.

Rob says, "He's been lying to you all along, Mary."

Skill adds, "This is just the tip of the iceberg, War Paint."

Tucker grunts, "Everything that fucker says is a lie. Don't trust him, Mary."

"They're right," Jonah says gently.

Dumbfounded, I stare at them.

Rob Fletcher and his merry men suddenly don't look very merry.

"No," I shake my head. "I don't believe you guys. Prince was in Honduras. He told me. He was gone that whole weekend! I know! He flew to Honduras with a bunch of security guards!"

"Which weekend?"

"The one before I gave the spy cameras back and broke your stupid router." I gasp.

"Show her the emails," Rob says.

Skill starts opening emails.

"See for yourself," Rob says.

I don't want to believe any of this. I want to run out of here and never look back, but Rob pushes me up to the desk next to Skill.

"Scroll through them," Skill says, handing me a mouse.

I take my time looking at the emails. Everything I read corroborates everything they said about Prince. The whole time I'm reading, I'm shaking my head in disbelief. "He was in Honduras!" I insist. "He told me!"

"May I?" Skill motions at the mouse.

I nod silently.

He takes it and opens a video. It plays and shows what looks like security camera footage of Prince walking into a cute brick building that looks like it belongs in downtown Castle Hill. There's an old-timey photography logo on the glass window. Prince opens the door and walks inside.

I gasp.

Rob says, "Look at the time and date stamp. Is that the weekend Prince said he was in Honduras?"

"Can I see a calendar?" I ask.

Skill opens one on the computer.

I cringe. "It is. That's the same weekend." My eyes are watering when I look over my shoulder at Rob.

"Sorry, Mary," he says sympathetically. "He's lying to you about Honduras and who knows what else."

"Did Prince even pay for those water purifiers?"

"Which ones?" Skill asks.

"The ones in all these pictures. Prince said he paid for a hundred of them to be given out around the world."

Rob sighs, "We've been monitoring his various email accounts but I don't remember seeing anything about any transactions with Water Of Life. Do you, Skill?"

Skill shakes his head, "No, nothing like that."

I scowl, "So he never paid them for the ones in the pictures?"

Skill says, "Let me check something." Skill does a bunch of computer wizardry for a few minutes and says, "These pics have been on the Water Of Life website for a while, some of them going back five years. Unless he's been giving money to them the past five years…" Skill trails off.

"No," I snort. "I don't think he thought of it until I mentioned it."

Rob says, "Then he never paid for them."

It's like a slap in the face.

"Why?" I whimper, cringing near tears. "Why would he go to so much trouble to lie to me?"

"That's what he does," Tucker grunts. "He's a fucking liar. Every other word out of his mouth is a lie."

"But why?" I demand. "I don't understand. I mean, why me? He can have any woman he wants. Why pick me?"

Rob says, "Why *wouldn't* he pick you?"

I shake my head in disbelief, "I don't understand. I'm a nobody. What could I possibly give him that a hundred other better looking women can't?"

"Love," Rob says.

"Wha-a-a-t?!" I stutter out a confused laughing cry because none of this makes one iota of sense.

"Love," Rob says, repeating that one word. "It's the only thing Prince can't buy."

Tucker growls, "But he'll lie his fucking ass off to get it. Rich people always fucking lie to get what they want. Always."

Jonah and Skill nod agreement.

I don't know what to say. I'm not processing much of what they're telling me because I'm fixated on Prince's lies. I feel completely betrayed. It doesn't matter we aren't hooking up, doesn't matter we're not officially dating. We kissed. Multiple times. I live in his guest bedroom. He got me *and* Mimi dresses for the winter formal. I was going to let him sleep with me! Thank goodness I didn't.

Suddenly, the pieces fall into place.

This is awful!

I'm a fool for trusting him!

If Prince would go to all this trouble just to fake a photo to make him look good, what else is he lying about? Everything? Can I trust a single word he says? Obviously not!

Rob says softly, "Mary, will you put our cameras back in Prince's suite?"

Skill adds, "And the router?"

"No-a!" I scowl angrily. "I'm never setting foot in his penthouse ever again! I don't even want to go in there for my stuff! Ew! He is so effing creepy! Just, gross!" I suddenly remember my backpack with my journal and my parents' rings. "I mean, I'll go back, but only long enough to get my stuff, then I'm out. I'm going back to live in the Convent. Screw Prince."

"At least put the router back," Skill says. "We need that more than the cameras."

"I broke it, remember? I gave it back to Mr. Hovarth."

"I rigged up another one," Skill says and walks to a nearby shelf. "Got it right here. All you have to do is swap it out like before." He offers it.

Rob says, "Will you, Mary? For us?"

I cringe, "Why do you want me to do this again? To take his family down or whatever?"

"For starters," Rob says.

"What do you mean for starters?" I scowl.

He turns to his friends, "Do we tell her?"

"Do it," Tucker says.

"The whole truth," Jonah says.

"All of it," Skill says.

"What?" I ask with trepidation. Then it hits me. I smirk sarcastically, "What part did *you* guys leave out that you accidentally forgot to tell me until now?"

They don't answer right away and exchange guilty looks.

"Spit it out," I snarl and fold my arms across my chest. "And it better be effing good, or I'm walking out of here and never talking to any of you ever again."

Chapter 41

Rob winces noticeably at my comment before saying, "Remember how I told you we want to take down the Fundies?"

"Yeah?" I prompt warily.

"Taking down was somewhat of a misleading term."

"Great," I groan. "What *did* you mean? Kill them?" As soon as I say it, I'm frightened out of my mind. I know what these four guys are capable of. I saw it with my own two eyes! Rob was covered in black blood the night I met him! I mean, it was probably red, but it was dark, and it looked black, but you know what I mean! I smelled blood! There was no mistaking it! Rob and his friends are killers! They shot the two cannibals in the GTO when I was locked in the trunk, and Rob murdered somebody in the woods before he walked out!

"No," Rob chastens, "we're going to rob them blind."

"Rob them?" I say, not believing it.

"Yes," Rob says.

"The Fundies?"

Rob nods.

Tucker says, "Every fucking cent."

I say, "You're going to rob every one of them? That's a ton of people."

Rob shakes his head, "Only the richest ones. We don't have the resources to heist them all, and some of them aren't worth the effort."

I say, "And, what, you wanted *me* to help?"

Rob nods slowly.

"Erm, I'll say it again for totally different reasons. Why me? Why do you need *my* help? The only stealing I've ever done is shoplifting. And an old motorcycle, but that's different."

Rob says, "No one has gotten close to Prince except you."

I think for a moment then smirk, "Oh, I get it, you want to *use* me. You're no better than he is." I slap my hands on my thighs. "Welp, I guess that's it." Furious, I stand up. "I'll be leaving now. I'm out."

Tucker chuckles, "The only person who wants to use you is Skill." He's obviously referring to sex.

"Me?!" Skill snorts. "I'm the only one who cut her in on any of our takes, in case you forgot! I haven't seen any of you fucks handing her any cash since."

I laugh, "He's right about that. When do I get paid for the spying I already did?" I hold out my hand expectantly.

Rob says, "Once we crack the codes on Prince's accounts."

"Don't you guys have access to his emails and credit cards or whatever? Isn't that enough?"

"We don't do credit cards. He can easily cancel those. We're here for the big haul. We want access to his family's bank accounts. Setting that up takes time. We're working him and the other Fundy whales at the same time. We don't make a move until everything is ready to go. Once we flip the switch, we'll have hours to transfer as many billions as we can offshore before they're onto us and shut us down."

"Billions?" I blurt.

"As many as we can get," Rob says.

My jaw drops. "You're going to steal *billions* with a B?"

"Fuck yeah we are," Tucker cackles.

"Ha!" I laugh.

They don't. They just sit there staring at me.

I frown, "You guys are serious."

They all nod.

"And you want *my* help?"

More nods.

I remember seeing Skill kick the shit out of those two cannibals. That boy can fight. I've had more than my fair share of scuffles, but we're talking grown men. I couldn't kick the ass of a grown man, not without a knife. That kind of thing is way out of my wheelhouse.

I suddenly shake my head and throw my hands in the air. "Why am I even talking about this?! All I have to do is keep my grades up, do my time at Castle Hill, and I'll get full tuition at any university I want! Why the F would I want to blow that?! No. No way. I'm not doing it. Sorry, guys. I really am out."

I start toward the door.

They move as one, prowling predators on the hunt.

The hair goes up on the back of my neck and I stop in my tracks. "Erm, I promise I won't tell?" I say it like a question because I'm now scared shitless. Here I am, in a serial killer bunker way out in the woods, with four hardened criminals surrounding me like rabid wolves. "Before you guys kill me and bury my body in a ditch, tell me one thing. Did you kill those guys in the GTO?"

"Wanted to," Tucker smirks.

Jonah said, "They tried to shoot us."

"I knocked their shit out as payback," Tucker adds.

"You didn't shoot them?"

"No," Jonah says with conviction.

Skill says, "Don't forget the two I hobbled."

I know the two he fought didn't die from their broken knees and ankles or whatever. They were moaning and groaning, but I assume they survived those injuries. I say, "What about you, Rob? You were covered in blood when you came out of the shadows."

"I wouldn't say covered," he says guiltily.

I roll my eyes. "Who'd you kill?"

"I didn't kill anybody."

"Was it *your* blood?" I demand, not caring that interrogating these four killers might get me killed if I push them too far. Then again, if they're going to off me anyway, what do I have to lose? May as well ask for a few answers. "Was it yours?"

"No," Rob says uncomfortably. "I had a little bit of a knife fight before I saw you. He had a gun."

"Did you kill him?"

"I defended myself when he tried to shoot me. Things got a little messy when I took away his gun. Had to use my knife. I didn't cut anything vital, I know that. He lived."

"Ha!" I blurt. "He probably bled out in the dark all by himself! Your hands were *covered* with blood, Rob! I saw!"

He scowls, "That's what happens when you tie tourniquets around the wrists of the man who threatened to shoot you in the face from point blank range before you took his gun away with your knife."

I picture it and cringe. It sounds truly horrifying any way you look at it. Assuming it's the truth.

"That's what happened," Jonah says.

Him I believe. That doesn't change how I feel.

"Sorry," I sigh, "I don't want any part of this, you guys. I won't tell anyone what I know, but seriously, I'd rather go back to being an indentured servant at Castle Hill until I finish my four years and go to college like a normal person. You totally understand, right?"

They don't answer.

"I mean, I swear on my life, I'll never tell anyone about you guys. If you knew the shit I've seen, you'd know I can keep my mouth shut. Believe me," I snort, "I know how to keep an effing secret."

Rob grunts, "Can we talk outside?"

Tucker barks, "Say it in here. You got anything to say, we all wanna hear it."

Rob's eyes darken like lightning and his hackles go up. He glares at Tucker with feral fury.

As dangerous as Tucker is, he wilts. "Fuck! Fine! Talk outside! I don't give a fuck!" He obviously does.

Rob looks ready to bite something with his fangs, bite it by the neck and shake it until it breaks.

Nearly scared out of my panties, I titter, "You're not going to kill me, are you?"

"No," he grunts. "Let's go." He grabs my elbow and hauls me out to the garage, then outside into the woods.

It may be December, but the sky is clear and the sun is out. Though the tall pine trees shade the forest, it's fairly bright compared to inside.

Rob pushes me into the woods.

"Where are we going?!" I demand, trying to hide my nervousness.

"For a little walk."

We trudge through pine needles and a scattering of broken branches between trees. From the looks of it, nobody comes out here. We're miles from town and the woods are whisper silent.

"Do you think we'll see any deer?" I ask casually.

"Probably. If you're quiet."

"Is that a hint?"

"No, but you're loud. You walk like a hippopotamus."

"Gee thanks," I say sourly. I keep my mouth shut and quickly realize Rob's footsteps are basically silent. Me? It's like bombs going off. I try to be more careful with my steps.

We continue for several more minutes.

"Not bad," he says.

"What?"

"Now you sound like a baby hippopotamus."

"Eff you," I snicker.

A little while later, we emerge from between trees to a sloping hillside in a hidden valley between steep peaks. Densely packed pines fill every square inch of the valley. All of a sudden, I feel like Rob and I are alone in the world.

"It's beautiful," I sigh. "Like, literally breathtaking."

"Have a seat," Rob points to a big boulder jutting out of the ground. It's large enough for two.

"You need romance lessons," I snark and sit down with my boots propping me up so I don't slide off the rock into the bed of pine needles, which are slippery. I wouldn't want to go sliding down the slope if I slipped. It's a long way to the bottom, and I'm sure I'd hit a tree or three along the way.

Rob sits next to me. "I come out here whenever I need to think."

"Think about killing me?" I quip.

"No, Mouth. I want you to join up with us. So do the other guys. We already talked about it. We want you to be a full-fledged member."

"Of what, your gang?"

"More like a brotherhood."

"Erm, have you noticed I'm a girl?" I smile. "I know my hair is short, but it is growing out. Do you like what I've done with it?" I'm joking because I haven't done anything with it and he's making me nervous.

He smirks, "I miss your mohawk. That was badass."

"Really?"

He nods, grinning at his large hands, which are laced around his knees. "What do you think?"

"You already asked me that. Back in your bunker. I mean, your Secret Fucking Hideout," I giggle.

He chuckles. Says nothing. Sighs. Looks at the view. "Yes or no?"

"I don't know, Rob. I mean, I could use a billion dollars."

He snorts.

I sigh, "But it's a huge risk. If we get caught... you know exactly what happens."

"We won't."

"I've heard that before," I laugh. "I've known a lot of criminals in my time. They always get caught."

"The dumb ones," he says with certainty. "We are planning this thing out to the very last detail. We won't get caught."

"Do you really need Prince's money too? I'm sure the other Fundy families have plenty. You don't really need me at all. I don't need your money either."

His mahogany eyes lock on mine. "Do you have any idea how much of his shit I've put up with since getting to Castle Hill?"

"A lot?" I grin. "How long have you been there?"

"The hideout or Castle Hill?"

"Either? Both?"

He nods, "We poured the foundation on the hideout two years ago. Finished construction and powered up the generators about six months later."

"Wait. You guys *made* that bunker?"

"Yeah. I landed myself in the can right after we finished construction and made my way to Castle Hill. So, I've been there a year and half. The boys started trickling in shortly after."

"Trickling?"

"Spaced out a few months apart. I didn't want us showing up at the same time. It'd look suspicious."

"You make it sound like you guys went to Castle Hill on purpose."

"We did."

"You never said why you went to jail. I remember Eliza-bitch insisting that you, um, you know..." I trail off. My first day at Castle Hill, she and the Silicones insisted that Rob was a rapist.

His mahogany eyes blacken with cancerous hate.

Oh no. I shouldn't have mentioned it! No, it's better I know the truth.

He growls low, "That lying cunt will say anything that comes to mind, no matter how hurtful it is. Anything to put herself above everyone else. She doesn't give a shit about anyone. Not one fucking person except herself."

"Erm, does that mean she was lying? About you and the..." I'm practically whispering it, I'm so afraid to speak.

"YES IT MEANS SHE'S FUCKING LYING!" Rob roars. "I WOULD NEVER—! FUCK HER! SHE HAS NO FUCKING IDEA WHAT SHE DOES WHEN SHE SAYS THE LYING SHIT SHE SAYS! I WAS THE ONE FUCKING RAPED, OKAY?! WHEN I WAS A LITTLE FUCKING KID! FUUUUCK!!!!"

Rob jumps off the boulder, bends down, picks up a nearby rock the size of a basketball, and hurls it one-armed against the nearest tree. It impacts with a huge boom, cracking off a thick branch and shaking the entire massive tree trunk from top to bottom. A bunch of birds flap squeaking angrily out of the pine-covered branches, wheeling away to safety.

"FUCK!" Rob storms forward, grabs the broken branch off the ground, and charges the sitting boulder where I'm looking at him over my shoulder in shocked surprise.

Frightened for my life, I slide off the rock thinking he's going to bash my head in from behind.

He doesn't. He starts beating the branch against the big sitting boulder.

Feet on the ground, I slip on the pine needles and land on my ass. There's a tense moment where I think I'll go sliding down the slope but I don't. I dust myself off and stand at a distance to watch Rob warily.

Splinters fly everywhere as he hammers away with his makeshift club.

The sitting boulder just takes it.

For ten or fifteen minutes, he shouts at it unintelligibly, bashing away with the branch, clearly intent on murdering it.

I cringe every time the branch crashes against the rock, one hand over my eyes to protect me from flying splinters. I don't know what to do, honestly. I want to hug him but I don't want to get hit by the battered branch, and I'm guessing hugging is not what he needs right now. I don't know what else to do except give him his space and wait for him to exhaust himself.

I feel awful.

Why'd I have to go opening that old wound?

When Rob runs out of gas, he stands there, heaving for air, red faced and sweat beading his brow, glaring and growling at the sitting boulder. Disgusted with himself, he throws the remaining stump of his battered branch into the pine needles.

He turns to me and hits me with a dark look.

I don't say an effing thing.

"Sorry," he grumbles. "You didn't need to see that."

"Do you want to talk about it or—" I stop myself. Of course he doesn't want to talk! He wants to kill! I am such an idiot.

"No." He squeezes his face with one big hand and scowls to himself, eyes closed.

"Sorry. I shouldn't have asked. I should've just—"

"It's not your fault," he grunts. "It's fucking Elizabeth's. If *she* hadn't said anything, *you* wouldn't have said anything. See how her lies propagate outward without her doing a thing? You see how she does one little careless thing and the repercussions amplify?"

"Totally. Like the butterfly effect."

"Exactly," he snarls. "She has no idea how she fucks up the world with her self-centered pettiness."

"Does she know?" I ask carefully. "About you, I mean?"

"Fuck no!" he snorts. "I'd never tell her."

But he told me. I'll admit, not under the best of circumstances, but he did tell me. My heart swells with tenderness. This man is letting me in. Letting down his guard.

For me.

Giddiness hits me and I want to laugh and cry at the same time.

"Fuck this shit," he grunts, startling me.

"What?"

"I suddenly don't want to look at the view. Let's head back to the hideout."

"Oh, right."

We start a slow stroll through the silent woods.

I say, "I hope I didn't ruin it for you."

"Ruin what?"

"The view."

"You're fine," he says dismissively. "I've been beating that shit out of my system for a long, long time. Sometimes I think I'm over it, then it comes back like it's happening all over again."

I nod silently, knowing all about—

(You stupid retard no good for nothing lousy sack of pig shit! Look what you did to my table! You roont it! Roont!)

—reliving shit.

"Anyway," he sighs. "I don't want to think about it right now. Can we talk about something else?"

"Erm, um, you were saying how you ended up at Castle Hill? You and the guys?"

"Right," he nods and relaxes into a smile. "We knew they wouldn't take us if we got caught for violent crime, right?"

"They wouldn't?"

"No," Rob shakes his head. "No one at Castle Hill is a murderer, or rapist," he grumbles, "or anything like that. No violent felons. It has to be non-violent crime or they won't take you."

"Obviously. Wait. Wait, wait, wait. That can't be right. I was going to jail for attempted murder. For supposedly stabbing Queen LaQueefa in the ears with *her* toothbrush shank. That's violent. How come they took me?"

Rob's eyes glimmer wickedly. "I pulled a few strings."

"You?" I wonder. "How?"

"Leverage."

"What does that mean? You have to give me more details than that."

He smirks, "Did you want to hear about how I got to Castle Hill or not?"

"Fine. Tell me."

He grins, "Okay, so I was dating this babe one time—" He stops himself. "You don't want to hear about her."

"No, it's fine," I smirk nervously, not sure I want to either.

"Anyway, her boyfriend was a complete dick, right? Rich as fuck and twice as much of a dick."

"Wait, her boyfriend?"

Rob shrugs. "When he found out—"

I roll my eyes.

"—he hired some guys to rough me up."

"How'd that turn out?" I venture.

Rob smirks, "You know the sitting boulder back there?"

"Yeah?"

"Let's just say those guys were the boulder and I was the branch."

"Wait, that's violent. I thought you said nobody gets into Castle Hill for doing anything violent."

"They were fine," he chuckles. "It wasn't like they were going to the cops after to say they got their asses kicked after being paid to kick mine."

"Oh, I guess that makes sense."

"Once I set the boyfriend's henchmen straight, I went after him."

"What'd you do?!" I ask, my eyes wide in trepidation.

"Stole the boyfriend's Lambo and drove it off a cliff."

"You did not!" I gape.

"Sure as fuck did," he grins. "By the time his two million dollar supercar hit bottom, there was nothing left."

"Oh my god, Rob!" I'm laughing. "That is insane!"

"He deserved it for paying to have my ass kicked."

"Is that why you went to jail?"

He nods, "Grand larceny. Totally worth it."

"So, what'd the other guys do to get into Castle Hill? What crimes did they commit?"

"They can tell you some time. Anyway, ever since I heard about Castle Hill, I don't know, I was itching to take the Fundies down, like it was in my blood. So many rich dicks in one place begging to get taken. It's so much easier when your marks are teenagers. They aren't as careful as their parents."

"Wow. How many people have you robbed, Rob?"

"Enough."

"Enough?" I snicker. "So this isn't your first robbing rodeo?"

"Not even close."

"Are you guys rich?"

"Enough," he chuckles.

"Wait, wait, wait," I snort. "Why are you robbing the Fundies if you're already rich?"

"Because they're dicks."

"And you're not?!" I laugh. "You rob people! How is that not a dickish thing to do?"

"We only steal from rich people. We only keep what we need to rob the next mark, and a little extra to live on."

"I don't believe you for a second," I smile.

"Do you see any yachts or helicopters out here?"

"No-a."

"Exactly."

"Wait, you said you only keep what you need. What do you do with the extra?"

"Give it to people who need it."

"Who would that be?"

"People who don't have money."

"Like who?"

"The poor, for starters. And a lot of charities."

"Nuh uh. I don't believe that for a second either."

"Why not?"

"You guys just told me how Prince is lying about buying water purifiers! Why should I believe you guys aren't lying too?!"

"You shouldn't. I'll show you."

"I'm not going to believe a bunch of internet photos."

"That's not what I'm going to show you."

Chapter 42

Rob walks me back to the Secret Fucking Hideout and tells the others he and I are going for a ride. We suit up and he tosses me on his motorcycle and we blaze out of there. An hour later, we end up in a small mountain town called Cedar Creek. The sign says the population is 942. It doesn't even have a downtown. It's just a few dilapidated storefronts adjacent to the main road, and you can see aging houses between the old trees climbing up the hillside. Honestly, the town looks like it's on its last legs.

We park in front of a liquor store and gas station combo that sells groceries too. Not one of the big brand name ones. Just a generic local place with a sign that says Liquor - Gas - Food.

Rob buy several bags worth of staples. Milk, juice, frozen hamburger, frozen vegetables, bread, breakfast cereal, apples, bananas.

"Is this lunch?" I joke while the cashier rings us up.

"No," he says.

I roll my eyes.

Outside, we walk up a sloping road between houses. They're all run down. Sagging roofs that need replacing, peeling paint, dirty windows, rundown yards, rusty old cars parked in the weeds. It's sad, really.

Then we get to a house that looks brand new with a green lawn. There's a brand new Toyota something in the driveway. Rob walks up the cute little walk like he owns the place.

"Is this your house, Rob?" I ask.

"No. Don't call me Rob here," he mutters as he rings the doorbell. "I'm someone else."

"What?!" I hiss, confused.

"Shhh."

I hear screaming kids in side. Good screaming, like they're playing and having the time of their lives.

Laughing and thumping as someone rushes to the door. A beautiful woman opens the door. She could be the cover girl for an outdoorsy magazine. No makeup, lush gold hair in a ponytail, a flannel buttoned over a turtle neck, jeans over slender legs, patterned socks on her feet.

"Carter!" she gushes when she sees him and practically jumps into his arms, throwing her arms around his muscled neck and hugging him hard. It takes a moment for her to realize I'm standing there holding a grocery bag. "I'm so sorry! I didn't realize you brought a friend!" She breaks away from Rob, slightly embarrassed.

Rob says, "Misty, this is Jewel."

"Hi," I smile, not sure if I'm supposed to be Misty or Jewel.

"Oh, hi!" the blonde beauty says. "*You're* Jewel! Carter told me all about you!" She holds out her hand for me to shake it.

I shake. "Hi. Ruh-*Carter* never mentioned you." Oops. Misty doesn't notice my slip, but Rob smirks at me. I smirk back. He should've told me to call him effing Carter!

"Come in, come in," Misty says. The kids inside are all little with big eyes staring at me.

When Rob and I step into the house, the kids scream, "Carter!" and jump all over him. He hastily hands grocery bags to Misty. A bunch of rough-house wrestling ensues with Rob in the middle of it on the living room floor. I help Misty unload groceries in the kitchen and we make small talk about the weather. After we finished putting everything away, she makes tea and tells me to help "Carter" with the kids.

Rob knows all their names and introduces me to each one. I can't keep their names straight, especially after the girls show me their dolls and plushies and name all twenty of them.

"Who wants juice and cookies?!" Misty calls out, carrying a tray into the living room.

A chorus of "I do!" sounds from the kids.

Rob sits on the couch surrounded by girls snuggling up with him and boys still trying to wrestle him. Rob is laughing when he says, "Can't I eat my cookies?"

A little boy grabs the cookie Rob is about to munch on and eats it himself.

Rob looks at me and laughs, "Did you see that little thief?"

The boy snickers around a mouthful of half-eaten cookie.

"Which one?" I wink at Rob.

He rolls his eyes.

The kids eventually settle down. Rob asks how the kids are doing. Misty says great, and details the doings of her little monsters, which she actually calls them. What a cool mom. I'm pretty sure they aren't all Misty's kids, because none of them look alike, unless she's had a lot of boyfriends. Ahem. There's seven kids in all. And now that I'm looking at her, I'm pretty sure Misty's too young to be all their moms.

I don't say much but I'm happy to listen while they talk at length about everything under the sun.

When the cookies and juice are gone, Rob says, "We should probably be going."

"Oh, I see how it is," Misty flirts. "You come for the cookies, then it's out the door with you."

"Something like that," he grins.

On the front porch, Rob pulls out his wallet, pulls out a bunch of cash, and offers it to Misty.

"What's that?" she smirks.

"For groceries. It's five hundred. It isn't much, but it's all I have on me."

"Oh no." Misty shakes her head and her ponytail waves. "No, no, no! You've given us more than enough already, Carter! First you pay off our mortgage. Then you pay the property taxes for the next *ten* years! Then a new car! No, Carter! No!" Misty is laughing. She smiles at me, "You're probably used to this. He's like this with you too. Mr. Generous. I know Carter."

"Yeah," I grin. What I want to say is, actually, no, he never gives me anything, but I know better than to spoil the mood.

Rob is insistent about Misty taking the money until she eventually relents. We say our goodbyes, and Rob and I walk slowly back down the road. The kids rush outside onto the lawn and wave, "Bye, Carter! We miss you!"

At the Liquor- Gas - Food store parking lot, I finally say, "Who was that? Your ex-wife?"

"No," Rob chuckles. "I was riding through town one day and bumped into her here. She had her kids with her."

"Are they all hers?"

"No. Two are. The rest are foster."

"Makes sense," I nod knowingly. I wish I'd had a foster mom like Misty. I never would've run away. Instead I had Gladys. And Dwight and Shayla. And so many other horror movies in between.

"She was broke when I met her. Her husband was a long haul trucker until he was killed in an accident. Some fucking drunk driver," Rob grunts. "Anyway, she'd just buried him the week before I met her. Her eyes were hollow, like she hadn't slept in days. A walking zombie taking care of those kids. She didn't know how she was going to pay rent when the insurance money ran out. When it did, she knew she'd have to give up some of the kids."

"How awful," I say sincerely.

"Tell me about it. So I paid everything off so she wouldn't have to worry about money. With the life insurance payout from her husband, and what I gave her, she has enough to raise those kids until they're eighteen."

"You did all that?"

"Wouldn't you?"

"If I was a billionaire," I bluster.

"You can do a lot of good with money." He arches a hopeful eyebrow, obviously hinting at me joining his good guy gang.

"I get it," I roll my eyes.

"Good," he says.

I change the subject. "Misty sure is pretty."

"You noticed?" he smirks.

"She sure likes you. Were you and her ever a thing?"

He glares at me, "Her husband *died* right before I met her. What kind of person do you think I am? She needed someone to help her, not take advantage of her."

That's a no. "Had to ask," I grin. "Wait, did you like, hire her and those kids to pretend they know you for today?"

He chuckles, "In the last hour?"

"Mmm-hmm," I nod.

"Please, Mouth. That kind of a scam would take days to set up."

"I don't know," I whine. "I'm not a scam artist."

"Rounding up the kids alone and getting comfortable with them would take days. Maybe weeks."

"Sorry for asking!"

"It's fine," he grins. "You hungry for lunch?"

"Am I ever! Misty's cookies were good, but I could use some real food."

"There's a great diner here in town."

"Sounds like a plan."

Mama Susie's Diner serves standard roadside burgers and fries, but they taste incredible. Their hot apple pie à la mode is the best I've ever had. Or maybe that's just the company. I can't tell. Sitting across a table staring into Rob's dreamy eyes while we attack the ice cream and pie makes our dessert taste better. It also makes the colors in the diner more vibrant, and the smells from the kitchen more delicious, making me want seconds, thirds, fourths, anything to drag out my time with Rob.

"We should get back," he says after paying the bill. Outside in the parking lot, Rob lifts me onto the black motorcycle and we race back to the bunker. There, he peels off his helmet and says, "Now do you believe me?"

"What, that you help people?"

He nods and sets his helmet on the gas tank. We're still outside, surrounded by the trees circling the bunker.

I unstrap my helmet and hang it from the handlebars. "Misty and her kids are *one* family. For all I know, they're the only family you help."

"They're one among many," Rob says. "There's organizations and charities we help too. We donate a lot of money to them. Doing daily grocery drop-offs ourselves is impossible with us working at the academy. You know how busy we are."

"But you find time for Misty," I smirk.

"That was a random thing. I've only been to her house a few times. For the most part, I just give her money and make suggestions about what to do with it."

"Money you stole," I snark.

"From rich people," he counters.

"It's still a crime."

"Is it? Ask yourself, where do rich people get their money in the first place?"

"They earn it?"

Rob snorts in amusement. "Have you ever heard the saying, behind every great fortune lies a great crime?"

I smirk, "Is the great crime the one where you steal someone's great fortune from behind when they aren't looking and you lie about it later?"

Rob grins in surprise, "Very clever, Mouth."

I bury my face in my elbow and throw out my other arm, hitting a casual Dab.

Rob chuckles.

I say, "So you guys *are* criminals."

"We only steal what's already been stolen. We pick our targets carefully. Take the Morgan-Hearsts, for example."

Having researched them myself, I know there's truth to what he's saying.

"Like I said," he adds, "we give most of what we take back to people who need it. That's the key difference. Me and the boys only steal enough to keep stealing. We don't waste our money on useless consumer bullshit."

"I can see that," I say, glancing at the bunker. It's hardly a mansion. "Unless you're hiding your yacht and castle at your own private Caribbean island or whatever."

He rolls his eyes, "We don't own any islands."

"How do you know them anyway? Jonah, Skill, and Tucker?"

"We met in foster care."

"Really?"

He nods. "Really nasty place. Our foster dad was a con artist. Taught us half the scams we know."

"No way!"

"It wasn't great. He was an alcoholic. Disgruntled ex-military plagued by PTSD. Beat the shit out of us as much as taught us how to steal and fight."

Old memories of Gladys suddenly punch me in the stomach.

(Please don't hit me! Ow! I didn't do anything!)

(Did too, dummy! Did! WHACK! Too! WHACK!)

(Leave me alone! Somebody help me! Help! Please!)

(You get back here, pig shit! WHACK! Stand still and take it like a lady! WHACK!)

I wish Gladys had taught me how to fight. The only thing she taught me was how to run away.

"Something wrong?" Rob asks.

"Nothing," I shake my head, my eyes watering. I sniff, "You were saying? About learning how to fight with Skill and them?"

He nods, "Me and the boys bonded over fighting. Became blood brothers. Vowed to always have each others backs, to always be there to catch each other if we fell. That's what we've been doing since we ran away."

"You too?! I ran away from foster care! That's how I ended up in juvi!"

"Happens to the best of us," he winks. He reaches into his pocket. "Oh, I keep forgetting to give this to you. I never have a chance on campus." He hands me a knife.

I gasp, "Grayson's knife! You remembered!"

"How could I forget?" he chuckles. "You wanted to stab me with it the day we met."

"I never thought I'd get it back." I'm tearing up as I throw my arms around him and hug him tight. I hardly have any possessions to my name, but the few I do, like this knife, mean the world to me.

"Use it the next time any Rich Girls try to lock you up."

"I can't do that! I'll get thrown in jail for assault with a deadly weapon!" I'm laughing but it's true.

"I didn't say stab them," he chuckles. "Just scare them."

"I'll still get in trouble! You know how Castle Hill works. The Fundies get away with murder and we get the shaft for every little thing."

"Don't worry, Mary." Rob puts both his big hands on my comparatively tiny shoulders. "No matter what happens, if you fall, I'll always be there to catch you."

"What if you can't?"

"I will."

"No, I mean, what if I get caught or blamed for having a knife or whatever, and I get hauled away? It *could* happen, you know. It's not like you're Prince and you can tell the faculty what to do. Wait, can you?"

"No. Me and the boys may have money, but we don't have the kind of power and influence he does at Castle Hill. Not yet, anyway. We're working on it."

"See?"

He sighs, "Do you not want the knife?"

"No-a, it's just, I don't know." I stare at Grayson's blade, torn about what to do with it. "I'm assuming you stole it from Mr. Ralston or whoever?"

He nods. "I can put it back if you want. Nobody'll ever know it was gone."

"Maybe you better." I offer it to him reluctantly. He reaches out to take it. Before he can, a series of images flash through my mind, starting with me running away on Dwight's Kawasaki and ending with Ms. Skelter forcing me to shave my pink mohawk. I'm never living under anyone's oppressive thumb. I snap my fingers closed over Grayson's knife. "No. I'm keeping it."

Rob's mouth eases into a wide smile. "Don't worry, Mary. If anything happens, I'll take the fall for you. Just don't stab anyone," he grins.

"I'll try. But if they push me into another iron maiden, I'll cut them all into one big fillet of bitch sandwich." Laughing, I flick the blade open with my thumb and wave it menacingly.

He laughs too.

I grin and close the blade before slipping it into my pocket.

He sighs, "If you stick with me, Mary, I won't ever let anything bad happen to you."

"Stick with you? Like one of your blood brothers?"

"Something like that," he says mysteriously, his mahogany eyes glimmering.

I'm speechless. What Rob has shown me today, and the things he's done in the months since I met him, are simply put, incredible. It's exciting to be around Prince and his money, sure, but Rob is something special. I can't put it into words. I've never met anyone like him, and I'm pretty sure I'll never meet anyone else like him as long as I live. It's like we have this special, magical, *timeless* connection. I can feel it. Like we're destined for each other. Not blood brothers.

Blood lovers.

Saying it sounds stupid, almost morbid, like we're vampires, which we're not. We're just two living, breathing regular people. But it feels like so much more than that. I can't explain it, but I feel it in my heart, this connection of ours. It's so beautiful, so complete, it's frightening and almost painful, but in a good way, like the hurting only happens when we're apart. When we're together, it's ecstasy. I've felt distant hints of this with other boys, but never with the power and intensity I'm feeling for Rob right now.

Does he feel it too?

I search his eyes.

If he's attracted to me, if he's feeling anything at all, he isn't sending any signals. But that night I spent cuddling with him in his bedroom in the Monastery? On Halloween? When we were in bed together then it was unforgettable. I still feel the imprint of Rob's body burned into mine like he never left. Like he entered me then and our souls rejoined after an eternity of separation and recombined for an eternity of union. It sounds crazy, but it's what I felt then and feel now. He *had* to have felt it too.

And you know what?

After the Silicones locked me in the iron maiden, Rob really *was* there to catch me when I fell. I have complete faith he'll be there the next time and the next. I don't know why, but that's what my heart is telling me.

Rob says in his deep singer's voice, "Whaddaya say, Mary? You want to help us take Prince's family's money and use it to help the people who actually need it?"

I wince. My feelings for Rob aside, he's asking me to spy on Prince for the express purpose of stealing his money. Part of me wants to say yes to anything Rob asks me because I trust him. The other part doesn't want to harm people for any reason, even those who might deserve it.

I bite my lower lip, "Erm, can I think on it? I'm supposed to go to the winter formal with Prince tonight. Can I decide after? This is all so much, you know?"

"Will this help you make up your mind?"

"Will what help?" I titter, confused.

Rob lunges at me and throws me onto the motorcycle seat. My feet kick up in surprise and I wrap my legs around his waist to keep from falling over backward onto the ground. Rob hooks an arm around my waist and jerks me toward him, leaning in for a kiss and stealing it with ease.

My arms wrap gently around his muscled neck. His lips are exquisite, claiming my mouth with his, taking full ownership, his tongue slipping and sliding in time with mine, owning every cell in my body with an overwhelming rush of electric energy that spins out from my heart and joins with his, an endless eternal connection that sizzles my nipples and lights a fire between my thighs, drenching everything.

"I'm in," I gasp, pulling his hips into mine.

Chapter 43

I'm out of breath after running from the Plant Services building where Rob dropped me off. I'm running late and Prince is probably wondering where I am. He told me to be ready to go at five o'clock and it's ten minutes past.

I burst from the elevator and dash down the hall to Prince's penthouse. He's opening the door while I'm digging out the key card he gave me.

"Marianne! What happened?" He grabs me by the arms and looks me over. "Are you okay? I was getting very worried."

"I'm fine," I sigh, trying to catch my breath while thinking of an excuse. I've got nothing. My mind is swimming with thoughts of kissing Rob. "It's, erm, I need to get ready." I push past him, barely noticing he's dressed up in a tuxedo, and march to the guest bedroom.

My dress is standing on a dress form and the designer's assistant from the other day is sitting in a chair by the window swiping through his phone looking bored.

"Sorry I'm late," I say. "Maurice, right?"

He nods.

"I didn't realize you'd be here."

"Not to worry, darling," Maurice smiles, sliding his phone into the pocket of his black and white checkerboard blazer. A red pocket scarf matches his red slacks, and his checkerboard shoes matches his jacket. He offers me a flirty wink, "Lateness is a sign of greatness, I always say."

"I like the sound of that," I laugh.

"It's what I tell all my boyfriends," he whispers conspiratorially and waves a dismissive hand. "What can I say? I'm worth it and you are too."

I notice a sharply dressed young woman sitting in the other chair next to a stack of cute little matching cases.

"Hi," I say. "Who're you?"

"I'm Claire. I'm here to do your hair and makeup."

"Oh. Erm, do we have enough time?"

Behind me, Prince says, "Barely."

I spin around and finally look at him.

His black tuxedo coat has tails. His satin vest and bowtie are white gold to match my dress. His black shoes shine with a mirror finish. The stunning outfit only accentuates his surfer good looks.

Prince says, "You have twenty minutes to turn her from a pauper into a princess."

"That's not enough time!" I blurt. "I need a shower! I'm totally gross!"

He grins, "That is a literal impossibility, fairest. Under the worst of circumstances you are nothing short of stunning. Your beauty outshines the stars above. It shines so bright, not even the sun itself can behold your exquisite perfection, lest he be dazzled into jaw-dropping awe."

"He?" I snort. "Shouldn't the sun be a she?"

Claire smirks in feminine solidarity.

Prince strokes a finger under my chin and lifts my eyes to his. "The sun shines for thee and thee alone, fairest Marianne. No maiden sun could look upon you without petty jealousy darkening her starfire and plunging the entire world into eternal night. No, fairest, the sun of our solar system was born to shine his light on you and you alone. Now that you have arrived, he shines ever brighter."

My entire body flutters with butterflies.

I am ready to swoon.

From the looks of Claire, I think she just did.

Maurice titters to himself, "I don't know about you all, but after that, I'm wet."

"Wait," I snicker, realizing something. "Prince, are you saying I'm responsible for global warming?"

"No," he chuckles, "but the mere sight of you on the day of your arrival here at Castle Hill did indeed melt the glacier encasing my heart and brought it beating back to life."

I grin, "Does that mean I get a few extra minutes to shower?"

"Make it quick," he winks and claps his hands with authority. "Chop-chop, everyone! Fairest and I have a formal to attend!" He closes the guest bedroom door on his way out.

I dash in and out of the shower so fast the water barely hits my skin. After toweling off and jumping into bra and panties, Claire makes quick work of my short hair, teasing it and freezing it into a mess of sexy spikes. Short on time, for makeup we settle on giving me smoky eyes and vampy lips.

Maurice says, "Now strip so we can get you in this dress."

I do as ordered until I'm down to my underwear.

"The bra too," Maurice says.

"Oh, right." I feel a moment's hesitation before taking it off. Maurice doesn't even notice when I do. I'm sure he's seen more boobs in the flesh working in fashion than most straight men see in their lifetimes.

It doesn't take long to get the dress on and I step into my heels, which I picked out the other day. Maurice and Claire hustle me out to the living room where Prince is waiting.

He stands there like a fashion model. When he sees me his lips widen into a sly grin and he says, "Perfection."

"You're not so bad yourself," I deflect.

"Can you help me with my boutonniere?"

"Sure." It takes me a few fumbling tries to pin it to his lapel.

He slips my matching corsage onto my wrist.

"It's beautiful," I sigh, admiring it. Never in my life did I think I'd be going to a winter formal or any sort of high school prom, let alone wearing a runway ready dress and going with one of the hottest young men on campus.

Maurice and Claire both insist on taking pictures for their look books. Maurice jokes about selling his photos to Vogue or Cosmo.

Prince grins, "If they don't start a bidding war, let me know and I'll make sure they do."

"Stop," I smile.

"I mean it, fairest. You look *that* good. Doesn't she look incredible?" He looks to Maurice and Claire.

They gush agreement because they're paid to.

I know better, but I appreciate it all the same.

"Shall we?" He offers his elbow.

"We shall," I sigh, doing my damnedest to focus on the now and not what Rob said and I read online about the Lancaster family earlier. "Oh wait! I forgot something!"

I rush back to the guest bedroom and fish Grayson's knife out of my jeans. Where to put it? Under my corsage. The knife is light and has a clip that slips around the elastic wristband of the corsage. You can't even tell it's there.

With any luck, I won't have any reason to use Grayson's knife tonight.

<(—)>

On our way past the Convent, I see a line of girls coming out wearing long-sleeve white lace above-the-knee dresses with jewel necklines. The lace detail and cut of the hem make them look like snowflakes. Their hair is done and so is their makeup. They all have the same white lace gloves, cute little white lace hairpiece, and matching low white kitten heels clacking the paving tiles on the walkway.

I recognize Luna from the salon and say, "Where are you guys going?"

"The winter formal," Luna says with a frustrated smile.

"Who're your dates? The work-study boys? Are they around here somewhere?"

Luna shakes her head and purses her lips. "We don't have dates. We're working it."

"I'll say," I grin. "You look savage in that dress."

"No, I mean we're *working* working it. We're waitressing."

"Oh," I say guiltily. That's when I notice the other work-study girls giving me dirty looks and grumbling about it. I grimace when I see one of them is Azzie, aka Elizabeth Morgan-Hearst.

She's going?

I thought she'd died.

Too bad.

I'll have to watch out for her. If she's a waitress, she might try and poison my food and drink or whatever. I check her fingernails for a fancy manicure like Elizabeth has, but I can't tell with her gloves. Not that it matters. I know they're the same person.

After walking a short distance, Prince pulls me away from the girls. They head toward the stairs that lead down to the parking garage. I notice a small group of Fundy boys and girls dressed in tuxes and gowns for the formal waiting for an elevator. There are several. The work-study girls don't wait for them. They shuffle down the stairs, their shoes echoing off the subterranean concrete as they go.

As always, the Fundies get the luxury option, and the work-study kids get the low-rent option.

"Aren't we taking your car?" I ask.

"The Bugatti?" Prince prompts.

I nod.

"Not tonight," he smiles. "I thought you might like something more comfortable." He leads me past the administration buildings to the huge roundabout and visitor parking area at the front of the school.

I see a line of white limousines and a couple charter buses filling the parking lot and backed up down the hill. "It's like everyone at the academy is going. This is crazy," I marvel.

"Winter formal always is. Our limo is around here somewhere."

"We're taking a limo?" I laugh. "I've never been in one!"

"First dance, first limo ride, what other firsts might you find waiting for you tonight?" Prince grins.

"I don't know," I laugh guiltily, partially because I notice a group of work-study boys lining up and boarding one of the charter buses. They wear white tuxedos and looking rather annoyed. I don't notice Rob or the other three Poor Boys among them. They're hard to miss.

We stop at a white limo and there's a guy in a white tuxedo and gloves waiting by the back door. "Mr. Lancaster," he says and opens the door.

"Thank you, Thomas," Prince says and motions for me to climb in the limo. "After you, fairest Marianne." He takes my hand and helps me in.

"Thanks." My dress isn't exactly movement friendly. Prince and Thomas have to help me pull the train into the limo, which is an entire production, but we manage.

Prince slides in after. Thomas closes the door and shortly after, we're creeping along past the limos and buses. I notice the work-study girls sitting in the windows of one bus looking decidedly unhappy and just a little bit pouty about it. We're supposed to have our Saturday nights free. Erm, I mean they, because I'm not working, am I?

I notice our limo has a sunroof and I feel like I should be opening it and standing in it so I can cheer about how epic tonight is going to be, but I don't want to rub it in the noses of the work-study kids.

So I sigh instead.

"Something wrong?" Prince asks, squeezing my hand.

"Nope, everything's perfect."

"It is from where I'm sitting," he grins, his blue eyes flashing and his sandalwood and cedar scent teasing my nose. "I'd kiss you but I don't want to ruin your makeup."

"Yeah," I sigh, thanking my makeup for ruining the moment.

"We'll make up for it later."

"Yeah," I practically whisper. If my mood doesn't change soon, there won't be a later. The mirror shine of every girl's dream come true princess ball is already starting to show cracks, and we haven't even left the parking lot.

"There they are," Prince says, eyes lighting up. "Stop the limo, Thomas."

"Yes, sir," Thomas says from up front through the little open compartment window.

Prince opens our back door from the inside and Chase climbs over him, followed by Mimi piling in giggling. She sits down next to me.

"Mare Bear!" she squeals and hugs me.

What a relief. Without her here, I don't think I could've done this. She wears the knee-length gown she picked out last night. An embroidered and embellished champagne-hued low V-neck that plunges well past her navel, showing cleavage and featuring her perfect legs. I could never pull off a gown that revealing, but she totally can.

"You look gorgeous," Mimi says. "Look at your makeup and hair!" She flicks a few of my spiky locks. "I love this!"

"Thanks," I grin, already perking up.

"You look fucking hot," Chase says.

"Who, me?" I giggle.

Mimi frowns dramatically, "You better not dump me for her tonight."

They're both just blowing smoke up my ass. Nobody would steal me over Mimi.

Chase says to Mimi, "I didn't say she was fucking hotter than you, babe. I just said she was fucking hot."

"Just making sure," Mimi says, sort of meaning it.

Chase says, "You're the hottest fucking babe in this school, babe. How many times do I have to tell you that?"

Mimi smiles at that, "You too, babe."

I love that they're calling each other babe. Mimi deserves a little romance in her life.

Mimi looks around herself for something, "Wears the sunroof button?"

"I got it," Prince says and opens it.

As soon as it's open, Mimi stands up. "Get up here, Mare Bear! Whoop, whoop!" Her enthusiasm is infectious.

Reluctantly, I stand up beside her.

Mimi is laughing and doing a sarcastic princess parade wave as we pass the line of limos waiting to pick up more Fundies. I don't feel so bad because we're past the work-study buses.

"Wave, Mares! Show them who the royals are!"

I don't have a problem shoving it in the faces of the Fundies. I do my own snooty princess parade wave and sneer at the few Fundy girls walking toward their limos.

Okay, maybe tonight might be fun.

Chapter 44

The limo stops and Thomas jumps out, opening the door for us. Mimi and I climb out first. We're on the outskirts of downtown Castle Hill. I immediately recognize the sports-slash-event arena from this morning. It has been fully transformed into what I can only describe as a fairytale snow castle.

"Oh my god!" Mimi gasps. "Would you look at this place?! It's insane!" Chase and Prince lead us up to the main doors. On our way, Mimi whispers in my ear, "Oh, look. The Snow Queen."

To my surprise, Ms. Skelter and Mr. Ralston flank the main doors. She wears a white dress and looks surprisingly good in it, and not at all ghostly or skeletal. Mr. Ralston wears a white and silver tuxedo that makes him look ten years younger.

"Mister Lancaster," Ms. Skelter says formally.

"Ms. S," Prince nods.

"What a beautiful young lady you've brought with you." She looks right at me, extending her hand and smiling, "Pardon my ignorance, I don't believe we've met."

"Erm," I mumble.

Her face ices over and she drops her hand to her side without shaking mine. "Mizz Angerman," she grumbles. "What are you doing here in *that* dress?" She obviously means not in one of the work-study snowflake waitress dresses.

Annoyed, I nod at Prince, "Ask him."

He says, "Isn't it obvious, Ms. S? Mary is my date for this evening."

"I can see that," Ms. Skelter scowls. She glares at Mimi, "You too, Mizz Barker?"

Chase steps forward, beaming with pride as he wraps a possessive arm around Mimi's waist. "No way I'm going to the winter formal with anyone other than the finest piece of ass on campus." He flashes a winning grin at Mimi and she eats it up.

"Mister Wendingham!" Ms. Skelter barks, furiously offended.

"What?" Chase chuckles. "You *don't* think Mimi has the best ass on campus?"

Mr. Ralston is blushing and trying not to laugh. Prince is chuckling.

Ms. Skelter is pissed, "Watch your tongue, Mister Wendingham! Foul language such as yours is *not* appropriate at an official school function!"

"Watch this tongue?" Chase flaps his tongue suggestively at Ms. Skelter. "I never do anything appropriate with it. You know that, Ms. S."

He blows her a dirty kiss and waggles his tongue expertly.

"Mister Wendingham!" Ms. Skelter harrumphs.

"Just say the word, Ms. S," he winks a laugh and leads a giggling Mimi past her and through the doors.

Ms. Skelter looks ready to explode, but she stands there impotent.

Prince says, "Don't mind us," and pulls me past her. We cross the big lobby, which is lightly decorated with silver and white streamers and garland.

Mimi hisses, "Can you believe that bitch?"

"Yes," I snort.

When we walk through the last set of doors and see the inside of the arena, I'm stunned. It has been transformed into a winter wonderland. Pools of cool colored lighting artfully reveal a sweeping snowscape. It's like walking into another world.

"Oh my god," Mimi marvels. "It's like we're *in* the movie Frozen!"

"Right?" I laugh.

"Oh my god, look!" Mimi points. "It's Santa!" Sure enough, hanging from the ceiling is a life-size Santa Claus in a big red sleigh full of colorful presents and pulled by nine life-size reindeer, their legs moving in slow motion with Rudolph in front, his red nose glowing bright, lighting the way through the twinkling snowflakes, which are sparkling lit up fixtures, hundreds of them hanging from the rafters.

"Wow." I can't imagine how much the decorations cost. A million dollars? Two? It's astonishing.

Prince and Chase lead us down the steps toward the main floor. I can see dinner tables laid out, only they're not in neat rows because the floor of the arena isn't flat. There's little snowdrift mountains of varying levels, with some tables on floors, but others set atop the fluffy mounds of varying heights, with the highest mounds and tables at the far end. Some of the tables are already occupied with groups of Fundies in their finest formal attire.

In the middle of it all is a shimmering silver dance floor.

"Is that ice?" I ask.

"It's supposed to look like ice," Prince offers as he leads us weaving past the table mounds to the tallest one in back. A curving white staircase circles around the snow, which is obviously fake, and we work our way to the top.

"This is *our* table?" Mimi gawks as we near the top of the staircase.

"It is," Prince says.

The table is draped in a sparkling white table cloth and covered with expensive place settings. A huge white floral centerpiece sits in the center of the table. There's seating for eight. I cringe when I see who is already here. Sitting in four of the chairs are Duke, Victoria, Jacqueline, and Skill, in that order, the girls between the men, probably so they don't fight.

"Oh, look!" Victoria gushes. "It's the gutter sluts!"

Jacqueline laughs.

Prince smiles, "Would you two like to leave on your own two feet, or shall I have you thrown out?"

"Pfft," Jacqueline snorts.

"You wouldn't," Victoria sneers.

"I would," Prince insists politely. "I'm not kidding, Vicky. Find your manners or find the exit doors. You too, Jackie."

Both girls roll their eyes and pout.

Prince pulls out a chair for me. "Fairest?"

"Oh, thanks." I sit down and he pushes in my chair, then sits between me and Skill.

"Hey, War Paint," he says. Unlike every other guy here, Skill's tuxedo is a dark burgundy with black lapels that goes great with his scarlet hair.

"Hey," I mutter, not sure what to say after seeing him at the Secret Fucking Hideout and hearing Rob's story about the Poor Boys today. I can't help but think Skill's here with Jacqueline for reasons other than the obvious, aka his manwhorishness. I'm suddenly wondering if that has all been an act? Has Skill been playing Jacqueline *and* Victoria this whole time?

I don't really know.

Chase pulls out Mimi's chair next to mine and she sits, then he plops down next to Duke. They bump fists, happy to see each other.

Prince does not look exactly happy to see Skill sitting next to him. He turns his back on him and focuses on me.

I notice a little white gold gift box on my plate and everyone else's. "What's this?"

"I would assume some sort of confection," Prince offers.

Mimi rips hers open. "White chocolate! My favorite!"

I open mine and see the same. "Do I eat it now or…"

Prince grins, "Do whatever you want, fairest. Tonight is yours to enjoy."

"I'll save it," I smile. I don't want to spoil my appetite. We're obviously having dinner and I want to try everything without eating too much. My gown isn't exactly expansive around the waist. As it is, I have to suck my tummy in just to sit.

The work-study waiters and waitresses go around asking if we want fish, fowl, or honeyed ham. I'd pick chicken if they had it, but they don't, so I go with the ham, which isn't my favorite, but who wants fish on Christmas? I'm not even sure what fowl means, other than a bird that isn't chicken, so I skip it.

Do I feel guilty the work-study kids are waiting on me hand and foot? Of course I do. I'm constantly thanking them profusely as a result, almost begging them not to hold it against me.

They start serving soup a few minutes later. Some sort of creamy pumpkin bisque that is to die for. Salad and breadsticks come next. A dozen different shapes and flavors of bread, some crunchy, others fluffy. The salad is mixed greens, walnuts, dried cranberries, and a bunch of other yumminess tossed together. The ham is honey-glazed and served with a side of roasted butternut squash drizzled with brown butter and cinnamon molasses, turkey sausage & chestnut stuffing, and lastly creamed spinach and nutmeg, all of it artfully arranged and plated. It's melt-in-your-mouth excellent, the most gourmet Christmas dinner I've ever had.

Oh, and it turns out the fowl is glazed game hen, which Prince gets and shares with me. It's actually really good. Almost tastes like chicken.

It takes nearly two hours to get through everything. During that time, I start to notice something weird. Prince is acting like he's got a solid buzz going. Not drunk, but getting there, which is weird because none of our drinks are alcoholic. That I know of, anyway. They certainly aren't supposed to be, not with faculty here.

I start to wonder about the punch. We're all drinking it. It's some kind of red mulled hibiscus infusion that's not too sweet and not too flowery. It's quite good, actually. But it's not alcoholic. I'd notice if it was. I sniff mine to make sure. Smells normal to me.

I whisper to Mimi, "Is Prince acting weird?"

"Not any weirder than usual."

"Does he seem drunk to you?"

She turns and glances at him, watching while he says something to Jacqueline, talking past Skill. Mimi shrugs, "I don't know, maybe a little? Why?"

"Did someone spike the punch?" I whisper.

She sniffs her glass, sips thoughtfully, and shakes her head, "I don't think so. He's probably just nervous. Trying to impress you."

"I guess."

At some point, one of the work-study snowflake waitresses goes around our table filling our punch glasses from a pitcher. I think her name is Hannah, if I remember.

Actually, she holds two pitchers. I watch her go around the table. She fills every glass from the pitcher in her right hand. Never pours from the pitcher in her left. Until she gets to Prince's glass. She fills his with the left pitcher.

When she gets to mine, she has to lean between me and Prince to reach my glass. He doesn't notice because he's blabbing something to Victoria.

"Oh, sorry," I grab my glass and hold it out for the snowflake waitress so she doesn't have to lean for it. "Here."

"Thanks," she says with an edge and sets down the left pitcher on the table next to me so she can take my glass and fill it. She steps back and pours with the right pitcher, holding my glass away from the table and over the floor.

While she's distracted, I take a quick sniff of the left pitcher sitting on the table. I swear I smell alcohol.

"Isn't that right, fairest?" Prince spins in his chair and knocks the left pitcher from the table splashing onto me.

I stand up and gasp. Red punch soaks my gown from the boobs down. The alcohol smell wafts over me.

"What the fuck?!" Prince roars. "Who put that pitcher here?!" He fires a hateful look at the snowflake waitress. "You did that on purpose! I've been watching you all night! Giving dirty looks to fairest Marianne! Now look what you've done! You fucking idiot! You ruined her dress! Do you have any idea how much that dress cost?!" He stands up and towers over her glaring.

"I, I, I,—" the waitress is scared to death, her face tightly frightened. "You were—"

"Me?! Don't blame me! What the fuck did you put that pitcher here for?"

Now I'm mad at him. I don't care about the stupid gown. "Calm down, Prince! It was an accident! She didn't mean it!"

Prince is furious. Looks at me. Looks at her. Looks at my gown. "Fuck!"

"Would you relax?!" I scowl at him. "It's just a stupid dress!" I'm suddenly seeing Prince in a very different light that I very much don't like.

He clenches his jaw and hisses hatefully, "But it's *your* dress, *princess*."

"Don't call me that!" I snap.

"I'm sorry." He heaves a deep breath. "I lost my temper. I want your evening to be perfect. This is not what I'd call perfect," he snorts, his voice strained, motioning at my gown. He's trying to get himself under control but he's struggling.

I remind myself at least he's trying.

The waitress looks like she wants to fall to pieces. Her eyes brim with tears.

"Sorry, fairest," Prince says to me.

Still angry, I blurt, "Don't apologize to me! Apologize to her! You called her an idiot in front of everyone!"

"She is an idiot," Victoria chortles and sips her punch.

I scowl at her, wanting nothing more than to throw the other pitcher of punch in her face.

Duke says to Victoria, "Not now, Vee."

"Don't tell me what to do!" she barks at him. "You're not the boss of me!"

Duke rolls his eyes in frustration.

"Fundy cunt," Mimi mutters.

"What did you call me?!" Victoria demands, standing up at the table, holding her glass of punch at the ready.

"Go ahead and throw it," Mimi threatens, grabbing her own glass of punch.

I feel for Grayson's knife under my corsage, ready to pull it on these bitches if need be.

"STOP!" Duke shouts loud enough to shake the stadium. Background dinner music is playing, but it isn't loud enough to drown him out.

Everyone in the entire arena is looking at us.

With us on the highest snow mountain, we're easy to see.

Duke says in a more normal volume, but with his face fighting itself, "Vee, put your punch down before I put it down for you." He's not even standing up, but his words carry an immense weight.

"What did you say to me?" Victoria hisses with righteous indignation like he's never stood up to her before and he's doing it for the first time in front of the entire school, of all places.

"Put it down, Vee, or we're done. No wedding and you can explain why to both our parents." These are momentous words. Everyone knows it. Especially me.

"Oh yeah?" Victoria snorts. "Fuck you, Duke! You dumb fucking jock! I never wanted to marry you anyway, you worthless piece of shit!" She splashes her punch in his face before storming off. She stops at the top of the staircase, "Come on, Jackie! We're going!"

Jacqueline looks at Skill.

Skill smirks at her, not moving from his seat.

"Come on, Skill!" Jacqueline demands.

"I haven't had dessert," Skill suggests.

Jacqueline snorts in surprise. "Fine! I hope you like not getting laid tonight!"

Skill stands up with a sigh and follows.

Jackess Jacqueline looks pleased. She, Vicious Victoria, and Skill disappear down the stairs.

"That happened," Chase chuckles, sipping his punch.

I realize the snowflake waitress is standing there paralyzed.

Prince turns to her. "I'm supposed to apologize to you."

"Her name's Hannah," I say. To her, "It is Hannah, right?"

She nods.

"Say you're sorry, Prince," I insist.

"My dear Hannah," he says somewhat drunkenly, "I am very sorry for losing my temper. Will you accept my most sincerest apology?"

"It's okay," Hannah mutters. "I'm sorry for spilling. It was an accident."

Prince gives her a smirky grin.

At least he apologized.

Hannah scurries off.

The rest of us sit down.

Prince says, "Duke, aren't you going to follow your fiancée?"

"Fuck her," he grumbles behind his fisted hands, which he clasps in front of his brooding mouth, elbows resting on the table top. "She can go fuck herself. Or fuck Skill. Or fuck Jacqueline. Or fuck them both. I'm done with her."

"Good for you," Prince says. "Show her who's boss."

Chase raises his eyebrows, a silent sign of doubt? Hard to say. He knows Duke better than I.

Dessert arrives at that point, distracting us. Two work-study waiters set out eight plates of white cake covered in thick drifts of sparkling frosting and accented with silver candy pearls.

"Who wants dessert?" Mimi says sarcastically.

Nobody laughs.

Duke digs in anyway, staring off into space and stabbing his cake with his fork and chomping on every bite like he's chomping on Victoria's head.

Chapter 45

When the dancing music starts, Mimi pulls all four of us off our snowy mountain top and down to the dance floor, Duke included.

Let me tell you, Mimi can move. She really knows how to dance. Her knee-length gown doesn't hurt. I wish I'd worn something shorter. I do my best, holding my train in one hand.

Mimi entertains us for well over an hour, dancing nonstop with Chase, switching to Duke, dancing with them both, then dancing with Prince, then with me, then all of us together.

After she wears us out, the boys insist on taking a break.

We make our way back up to our snow table on high to refresh ourselves on cake and punch. The glasses have all been refilled. I switch my glass with Prince's when he isn't looking. Sipping it, I taste the alcohol from earlier.

I have to wonder, who told Hannah to put alcohol in Prince's glass? She was obviously doing it on purpose. Did Skill tell her? He isn't here to ask. I'll have to grill him later. He must've known.

Duke busies himself eating the two untouched cake slices left for Victoria and Jacqueline. Chase eat's Skill's cake. When they finish, Mimi drags them away from the table and pushes them toward the stairs, ready for more dancing.

"You guys coming?" she asks me and Prince from the top of the stairs before going down.

"You go," Prince says. "I need a few more minutes."

"Oh, I get it," Mimi says knowingly. "You want some alone time with Mare Bear. Don't let me stop you!" She rushes down the stairs, giggling.

Despite being in plain view of everyone from up here, there's a sense of privacy with our height above the crowd and the dance music filling the arena. It's not concert loud, but it's loud enough.

"What a fucking night," Prince sighs, sitting next to me at the table. "I hope I haven't ruined it for you."

"It's fine," I say. "That dancing did you good."

"Yeah. Helped me blow off some steam." And maybe sobered him up a little. It wasn't like he was wasted. Just buzzed. He seems slightly less so now. "Sorry I was such a dick earlier."

"You apologized," I shrug.

"It pisses me off she disrespected you like that."

"Like how?"

He frowns, "She spilled punch all over you."

"Is that what *she* did?" I purse my lips.

"Forget it," he grunts and reaches for his water, sipping it. He stares off at the silvery dance floor.

Grimacing, I find myself remembering what Rob and the Poor Boys showed me earlier in their Secret Fucking Hideout. Prince's emails and Photoshopped photos.

I muse, "What was it like in Honduras? You never really said."

"Yes I did," Prince grumps. "It was dangerous."

"No, I mean, was it hot? Did it rain?"

"Yes and yes."

I nod, thinking. "Were the people nice?"

He throws back a swallow of water and winces, "The nicest. Why are you asking?"

I shrug. "How was the food?"

"Excellent."

"Hmm. What *kind* of food did you eat?"

He glares at me for several seconds. "What is up with you right now? Why are you asking so many questions? Don't you believe I was there?"

"Erm, why would you say that?"

"You tell me." He looks around. "Where's that fucking waitress? I need a refill."

"You mean Hannah? She has a name," I smirk.

"Whatever. Where is she? The least she could do after spilling punch all over you is refill our fucking drinks."

"You weren't there, were you?"

"Yes I was. She knocked the— okay, fine. *I* knocked the stupid fucking pitcher of punch on your dress. But she put it on the table. Who does that?"

"Honduras."

"What?!"

"You weren't in Honduras," I mutter quietly.

"What the fuck are you talking about, Mary?" He isn't calling me Marianne or fairest for obvious reasons.

"You never brought a water purifier to that village, did you?"

"What?" he chuckles in disbelief. "Have you lost your mind? I was there! I showed you the photos!"

"One photo."

"I told you I only went to one village. I didn't have time to go to the others."

"You didn't go anywhere."

He stares at me, his face making an escape plan for a moment, then settling into superiority. He smirks, "Where'd you get that idea? Did somebody tell you?"

I shrug. I know enough not to show my hand. I'm not telling him what Rob showed me.

He sneers, "Were *you* there? Did *you* go to Honduras?"

"No-a."

"Well, I fucking did."

"Do you have other photos?"

"Of Honduras?"

"Yeah, from your trip. Did you take any other pictures? Or just the one?"

For a moment, his face is frozen. Then it flips into a snicker. "You think I'm lying."

"I didn't say that." I mean that, but I'm not saying that.

"Who told you I wasn't there?" he snorts.

"Nobody told me," I say firmly. I mean *lie* firmly.

"Bullshit. Somebody told you something. It's written all over your face."

"What?!" I laugh to cover up my lie.

He smirks and shakes his head. "Who was it? Elizabeth? Is she trying to sabotage us? Is that it? She's pissed you and I are together so she told you a bunch of lies, right?"

I play dumb.

"That fucking bitch," Prince snorts sourly. He leans forward on the edge of his seat and takes one of my hands in both of his. "Listen to me, fairest Marianne. I don't know what she told you, but I—"

I blurt, "She told me she saw you wandering around downtown Castle Hill the weekend you said you were in Honduras."

Prince freezes. "She said that?"

I nod, emphasizing my lie. No, semi-lie. It doesn't matter who told me the truth.

He snorts. "What kind of cooked up story did she tell you?"

"She didn't. She just said she saw you."

"Well she didn't," he spits. "That woman has lost her mind. She's trying to fool you. She doesn't want us together so she's spinning lies to turn you against me, anything she can think of to break us apart. That's what she does. She plants a seed and lets it fester. She never takes the direct approach."

Suddenly I'm wondering if that's exactly what Rob did, plant a seed of doubt in me. But I saw those photos! I saw Prince in that Water Of Life T-shirt in the photo studio!

Prince says, "Whatever she told you, fairest, it's not true."

Is it possible Rob and the Poor Boys Photoshopped that logo onto the

T-shirt to trick me? That they were lying when they said he ordered the shirt online specifically for the photo shoot? Of course it is. Is it possible they faked all the emails they showed me? Of course it is.

No! I'm making excuses for Prince!

I blurt, "It wasn't Elizabeth! *I* saw you go into that shop!"

"What?" he chuckles.

"I saw you downtown!" I lie emphatically. "I snuck off campus that day just to get out! I went downtown and saw you walk into a photography studio! You said you were in Honduras! You weren't! You were here! You lied to me, Prince! You never bought any water purifiers for anybody, did you?! It was all a lie to make me like you, wasn't it?!"

Deer, meet Prince J. Lancaster caught in headlights.

My crazy gamble paid off.

He's stunned. He releases my hand. Sits back in his chair staring at me for a long time.

"Aren't you going to say something?" I mutter.

His placid face puckers with rage, "So what? So what if I *fucking* lied? You kissed Chase on Halloween! At *my* party! Right after we fucking kissed! Minutes after, Mary! Minutes! Did you mention that?! Huh?! Did you tell me about kissing my best friend on *our* date?! Did you, Mary? Did you?!"

I scowl, "Don't turn it around on me! We're talking about you lying!"

"I lied for you, Mary! Did you kiss Chase for me?"

"Unh!" I gawk at him.

"Did you? Did you let him put his tongue in your mouth for our sake? Was that the idea? Kiss another man to bolster our relationship?"

"Relationship?!" I snort. "What relationship?! All you and I did was kiss! We never made anything official!"

"You moved in with me, Mary! You live in my fucking guest room! How more official do I need to be?!"

"It isn't official if you don't even say it!"

"Fine! I fucking love you, Mary! I love you! Is that official enough for you?!" His face swims with pent up passion.

I'm stunned into silence.

He continues, "That's right, I faked a bunch of photos because I don't have fucking time to fly to fucking Honduras to impress you! So what?! But I bought those fucking water purifiers! I bought a hundred of them! It cost me seventy-five thousand fucking dollars! I showed you the photos!"

"Every picture you showed me are old photos from the Water Of Life website! From before we ever met! How do you explain that?!"

He smirks, "Oh, I see you're checking up on me."

"So?" I whine. "I wanted to make sure. They're old photos."

"I bought the purifiers! If you don't believe me, talk to them yourself!" Prince pulls his phone out of his tuxedo and swipes through it for almost a minute. Punches something in. Hands it to me. "Ask them."

I hear the phone ringing in my ear. "Who're you calling?"

"Water Of Life. Ask someone there. They'll tell you."

I take the phone in shaky hands. It rings then goes to voicemail for Water Of Life. "Voicemail," I say.

"Of course," he says. "It's Saturday night. They're probably closed. Call them tomorrow. Or Monday. Just fucking call them. They'll tell you."

Now I don't know what to believe. Or who. Rob or Prince?

"Do you believe me now?" Prince presses.

"Can I wait until I talk to Water Of Life?"

He grinds out a hard glare, "Do you believe me or don't you, Mary?"

"I don't know!"

"Make up your mind!"

"I need time!"

"I need you to make up your mind!" He shoots to his feet. "I told you I love you and you call me a liar?! How fucked up is that?!"

"You *did* lie!"

"For you, Mary! I lied for you!"

I don't know how to respond to that.

His face pained, he grumbles, "You know what?! Fuck this! You don't love me! I can fucking tell! You hate that I have money, which means you hate me for who I am! I didn't pick my parents! Nobody does!" He shakes his head in frustration. Leans down and hisses in my face, "I thought you were different, Mary. Thought because you're poor, you wouldn't be like everyone else at Castle Hill. But you *are* like them, you just don't realize it. You don't need to want money to be greedy, Mary. You just need to want more, always fucking more. Nothing is ever enough. No matter what I do, it's not good enough for you, is it? You always want more, more, more! Tell me I'm wrong!"

I want to tell him about Rob, tell Prince everything, admit I was spying on him, admit I put spy cameras and a hacked router in his penthouse, then apologize profusely, beg forgiveness for the things I did that are ever so messed up. I'm not perfect and I don't need Prince to be. But I don't know where to start in a tense moment like this.

Prince sneers at me in disgust, shaking his head, "You know what? Fuck this. I'm out." He spins and storms down the stairs, leaving me sitting alone on top of the fake snow mountain with the Fundies at the nearby tables staring at me.

Some of them laugh and point.

I ignore them because I'm reeling, my mind vortexing in a tornado of confusion like my brain might fly apart at any moment, remembering all the things Rob said about Prince, trying to make sense of it in relation to what Prince just admitted, but not being able to wrap my head around any of it.

For several minutes I just sit there, trying to calm myself but not succeeding. Eventually, one theme emerges from my mental hurricane.

Rob is a thief.

Rob steals.

Rob wants me to lie.

Rob wants me to spy.

Everything Rob does is criminal.

Everything!

Why should I believe anything he says about Prince?

Prince came clean. He told me the truth. He told me he lied because he loved me.

Rob said he lied because he wants me to help him rob Prince's family blind.

Which lie is worse?

The answer is obvious.

I get up and go looking for Prince.

Who am I to judge him?

I owe him an apology.

Chapter 46

"Is everything okay?" asks a demure voice that startles me as I emerge from the comparatively loud main floor of the arena into the quiet lobby area. In the near quiet, I recognize that feeble voice immediately.

I spin and snarl, "Azzie. Or should I say Elizabeth. You spiked his punch, didn't you? It was you who told Hannah what to do, wasn't it?"

"What are you talking about, Mary?"

"Don't bullshit me, Elizabeth! You dressed up as Azzie and spiked Prince's punch so we'd fight and you'd get him back!"

"I'm not Elizabeth," she protests meekly. "How many times do I have to tell you?"

"You gaslighting bitch, you've always been Elizabeth." I'm so effing pissed right now, I whip out Grayson's knife and point it at her. "Take your gloves off."

"What?" She wears the white lace gloves that go with her white snowflake waitress dress.

"Your gloves. Show me your nails, *Elizabeth*."

She hesitates.

"Show me!" I jab the knife at her. It's not like I'm going to actually stab her, but I need to make a point, pun intended. Elizabeth has been fucking with me since day one. Trying everything in her power to make me miserable.

"Okay," Azzie whines, and peels off one glove.

"Show me your nails!"

"Wha-a-at?" she whimpers.

I jab my knife. "Show me your fucking fingernails!"

She holds up a shaking hand and pouts, "There! Are you happy now?!" She pretends like she's ready to cry. Such a lying gaslighter.

"Wait," I say. "Where's your manicure? The one with the gold and silver loops?"

"I never had a manicure," she snivels. "I work like you do, remember?"

"Show me your other hand. Take your glove off."

She sniffs petulantly and removes the other glove, showing me her natural nails.

Crap. The last time I saw Elizabeth and her brand new manicure was a week or two ago. She could easily have scrubbed it off since and cut them down to nothing.

"Is everything okay, Mary? I saw you fighting with Prince."

"So you *did* spike his punch!"

"What are you talking about? I don't know anything about any spiked punch!" Now she's getting mad.

But I'm madder and I have a knife. I lunge forward. "Tell me the truth, Elizabeth, or so help me, I will cut your nose job off!"

"Help!" she shrieks in sheer terror. "Somebody help me! Mary has a knife. Help! HELP!"

"I'm not going to cut you, Elizabeth." I lower the knife.

"HELP ME!" She really has a set of lungs on her for such a demure little thing. "SOMEONE HELP! MARY IS GOING TO STAB ME!" She turns and runs down the curving lobby, disappearing around the corner.

Instinct kicks in.

Time for me to run.

I pick up my dress train and start shuffling because running in this fricking gown is impossible.

I hear loud footsteps smacking the corridor floor coming toward me from around the corner.

I am fucked.

I shuffle toward the nearest door leading outside and slam my hands on the push bar. Thank my lucky stars it opens. Outside in the darkness, I close it slowly, quietly as I can until it latches, giving me a few precious seconds to work.

First, I peel off my heels. Then I grab a handful of jeweled gown above my knees and stab it, sawing through the material with Grayson's knife. The ripping sound of ruining this hundred thousand dollar gown, or however much it cost, is surprisingly gratifying.

It only takes a few seconds to cut all the way around and push the bottom of the dress down and kick it off. I rip off the hooked on train from my waist and drop it.

Ready to run, I pause long enough to grab the severed section of dress with the jewels. No telling how much money I'll need now that I am once again on the run. Good thing I'm a walking wallet.

When I hear doors burst open ahead, and see light pouring onto the concrete, I spin around and sprint into the darkness behind the arena building. Seconds later, I'm stopped by an unclimbable fence, tiny black steel mesh with holes too small for feet or fingers.

Boots smack the ground behind me.

I spin around pointing my knife.

Several big men who are obviously not students from the academy come running to a stop.

"Drop the knife!" one of them shouts.

The others pull guns.

I notice their black jackets say SECURITY over their breast pockets. Are you surprised they hired armed security for their winter formal? I'm not. There's like a million dollars worth of dresses inside. The winter formal would be the perfect place to pull a dress heist. I'm surprised Rob and the Poor Boys haven't thought of it. What do I know? Maybe they did.

I nod at the arena and say, "You better get in there before they steal all the dresses."

"What?" the front security guy says.

"The dresses. They're going to steal the dresses."

"Put the knife down, miss," the guy says, waving his gun.

You know what I just figured out?

Now I am *actually* fucked.

Why?

Pretty sure pulling a knife on another student, whether or not they're an effing gaslighter, is not approved student conduct.

Chapter 47

They make me sit handcuffed in the back of a black security car for over an hour while they figure things out. It's not a police car but it looks like one without the markings and lights. They left the back windows open an inch to give me air. Being that it's effing December, I'm freezing in my newly knee length gown.

I keep waiting for Prince to come knocking, open the door, and tell me everything is going to be fine.

He doesn't.

One guess why.

I also wait for Rob or Skill to swoop in and save me. They don't.

Why?

Because Rob is an effing liar. I'm starting to think he gave me Grayson's knife on purpose.

"Are you okay in there, Miss Angerman?" Mr. Ralston asks, leaning down to speak through the inch of open window.

"What's going on? Have they figured out if they're going to kick me back to prison yet?"

Mr. Ralston takes a moment to answer, sighs sympathetically, "I don't know, Miss Angerman. What you did tonight was—"

"Stupid, I know. I wasn't going to hurt anyone." I don't say stab. Never say stab. People hate that word.

I hear a commotion nearby.

"One second, Miss Angerman." Mr. Ralston steps away from the car.

I twist around, trying to see what it is.

Is it Prince coming to save me?

Riding in on a white stallion with his sword held high and his armor glimmering with a savior's glow?

Nope.

Ms. Skelter is standing there with her hands on her hips, surrounded by security, giving them instructions. They nod and disperse. One walks to my car and gets in the driver's seat. He starts the engine without saying a word.

"Where are we going?" I ask.

"Back to campus."

"Why?"

He doesn't answer.

A short time later, we're back at the castle, pulling into the roundabout, which is full of limousines. It's late enough that many of the

Fundies have returned to campus, done with the winter ball, or perhaps they're more interested in watching my drama. You know what else it's full of?

The flashing blue and red lights of a bunch of Hill County Sheriff's cruisers. A whole squad of them.

Great.

Guess who they're here for?

A bunch of Fundy kids snap pictures of me in the back of the black security car. I'd flip them off if my hands weren't handcuffed behind my back. Do I duck my head in shame? No effing way! I don't care what they think!

Ms. Skelter arrives with Mr. Ralston. They're met by several other faculty members, including Ms. Braunschott. They huddle up and discuss the situation, looking very adult and very annoyed. When they see the Fundy kids gawking at me, they dispatch several deputies and the private security men to lead me from the black security car into the courtyard proper.

As we walk past Ms. Skelter, I see Mr. Hovarth, aka Peanut Face, come trotting out of the darkness, carrying something under his arm.

Ms. Skelter frowns, "What are you doing here so late on a Saturday, Mister Hovarth? Shouldn't you be at home with your wife and children?"

"Ma'am, I just found—" Mr. Hovarth sees me and abruptly stops talking.

Ms. Skelter takes note of my arrival and barks at the deputies and security detail, "Take her to the administration building! Miss Braunschott, show them the way."

"Yes, ma'am," Brawny nods.

They start walking me and I look over my shoulder just in time to see Mr. Hovarth hold up whatever he's got in his hands, showing it to Ms. Skelter. It's a wifi router.

One exactly like the hacked router I planted in Prince's penthouse before breaking it and returning it Mr. Hovarth. I can even see the crack where I dropped it.

Oh, no.

Ms. Skelter glares at me while Mr. Hovarth chatters away.

Did I say I was fucked?

Now I am double fucked.

That's when I see Elizabeth stroll into the courtyard. She's not wearing the white snowflake waitress dress she had on at the arena. She's wearing a chic black blazer, black silk top bursting with cleavage, skintight black pencil pants, black belt, and black stilettos. Her blonde hair is perfectly coiffed and flowing, and her makeup is smoky and sultry. She looks like she just got back from going out clubbing.

She stops in front of me, Brawny, the deputies, and the security men, blocking our way.

"Step aside, miss," the lead deputy says, irritated that some teenage girl is stopping him from doing his job.

"YOU DO NOT TALK TO ME THAT WAY!" Elizabeth commands in a powerful voice, her words lashing the man with an undeniable entitlement that nearly slices his head off and stops everyone in their tracks.

I'm not surprised that *Azielbeth* the effing *Devil* has changed outfits, done her hair, *and* her makeup. She had more than enough time after I threatened her with Grayson's knife back at the arena.

Effing gaslighter!

She's just trying to cover her tracks!

She can't fool me!

Just then, a limousine pulls up. Out steps Mimi. Alone. Where's Chase? Did they have a falling out back at the winter formal? I don't know. I hope not. But I do know I'm desperately in need of an ally, and Mimi is the best one I've ever had. Once I explain everything to her, I know she'll be right by my side fighting for my freedom. Knowing I'm not alone gives me the strength to keep fighting.

When Mimi walks up to me, I nearly gasp, "Thank goodness you're here, Meems! You'll never believe what happened! I was back at the winter formal and I—" I suddenly stop talking when I see a slender white female leg stretch out of Mimi's limo.

Azzie stands up behind Mimi.

That's right.

Azzie.

Not clubby black-clad Elizabeth.

Effing Azzie.

In her white snowflake dress, hair tied back, and minimal makeup. When she sees me, an evil smirk spreads across her angelic face.

Mimi *knows* how I feel about Azzie. What the F is she doing riding around in a limo alone with effing Azzie?

"Hey, *Mary*," Mimi says strangely.

Mary?

What happened to Mare Bear?

Now I'm *Mary*?

"Say hi to Azzie," Mimi snickers.

Oh no.

My chest seizes with fear.

Has Mimi been gaslighting me too?

Has her friendship been bullshit?

This whole time?

Was I *ever* her bestie? Or did she just say that so I'd trust her and she could betray me that much harder?

Has everything been some elaborate scheme the Silicones *and* Azzie *and* Mimi cooked up together, and they've *all* been in on it from the start?

No, it can't be.

But it is.

Everything *everyone* has said to me since I got here was one big lie! The same as it has always been everywhere I've ever gone!

I'm ready to either break down crying or have a mental breakdown or both.

Just then, Rob steps out of nowhere into the light. He's dressed in a tight shimmery shirt, dark jeans, and brand new black boots. I've never seen him wearing new boots. He always wears old work boots. If I didn't know better, I'd say he just got back from clubbing.

From clubbing…

I look at Elizabeth in her black clubbing outfit.

And Rob in his.

Oh.

No.

That's when the world tilts and starts a slow spin around me.

I struggle to stand up.

I am literally losing my mind.

I can't even swallow the rock of despair clogging my throat. It's impossibly large.

I want to die.

If I don't start breathing soon, I will.

I try to inhale but I can't.

The suffocation of my betrayal is complete and total and it's going to kill me where I stand.

Fine.

Let it.

But I won't fall.

I'll die standing in front of these assholes if it's the last thing I do.

Fuck. Them.

FUCK ALL OF THEM!

Chapter 48

Elizabeth and Azzie converge on me, one on each side. They are freakishly identical.

Rob stands behind Elizabeth, his face blank.

I glare at him. With a gasp of righteous rage, I suddenly put it all together and suck in a saving breath that keeps me standing.

How could I have been so stupid?! Rob has been using me all along! Since the day I got to Castle Hill, he was playing me every step of the way! His kiss today didn't mean a thing! We aren't soulmates or blood lovers! We never were! We're nothing!

I scream at Rob, "Did you ever have *any* feelings for me?! Or was all of it an act to manipulate me?!"

Rob doesn't answer.

Ms. Skelter barks at Brawny, "Get Mizz Angerman to the administration building immediately, Ms. Braunschott!"

"Wait," Elizabeth says, her words a quiet knife at Brawny's throat.

"Yes, Ms. Morgan-Hearst," Brawny minces, head bowed respectfully. I've never seen her so cowed.

"Now, Mizz Braunschott!" Ms. Skelter insists, having not heard Elizabeth.

Elizabeth tosses a comment over her shoulder at Skelter without looking, "Shut up and stay in your lane, you dusty old bag." Her words land like a hand grenade.

Ms. Skelter's face explodes with indignation, but she says nothing.

Elizabeth sneers at me, "So you thought you could steal my boyfriend, did you?"

I smirk at Rob and say to her, "Which one? Prince or Rob?"

"Hmph," Elizabeth snorts. "Both."

"I knew it!" I rage. "You've been with them both this whole time, haven't you?!"

She shrugs.

That's a yes if I've ever seen one. I glare at her and shake my head thinking, wait till Prince hears. I bet he'll be thrilled to find out she was cheating on him with Rob for who knows how long. Not that I'll get the chance to tell him. He isn't here and I have a sneaking feeling I will be in jail long before he arrives, and prison not long after.

Just then, Skill comes shuffling out of one of the limos with Jacqueline on his arm. "War Paint," he drawls.

I blurt, "Screw you, Skill! You're in on it too, aren't you?!"

"In on what?" he says innocently.

"Don't play dumb," I seethe. "You knew!"

He sighs, "Whatever, War Paint."

Elizabeth says to me, "You tried to steal him too, didn't you?"

"Who, Skill?" I snort. "Who'd want him?!"

"Me," Jacqueline says. Her eyes blaze with naked desire and she tiptoes up for a kiss, which Skill gladly gives. They busy themselves swallowing each other's tongues.

Disgusting.

Work-study kids wander out of the Convent and Monastery to see what the commotion is about. These kids didn't work the winter formal. They're wearing sweats or pajamas or whatever they usually sleep in. One of them is Jonah. He walks up warily behind Rob, watching from a distance.

"What's all the noise?" Tucker says, walking out of the shadows from the opposite direction. He's wearing his kitchen whites. Was he cooking food for the formal? Here in the Palace kitchen?

I don't know.

Not that it matters.

I don't care what these four Poor Boys are doing. Not anymore. I don't care if I ever see them again. They're in on it too. I just know it.

"I HAVE HAD ENOUGH!" Ms. Skelter snaps at the group of faculty surrounding her and everybody looks her way. "I have made my final decision and that is final!" She whips a snarl at Elizabeth before striding over to me with purpose. "Mizz Angerman, what you have done tonight is a most egregious offense! I will not tolerate such a violation on *my* campus!"

"Your campus," Elizabeth titters to herself, examining her manicured nails.

Ms. Skelter's eyes flick at her for a moment then return to me. "You are done here, Mizz Angerman. You had your chance at redemption, but you had to go and waste it, didn't you?"

"Fuck your redemption!" I spit. "I don't need you or this fucking place! It's worse than jail! I wish you'd left me there in the first place!"

"Oh do you?" she snorts a superior laugh. "Then your wish shall be granted, Mizz Angerman, and then some! You have broken the law more times than I can count!"

"Once! I broke the law once! And I didn't even stab anyone!" There, I said it. Stab, stab, stab. "Check Azzie! She isn't hurt! She's fine! The only thing I hurt is her feelings!"

"You have done more than that, Mizz Angerman! According to Mister Hovarth, you have broken into the academy's computer system!

Cybercrime is a felony, Mizz Angerman! Or did you not know that?!"

"You don't even know what cybercrime is!" I seethe. "You and your stupid old-timey everything!"

"I know that cybercrime is a felony under state law! And *that* is in direct violation of the student code!"

"Fuck your student code, *Mizz* Skeleton! That's right! You're a bag of living sticks! I don't need you or this stupid fucking school!"

Ms. Skelter shakes with rage. "We are done here, MIZZ ANGERMAN!" She motions to the deputies surrounding me. "Get her out of my sight!"

While the Castle Hill deputies drag me handcuffed and kicking across the moonlit courtyard, I scream at the four Poor Boys, "You lied to me! You said we wouldn't get caught! You said you'd take the fall for me if we did! I'm falling now! Why aren't the four of you falling with me?! You're in this too! This was your guys's idea! Not mine!"

Rob doesn't answer. He's stoic as a stone.

I shout, "Say something, Rob! Tell them! Tell them this was your idea! Tell them you're the mastermind!"

Rob refuses to speak. He truly doesn't care.

I'm not stopping. "I put my faith in you! I did exactly what you said! Look what happened! Don't you have anything to say?"

Rob's stoicism gives way to the curl of his cocky grin.

"Damn you, Rob! Say something!"

Elizabeth wraps her arms seductively around his big bicep. He rests his hand possessively on her flared hip, pulling her close. Elizabeth nuzzles into him and they kiss passionately.

I'm horrified. I should know better, but I can't believe he is actually kissing her!

How can he?!

After everything she's done to him?!

She accused him of being a rapist! When he told me he was the one who got raped when he was a little kid, he flew off the handle and started murdering that sitting boulder with that branch! That was real feelings! I saw! I could feel them like they were mine! Rob was ready to crack from the misery! Does Eliza-*bitch* not have a single scintilla of compassion in her beautifully awful body?

Wait.

Wait, wait, wait!

Was Rob *lying* to me about being raped?

I gasp.

Was that all some stupid act he put on to trick me into caring for him? To sucker me into feeling sympathy for poor little Rob Fletcher the foster kid? He probably wasn't even ever *anyone's* foster kid! He's probably as rich as they are! Look at his clothes! He's no Poor Boy! He's a Rich Boy if there ever was one! He probably has his own fucking trust fund!

I am so stupid!

Stupid, stupid, stupid!

Rob is the worst liar of all! *He's* the one filling the world full of butterfly effect lies!

Billions of them!

Trillions!

Disgust knots my guts. That's when I know for certain this was all a lie. One big gaslight. From day one, Rob was using me. I was always his pawn. Nothing more. A gullible little girl who didn't know any better. How could I have possibly thought a hottie like him would *actually* be into a nobody like me?

I am a fucking idiot.

A stupid fucking idiot!

As the deputies drag me along, I fight back tears even though I want desperately to fall sobbing to my knees. I say to Rob as I pass, "You never cared about me, did you?! You only cared about what I could do for you! I never should've trusted you! I hate you, Rob Fletcher! You're dead to me! Do you hear me?! Dead!"

Elizabeth laughs.

Rob's eyes glimmer for a moment before he breaks his superior stare and turns his back on me.

Tucker, Skill, and Jonah turn too.

Surprisingly, Jonah turning away hurts most of all. He was supposed to be the perfect big brother every girl wishes she had. Now he's showing his true colors. He's as much of a lying conniver as the rest of those pathetic Poor Boys.

And me?

Now I'm going to prison.

Actual adult women's prison.

What did I tell you in the beginning?

You can't ever run away from your problems.

They *always* catch up to you.

I knew this place was too good to be true.

Good fucking riddance, Castle Hill.

I'd rather be behind bars.

My heart is shattered and I'm dying inside but hiding it as the deputies lead me out of the gatehouse to the visitor parking lot. It's buzzing with patrol cars, their red and blue lights bouncing eerily off the castle's tall stone walls.

"WAIT!" a familiar voice roars booming across the courtyard.
My heart stops me where I stand.
When I turn, I see Prince.
When I see his eyes, I know.
He came back for me.
He came back!
And he brought reinforcements.
Right behind him are Duke and Chase looking righteously pissed.
They came too!
My heart soars.

Epilogue

I've been sitting in a cramped and windowless interrogation room inside the Hill County sheriff's office for five hours. They have been interrogating me the entire time. I'm dying of thirst and I'm starving. Whoever is supposed to be playing "good cop" forgot to be nice. Where's my complimentary bottle of water? How about a fricking Snickers bar? Or some Lay's potato chips? Don't you guys have an effing vending machine around here somewhere? Or a box of fricking doughnuts?

No?

How about some day-old cop coffee?

Or some freaking tap water?

Do you not have water pipes in this stupid place?

Or anything?

No?

Fuck you, good cop.

And the rest of them.

Just *fuck* you.

I sigh and slump in my seat, a hard plastic chair that is totally unforgiving after five hours of slouching in it.

At least they uncuffed me.

I don't look dangerous.

If they only knew.

Idiots.

If I was anyone else, I would want more than anything right now to go home and be done with this bad dream that is my life. But I'm not anyone else.

I'm me, Mary Angerman.

I don't have a home.

All I want to do is get the F out of here.

You know how I told you at the beginning that "they" say you can't run away from your problems?

Welp, guess what?

"They" are wrong.

Running away is the *only* thing you can do.

As soon as I have a chance, I'm running the F out of here. I swear to all that is holy, the next time a deputy or a detective opens the interrogation room door, I am running past whoever it is and never looking back. If they try to grab me, I will start biting hands and kicking man balls and/or lady balls (thank you for teaching me that trick, Emily Calhoun and your reptile friends) until whoever it is lets go. Then I will run out of this damn building and into the darkness. Screw the infrared cameras on their stupid helicopters. I am out, no matter what they try and do.

Bye, bitches!

Am I blustering?

You bet your ass I am.

It's all I have left.

Next stop, women's prison.

I'll—

((((pitch black))))

((((pain))))

((((it hurts!))))

((((please not again!))))

—deal.

Loud muffled sounds from outside the door startle me. They soundproof these rooms so I can't hear anything clearly, but it's people talking. No, shouting. The shouting continues for almost five minutes until someone rips the interrogation room door open an inch.

I gasp.

Something slams the door closed from outside before I see who it is.

I gasp again.

More shouting and now bumping.

The door opens again.

"I don't give a fuck what you think, Sheriff Clemmons!" Prince Lancaster shouts. "I am taking her with me! You and your deputies can go fuck yourselves!"

"I can't let you go in there, Mr. Lancaster!" someone says from the hallway.

"Talk to my fucking lawyers!" Prince roars before barging through the interrogation room door.

Behind him, I see who I assume is Sheriff Clemmons surrounded by an intimidating army of lawyers wearing power suits and looking eminently badass and fully equipped to fight the greatest legal battle of all time. Standing amongst them are Duke and Chase, both of them pushing toward the door to my interrogation room. As for any deputies, I don't see a single one. There isn't room in the crowded hallway.

Still wearing his winter formal tuxedo, Prince forces his way inside the interrogation room first. When he sees me, relief calms his furious and slightly frightened face. "Mary! I thought I'd lost you!" He strides over to me, arms open.

I jump up from my chair and rush into his hug.

He hugs back hard, whispering in my ear and kissing my cheek repeatedly, desperately, "This is all my fault, Mary. I never should've lied to you. I am such an idiot. You don't deserve this. If I hadn't been such a self-centered fucking asshole, you wouldn't be here right now. I am so sorry. Can you ever forgive me?"

"Yes, Prince! Yes!"

When we kiss, it's heaven.

No, it's home.

Twenty minutes later, I am a free woman.

That's right, woman.

I'm only sixteen, I know, but they were going to try me as an effing adult. That makes me a woman in my book, and this *is* my effing book, so screw anyone who disagrees.

My three kings walk me out the front doors of the sheriff's office into the parking lot. The sun has just crested the eastern hills, coating everything in a golden glow. Behind us, the army of lawyers start to filter out after us and head for their cars. Mercedes and BMWs that weren't here when I arrived. I also see a white limousine. It's Prince's. Not a valiant white stallion, but close enough.

"I told you I got this," Duke chuckles beside me.

"No, *we* got this," Chase emphasizes with a sly smile.

"We did, didn't we?" Prince grins, his arm around my shoulder and pulling me close.

"You did," I giggle, smiling so hard it hurts.

It's a good hurt.

I sniff back tears and snort a happy laugh, "You guys, I don't know what to say."

"Don't say anything, Mary," Prince soothes, kissing the top of my head affectionately. "You've had a long night. Now it's time for you to go home and sleep."

"Home?" I say hopefully. "Which home?"

Prince John grins, "Castle Hill Academy. Where else?"

I cringe.

No.

No, no, no, no!

Why does that sound so wrong?

Why do I suddenly feel like I'm his prisoner?

Because I am!

I am Prince's fucking prisoner!

He leads me to his waiting white limousine and opens the back door for me.

My hands are shaking insanely as I reach for the doorframe.

I'm about to shatter, I'm so afraid of what comes next.

What have I gotten myself into?

This is messed up!

I should run!

Run, Mary!

Run!

Loud sounds at the end of the parking lot startle me.

Four black motorcycles roll to a stop on the main road.

Four black-clad men straddle them.

They wear black helmets, visors down.

Their blank-faced helmets are looking at me.

I can feel their eyes prying into my heart.

Rob and his not so merry men.

I swear I feel them seething.

Their engines rev angrily and they roar into the morning.

Is that it?!?!

Is that the effing cliffy ending we're left with, Devon?!

Don't worry, I'm already writing Book 2. :-)

Anywho, thank you so much for reading Rich Boys vs. Poor Boys, the Cruel Kings of Castle Hill Academy, Book 1. It means the world to me. While you're still here, can I ask you to leave a review online where you purchased this book? Every review matters, but yours means the most. :-)

If you want to chit chat with Devon about what's next for Mary, or rail on him about how he left you hanging on the edge of a mile-high cliff over a pool of hungry alligators who want to chomp on your heart like Devon so ruthlessly did with the ending of this book, join his Facebook group and tell him what's what on Devon Hartford's Heartbreakers here:

www.facebook.com/groups/devonhartford

Lastly, if you'd like an email telling you when Book 2 of The Cruel Kings of Castle Hill Academy drops (that's hip lingo for "is available for purchase"), sign up for Devon's newsletter here:

devonhartford.com

ABOUT THE AUTHOR

Devon Hartford spent most of his life in Southern California.
Devon also paints. His background in the arts was the inspiration
for his #1 bestselling romantic comedy series The Story of
Samantha Smith.

Devon Hartford's Heartbreakers

Join Devon's Facebook group to chat with Devon and stay
up to date on his new releases. Here's the link:

www.facebook.com/groups/devonhartford

A gift from Devon

Would you like a free copy of Devon's #1 bestselling romantic new adult comedy? To read it free, sign up for the Devon Hartford Newsletter here:

devonhartford.com

Warning: Fearless contains adult sexual situations that are consensual. All characters are age 18 or over.

OTHER BOOKS BY DEVON HARTFORD:

COLLEGE ROMANTIC COMEDY
Fearless (The Story of Samantha Smith #1)
Reckless (The Story of Samantha Smith #2)
Painless (The Story of Samantha Smith #3)

NEW ADULT ROMANTIC COMEDY
Cover Model
Stealing Chastity

HIGH SCHOOL ROMANTIC COMEDY
Stepbrother Obsessed

ADULT ROMANTIC COMEDY
Taking Back Beautiful
Broken Lion

SLIGHTLY PARANORMAL ROMANCE
If I Were Beautiful (If I Were... #1)

BILLIONAIRE ROMANCE
ONE YEAR LOVE - Part One
ONE YEAR LOVE - Part Two
ONE YEAR LOVE - Part Three
ONE YEAR LOVE - Part Four
ONE YEAR LOVE - Collected Edition (Parts 1-4)

ROCKER ROMANCE
Victory RUN 1 (The Story of Victory Payne)
Victory RUN 2 (The Story of Victory Payne)
Victory RUN 3 (The Story of Victory Payne)
Victory RUN 1-2-3 (The Story of Victory Payne - Collecting Parts 1-2-3)

ACKNOWLEDGMENTS

A HUGE thanks to:

Jackie Barnett for her usual genius

Jessie Duchannes for all things Sailor Moon.

Bethanie "The Typo Hammer" Melander for killing those typos

Her Highness Samantha Sheeley, Queen of All Typos and Ouster of Oopsies!

Michele McKenzie for equally all-star eagle-eyed typo-snyping.

For last minute typo-snyping of the highest order and in the face of great personal danger, I award a Typo Heart to the recently promoted **Brigadier General Melanie Starr**, the one and only **Comma Bomber**, who saved this mission from certain disaster at the 11th hour, but not without significant personal sacrifice on her part. General, I salute you!

The HUGEST thanks to all my passionate and fantastic sneaky peeking readers: Hayley Picknell, Maria Combee, Sarah Patton, Sarah Lintott, Natasha Slater, Tamara, Muriel Garcia, Elizabeth P., Lynn Walters, Megan Christmas, Mandy Jamerson, Clare Harrison, Dr. Ooooh!!!!, Kimber, Sandy England, Nicki HH, Sarah Frost, Ashley Hall, Julez, Mandy Karsa, Anna Lamonica, Michelle Crane, Paula DeBoer, Jessica Janis, Esther Blair, Ellie, Lori L Roberson, Deanna Dodge, Lisa Venn Sims, Jessica Laws, The REAL Julie England, Genice Cassidy, Mylinda Powell, Erika Jackson, Kim Byrd, Brandi Morrone, Rosanne Triegaardt, Tina Lewis, Meghean Alejandro, STEFFINI R WALKER (she's not shouting but I am), Meledy Blumberg, Lori JoRay, Sade, Melissa Seay, Cyndi Dieter, Lynn Walters, and The Ever Special Mel Bushell for invaluable feedback and encouragement! You guys rock the typo sauce!

Last but most of all, a thousand GINORMOUS thank-yous to everybody else who helped make this book a reality!